FRANKIE'S WORLD

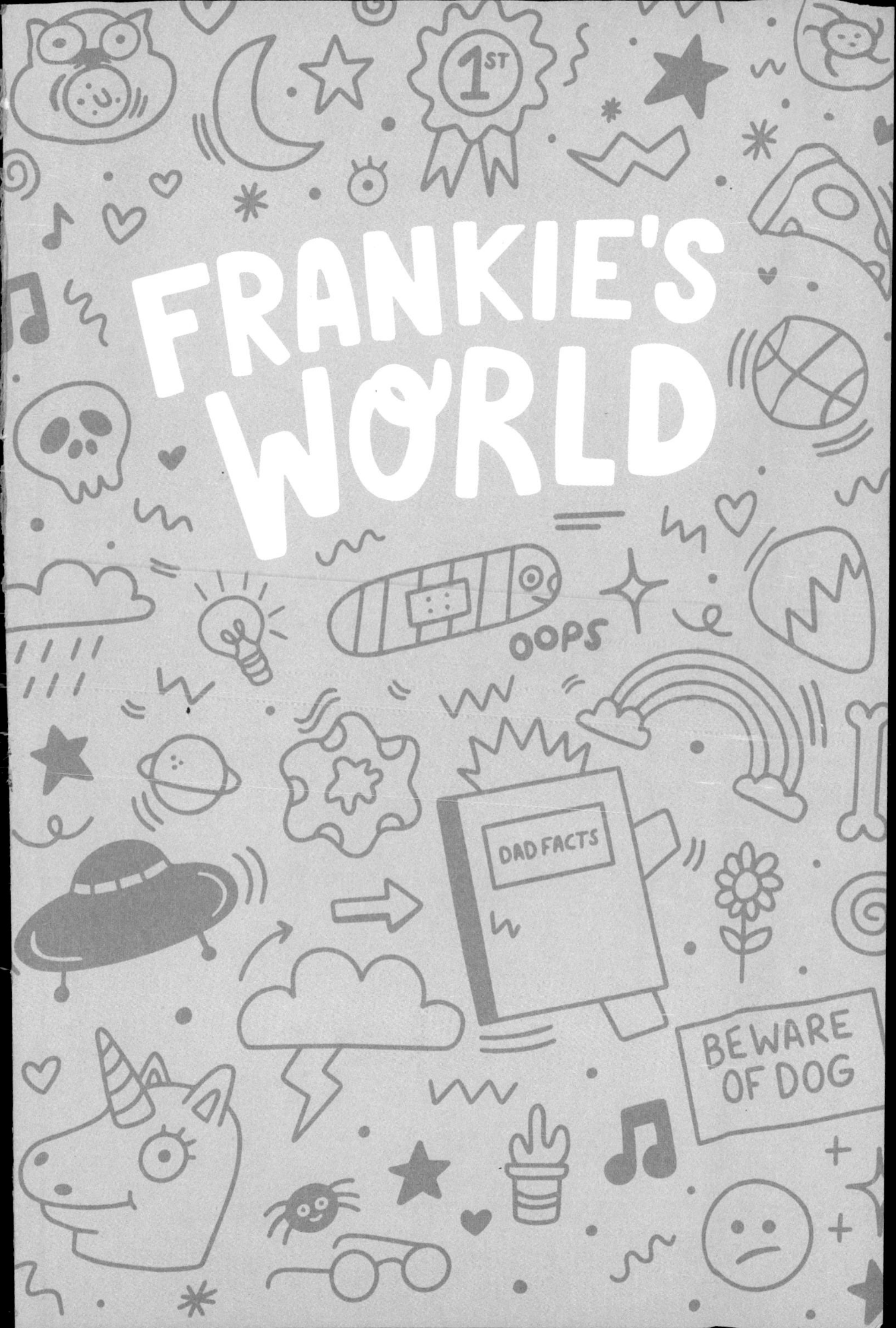
1ST
OOPS
DAD FACTS
BEWARE OF DOG

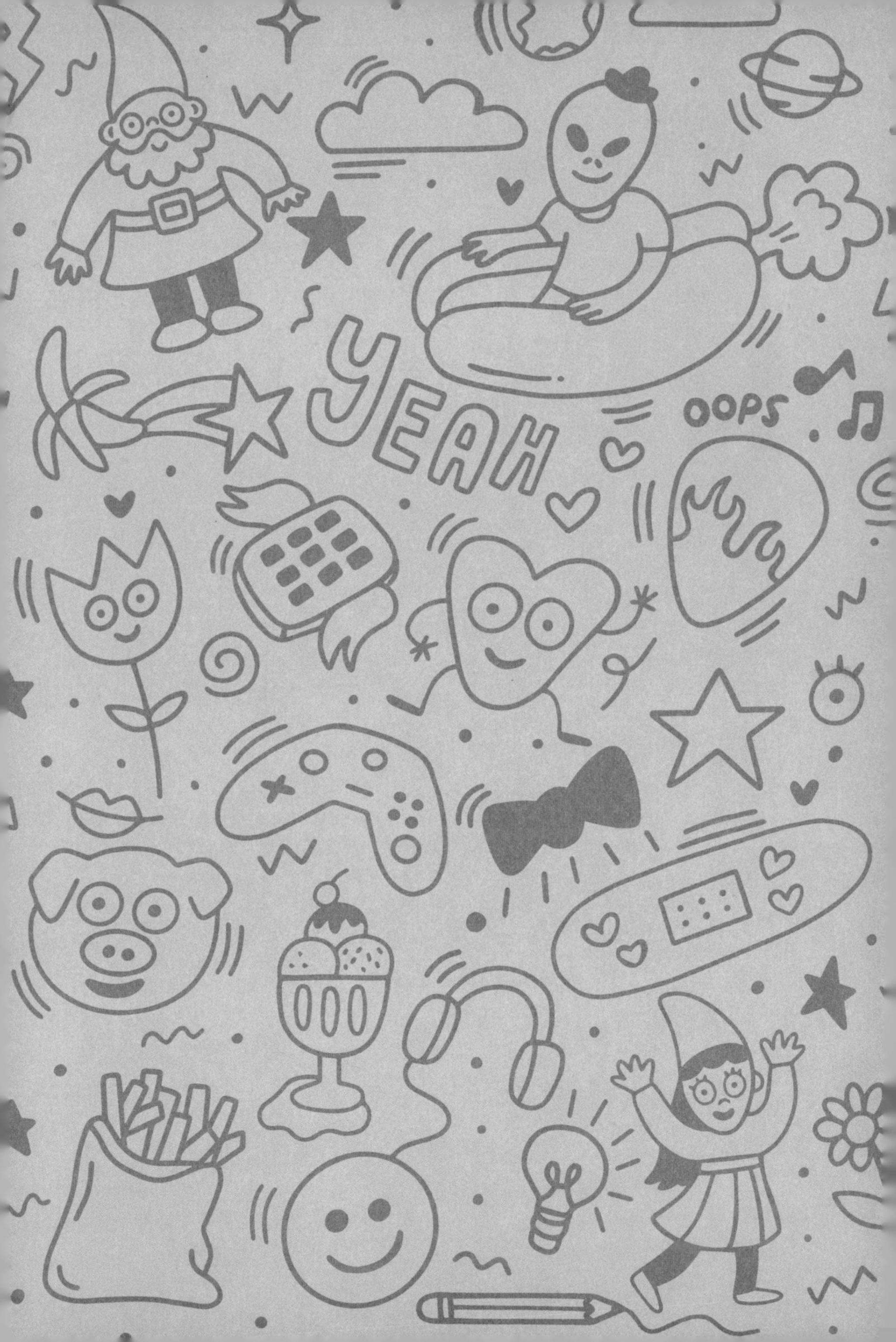
YEAH
OOPS

FRANKIE'S WORLD

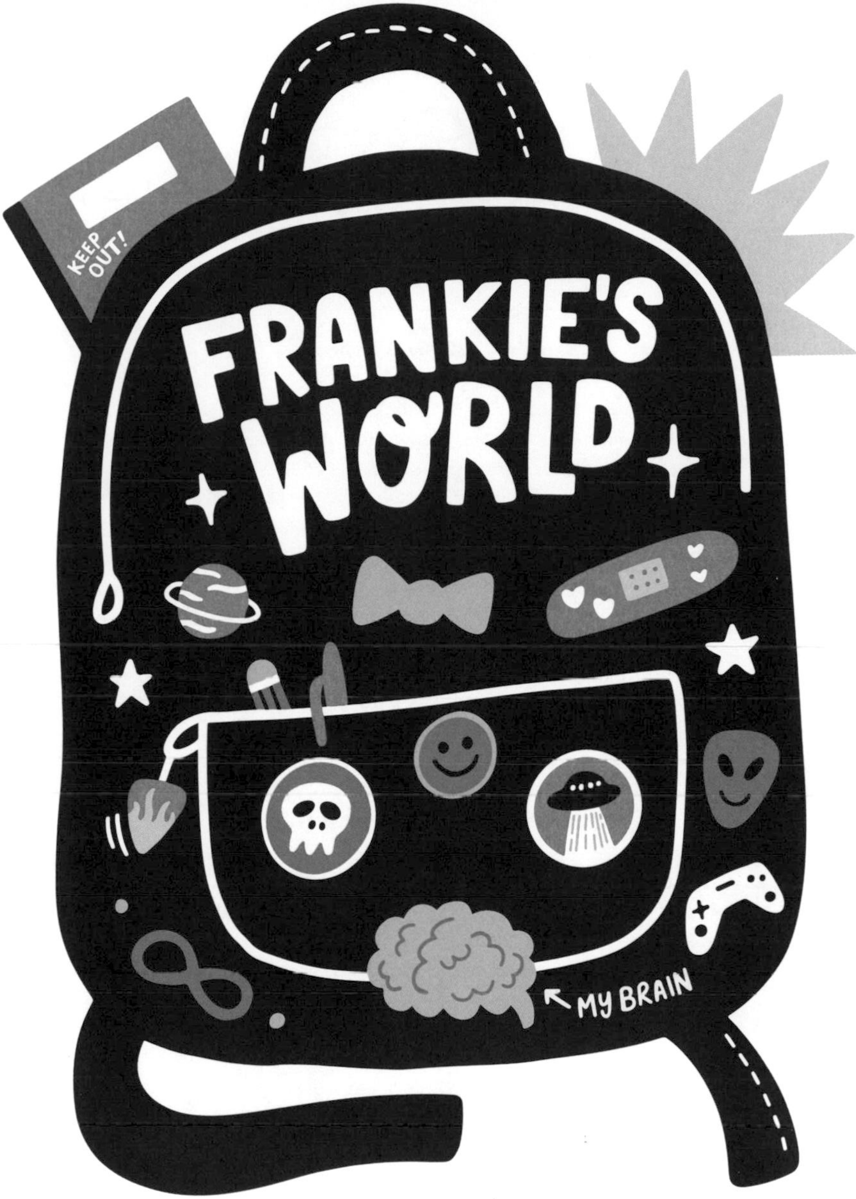
KEEP OUT!
MY BRAIN

AOIFE DOOLEY

graphix
An Imprint of
SCHOLASTIC

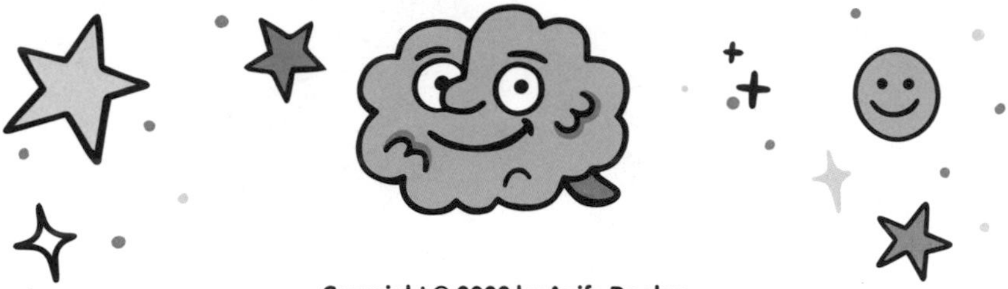

First published in the United Kingdom in 2022 by Scholastic UK.

Library of Congress Control Number: 2021948451

ISBN 978-1-338-81312-8 (hardcover)
ISBN 978-1-338-81311-1 (paperback)

10 9 8 7 6 5 4 3 2 1 22 23 24 25 26

Printed in the U.S.A. 113
This edition first printing, August 2022

For anyone and everyone who
feels like they don't fit in

me

KETCHUP

MY BRAIN

NAME: FRANKIE

AGE: 11 YEARS OLD

HEIGHT: SMALLEST IN MY CLASS

THINGS I LOVE: ART, PIZZA, AND ROCK MUSIC

THINGS I DON'T LOVE: SCHOOL, THE HOSPITAL,

AND POP MUSIC

CHAPTER 1

WELCOME TO MY WORLD

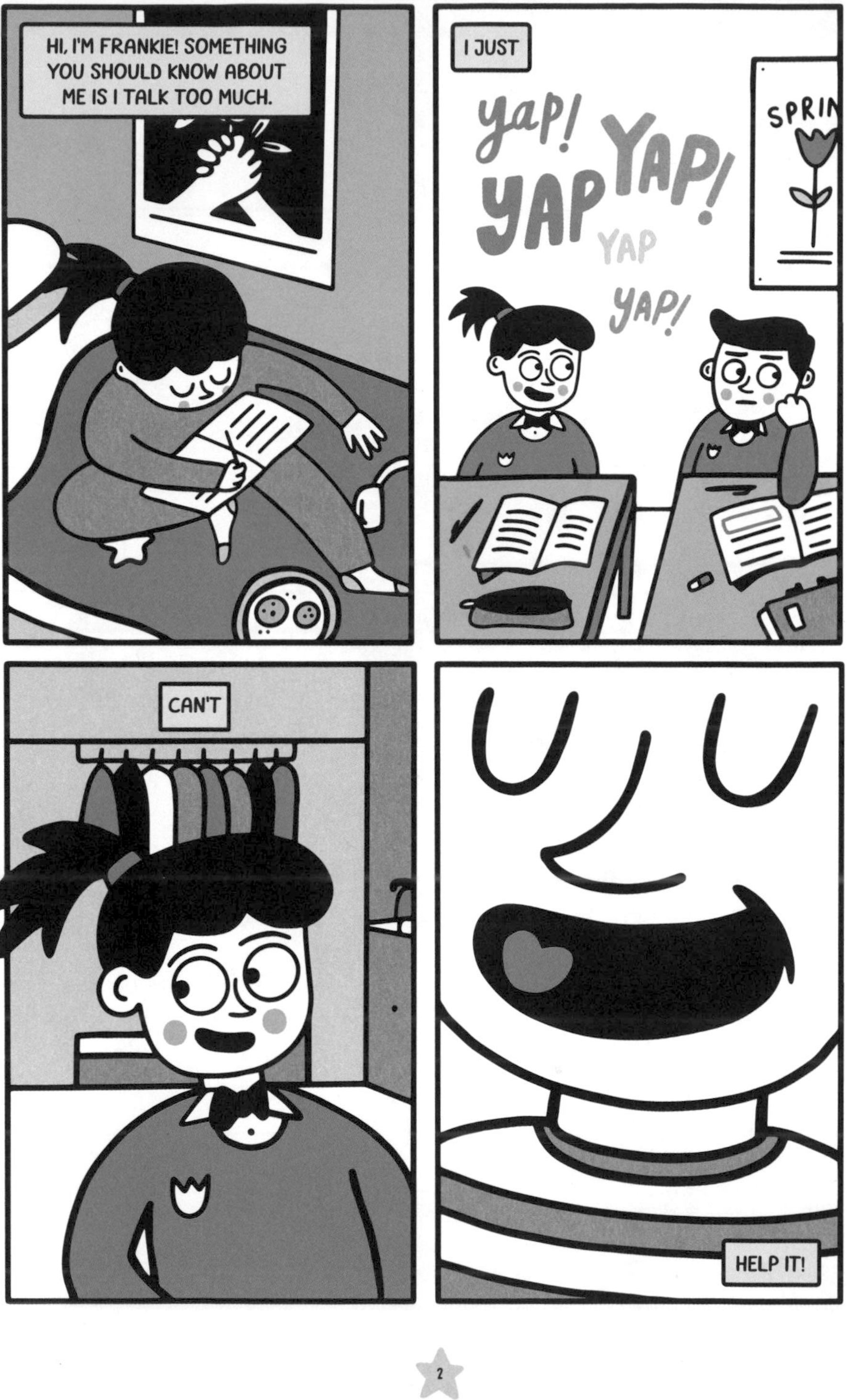
HI, I'M FRANKIE! SOMETHING YOU SHOULD KNOW ABOUT ME IS I TALK TOO MUCH.
I JUST
yap!
YAP!
YAP
YAP
yap!
SPRIN
CAN'T
HELP IT!

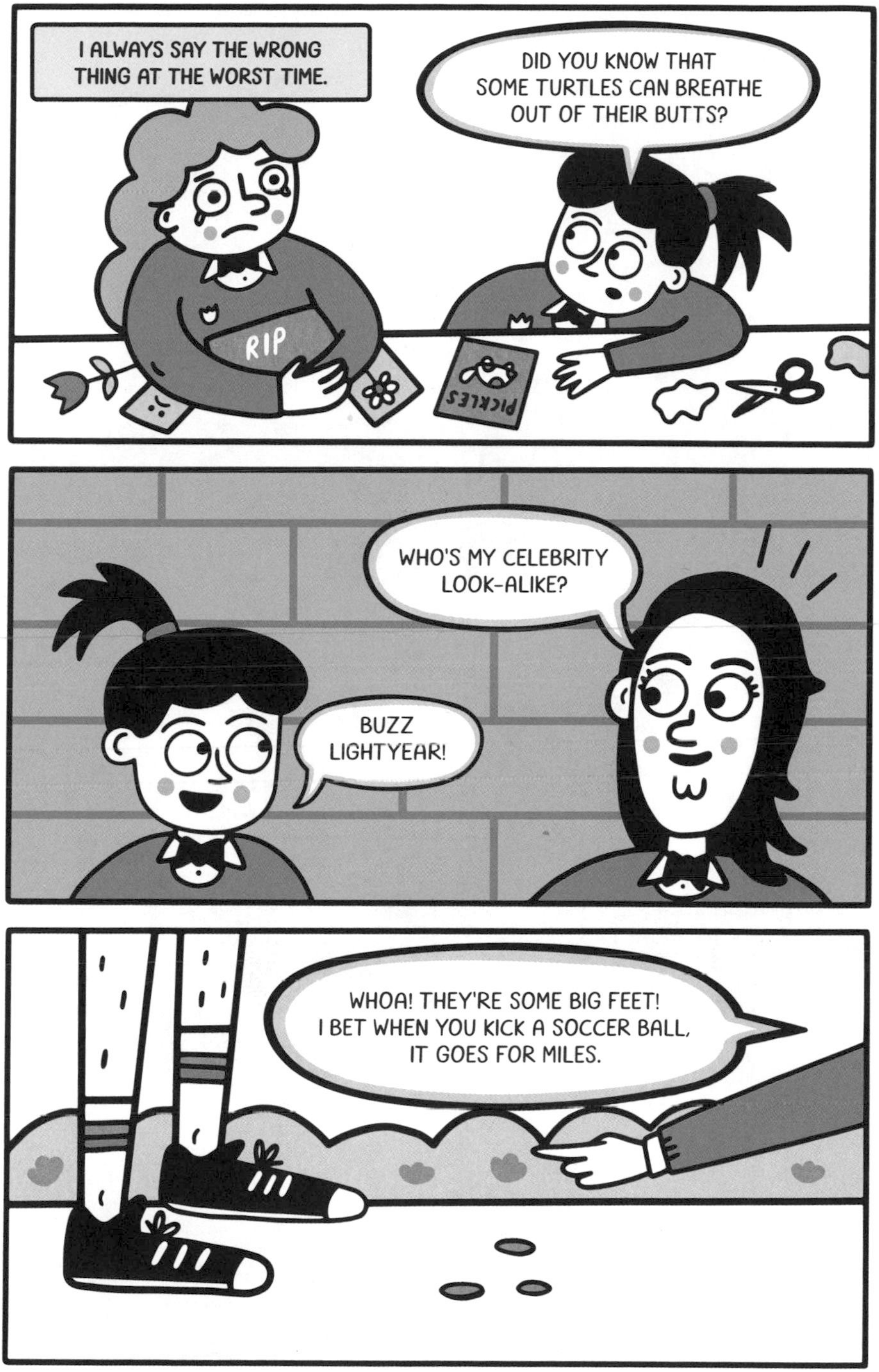
I ALWAYS SAY THE WRONG THING AT THE WORST TIME.
DID YOU KNOW THAT SOME TURTLES CAN BREATHE OUT OF THEIR BUTTS?
RIP
PICKLES
WHO'S MY CELEBRITY LOOK-ALIKE?
BUZZ LIGHTYEAR!
WHOA! THEY'RE SOME BIG FEET! I BET WHEN YOU KICK A SOCCER BALL, IT GOES FOR MILES.

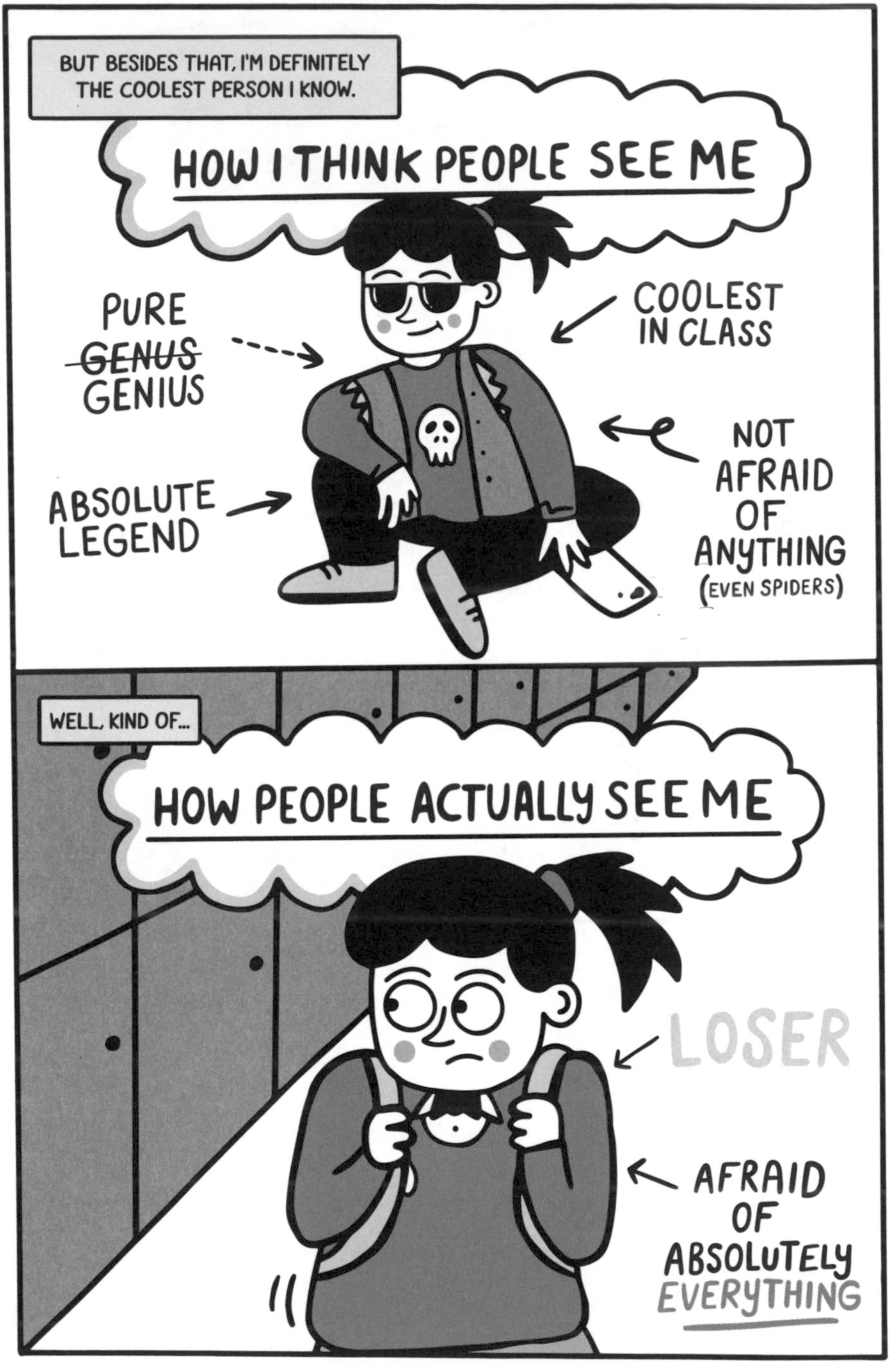
BUT BESIDES THAT, I'M DEFINITELY THE COOLEST PERSON I KNOW.
HOW I THINK PEOPLE SEE ME
PURE ~~GENUS~~ GENIUS
COOLEST IN CLASS
NOT AFRAID OF ANYTHING (EVEN SPIDERS)
ABSOLUTE LEGEND
WELL, KIND OF...
HOW PEOPLE ACTUALLY SEE ME
LOSER
AFRAID OF ABSOLUTELY EVERYTHING

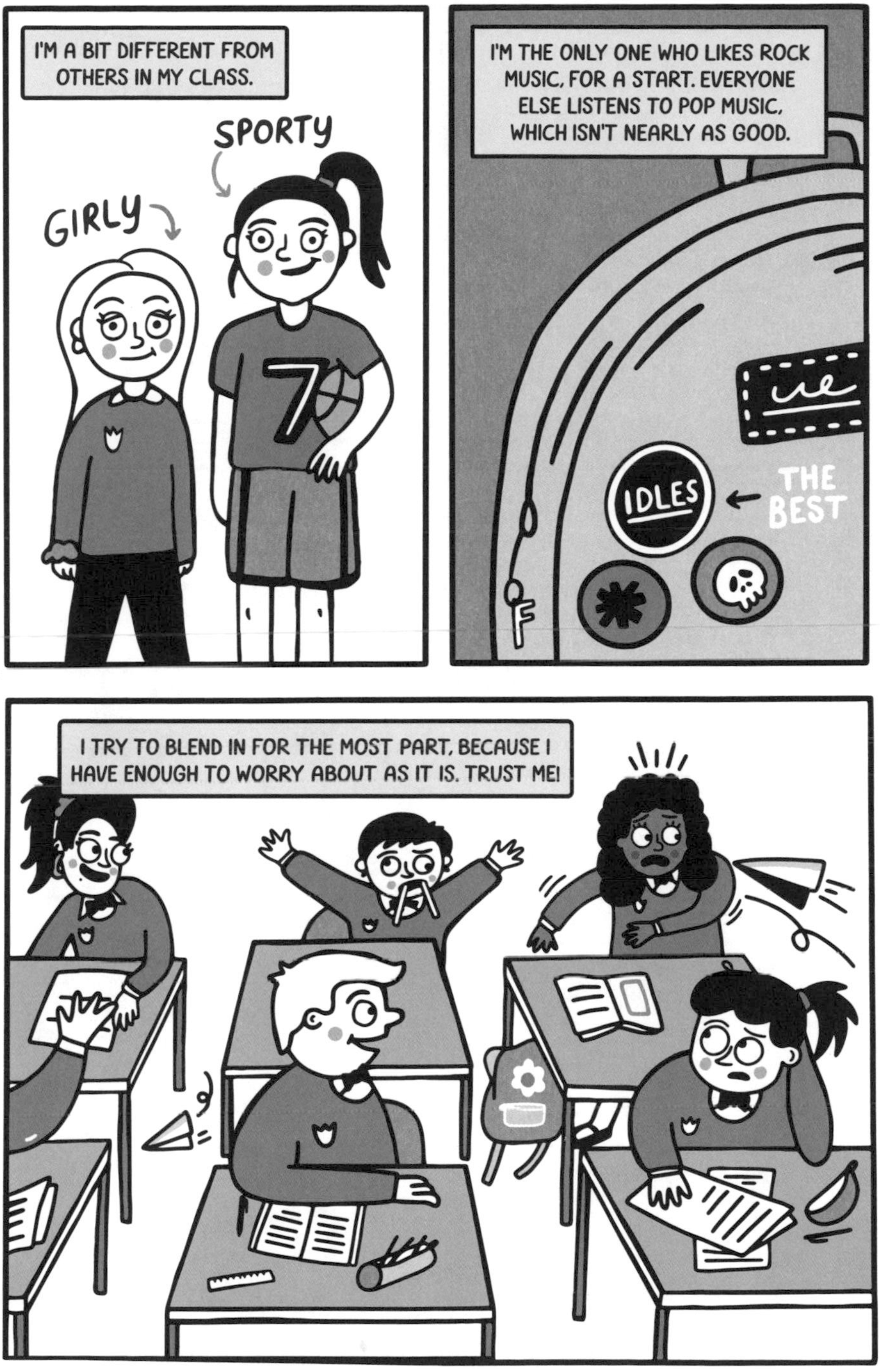
I'M A BIT DIFFERENT FROM OTHERS IN MY CLASS.
SPORTY
GIRLY
7
I'M THE ONLY ONE WHO LIKES ROCK MUSIC, FOR A START. EVERYONE ELSE LISTENS TO POP MUSIC, WHICH ISN'T NEARLY AS GOOD.
IDLES
THE BEST
I TRY TO BLEND IN FOR THE MOST PART, BECAUSE I HAVE ENOUGH TO WORRY ABOUT AS IT IS. TRUST ME!

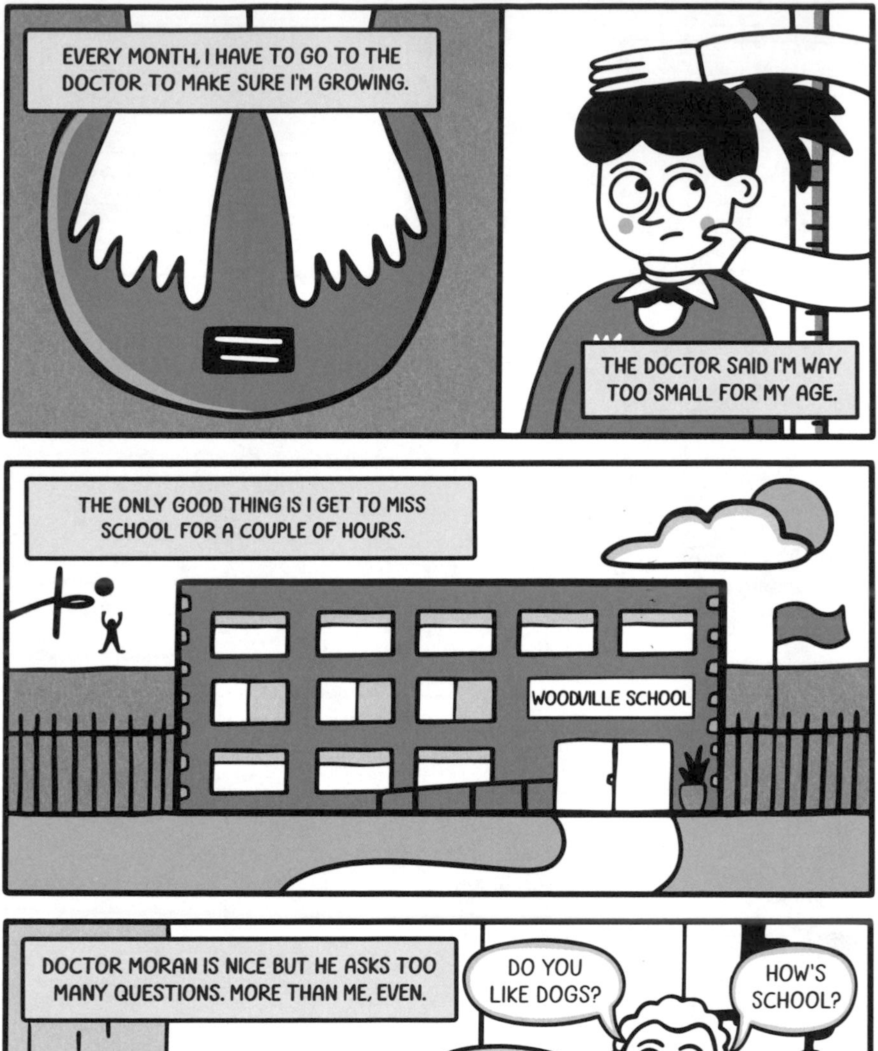
EVERY MONTH, I HAVE TO GO TO THE DOCTOR TO MAKE SURE I'M GROWING.
THE DOCTOR SAID I'M WAY TOO SMALL FOR MY AGE.
THE ONLY GOOD THING IS I GET TO MISS SCHOOL FOR A COUPLE OF HOURS.
WOODVILLE SCHOOL
DOCTOR MORAN IS NICE BUT HE ASKS TOO MANY QUESTIONS. MORE THAN ME, EVEN.
DO YOU LIKE DOGS?
HOW'S SCHOOL?
HOW ARE YOU FEELING?
O Z
P E D

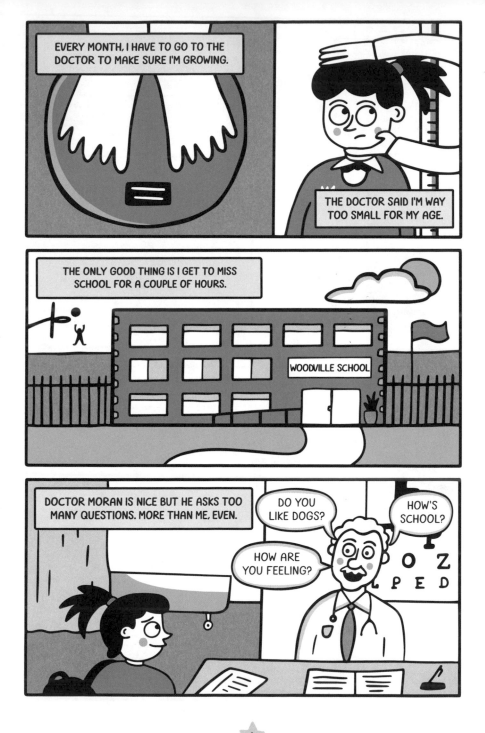

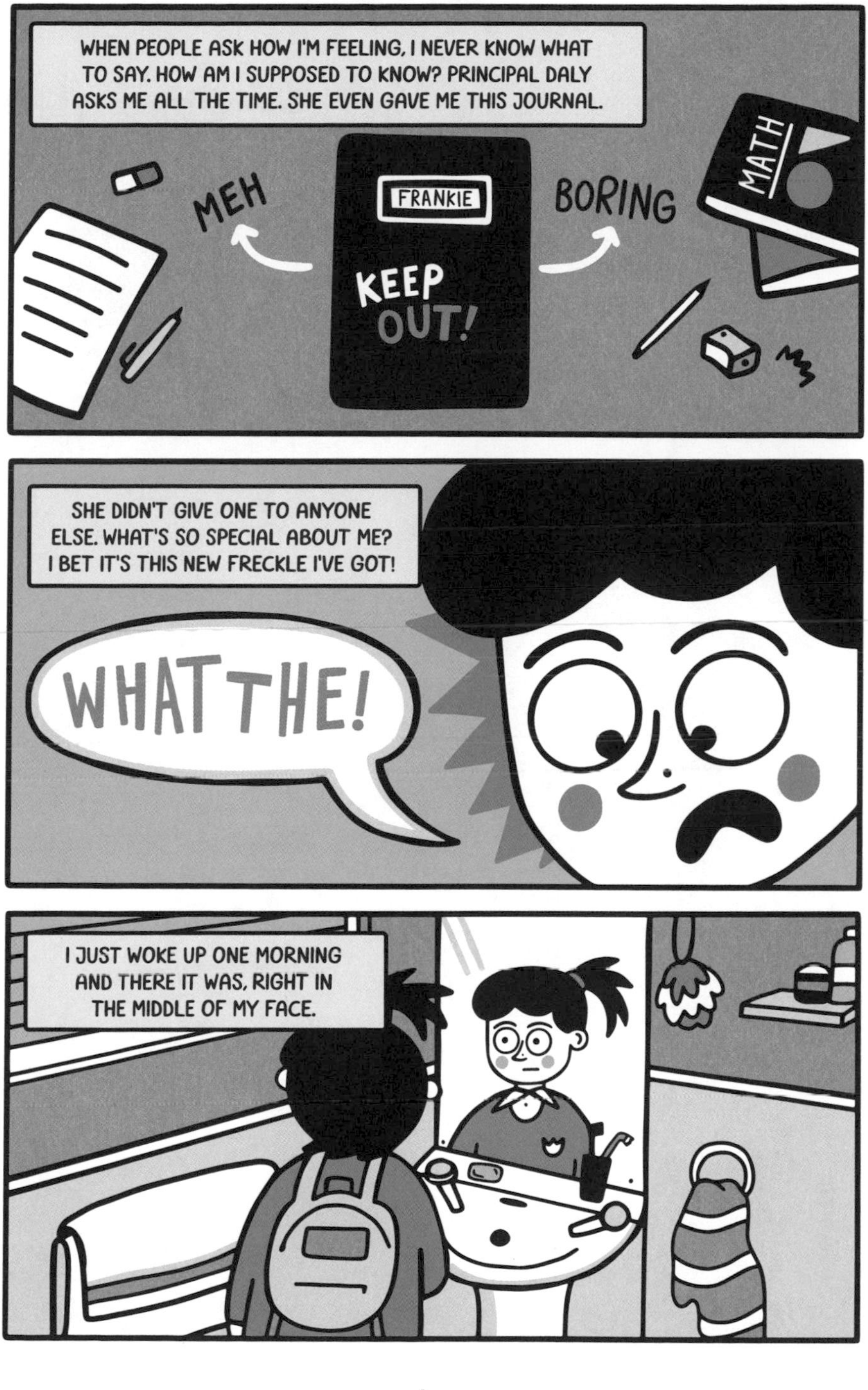

WHEN PEOPLE ASK HOW I'M FEELING, I NEVER KNOW WHAT TO SAY. HOW AM I SUPPOSED TO KNOW? PRINCIPAL DALY ASKS ME ALL THE TIME. SHE EVEN GAVE ME THIS JOURNAL.
MEH
FRANKIE
KEEP OUT!
BORING
MATH
SHE DIDN'T GIVE ONE TO ANYONE ELSE. WHAT'S SO SPECIAL ABOUT ME? I BET IT'S THIS NEW FRECKLE I'VE GOT!
WHAT THE!
I JUST WOKE UP ONE MORNING AND THERE IT WAS, RIGHT IN THE MIDDLE OF MY FACE.

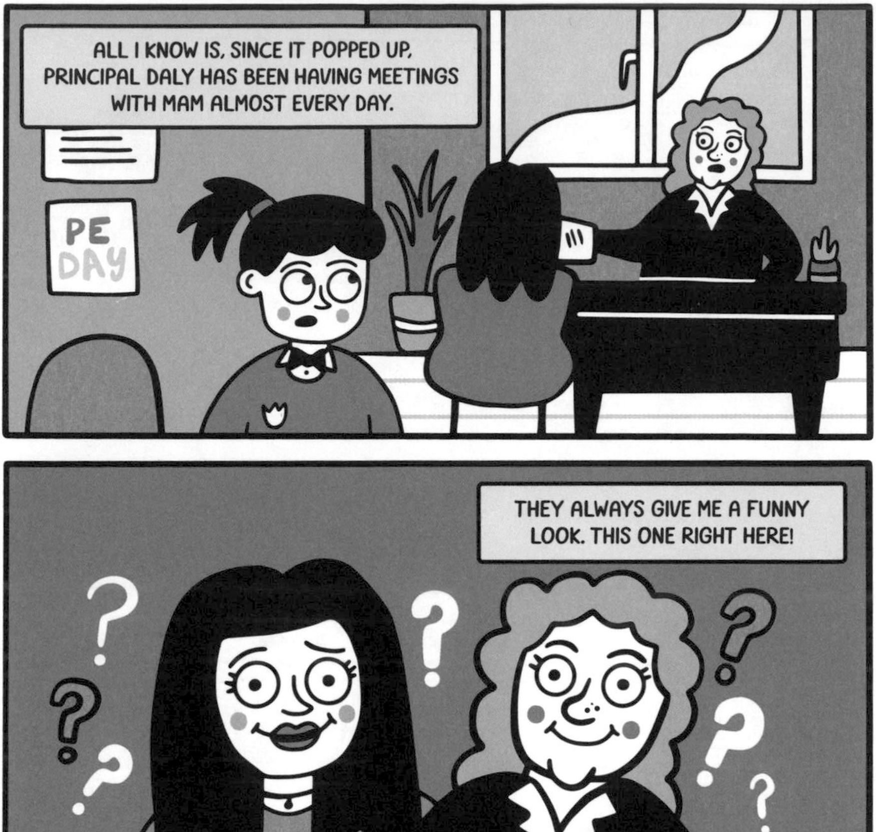
ALL I KNOW IS, SINCE IT POPPED UP, PRINCIPAL DALY HAS BEEN HAVING MEETINGS WITH MAM ALMOST EVERY DAY.
PE DAY
THEY ALWAYS GIVE ME A FUNNY LOOK. THIS ONE RIGHT HERE!
MAYBE THEY'RE THINKING OF REMOVING MY FRECKLE AND PUTTING IT IN A MUSEUM...
WOW!
IT'S SO FAMOUS, IT EVEN HAS ITS OWN NETFLIX SERIES. SEASON 7 IS COMING THIS SPRING!
DO NOT TOUCH

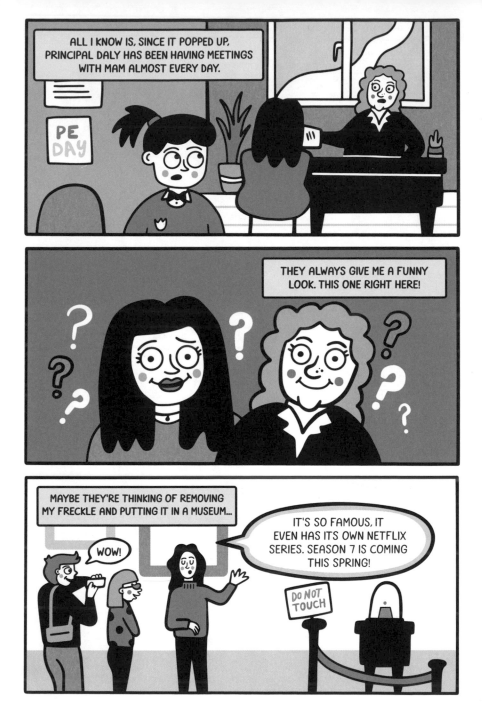

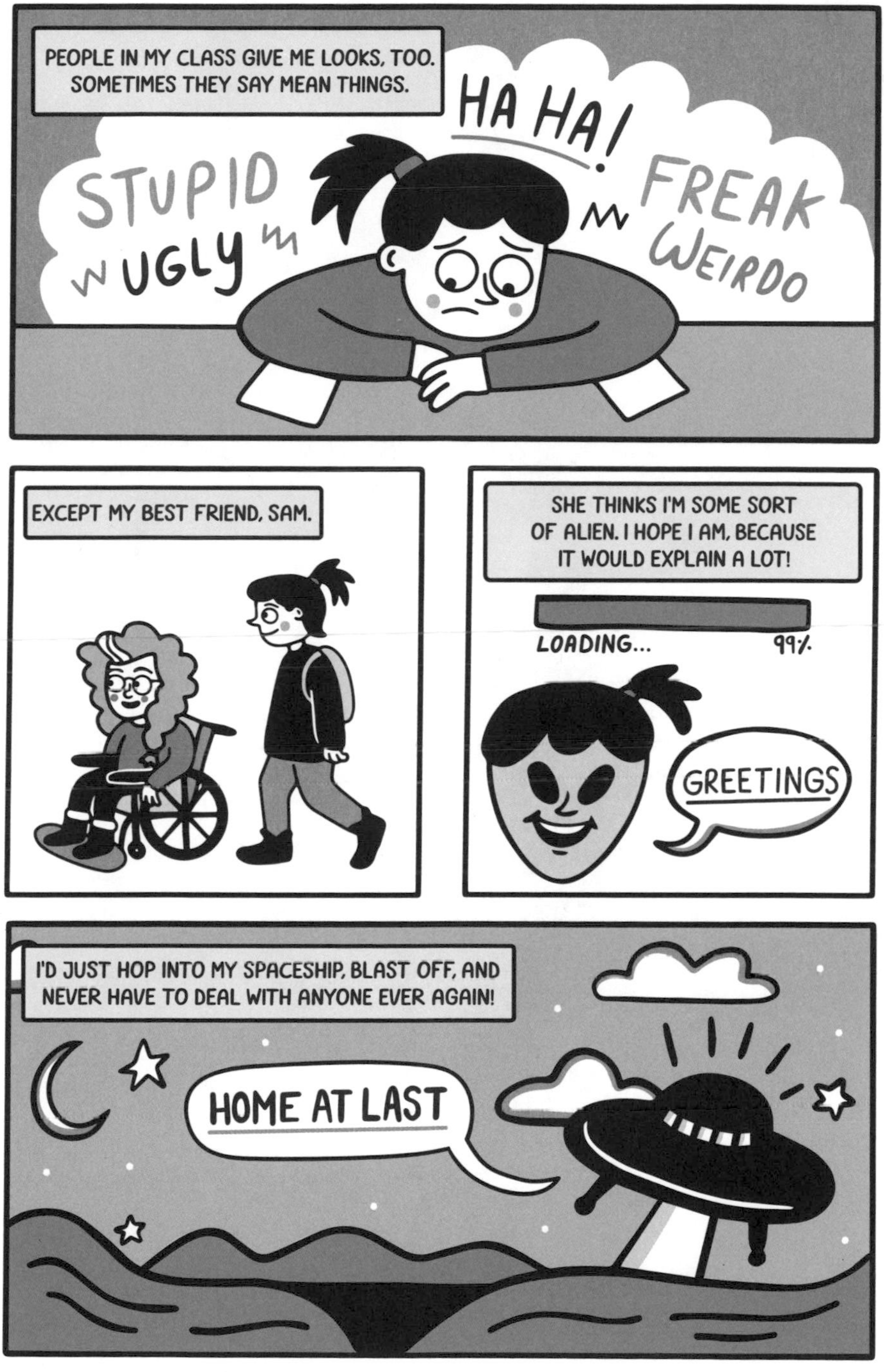
PEOPLE IN MY CLASS GIVE ME LOOKS, TOO. SOMETIMES THEY SAY MEAN THINGS.
HA HA!
STUPID
UGLY
FREAK
WEIRDO
EXCEPT MY BEST FRIEND, SAM.
SHE THINKS I'M SOME SORT OF ALIEN. I HOPE I AM, BECAUSE IT WOULD EXPLAIN A LOT!
LOADING... 99%
GREETINGS
I'D JUST HOP INTO MY SPACESHIP, BLAST OFF, AND NEVER HAVE TO DEAL WITH ANYONE EVER AGAIN!
HOME AT LAST

ONE PERSON I'D LIKE TO NEVER SEE AGAIN IS MS. CRACKLE, MY TEACHER. SHE'S SCARY! HER SKIN LOOKS LIKE A RAISIN, AND HER BREATH SMELLS LIKE A BIN FULL OF ROTTEN CABBAGES. I'VE NO IDEA WHAT THAT SMELLS LIKE, BUT I'M GUESSING IT'S PRETTY BAD.

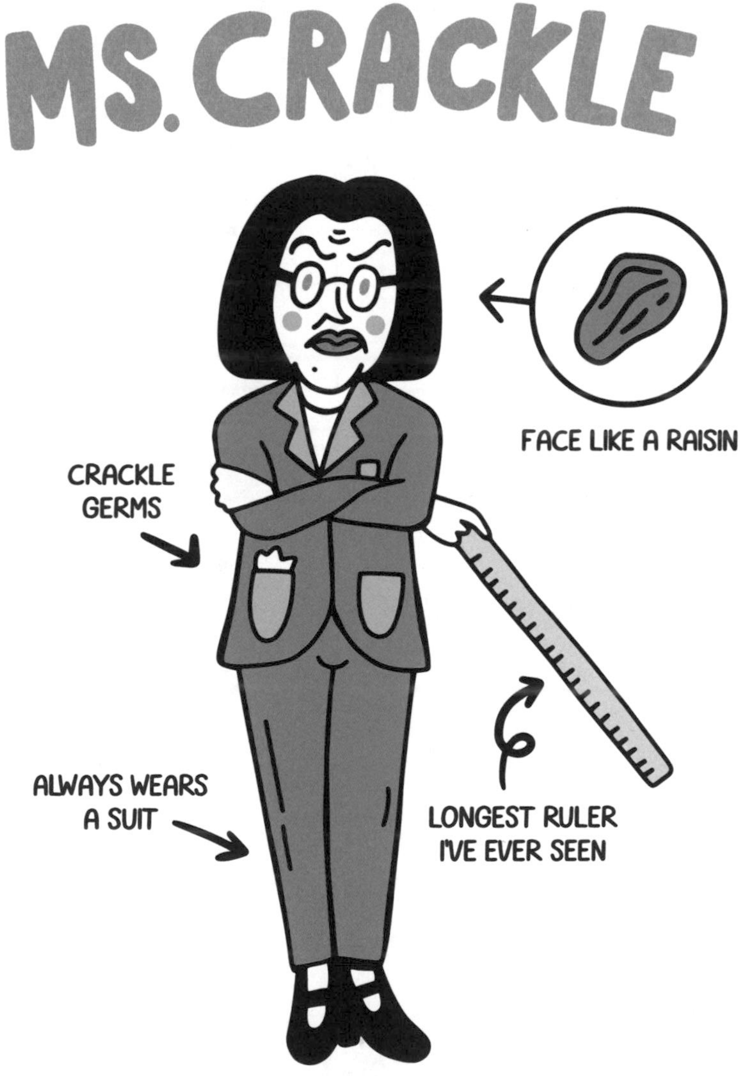
MS. CRACKLE
FACE LIKE A RAISIN
CRACKLE GERMS
ALWAYS WEARS A SUIT
LONGEST RULER I'VE EVER SEEN

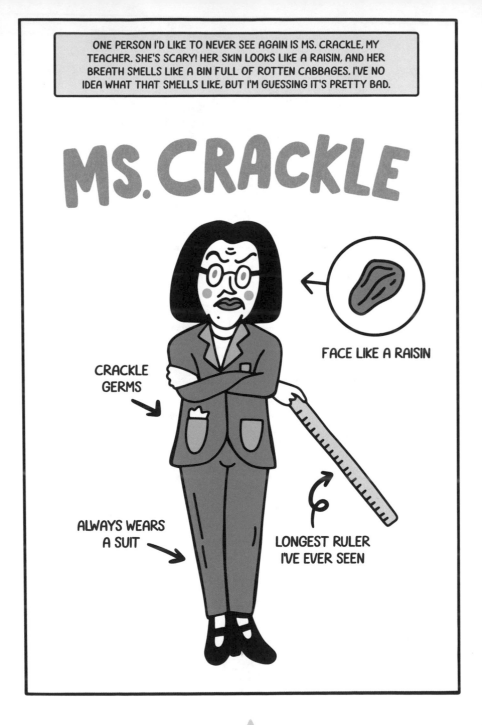

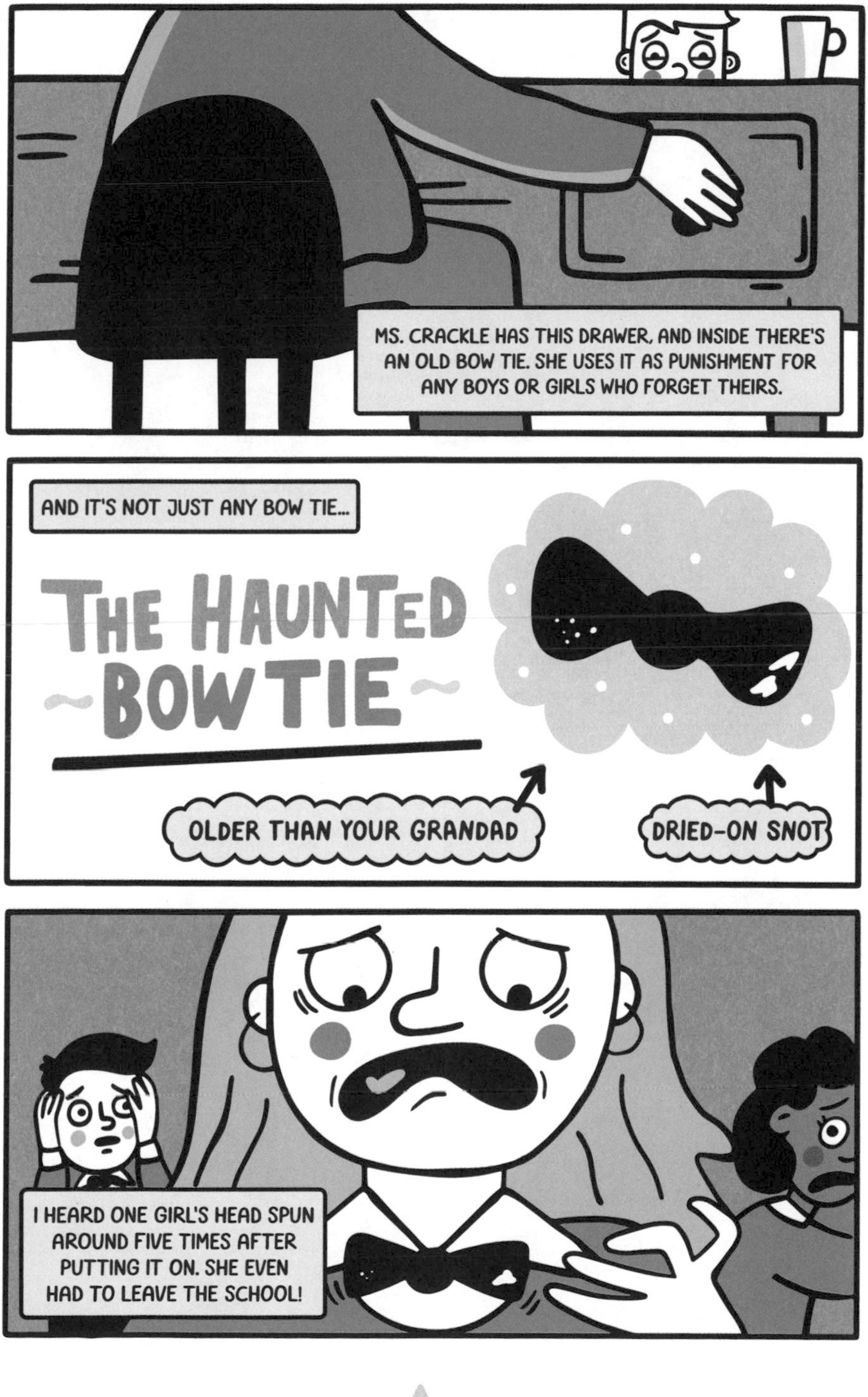
MS. CRACKLE HAS THIS DRAWER, AND INSIDE THERE'S AN OLD BOW TIE. SHE USES IT AS PUNISHMENT FOR ANY BOYS OR GIRLS WHO FORGET THEIRS.
AND IT'S NOT JUST ANY BOW TIE...
THE HAUNTED BOW TIE
OLDER THAN YOUR GRANDAD
DRIED-ON SNOT
I HEARD ONE GIRL'S HEAD SPUN AROUND FIVE TIMES AFTER PUTTING IT ON. SHE EVEN HAD TO LEAVE THE SCHOOL!

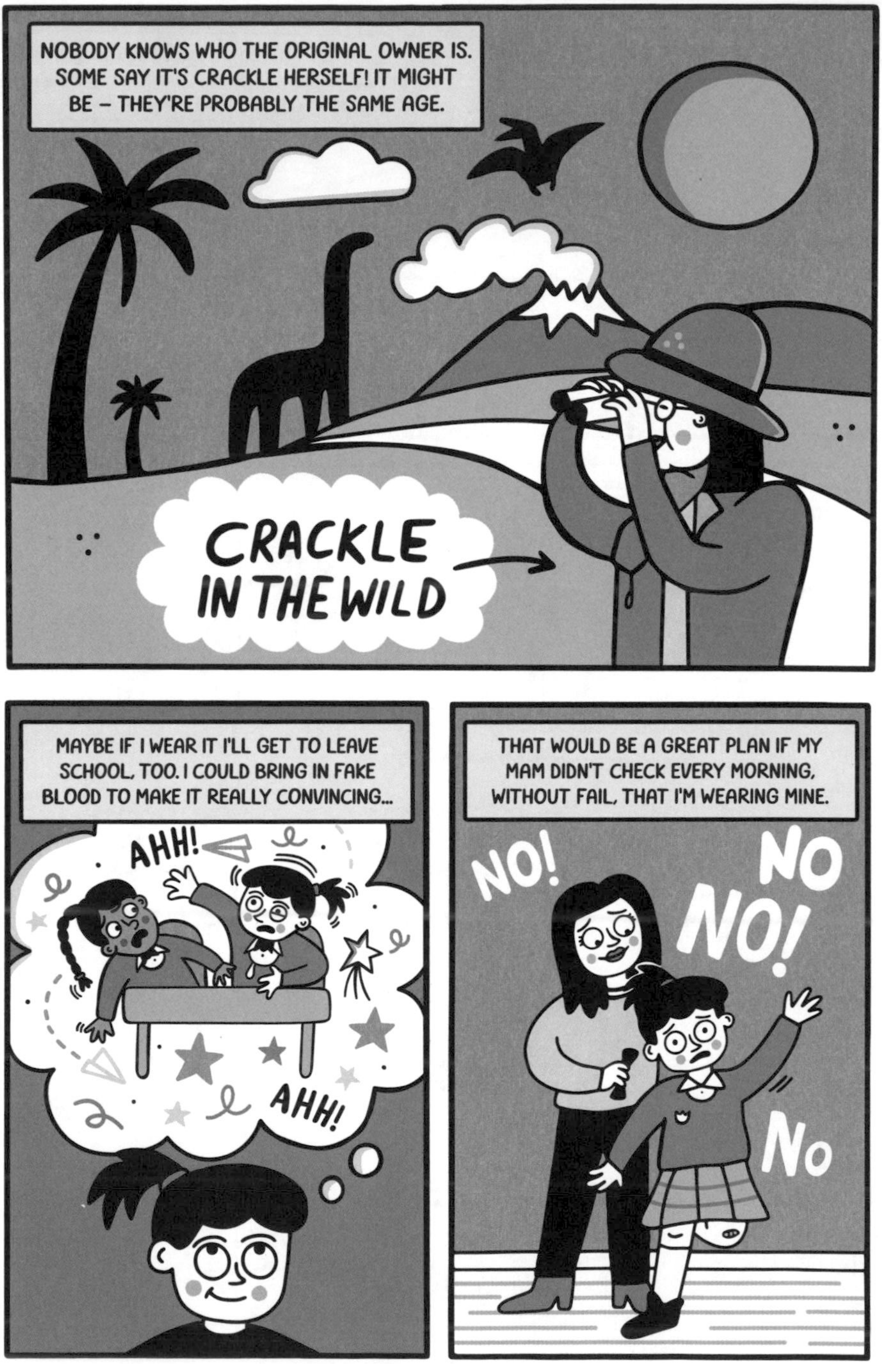
NOBODY KNOWS WHO THE ORIGINAL OWNER IS. SOME SAY IT'S CRACKLE HERSELF! IT MIGHT BE – THEY'RE PROBABLY THE SAME AGE.
CRACKLE IN THE WILD
MAYBE IF I WEAR IT I'LL GET TO LEAVE SCHOOL, TOO. I COULD BRING IN FAKE BLOOD TO MAKE IT REALLY CONVINCING...
AHH!
AHH!
THAT WOULD BE A GREAT PLAN IF MY MAM DIDN'T CHECK EVERY MORNING, WITHOUT FAIL, THAT I'M WEARING MINE.
NO!
NO
NO!
No

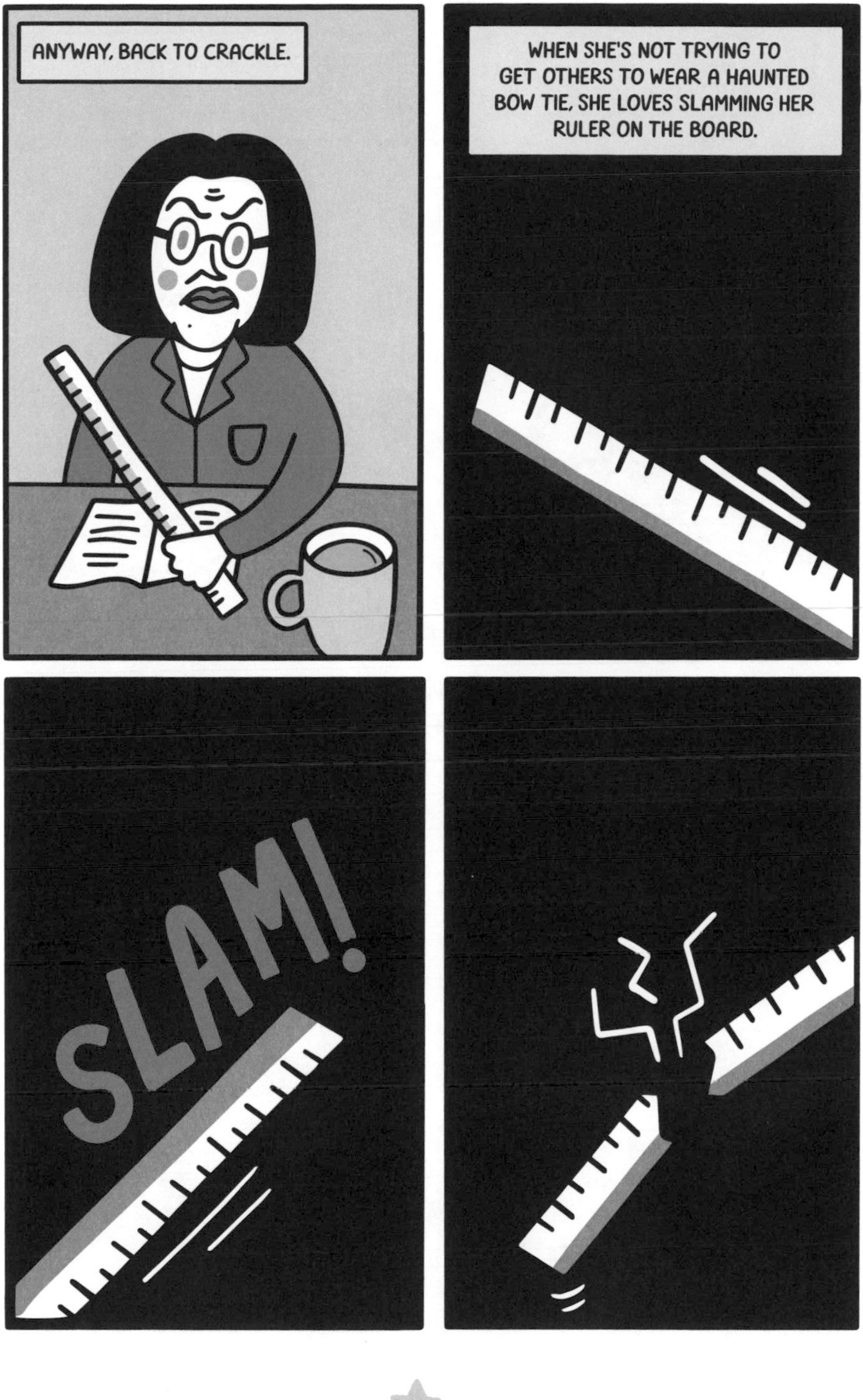
ANYWAY, BACK TO CRACKLE.
WHEN SHE'S NOT TRYING TO GET OTHERS TO WEAR A HAUNTED BOW TIE, SHE LOVES SLAMMING HER RULER ON THE BOARD.
SLAM!

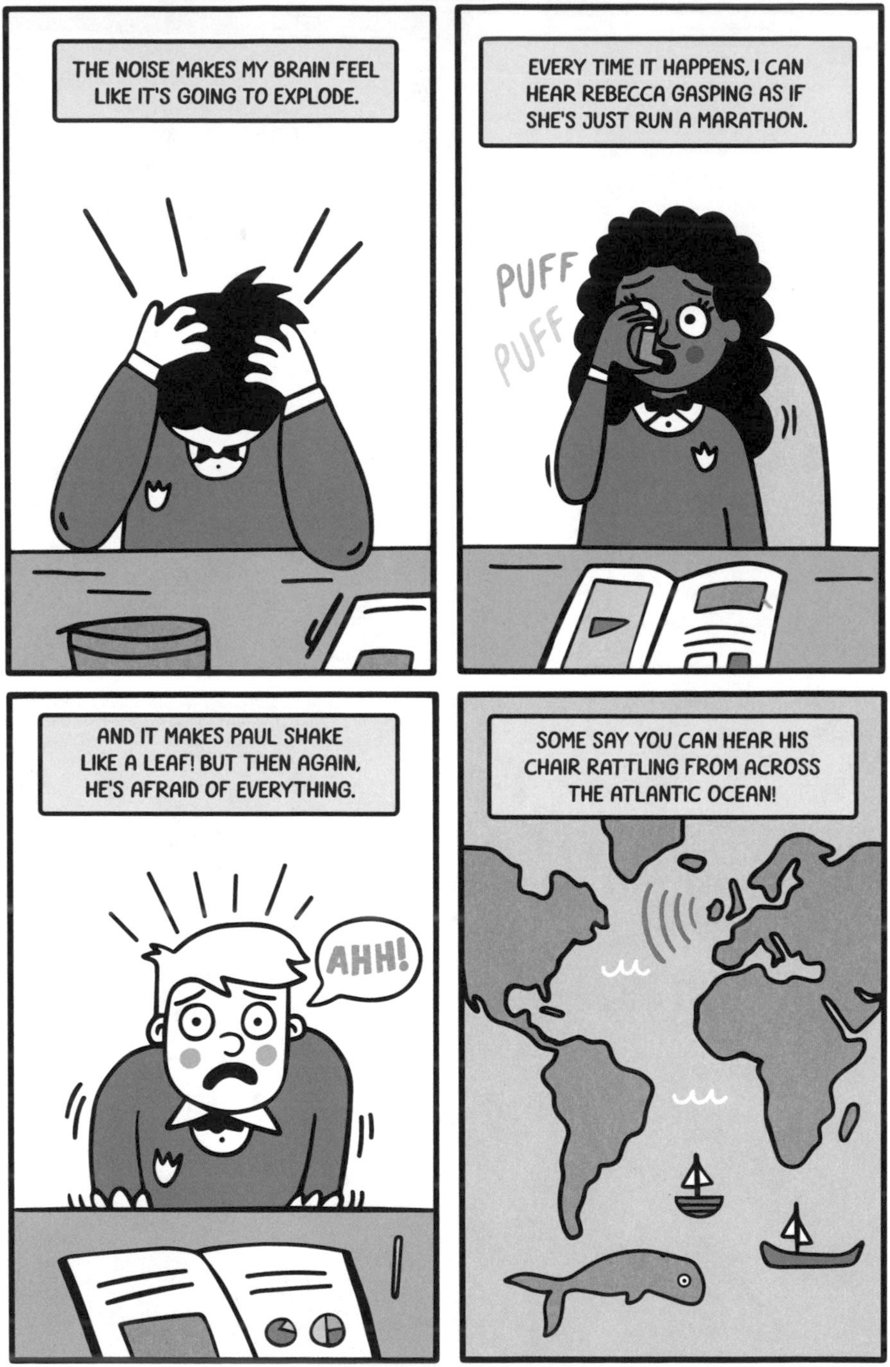
THE NOISE MAKES MY BRAIN FEEL LIKE IT'S GOING TO EXPLODE.
EVERY TIME IT HAPPENS, I CAN HEAR REBECCA GASPING AS IF SHE'S JUST RUN A MARATHON.
PUFF
PUFF
AND IT MAKES PAUL SHAKE LIKE A LEAF! BUT THEN AGAIN, HE'S AFRAID OF EVERYTHING.
AHH!
SOME SAY YOU CAN HEAR HIS CHAIR RATTLING FROM ACROSS THE ATLANTIC OCEAN!

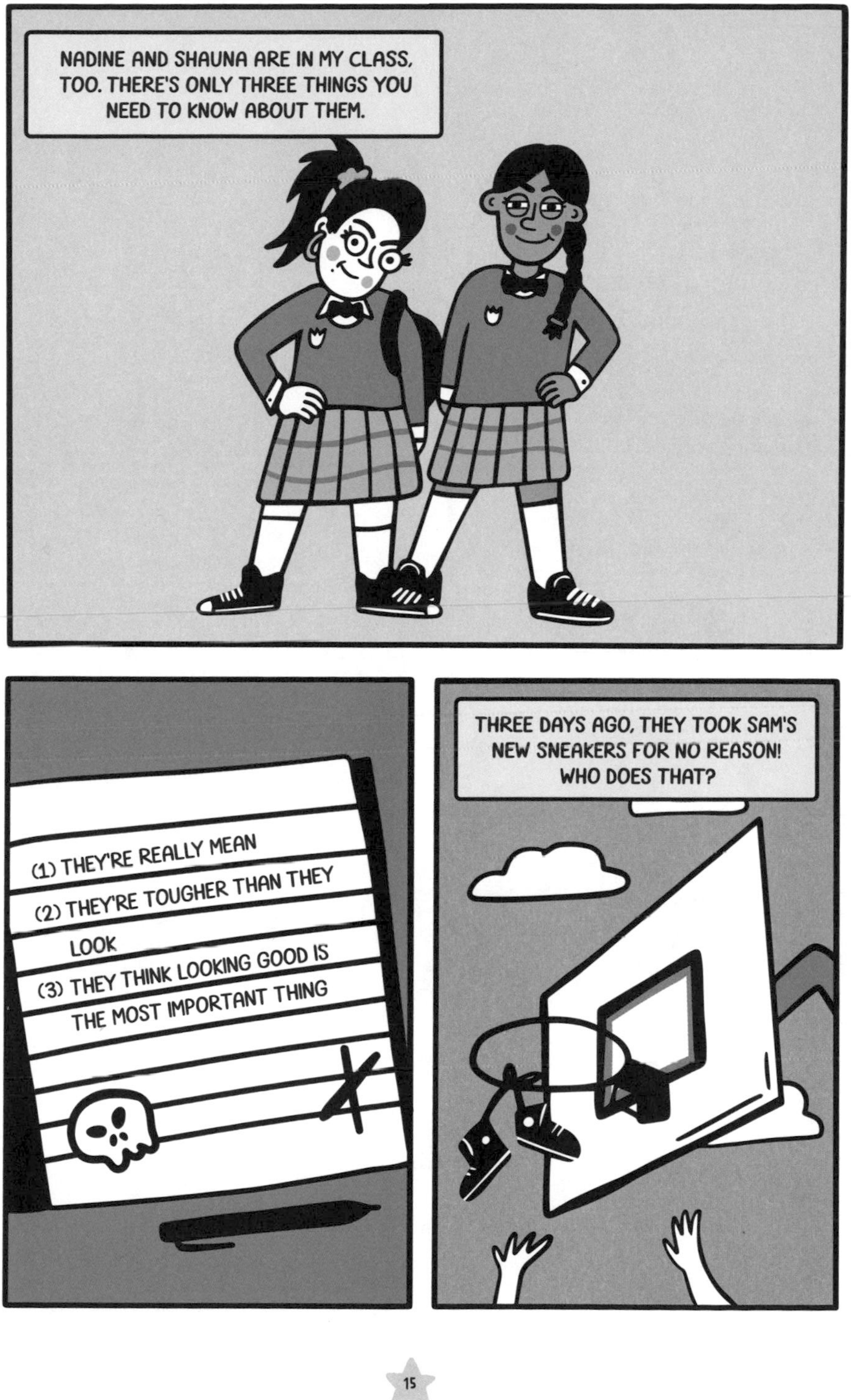
NADINE AND SHAUNA ARE IN MY CLASS, TOO. THERE'S ONLY THREE THINGS YOU NEED TO KNOW ABOUT THEM.
(1) THEY'RE REALLY MEAN
(2) THEY'RE TOUGHER THAN THEY LOOK
(3) THEY THINK LOOKING GOOD IS THE MOST IMPORTANT THING
THREE DAYS AGO, THEY TOOK SAM'S NEW SNEAKERS FOR NO REASON! WHO DOES THAT?

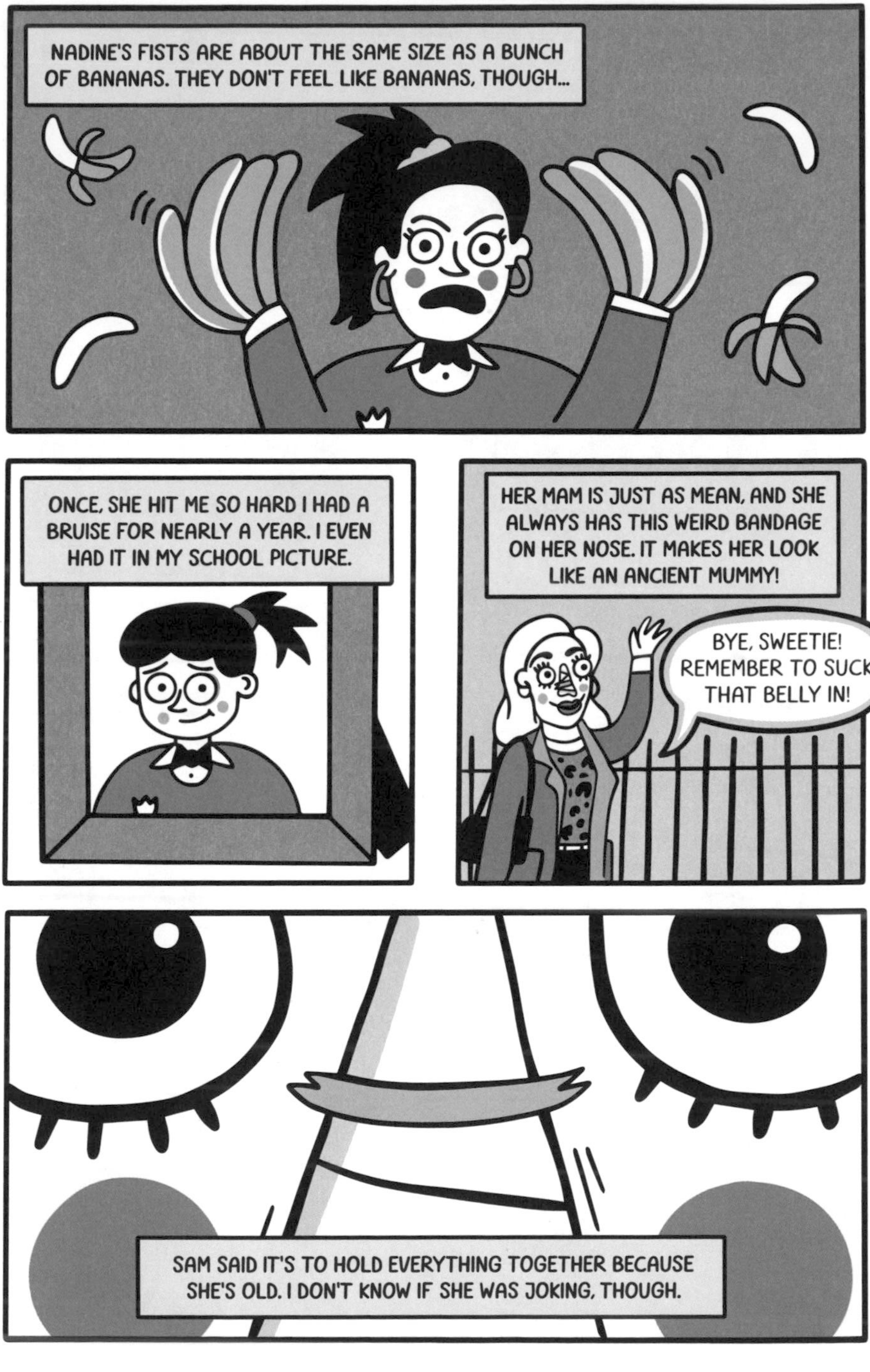
NADINE'S FISTS ARE ABOUT THE SAME SIZE AS A BUNCH OF BANANAS. THEY DON'T FEEL LIKE BANANAS, THOUGH...
ONCE, SHE HIT ME SO HARD I HAD A BRUISE FOR NEARLY A YEAR. I EVEN HAD IT IN MY SCHOOL PICTURE.
HER MAM IS JUST AS MEAN, AND SHE ALWAYS HAS THIS WEIRD BANDAGE ON HER NOSE. IT MAKES HER LOOK LIKE AN ANCIENT MUMMY!
BYE, SWEETIE! REMEMBER TO SUCK THAT BELLY IN!
SAM SAID IT'S TO HOLD EVERYTHING TOGETHER BECAUSE SHE'S OLD. I DON'T KNOW IF SHE WAS JOKING, THOUGH.

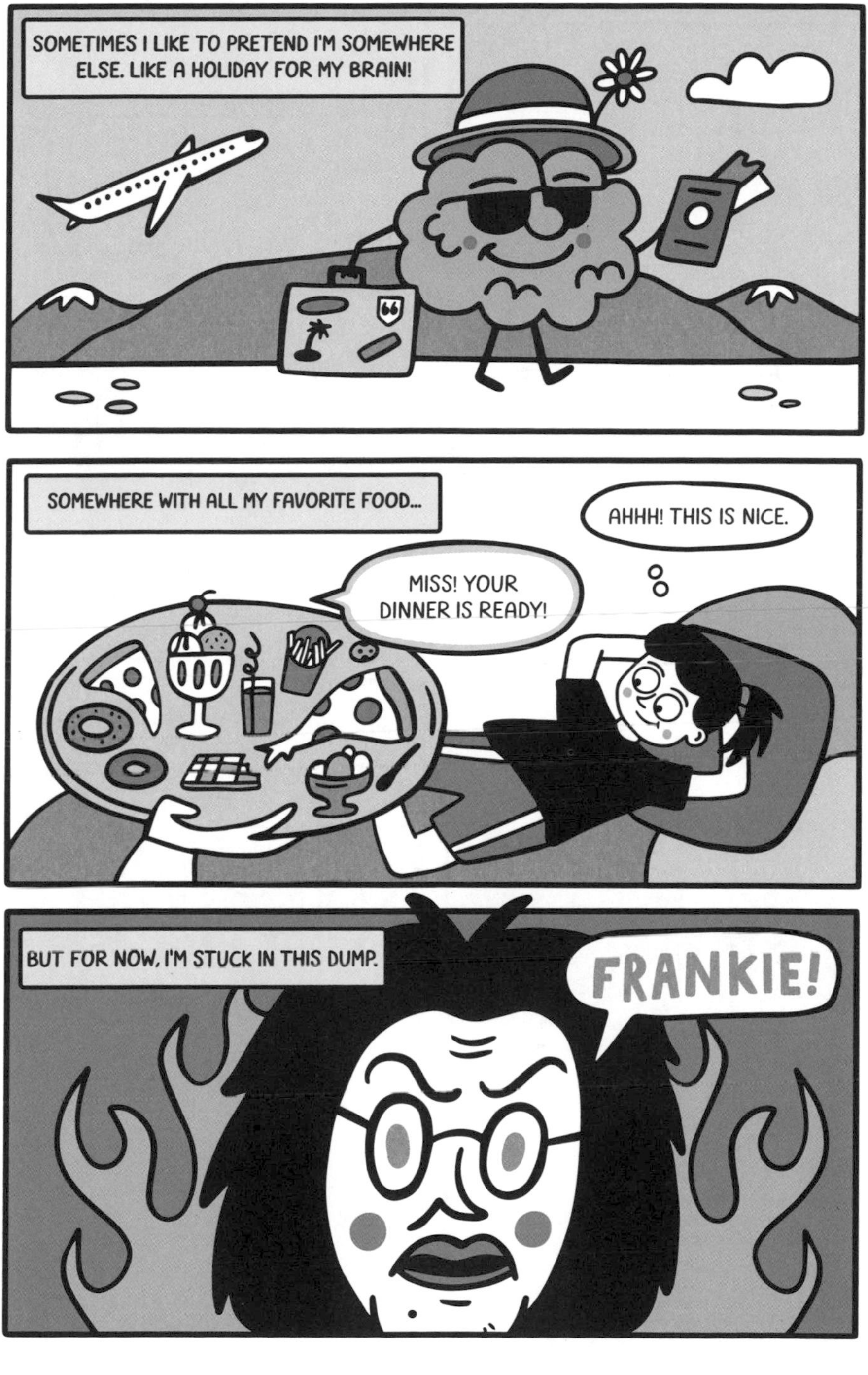
SOMETIMES I LIKE TO PRETEND I'M SOMEWHERE ELSE. LIKE A HOLIDAY FOR MY BRAIN!
SOMEWHERE WITH ALL MY FAVORITE FOOD...
AHHH! THIS IS NICE.
MISS! YOUR DINNER IS READY!
BUT FOR NOW, I'M STUCK IN THIS DUMP.
FRANKIE!

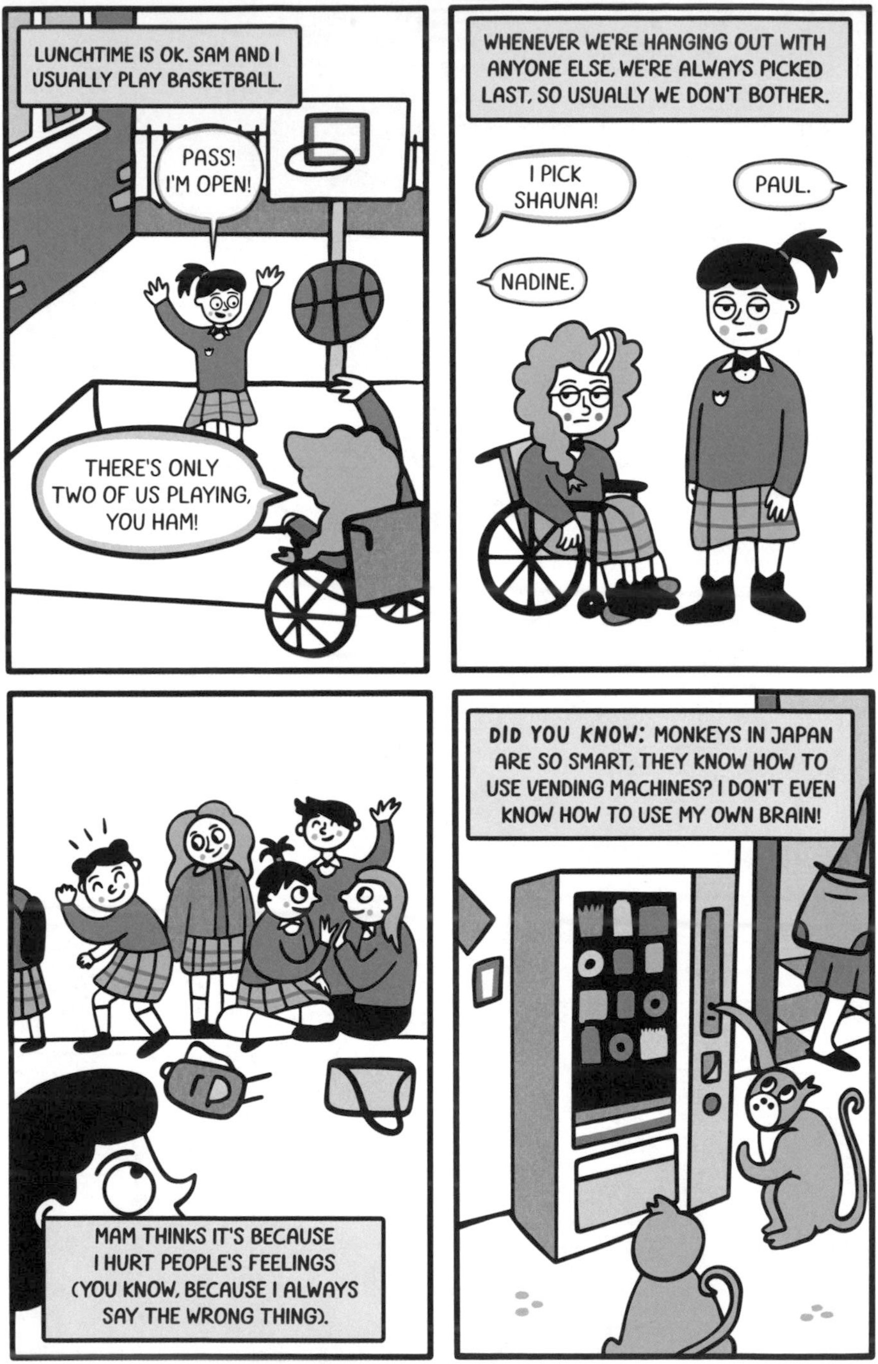
LUNCHTIME IS OK. SAM AND I USUALLY PLAY BASKETBALL.
PASS! I'M OPEN!
THERE'S ONLY TWO OF US PLAYING, YOU HAM!
WHENEVER WE'RE HANGING OUT WITH ANYONE ELSE, WE'RE ALWAYS PICKED LAST, SO USUALLY WE DON'T BOTHER.
I PICK SHAUNA!
PAUL.
NADINE.
MAM THINKS IT'S BECAUSE I HURT PEOPLE'S FEELINGS (YOU KNOW, BECAUSE I ALWAYS SAY THE WRONG THING).
DID YOU KNOW: MONKEYS IN JAPAN ARE SO SMART, THEY KNOW HOW TO USE VENDING MACHINES? I DON'T EVEN KNOW HOW TO USE MY OWN BRAIN!

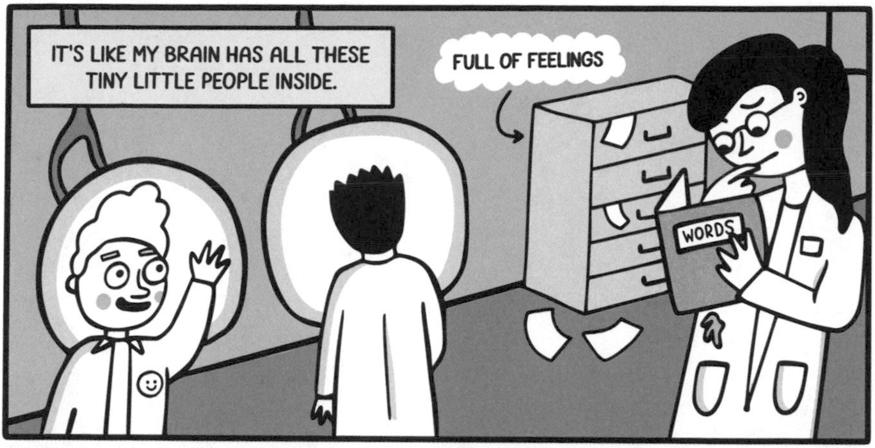
IT'S LIKE MY BRAIN HAS ALL THESE TINY LITTLE PEOPLE INSIDE.
FULL OF FEELINGS
WORDS

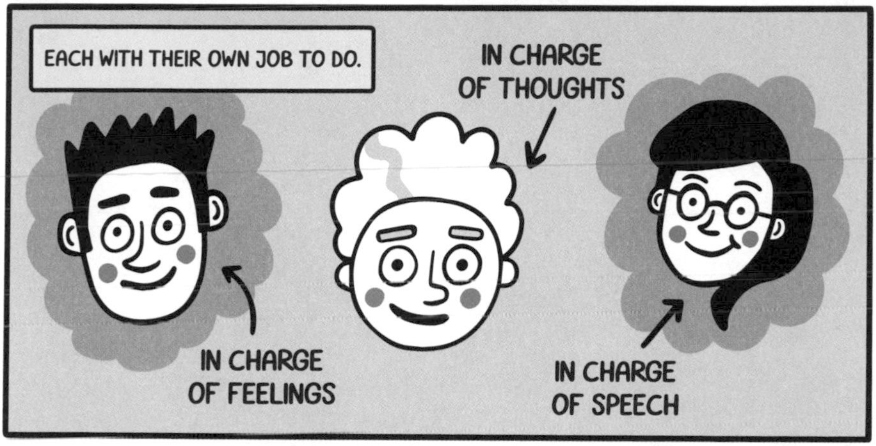
EACH WITH THEIR OWN JOB TO DO.
IN CHARGE OF THOUGHTS
IN CHARGE OF FEELINGS
IN CHARGE OF SPEECH

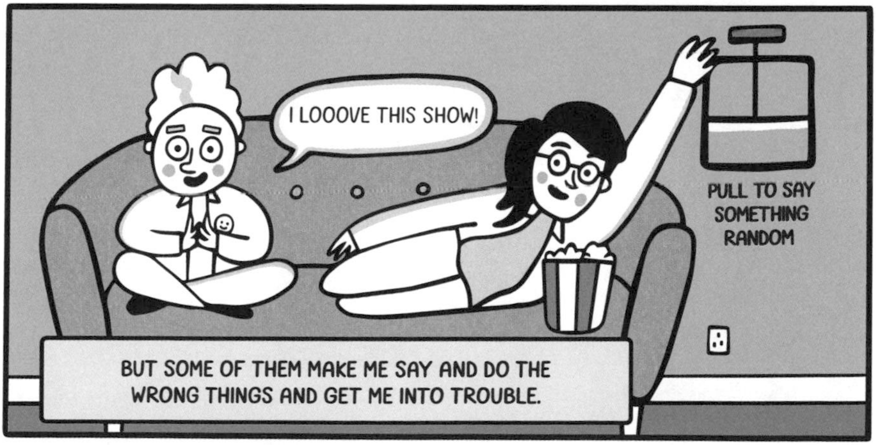
I LOOOVE THIS SHOW!
PULL TO SAY SOMETHING RANDOM
BUT SOME OF THEM MAKE ME SAY AND DO THE WRONG THINGS AND GET ME INTO TROUBLE.

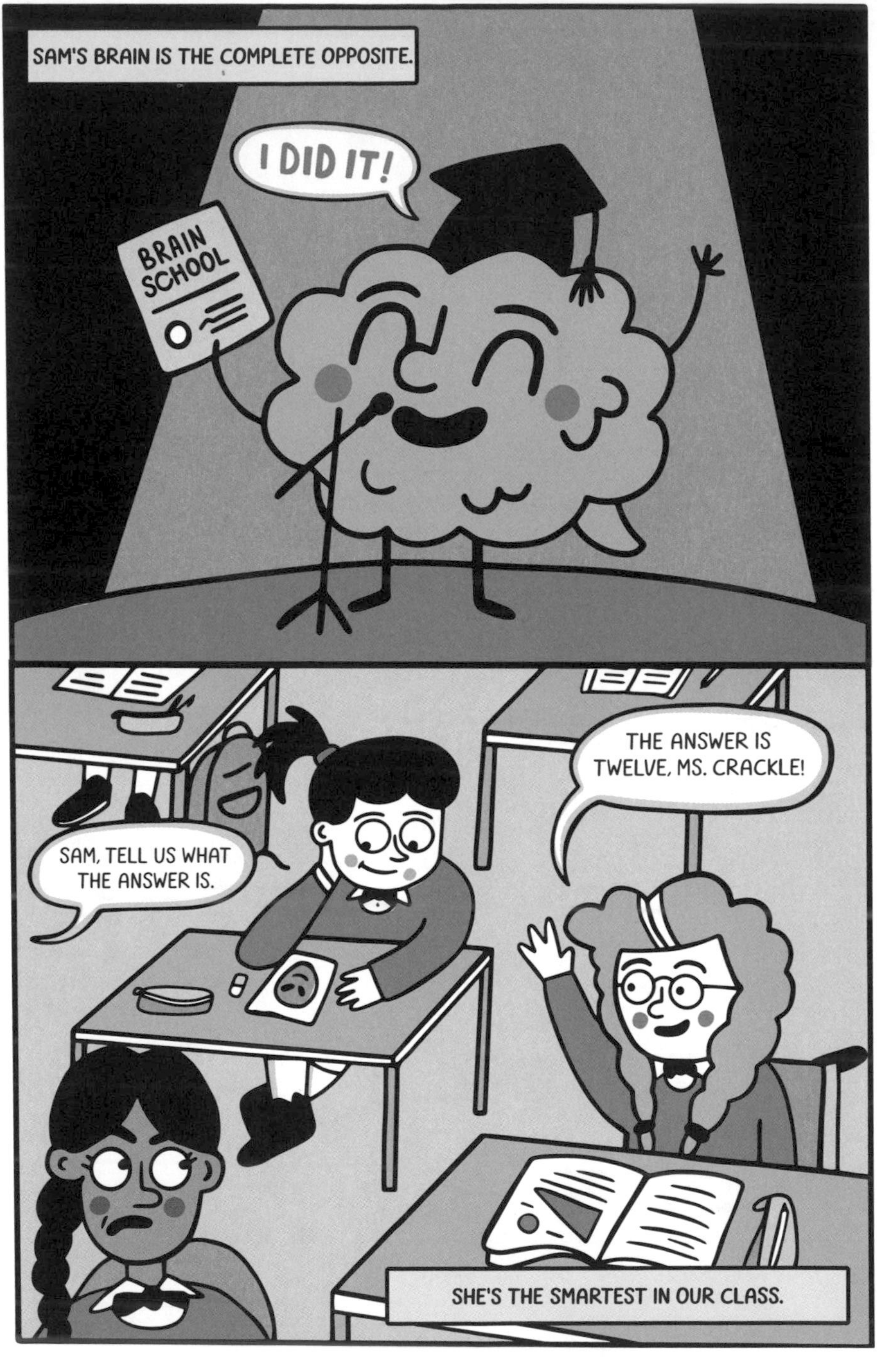
SAM'S BRAIN IS THE COMPLETE OPPOSITE.
I DID IT!
BRAIN SCHOOL
SAM, TELL US WHAT THE ANSWER IS.
THE ANSWER IS TWELVE, MS. CRACKLE!
SHE'S THE SMARTEST IN OUR CLASS.

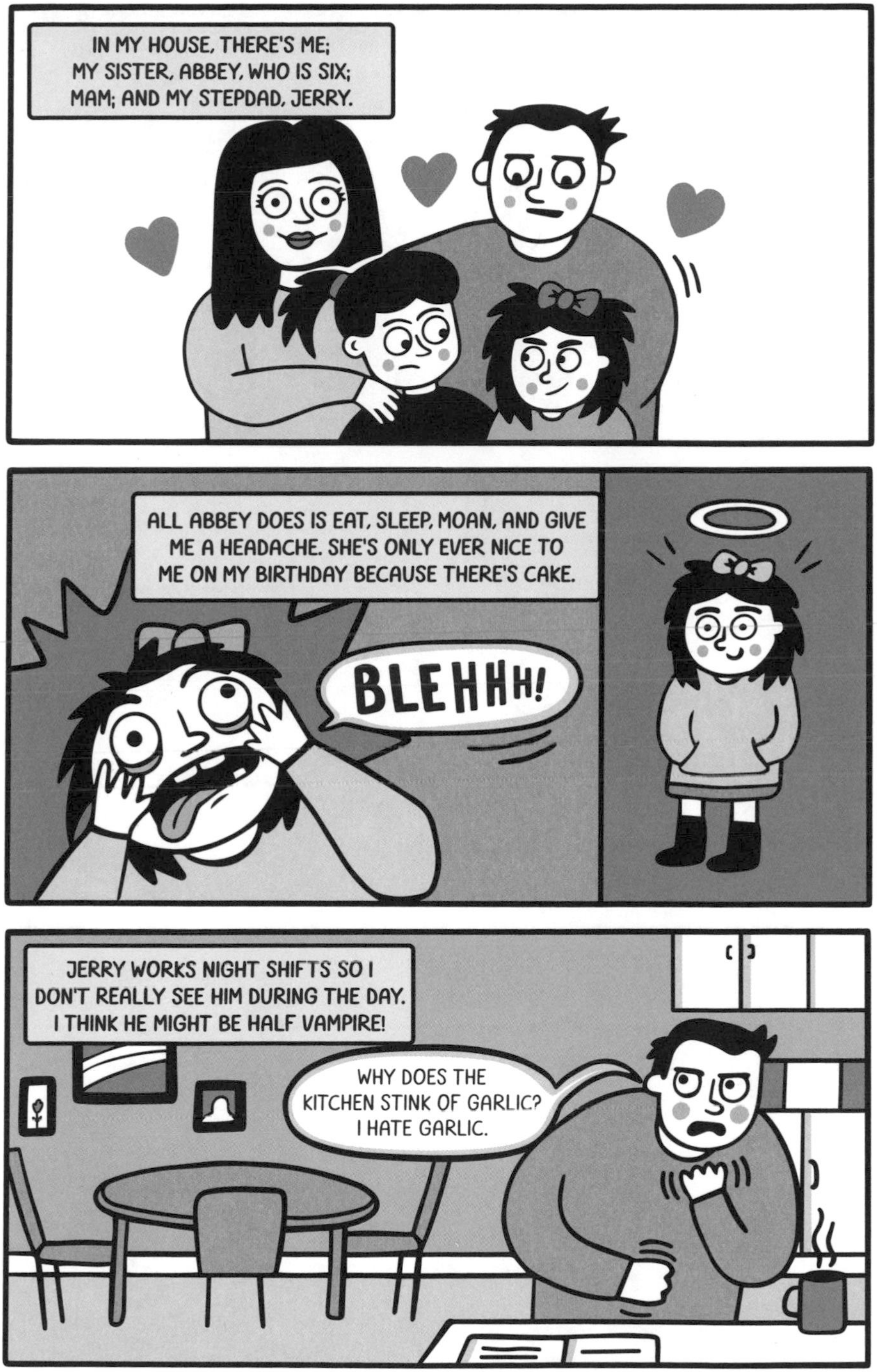
IN MY HOUSE, THERE'S ME; MY SISTER, ABBEY, WHO IS SIX; MAM; AND MY STEPDAD, JERRY.
ALL ABBEY DOES IS EAT, SLEEP, MOAN, AND GIVE ME A HEADACHE. SHE'S ONLY EVER NICE TO ME ON MY BIRTHDAY BECAUSE THERE'S CAKE.
BLEHHH!
JERRY WORKS NIGHT SHIFTS SO I DON'T REALLY SEE HIM DURING THE DAY. I THINK HE MIGHT BE HALF VAMPIRE!
WHY DOES THE KITCHEN STINK OF GARLIC? I HATE GARLIC.

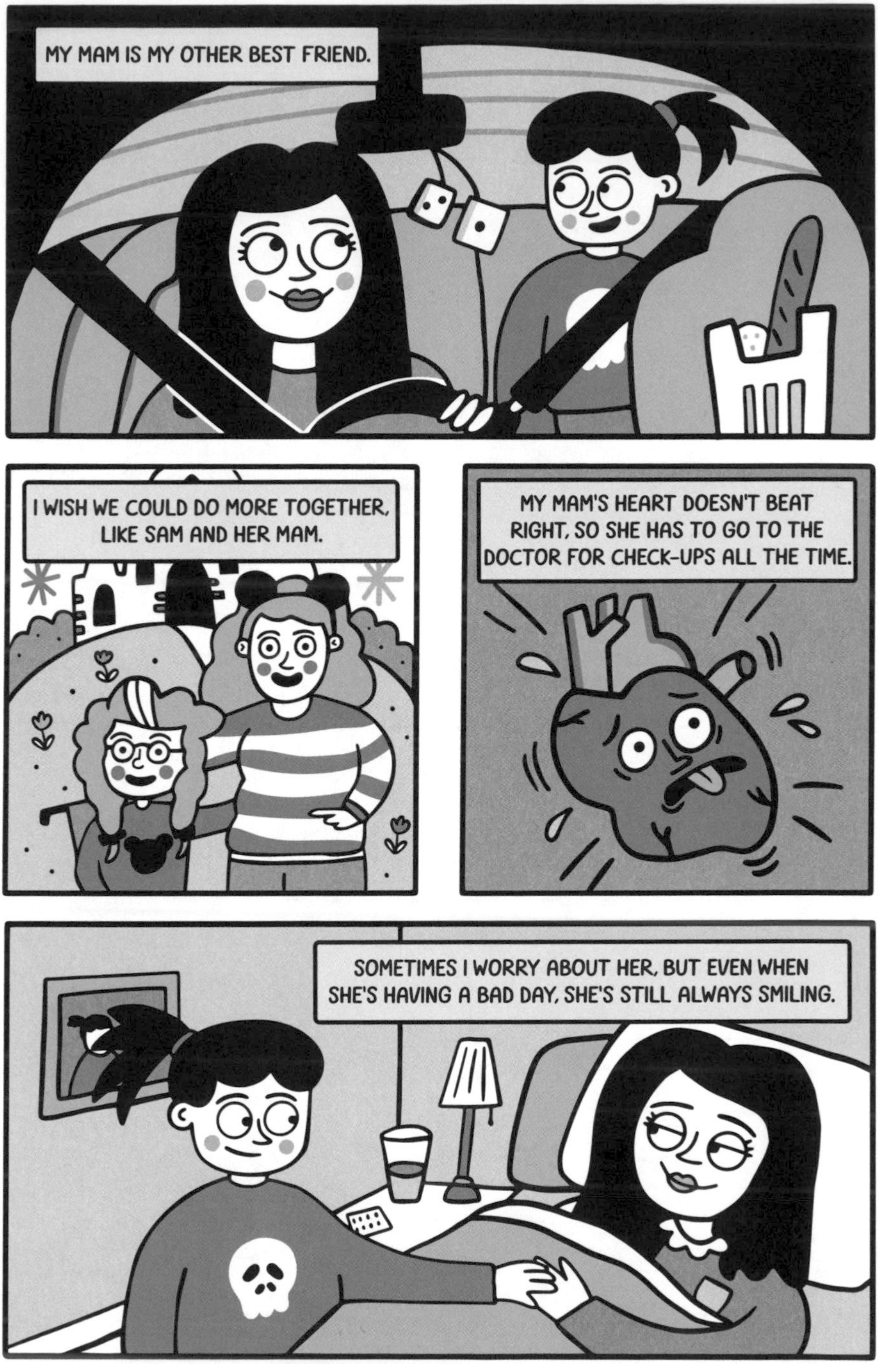
MY MAM IS MY OTHER BEST FRIEND.
I WISH WE COULD DO MORE TOGETHER, LIKE SAM AND HER MAM.
MY MAM'S HEART DOESN'T BEAT RIGHT, SO SHE HAS TO GO TO THE DOCTOR FOR CHECK-UPS ALL THE TIME.
SOMETIMES I WORRY ABOUT HER, BUT EVEN WHEN SHE'S HAVING A BAD DAY, SHE'S STILL ALWAYS SMILING.

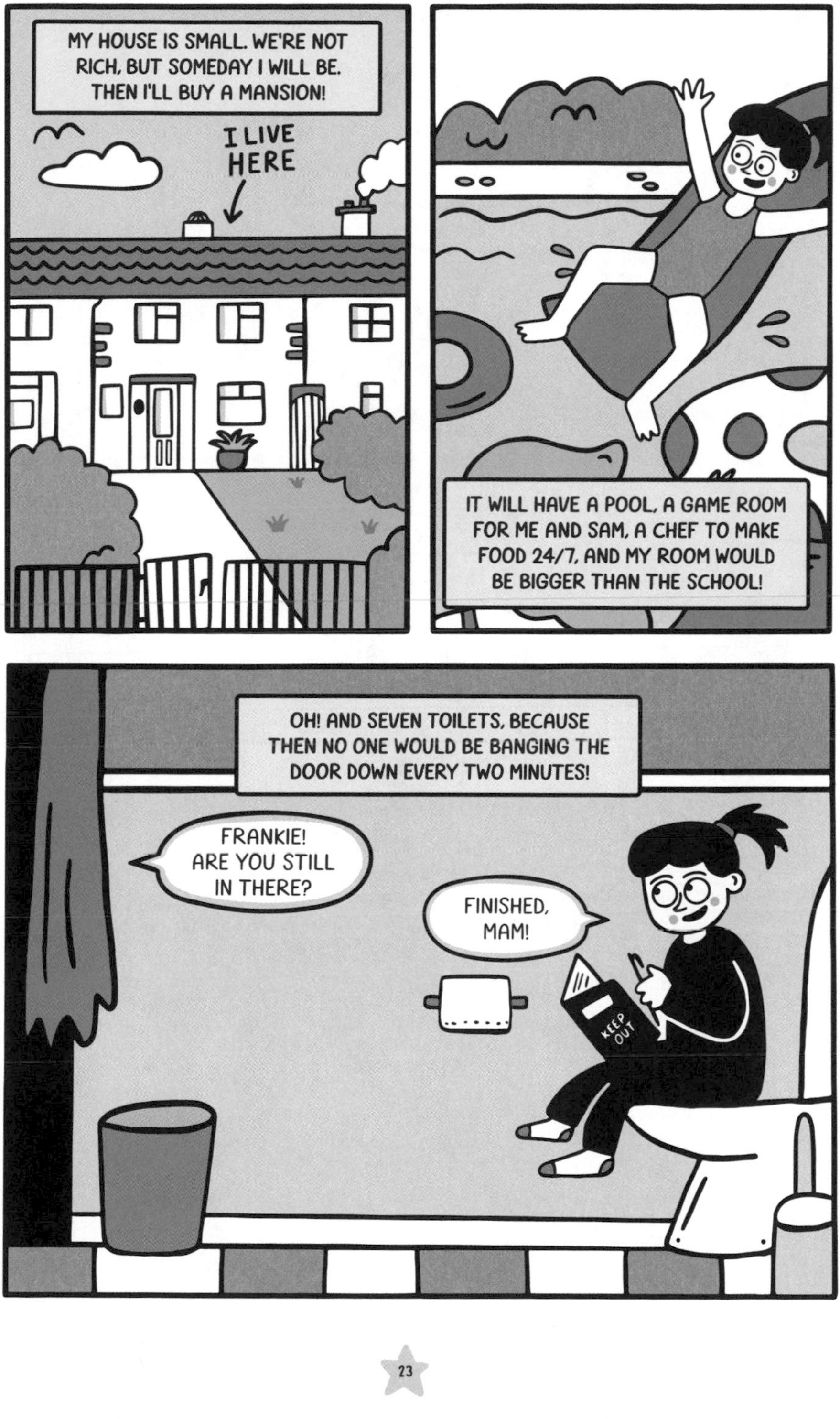
MY HOUSE IS SMALL. WE'RE NOT RICH, BUT SOMEDAY I WILL BE. THEN I'LL BUY A MANSION!
I LIVE HERE
IT WILL HAVE A POOL, A GAME ROOM FOR ME AND SAM, A CHEF TO MAKE FOOD 24/7, AND MY ROOM WOULD BE BIGGER THAN THE SCHOOL!
OH! AND SEVEN TOILETS, BECAUSE THEN NO ONE WOULD BE BANGING THE DOOR DOWN EVERY TWO MINUTES!
FRANKIE! ARE YOU STILL IN THERE?
FINISHED, MAM!
KEEP OUT

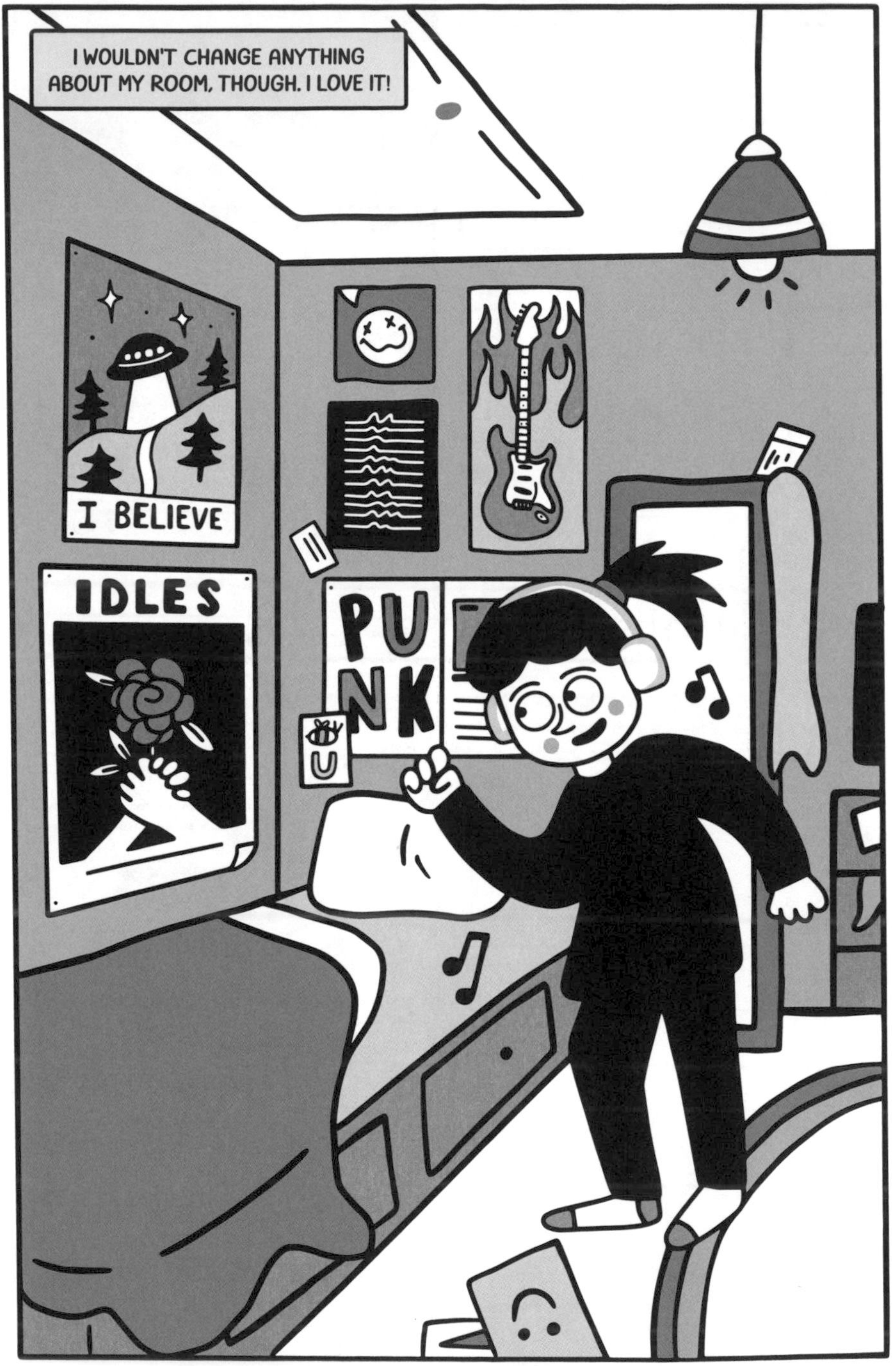
I WOULDN'T CHANGE ANYTHING ABOUT MY ROOM, THOUGH. I LOVE IT!
I BELIEVE
IDLES
PUNK

CHAPTER 2

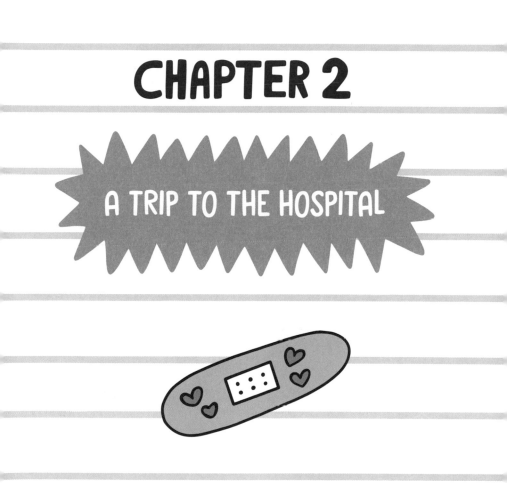

A TRIP TO THE HOSPITAL

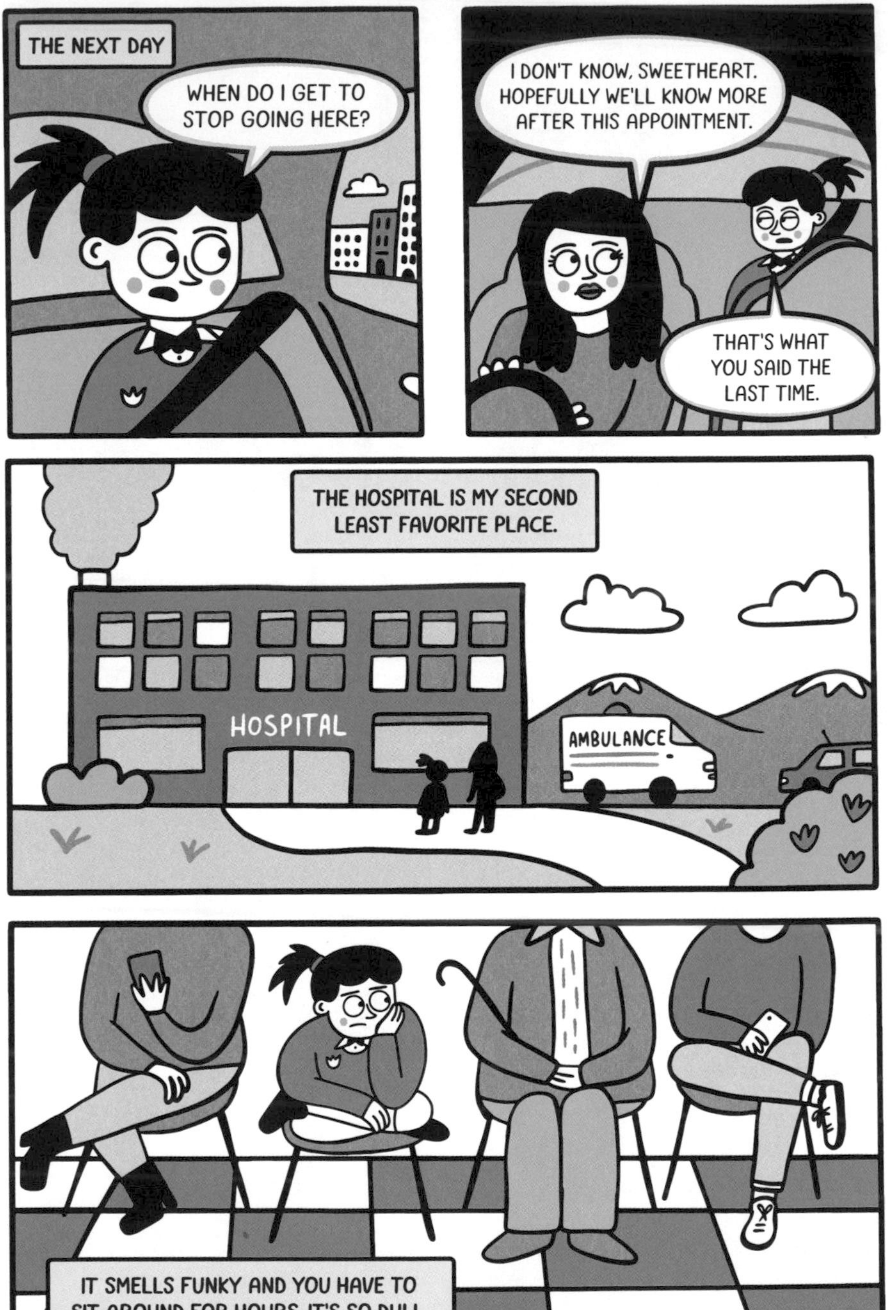
THE NEXT DAY
WHEN DO I GET TO STOP GOING HERE?
I DON'T KNOW, SWEETHEART. HOPEFULLY WE'LL KNOW MORE AFTER THIS APPOINTMENT.
THAT'S WHAT YOU SAID THE LAST TIME.
THE HOSPITAL IS MY SECOND LEAST FAVORITE PLACE.
HOSPITAL
AMBULANCE
IT SMELLS FUNKY AND YOU HAVE TO SIT AROUND FOR HOURS. IT'S SO DULL.

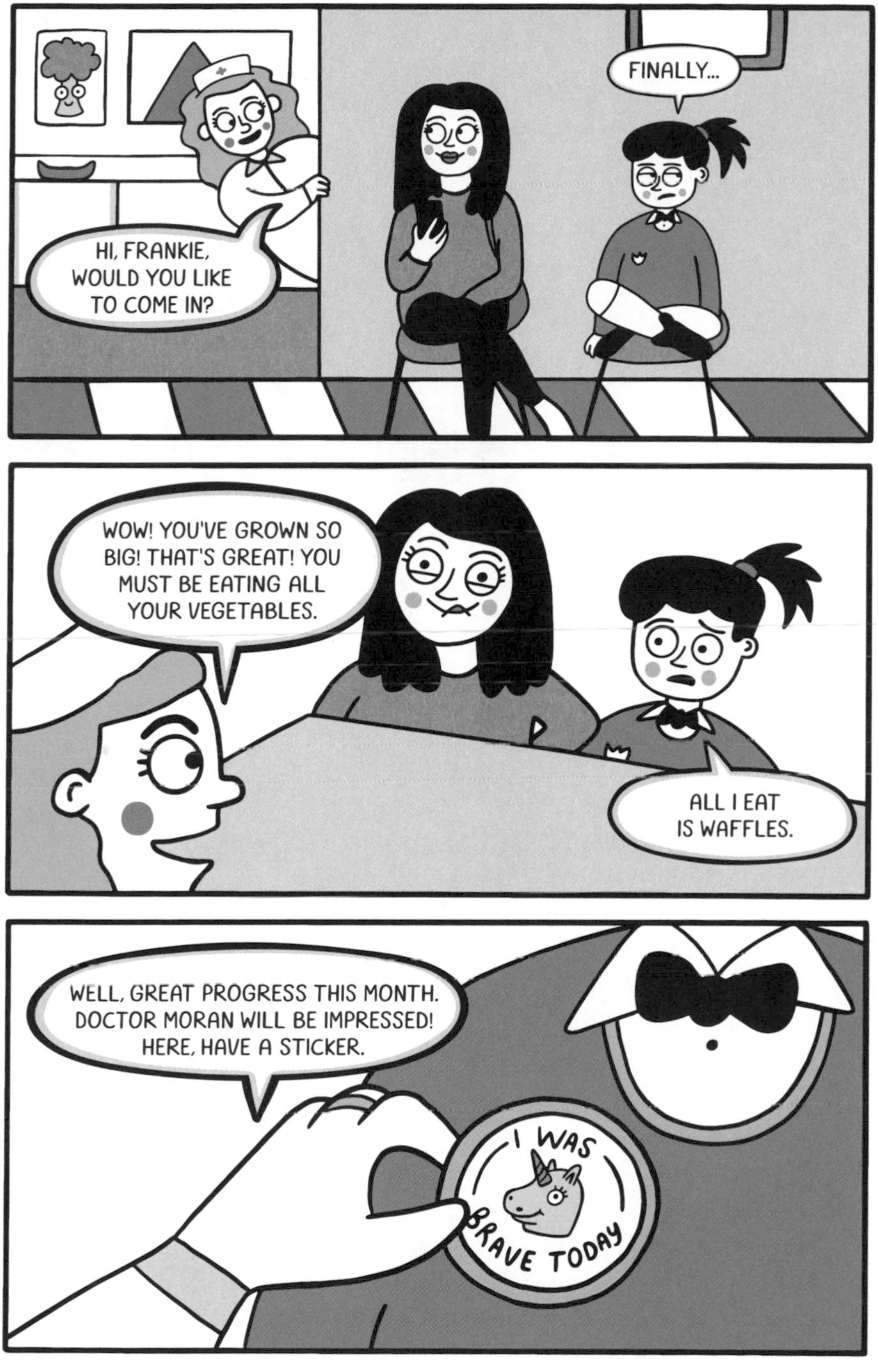
FINALLY...
HI, FRANKIE, WOULD YOU LIKE TO COME IN?
WOW! YOU'VE GROWN SO BIG! THAT'S GREAT! YOU MUST BE EATING ALL YOUR VEGETABLES.
ALL I EAT IS WAFFLES.
WELL, GREAT PROGRESS THIS MONTH. DOCTOR MORAN WILL BE IMPRESSED! HERE, HAVE A STICKER.
I WAS BRAVE TODAY

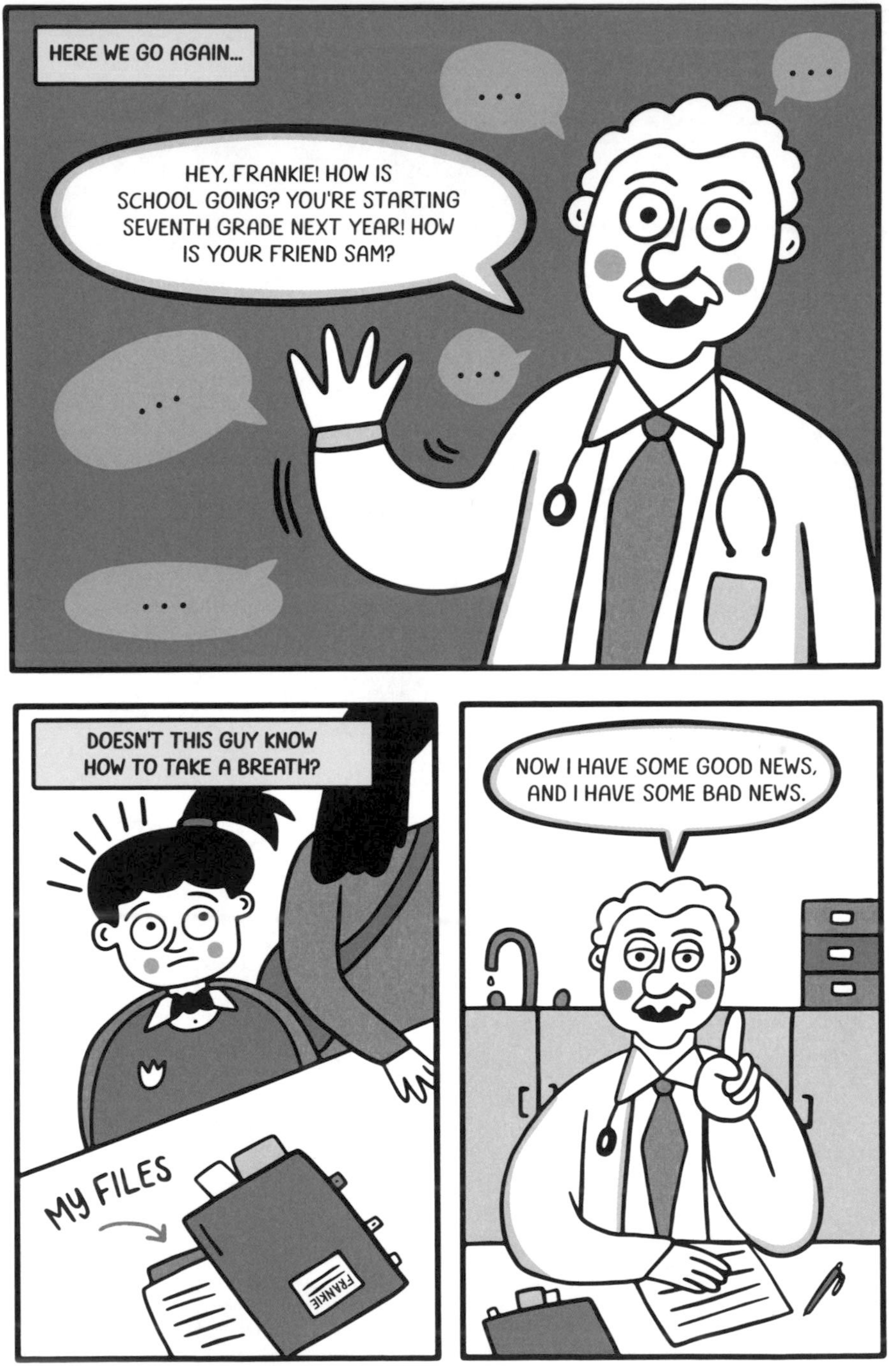
HERE WE GO AGAIN...
...
...
HEY, FRANKIE! HOW IS SCHOOL GOING? YOU'RE STARTING SEVENTH GRADE NEXT YEAR! HOW IS YOUR FRIEND SAM?
...
...
...
DOESN'T THIS GUY KNOW HOW TO TAKE A BREATH?
MY FILES
FRANKIE
NOW I HAVE SOME GOOD NEWS, AND I HAVE SOME BAD NEWS.

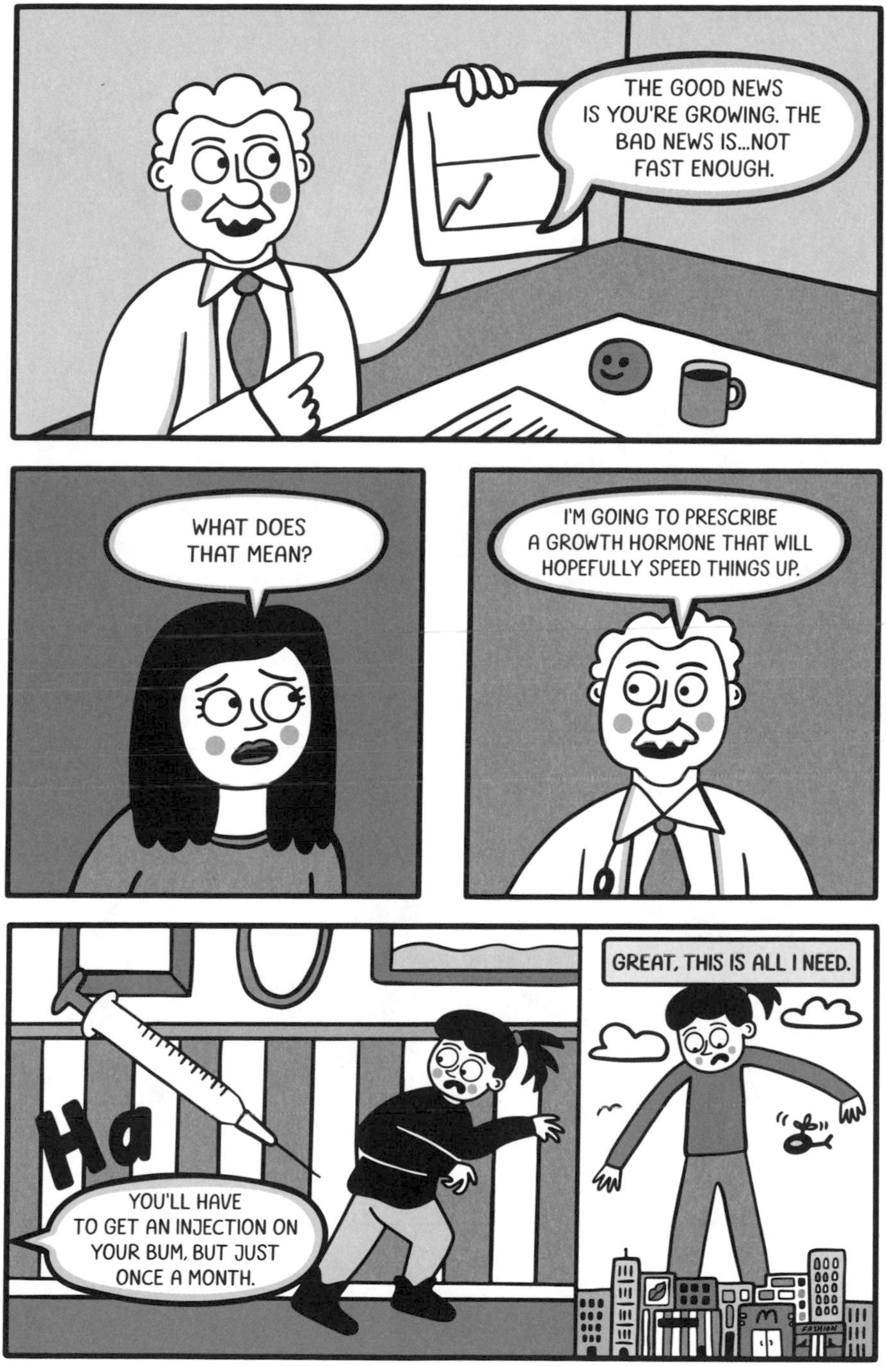
THE GOOD NEWS IS YOU'RE GROWING. THE BAD NEWS IS...NOT FAST ENOUGH.
WHAT DOES THAT MEAN?
I'M GOING TO PRESCRIBE A GROWTH HORMONE THAT WILL HOPEFULLY SPEED THINGS UP.
Ha
YOU'LL HAVE TO GET AN INJECTION ON YOUR BUM, BUT JUST ONCE A MONTH.
GREAT, THIS IS ALL I NEED.
FASHION

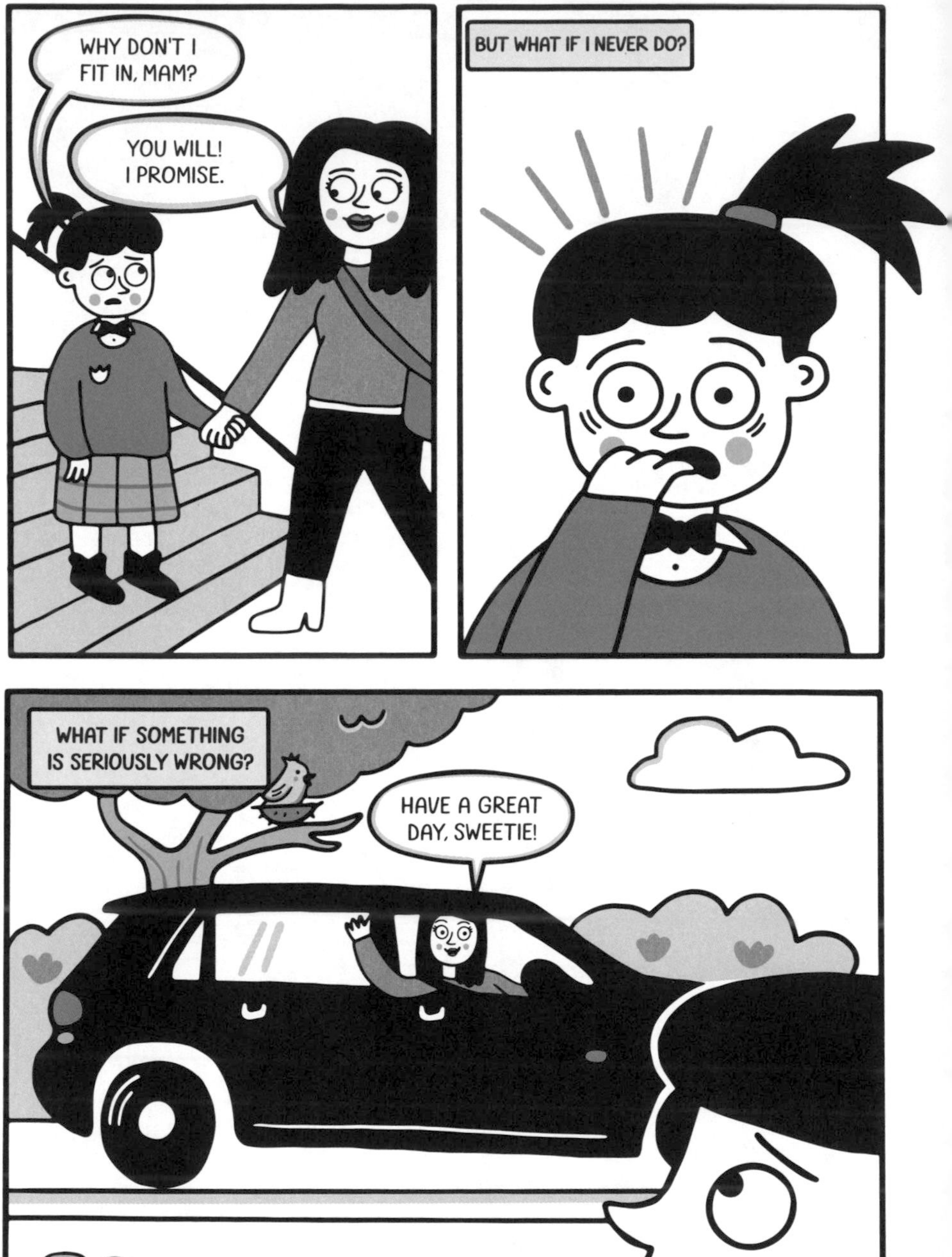
WHY DON'T I FIT IN, MAM?
YOU WILL! I PROMISE.
BUT WHAT IF I NEVER DO?
WHAT IF SOMETHING IS SERIOUSLY WRONG?
HAVE A GREAT DAY, SWEETIE!

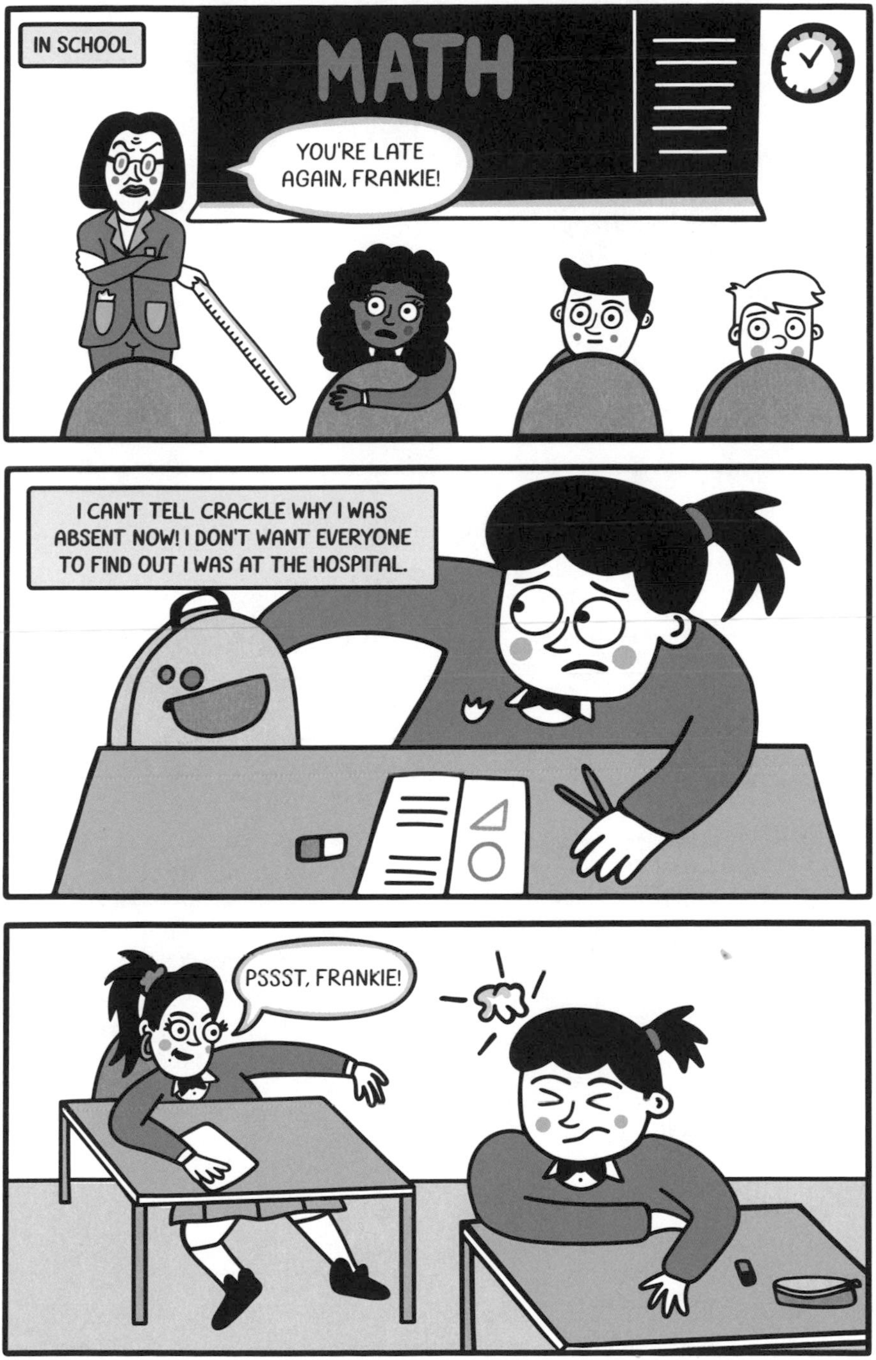
IN SCHOOL
MATH
YOU'RE LATE AGAIN, FRANKIE!
I CAN'T TELL CRACKLE WHY I WAS ABSENT NOW! I DON'T WANT EVERYONE TO FIND OUT I WAS AT THE HOSPITAL.
PSSST, FRANKIE!

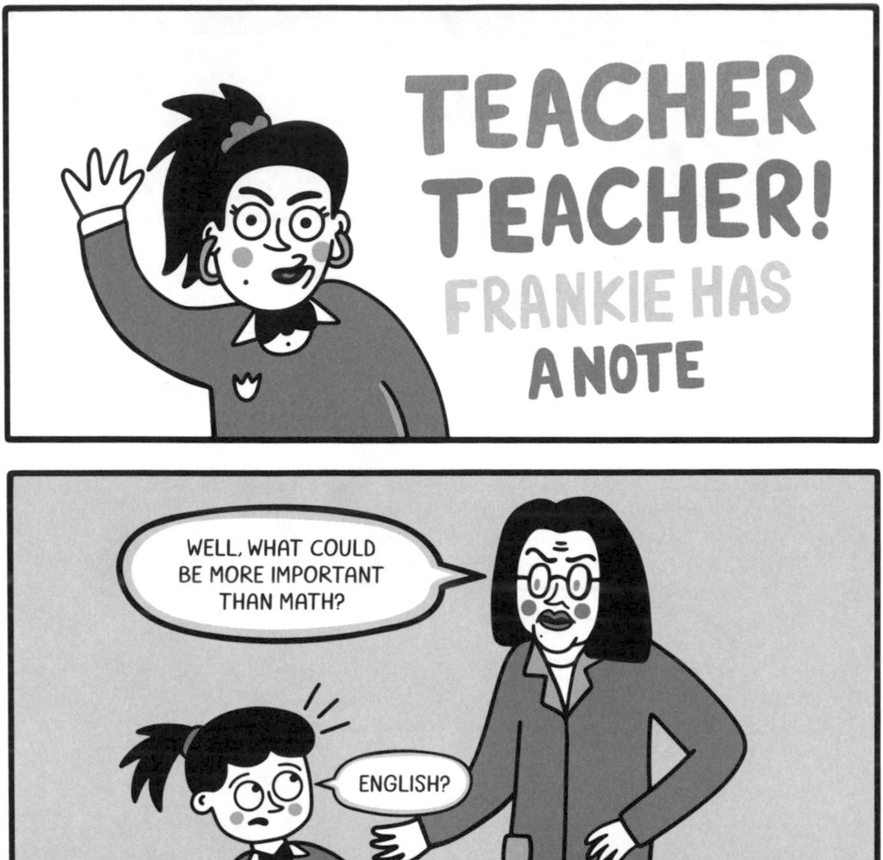
TEACHER TEACHER!
FRANKIE HAS A NOTE
WELL, WHAT COULD BE MORE IMPORTANT THAN MATH?
ENGLISH?
THAT WASN'T A QUESTION, YOU SILLY GIRL! GO TO PRINCIPAL DALY.
PRINCIPAL

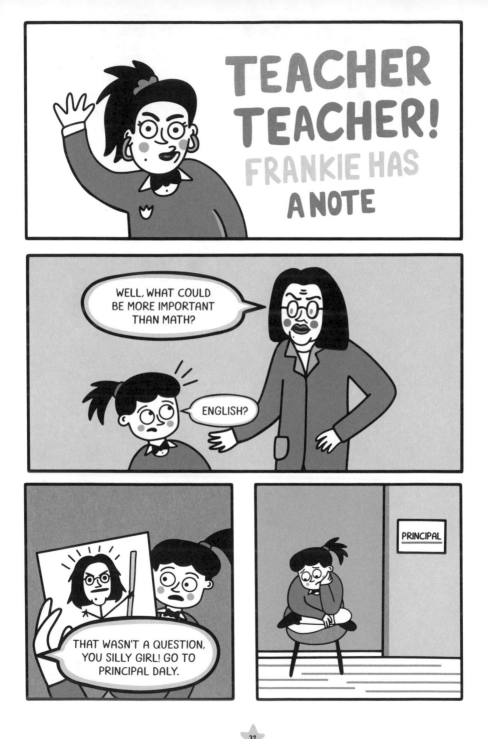

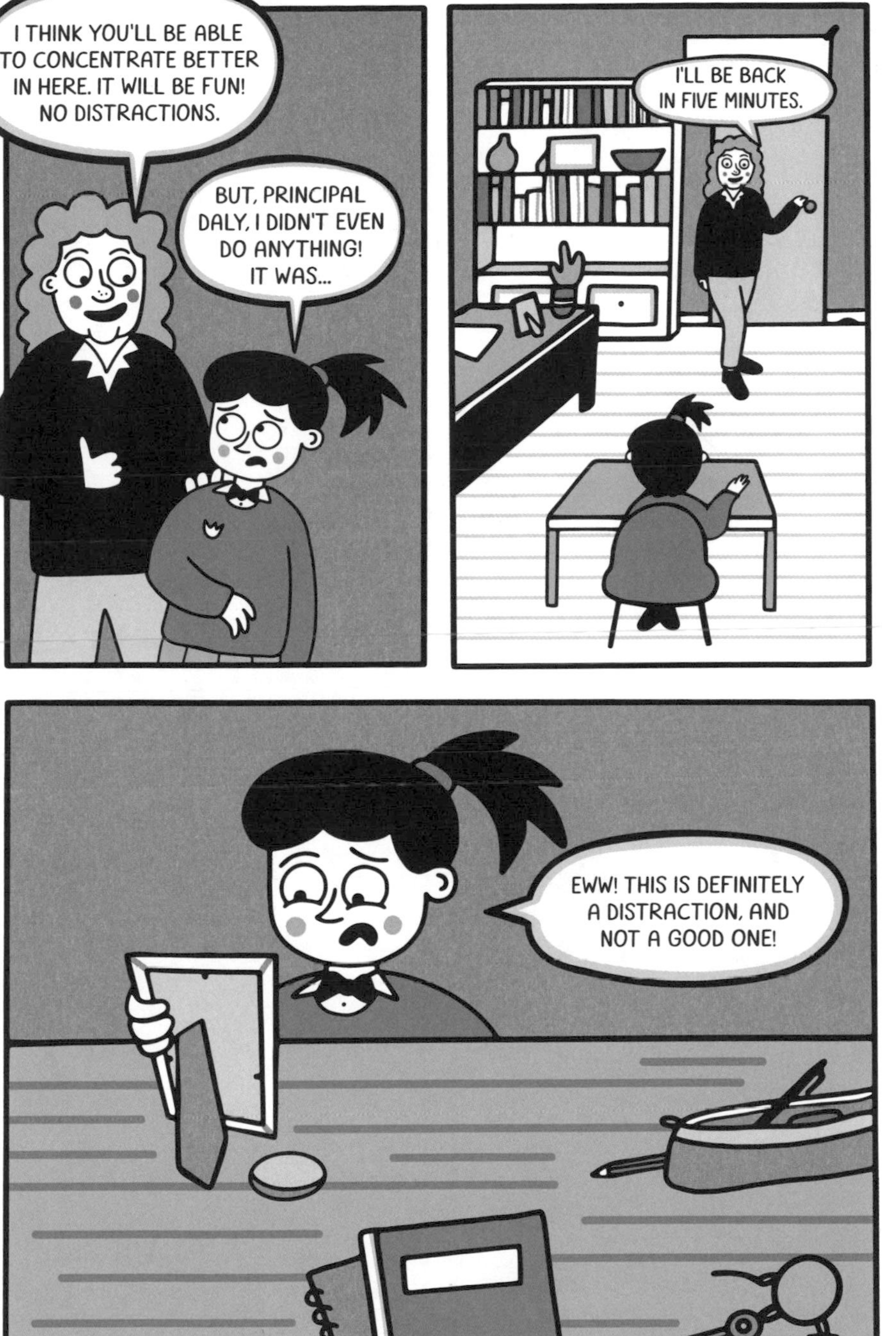
I THINK YOU'LL BE ABLE TO CONCENTRATE BETTER IN HERE. IT WILL BE FUN! NO DISTRACTIONS.
BUT, PRINCIPAL DALY, I DIDN'T EVEN DO ANYTHING! IT WAS...
I'LL BE BACK IN FIVE MINUTES.
EWW! THIS IS DEFINITELY A DISTRACTION, AND NOT A GOOD ONE!

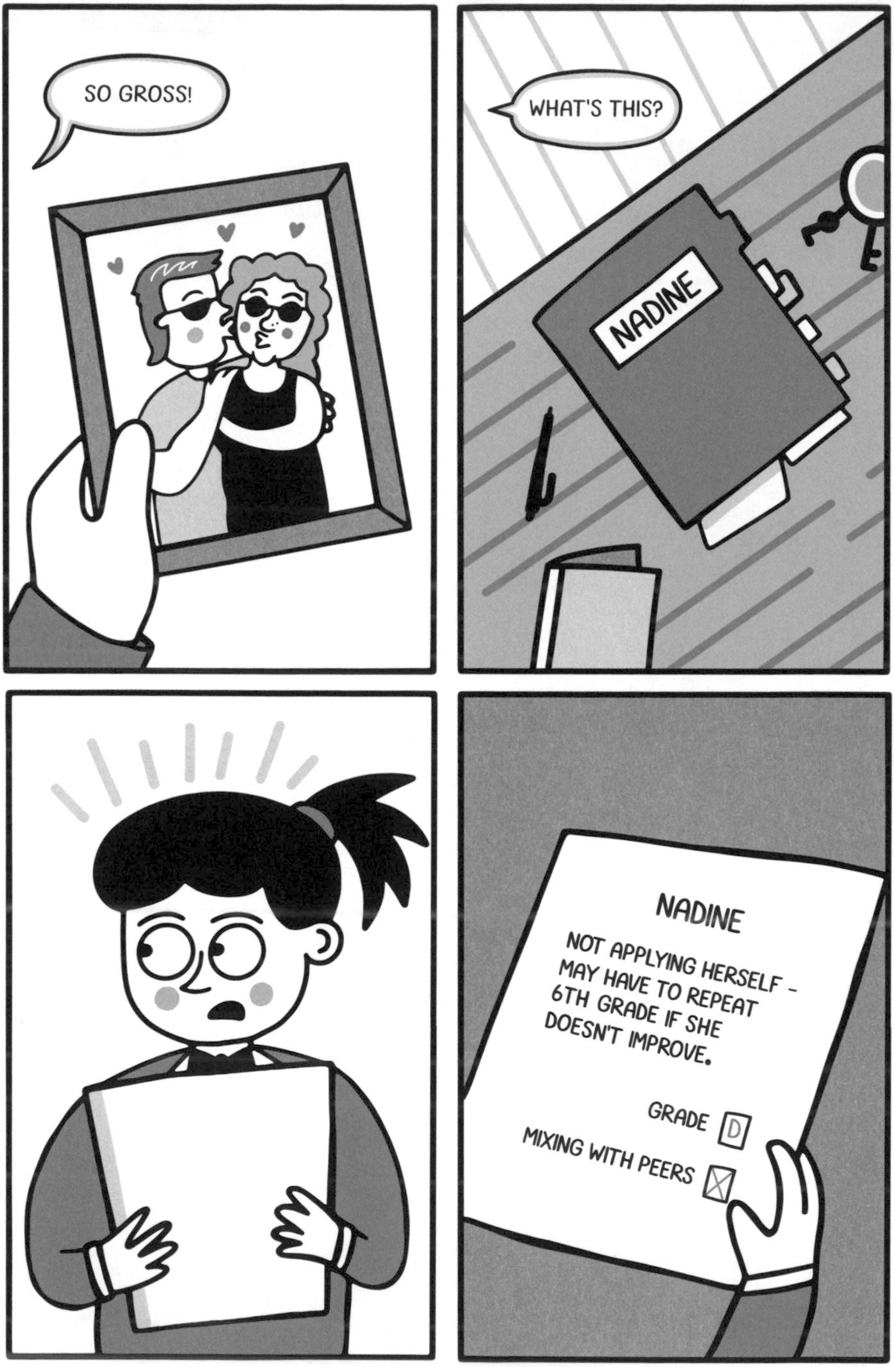
SO GROSS!
WHAT'S THIS?
NADINE
NADINE
NOT APPLYING HERSELF - MAY HAVE TO REPEAT 6TH GRADE IF SHE DOESN'T IMPROVE.
GRADE D
MIXING WITH PEERS

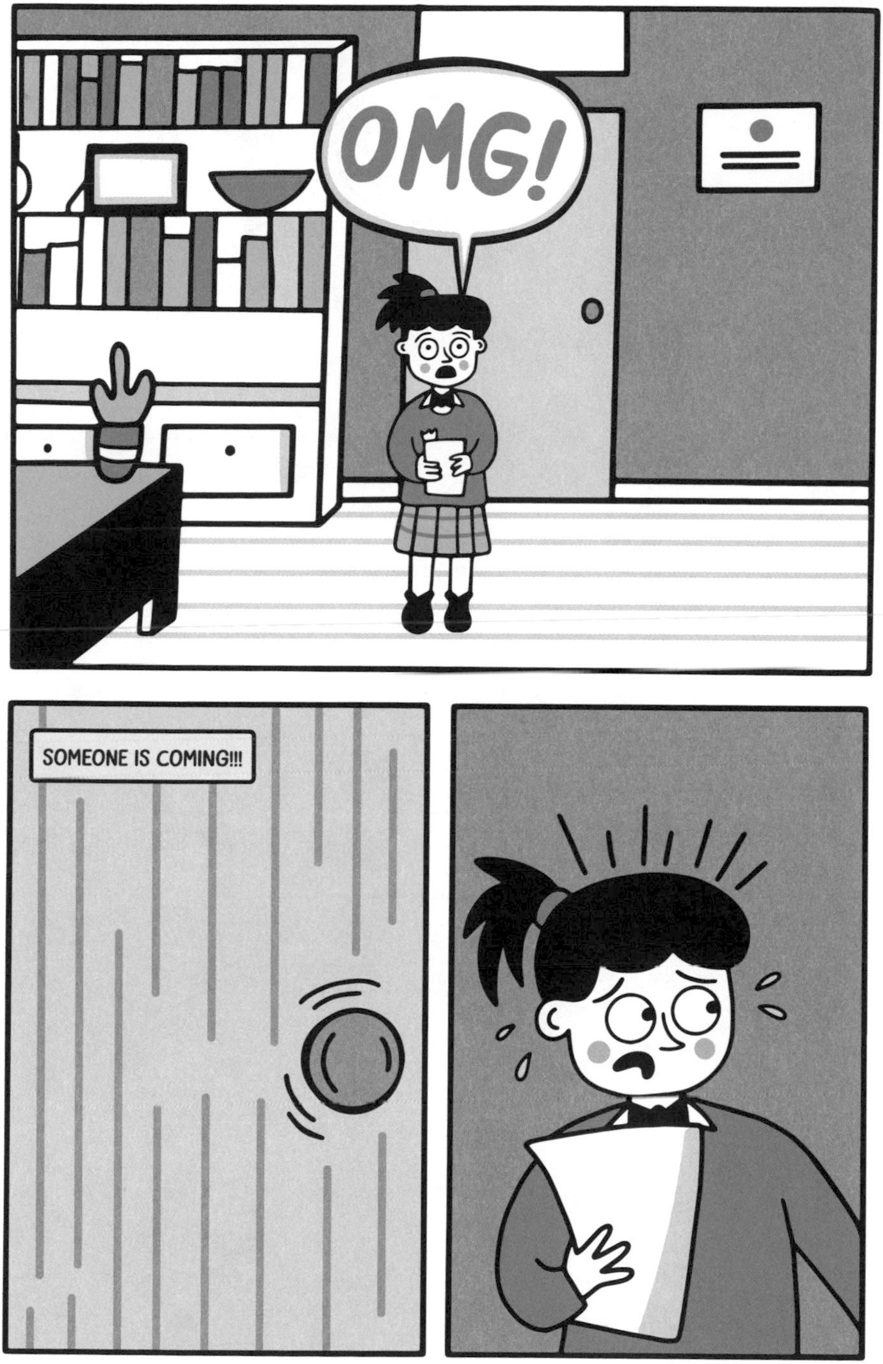
OMG!
SOMEONE IS COMING!!!

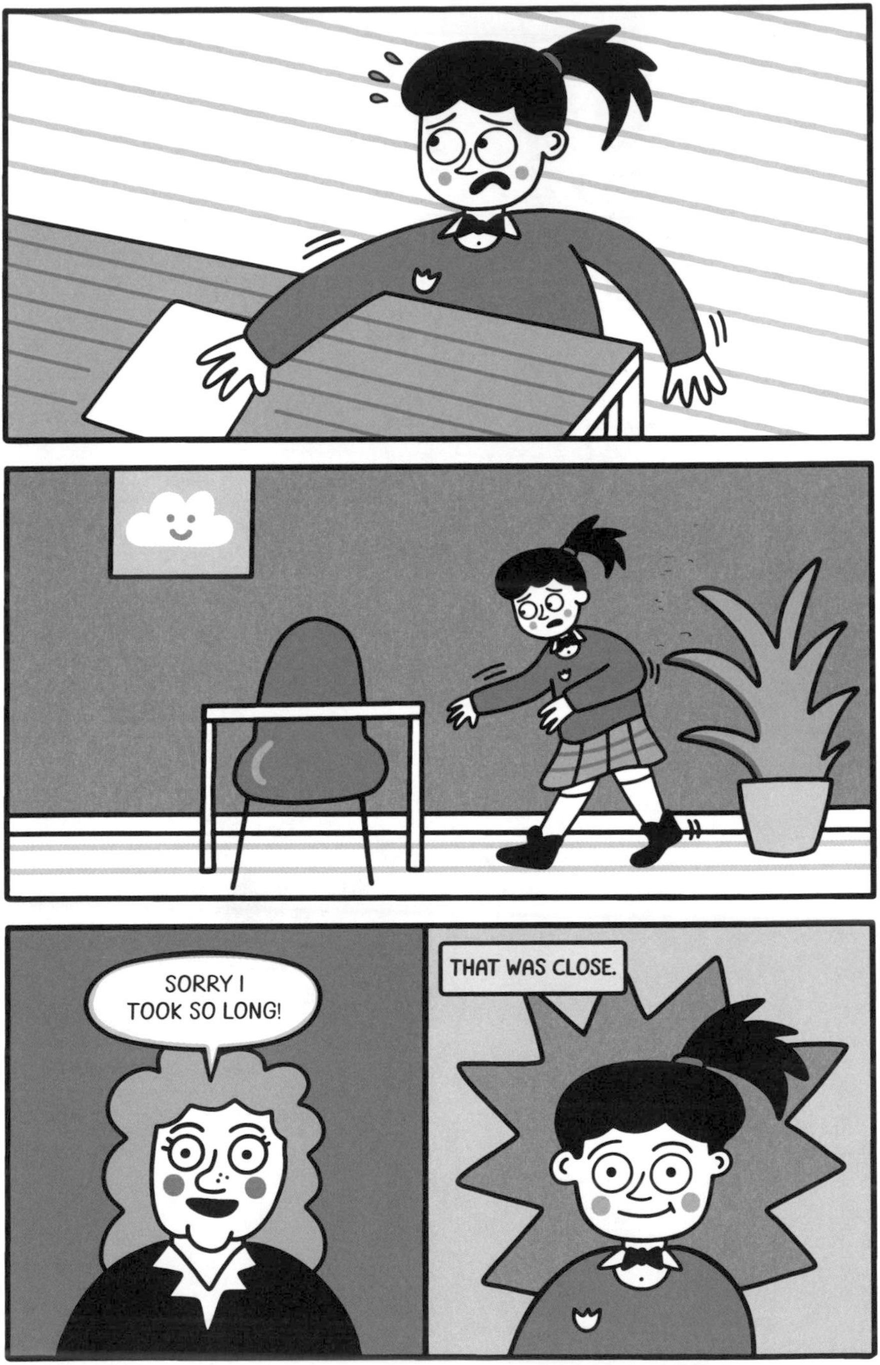
SORRY I TOOK SO LONG!
THAT WAS CLOSE.

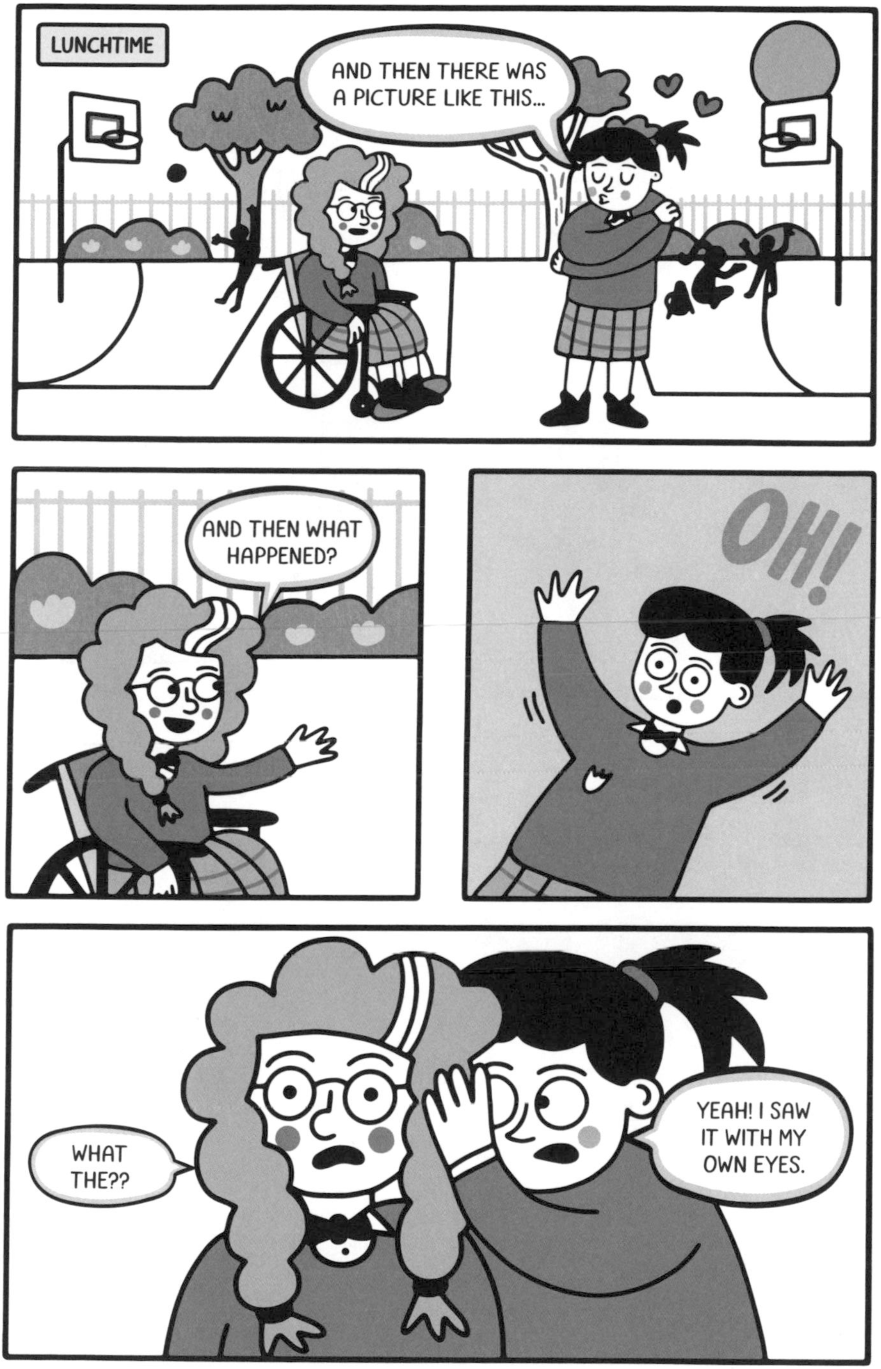
LUNCHTIME
AND THEN THERE WAS A PICTURE LIKE THIS...
AND THEN WHAT HAPPENED?
OH!
WHAT THE??
YEAH! I SAW IT WITH MY OWN EYES.

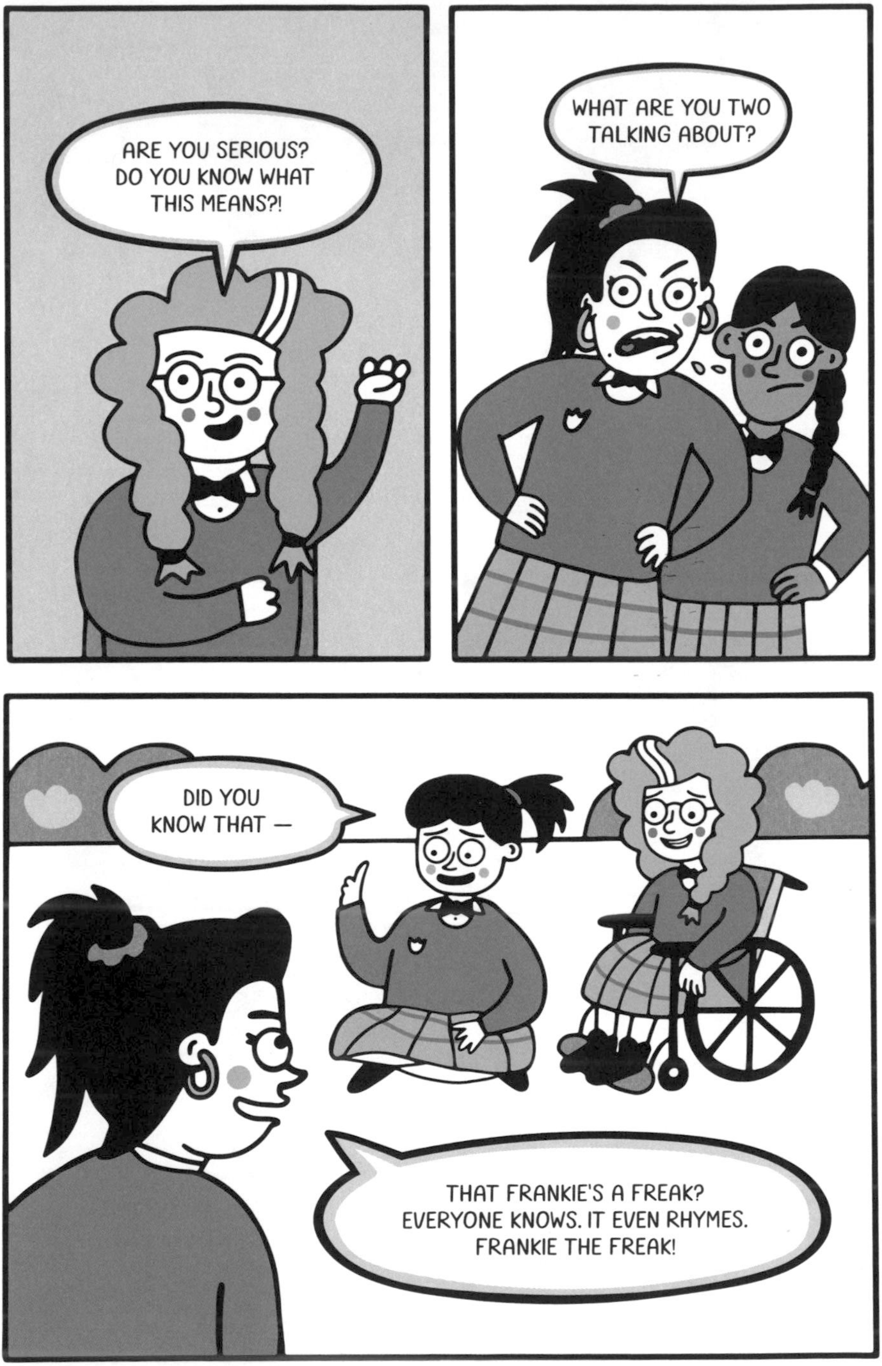
ARE YOU SERIOUS? DO YOU KNOW WHAT THIS MEANS?!
WHAT ARE YOU TWO TALKING ABOUT?
DID YOU KNOW THAT —
THAT FRANKIE'S A FREAK? EVERYONE KNOWS. IT EVEN RHYMES. FRANKIE THE FREAK!

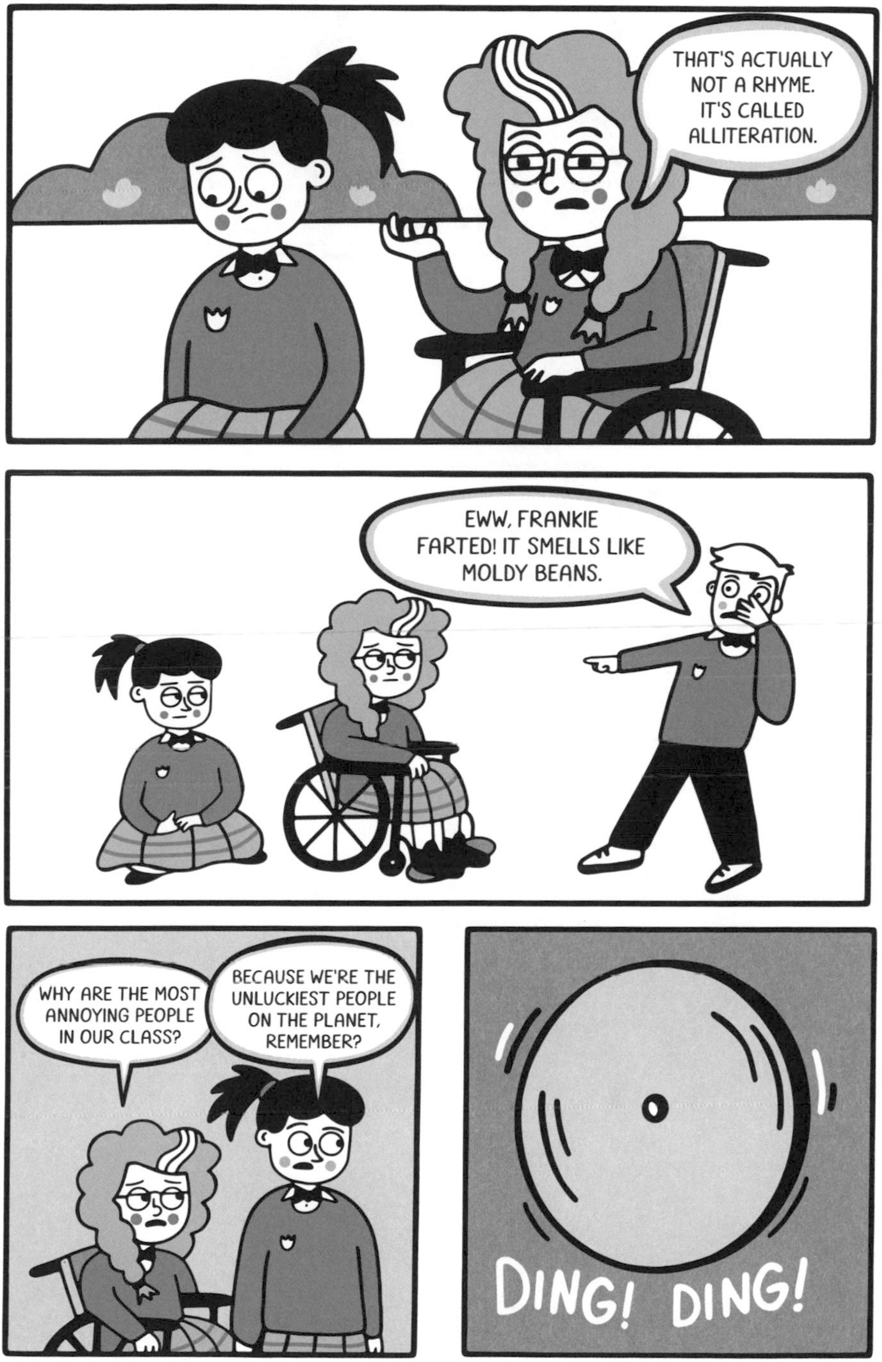
THAT'S ACTUALLY NOT A RHYME. IT'S CALLED ALLITERATION.
EWW, FRANKIE FARTED! IT SMELLS LIKE MOLDY BEANS.
WHY ARE THE MOST ANNOYING PEOPLE IN OUR CLASS?
BECAUSE WE'RE THE UNLUCKIEST PEOPLE ON THE PLANET, REMEMBER?
DING! DING!

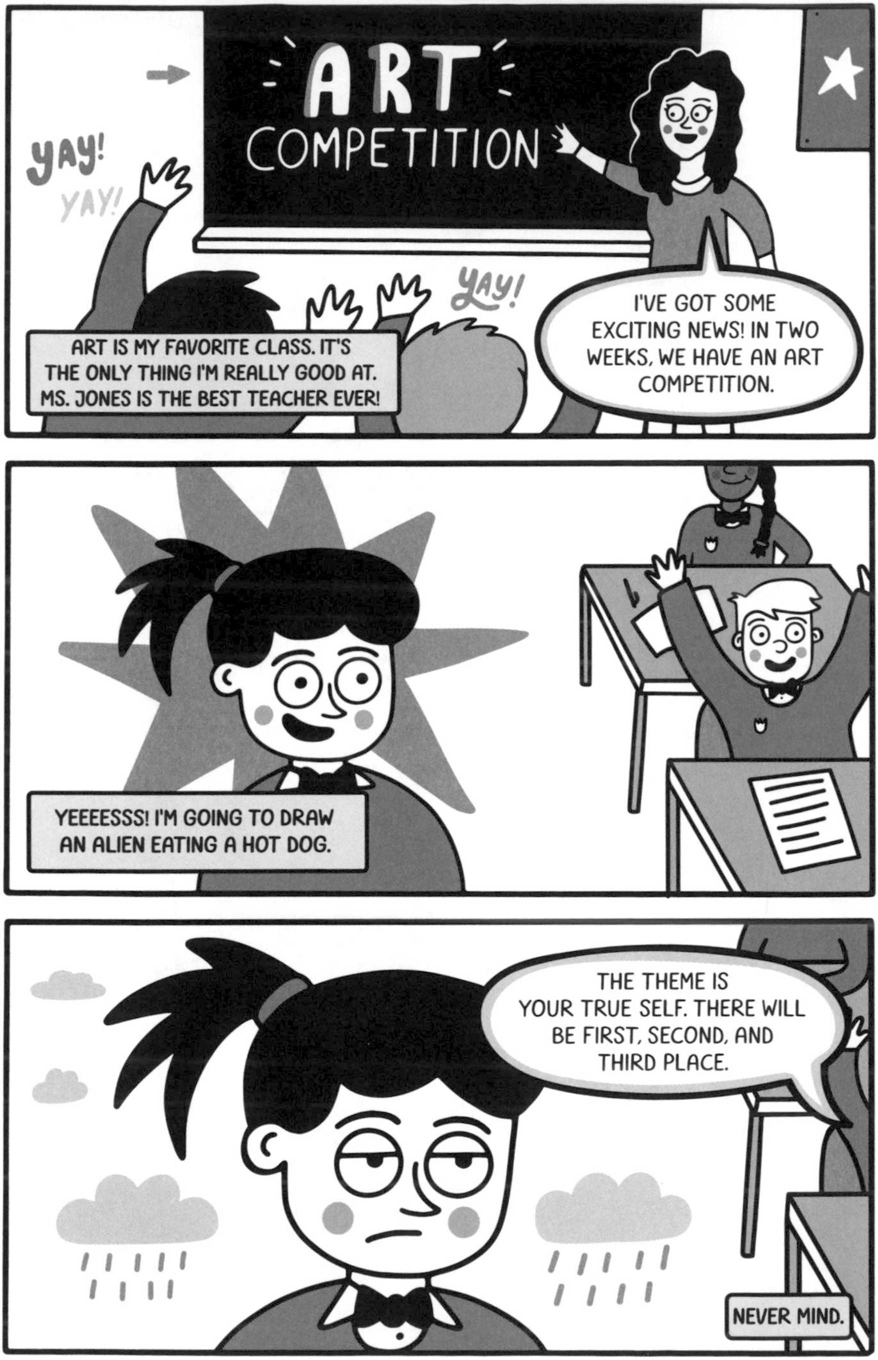
ART
COMPETITION
YAY!
YAY!
YAY!
ART IS MY FAVORITE CLASS. IT'S THE ONLY THING I'M REALLY GOOD AT. MS. JONES IS THE BEST TEACHER EVER!
I'VE GOT SOME EXCITING NEWS! IN TWO WEEKS, WE HAVE AN ART COMPETITION.
YEEEESSS! I'M GOING TO DRAW AN ALIEN EATING A HOT DOG.
THE THEME IS YOUR TRUE SELF. THERE WILL BE FIRST, SECOND, AND THIRD PLACE.
NEVER MIND.

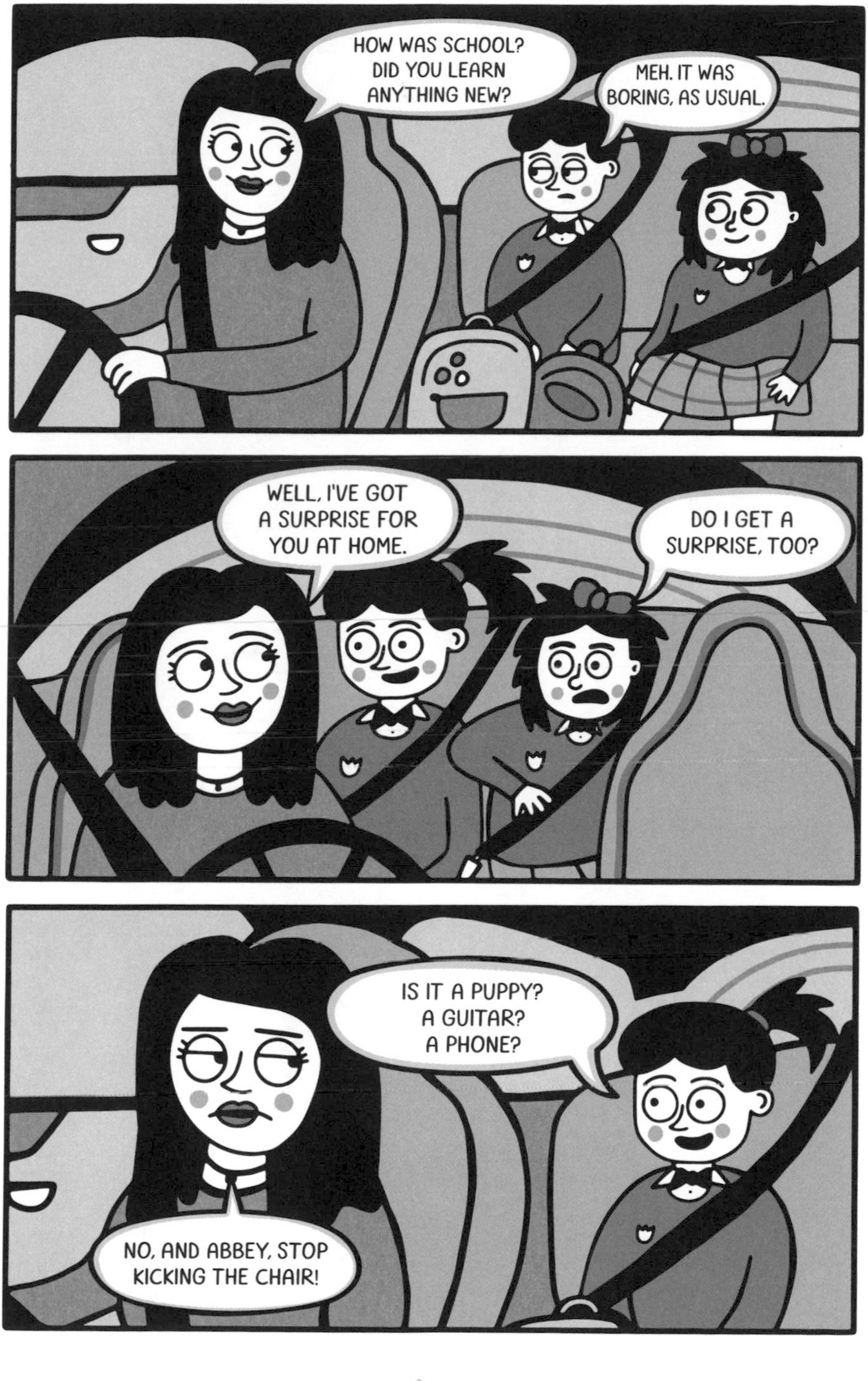
HOW WAS SCHOOL? DID YOU LEARN ANYTHING NEW?
MEH. IT WAS BORING, AS USUAL.
WELL, I'VE GOT A SURPRISE FOR YOU AT HOME.
DO I GET A SURPRISE, TOO?
IS IT A PUPPY? A GUITAR? A PHONE?
NO, AND ABBEY, STOP KICKING THE CHAIR!

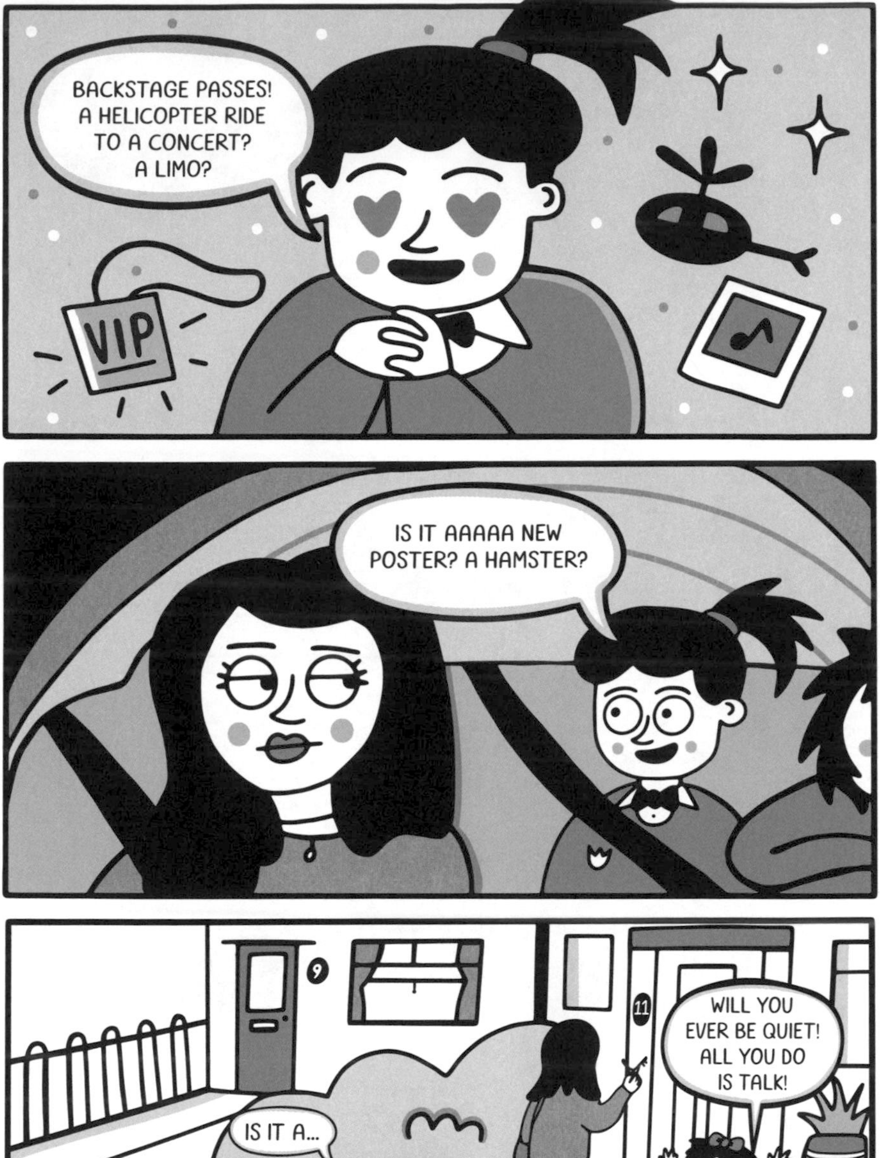
BACKSTAGE PASSES! A HELICOPTER RIDE TO A CONCERT? A LIMO?
VIP
IS IT AAAAA NEW POSTER? A HAMSTER?
9
11
WILL YOU EVER BE QUIET! ALL YOU DO IS TALK!
IS IT A...

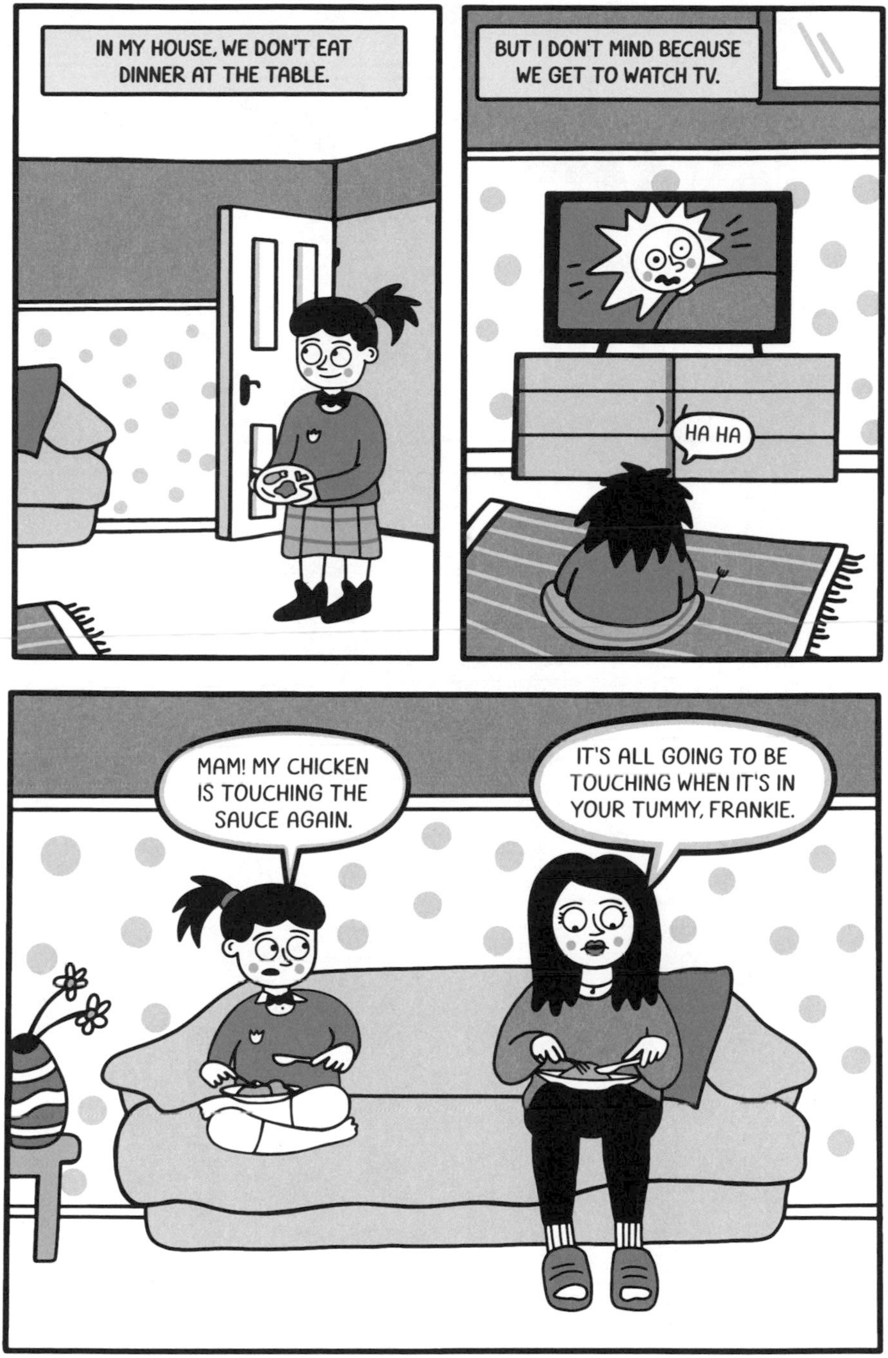
IN MY HOUSE, WE DON'T EAT DINNER AT THE TABLE.
BUT I DON'T MIND BECAUSE WE GET TO WATCH TV.
HA HA
MAM! MY CHICKEN IS TOUCHING THE SAUCE AGAIN.
IT'S ALL GOING TO BE TOUCHING WHEN IT'S IN YOUR TUMMY, FRANKIE.

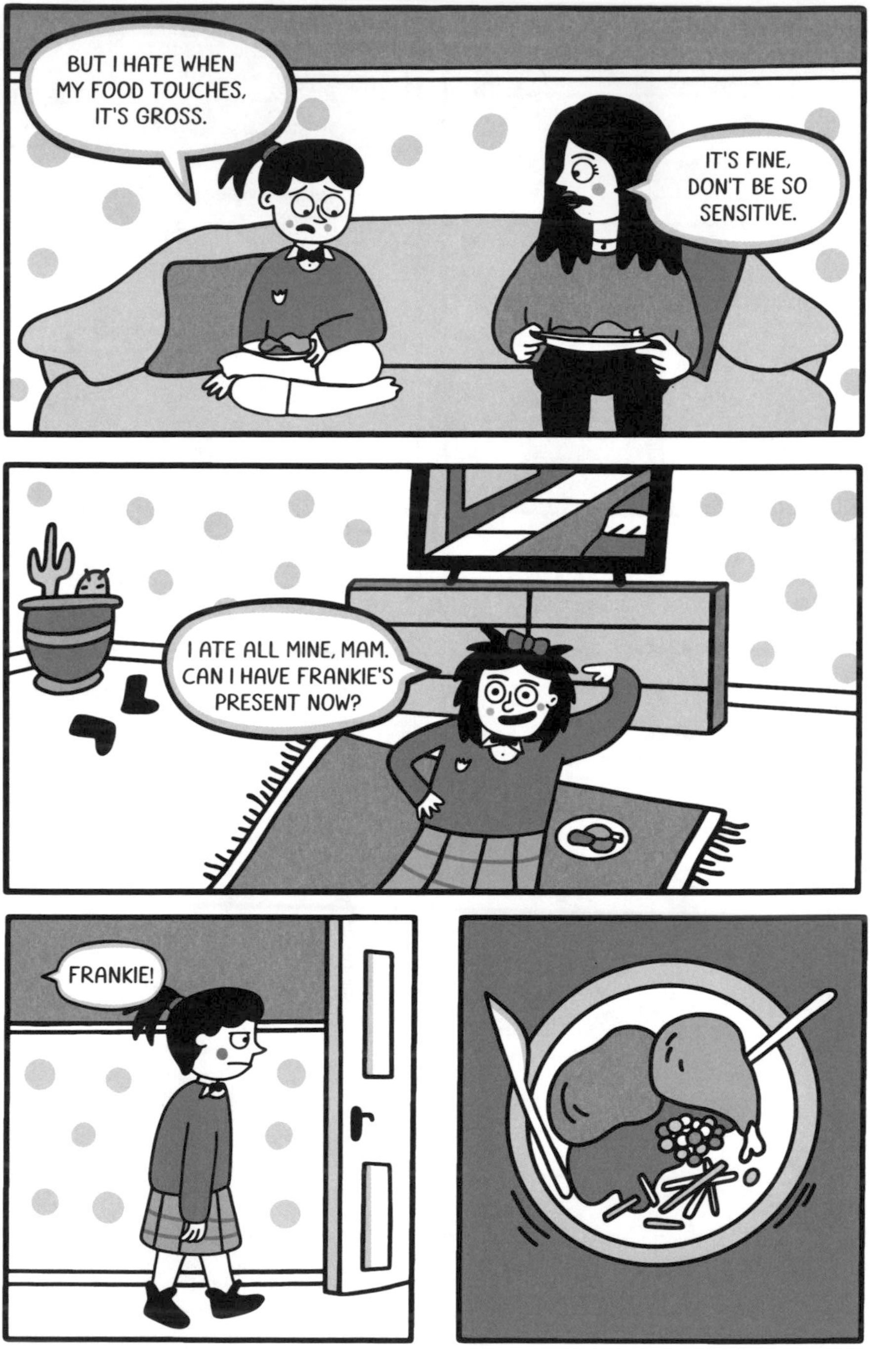
BUT I HATE WHEN MY FOOD TOUCHES, IT'S GROSS.
IT'S FINE, DON'T BE SO SENSITIVE.
I ATE ALL MINE, MAM. CAN I HAVE FRANKIE'S PRESENT NOW?
FRANKIE!

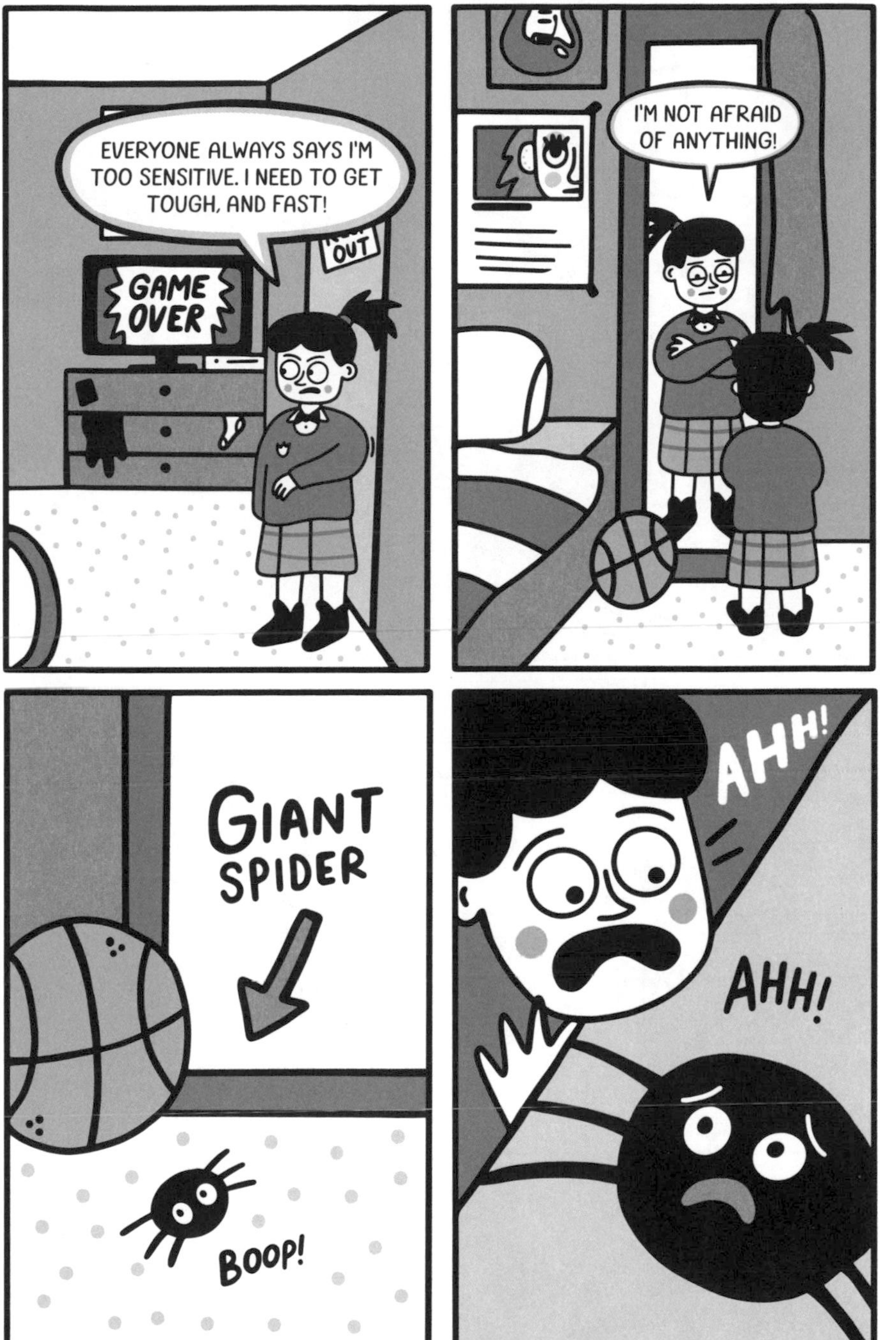
EVERYONE ALWAYS SAYS I'M TOO SENSITIVE. I NEED TO GET TOUGH, AND FAST!
GAME OVER
OUT
I'M NOT AFRAID OF ANYTHING!
GIANT SPIDER
BOOP!
AHH!
AHH!

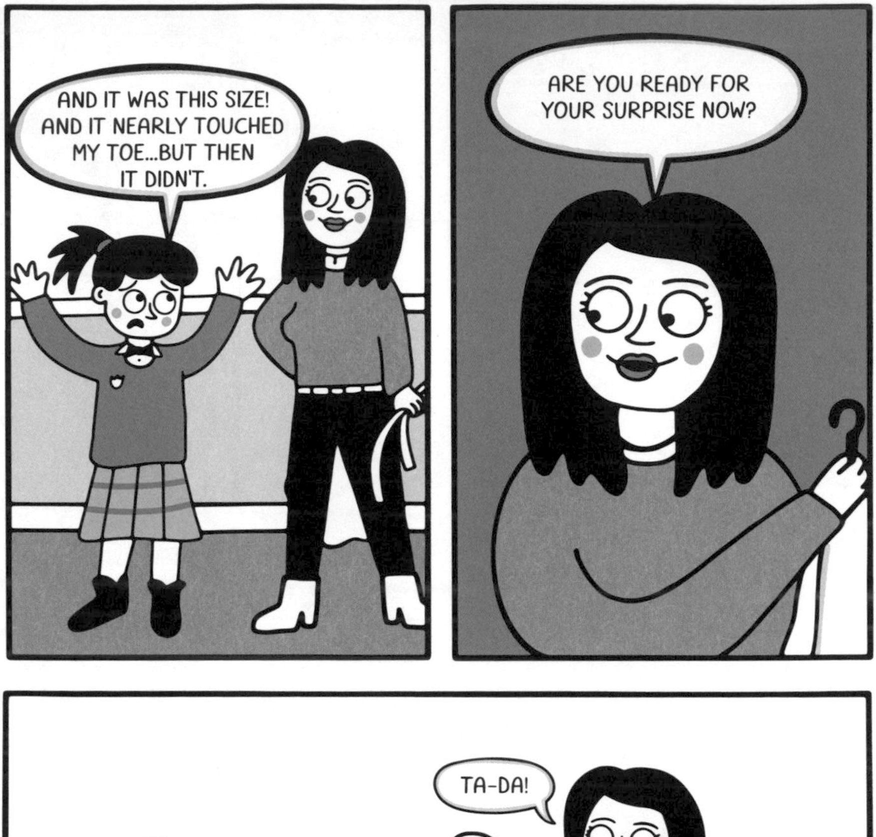
AND IT WAS THIS SIZE! AND IT NEARLY TOUCHED MY TOE...BUT THEN IT DIDN'T.
ARE YOU READY FOR YOUR SURPRISE NOW?
TA-DA!

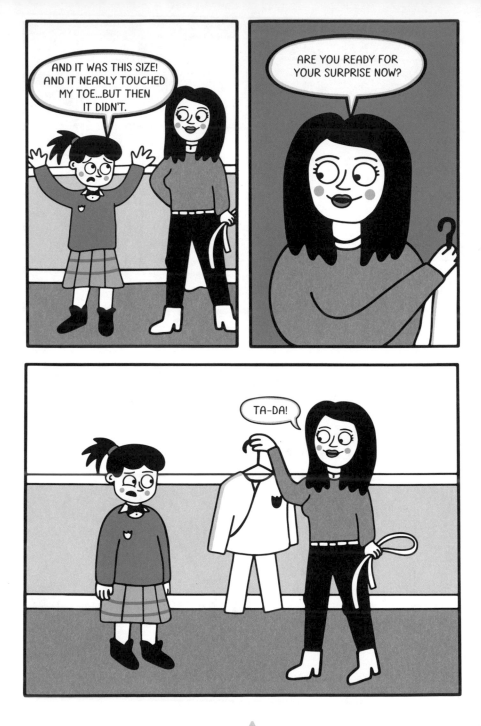

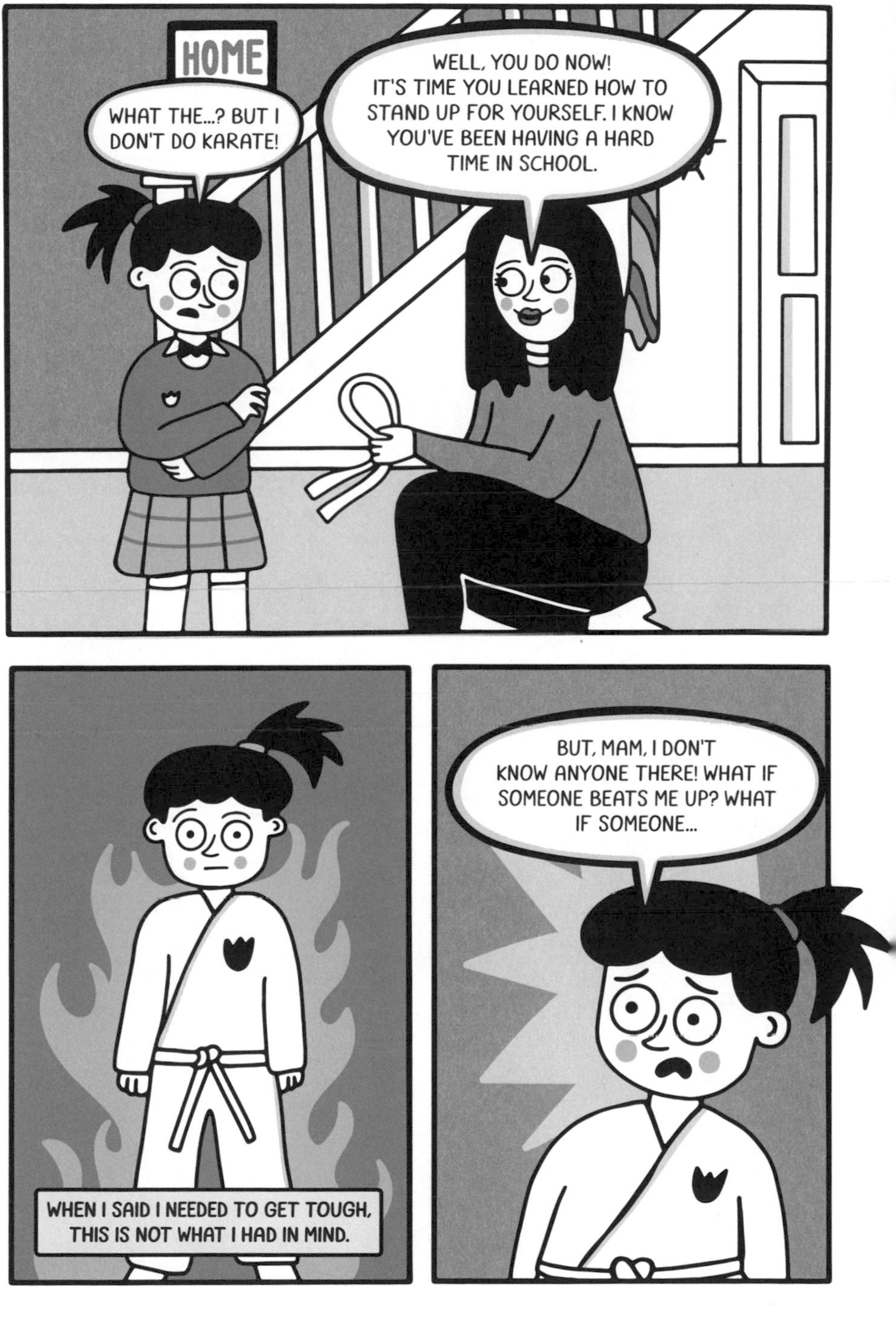
HOME
WHAT THE...? BUT I DON'T DO KARATE!
WELL, YOU DO NOW! IT'S TIME YOU LEARNED HOW TO STAND UP FOR YOURSELF. I KNOW YOU'VE BEEN HAVING A HARD TIME IN SCHOOL.
WHEN I SAID I NEEDED TO GET TOUGH, THIS IS NOT WHAT I HAD IN MIND.
BUT, MAM, I DON'T KNOW ANYONE THERE! WHAT IF SOMEONE BEATS ME UP? WHAT IF SOMEONE...

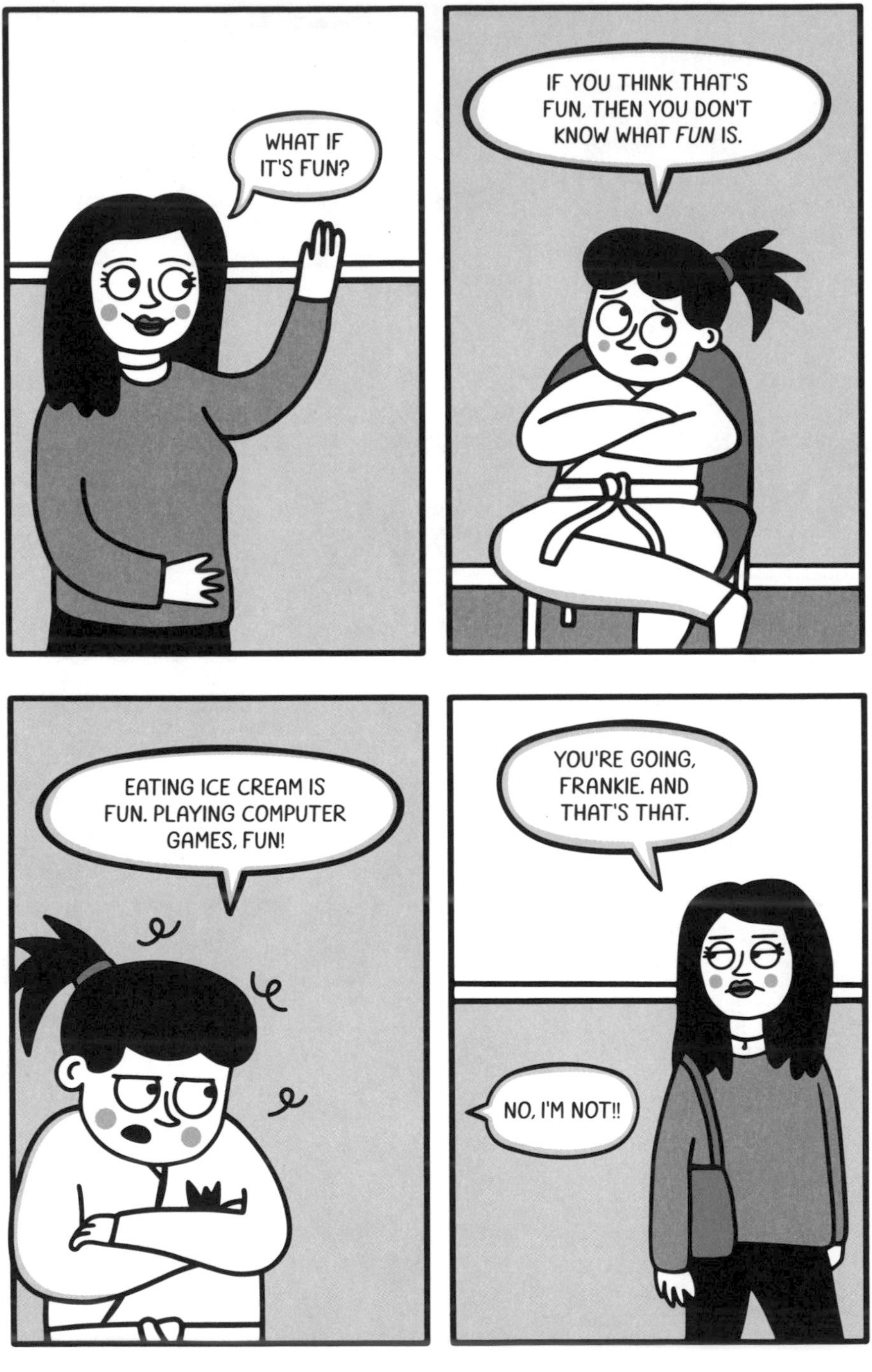
WHAT IF IT'S FUN?
IF YOU THINK THAT'S FUN, THEN YOU DON'T KNOW WHAT *FUN* IS.
EATING ICE CREAM IS FUN. PLAYING COMPUTER GAMES, FUN!
YOU'RE GOING, FRANKIE. AND THAT'S THAT.
NO, I'M NOT!!

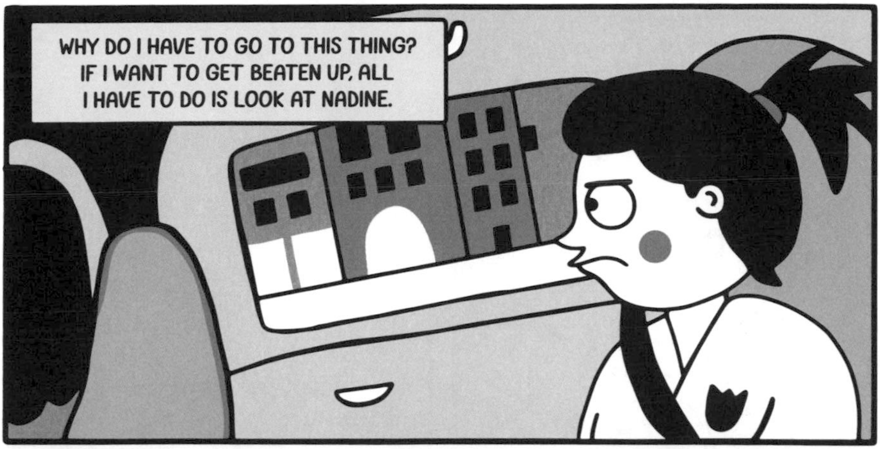
WHY DO I HAVE TO GO TO THIS THING? IF I WANT TO GET BEATEN UP, ALL I HAVE TO DO IS LOOK AT NADINE.

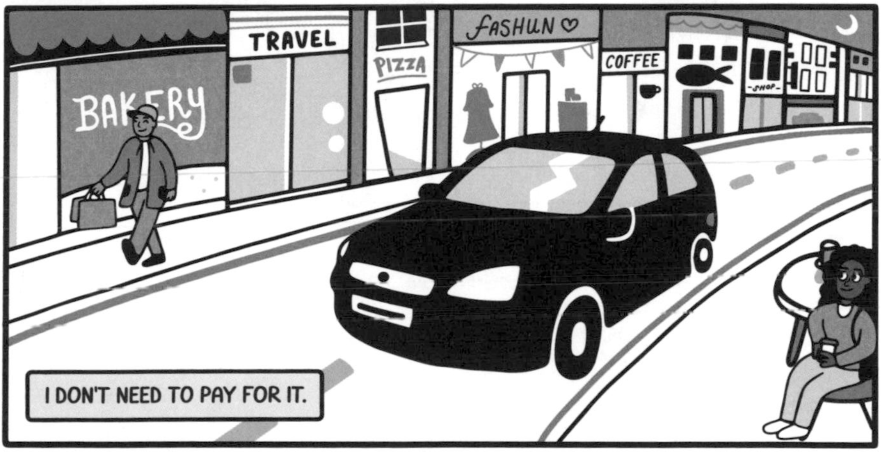
TRAVEL
PIZZA
FASHUN
COFFEE
BAKERY
SHOP
I DON'T NEED TO PAY FOR IT.

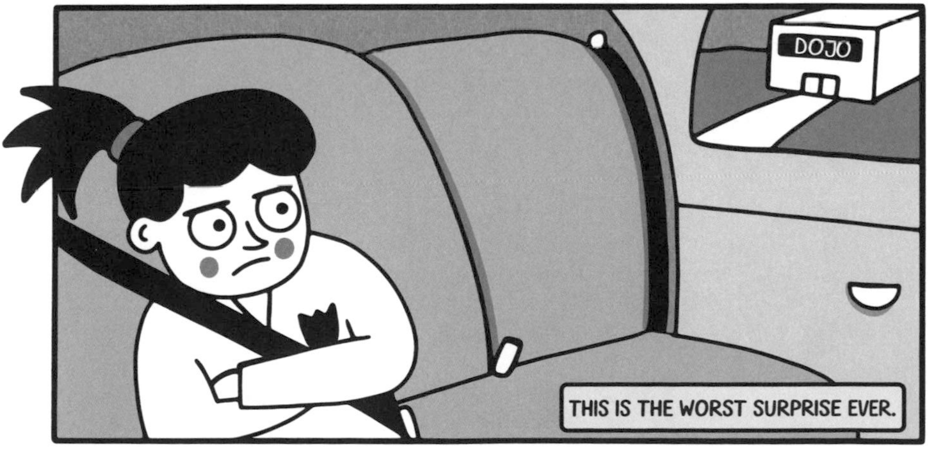
DOJO
THIS IS THE WORST SURPRISE EVER.

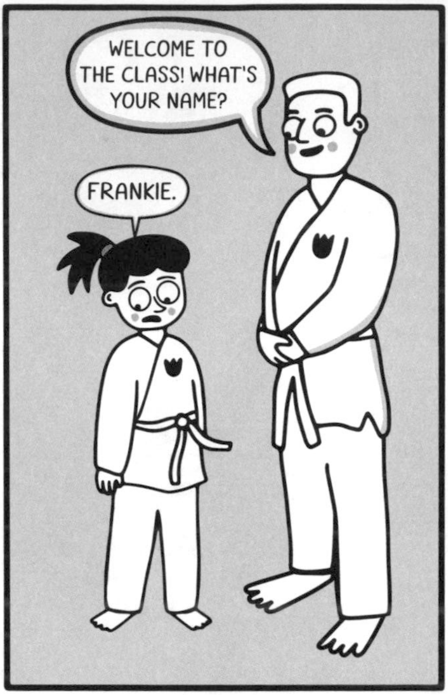
WELCOME TO THE CLASS! WHAT'S YOUR NAME?
FRANKIE.

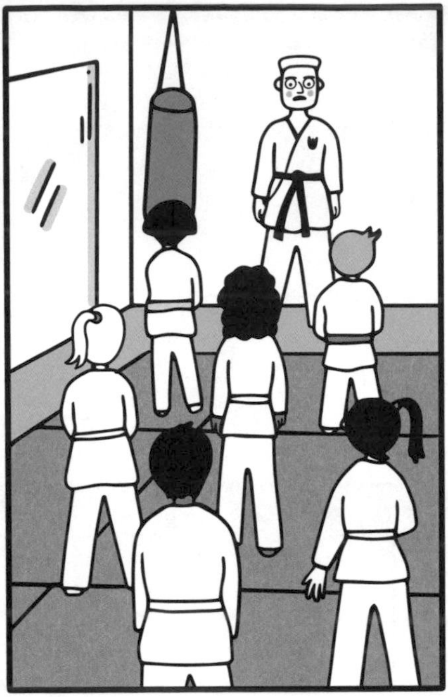

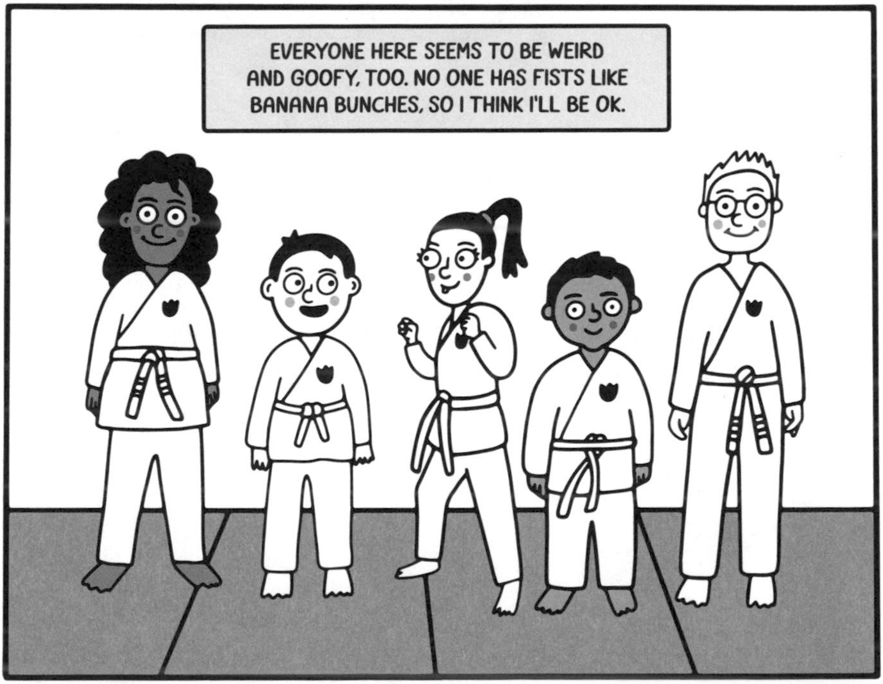
EVERYONE HERE SEEMS TO BE WEIRD AND GOOFY, TOO. NO ONE HAS FISTS LIKE BANANA BUNCHES, SO I THINK I'LL BE OK.

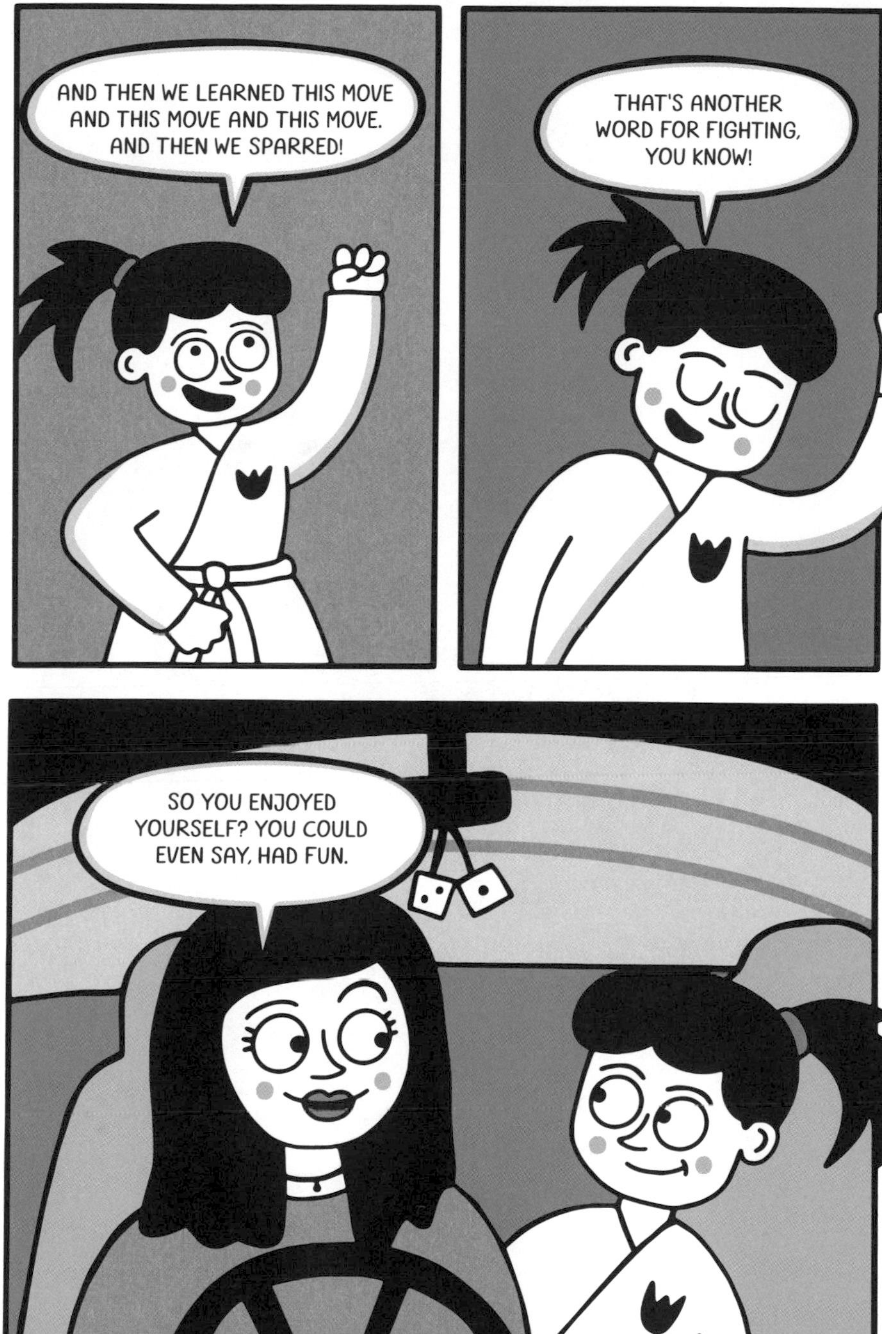
AND THEN WE LEARNED THIS MOVE AND THIS MOVE AND THIS MOVE. AND THEN WE SPARRED!
THAT'S ANOTHER WORD FOR FIGHTING, YOU KNOW!
SO YOU ENJOYED YOURSELF? YOU COULD EVEN SAY, HAD FUN.

CHAPTER 3

MY DAD'S AN ALIEN!

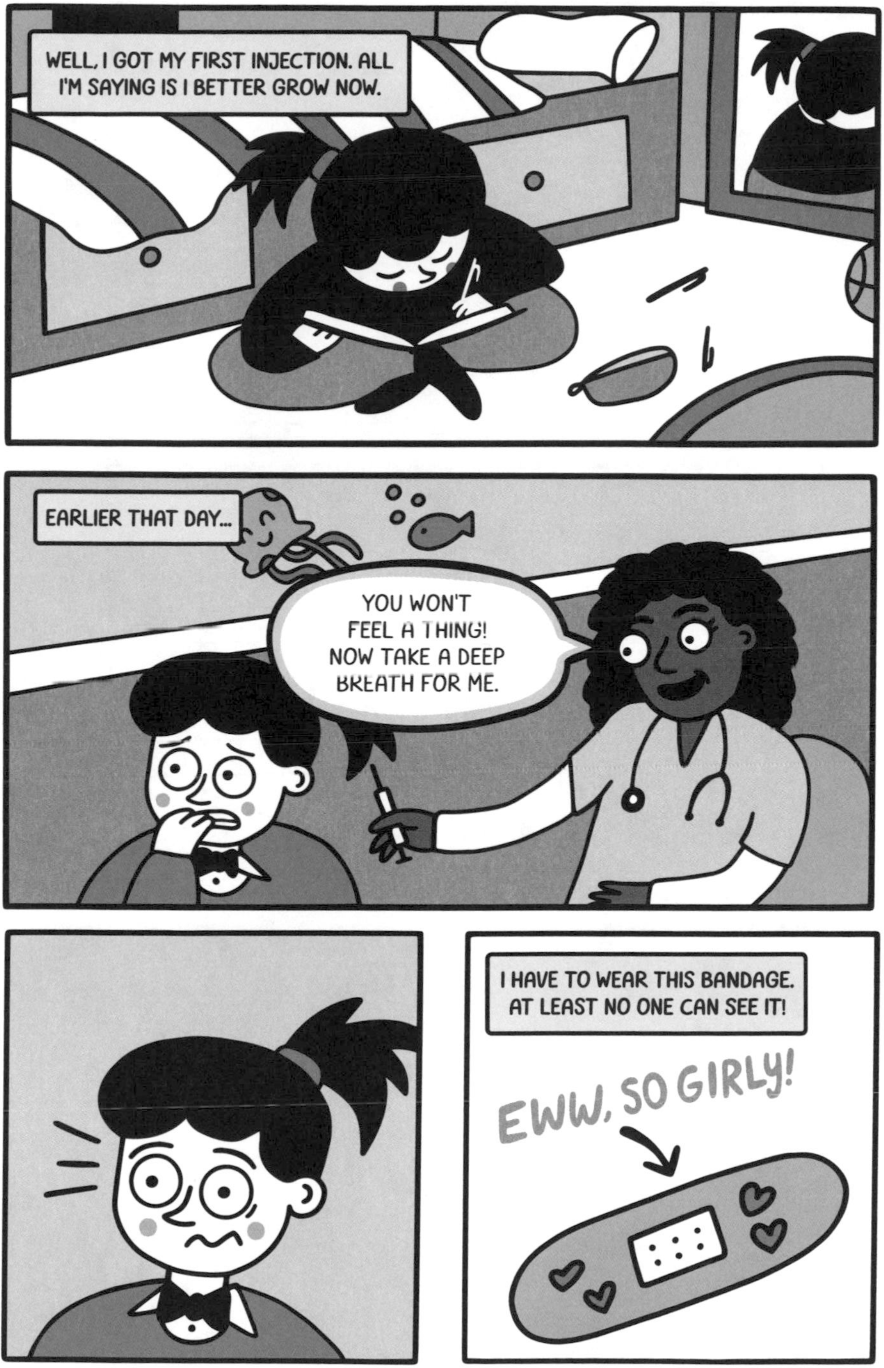
WELL, I GOT MY FIRST INJECTION. ALL I'M SAYING IS I BETTER GROW NOW.
EARLIER THAT DAY...
YOU WON'T FEEL A THING! NOW TAKE A DEEP BREATH FOR ME.
I HAVE TO WEAR THIS BANDAGE. AT LEAST NO ONE CAN SEE IT!
EWW, SO GIRLY!

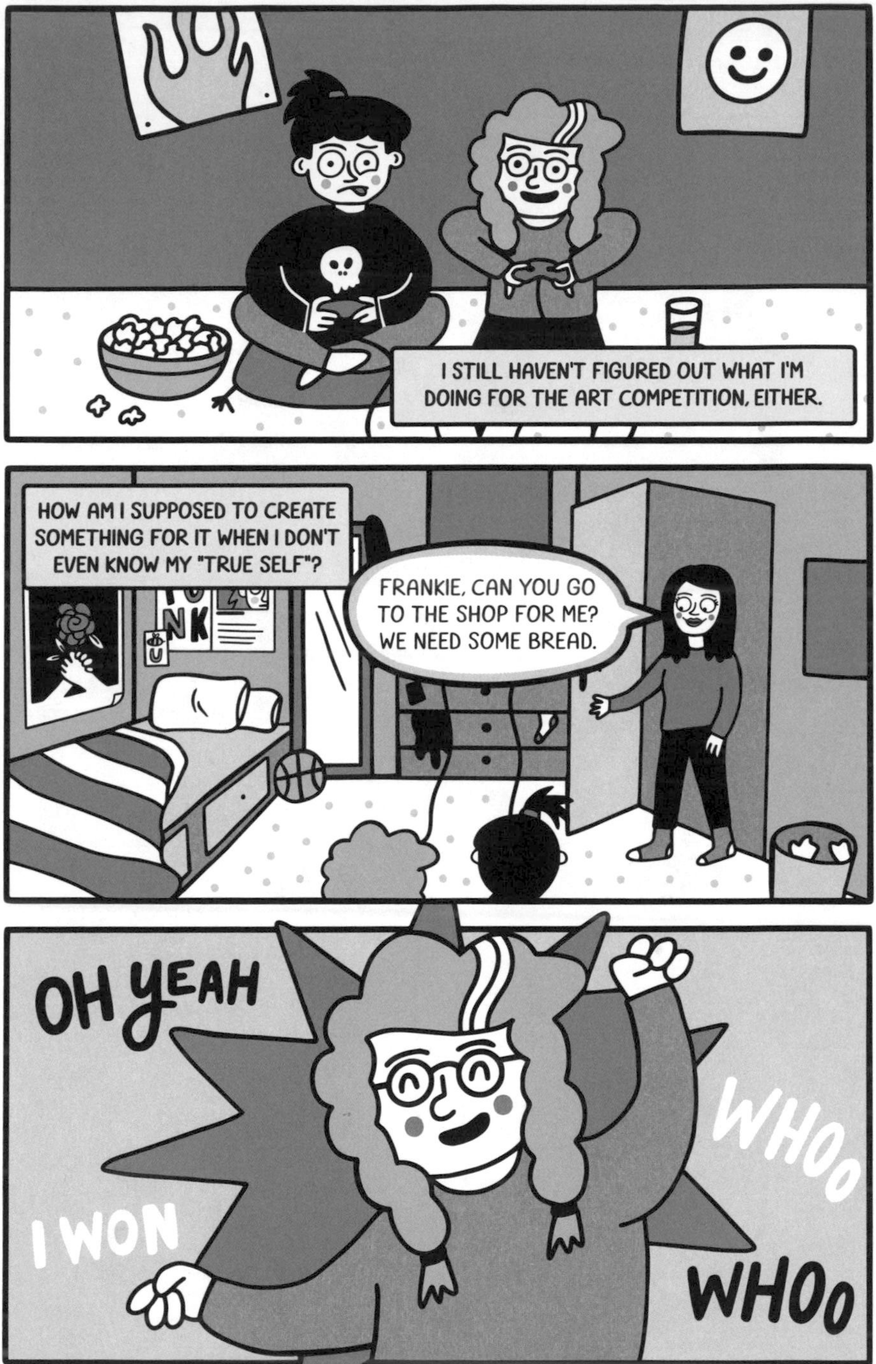
I STILL HAVEN'T FIGURED OUT WHAT I'M DOING FOR THE ART COMPETITION, EITHER.
HOW AM I SUPPOSED TO CREATE SOMETHING FOR IT WHEN I DON'T EVEN KNOW MY "TRUE SELF"?
FRANKIE, CAN YOU GO TO THE SHOP FOR ME? WE NEED SOME BREAD.
OH YEAH
WHOO
I WON
WHOO

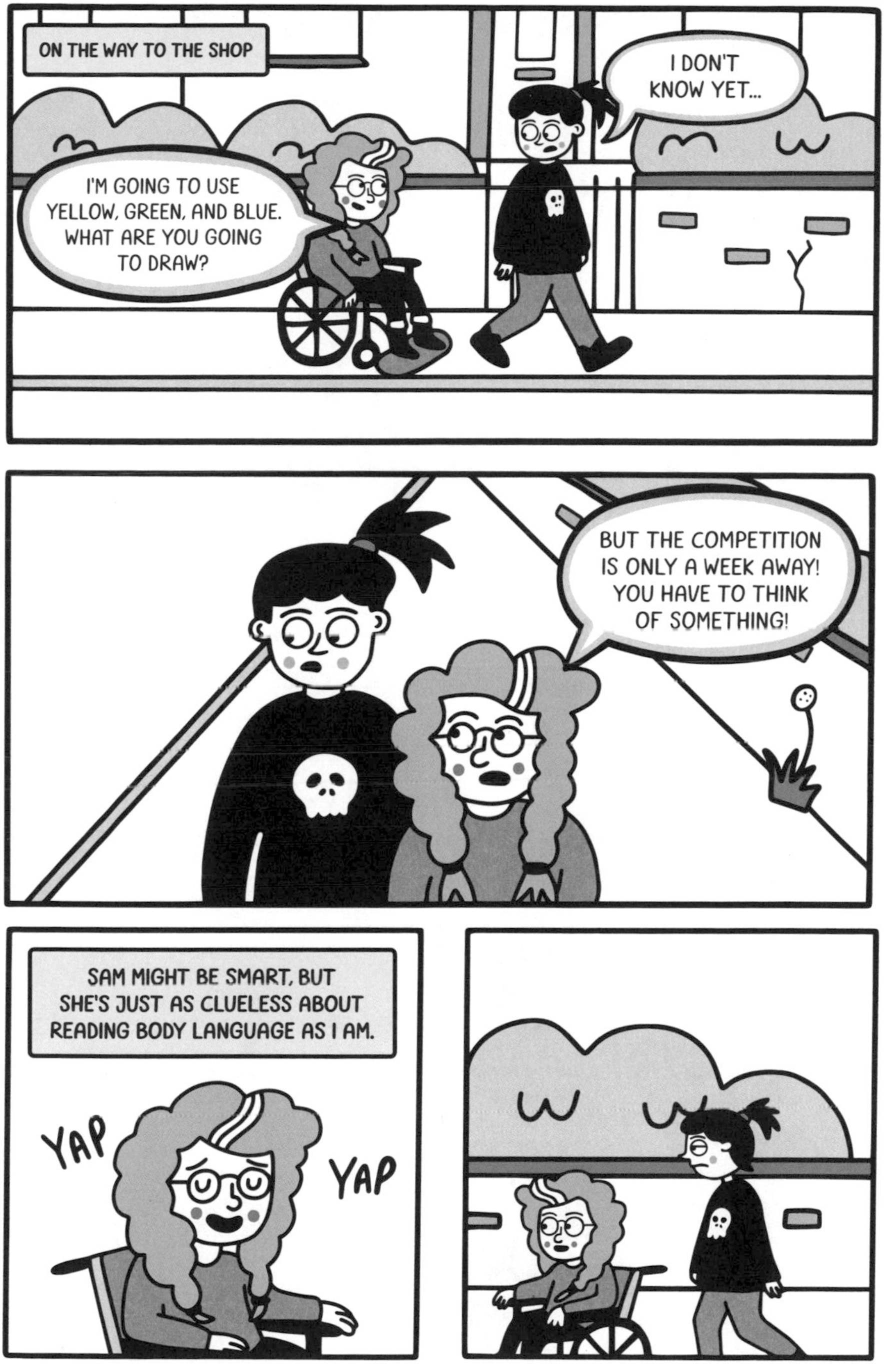
ON THE WAY TO THE SHOP
I'M GOING TO USE YELLOW, GREEN, AND BLUE. WHAT ARE YOU GOING TO DRAW?
I DON'T KNOW YET...
BUT THE COMPETITION IS ONLY A WEEK AWAY! YOU HAVE TO THINK OF SOMETHING!
SAM MIGHT BE SMART, BUT SHE'S JUST AS CLUELESS ABOUT READING BODY LANGUAGE AS I AM.
YAP
YAP

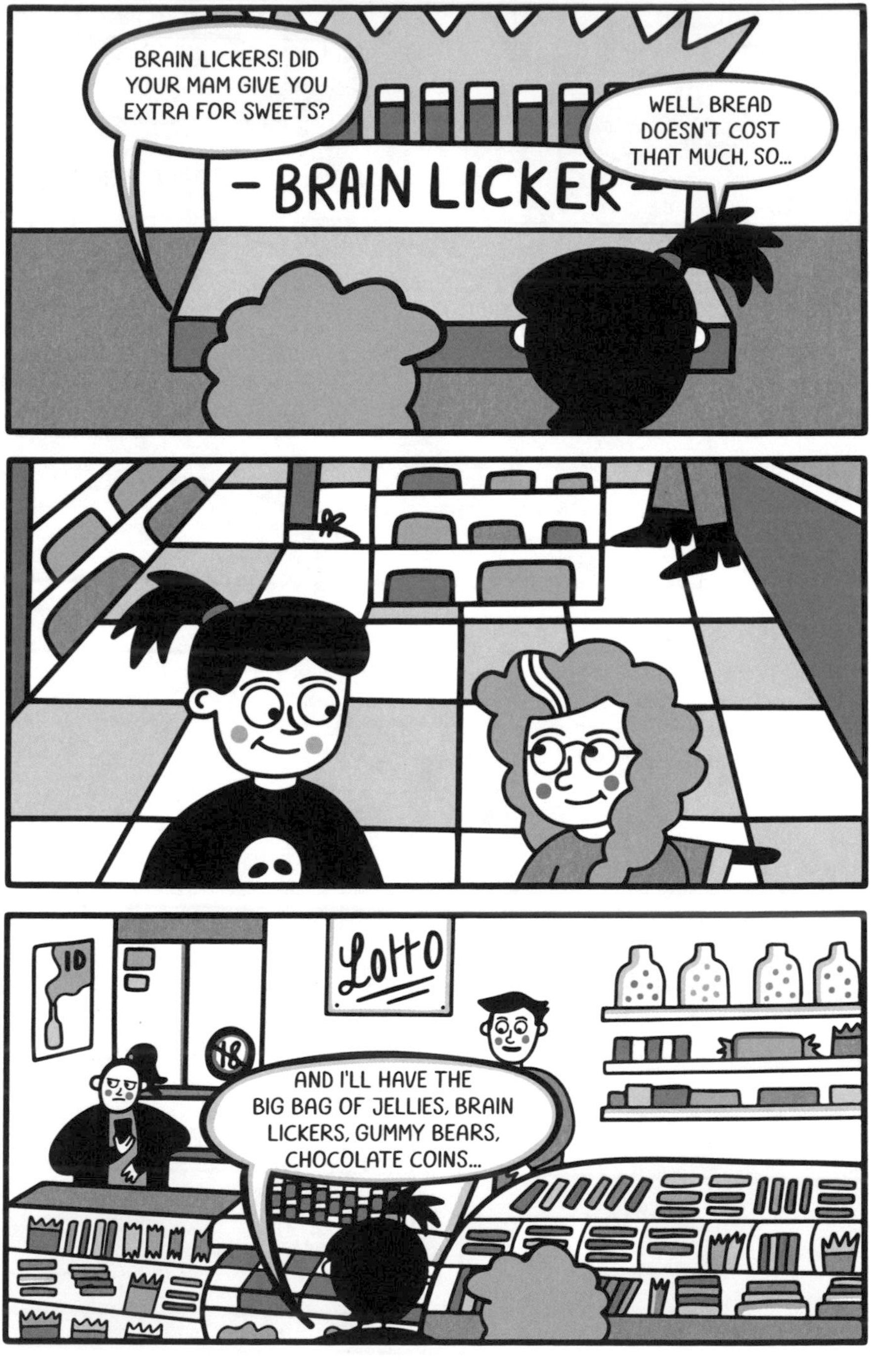
BRAIN LICKERS! DID YOUR MAM GIVE YOU EXTRA FOR SWEETS?
WELL, BREAD DOESN'T COST THAT MUCH, SO...
- BRAIN LICKER -
ID
18
Lotto
AND I'LL HAVE THE BIG BAG OF JELLIES, BRAIN LICKERS, GUMMY BEARS, CHOCOLATE COINS...

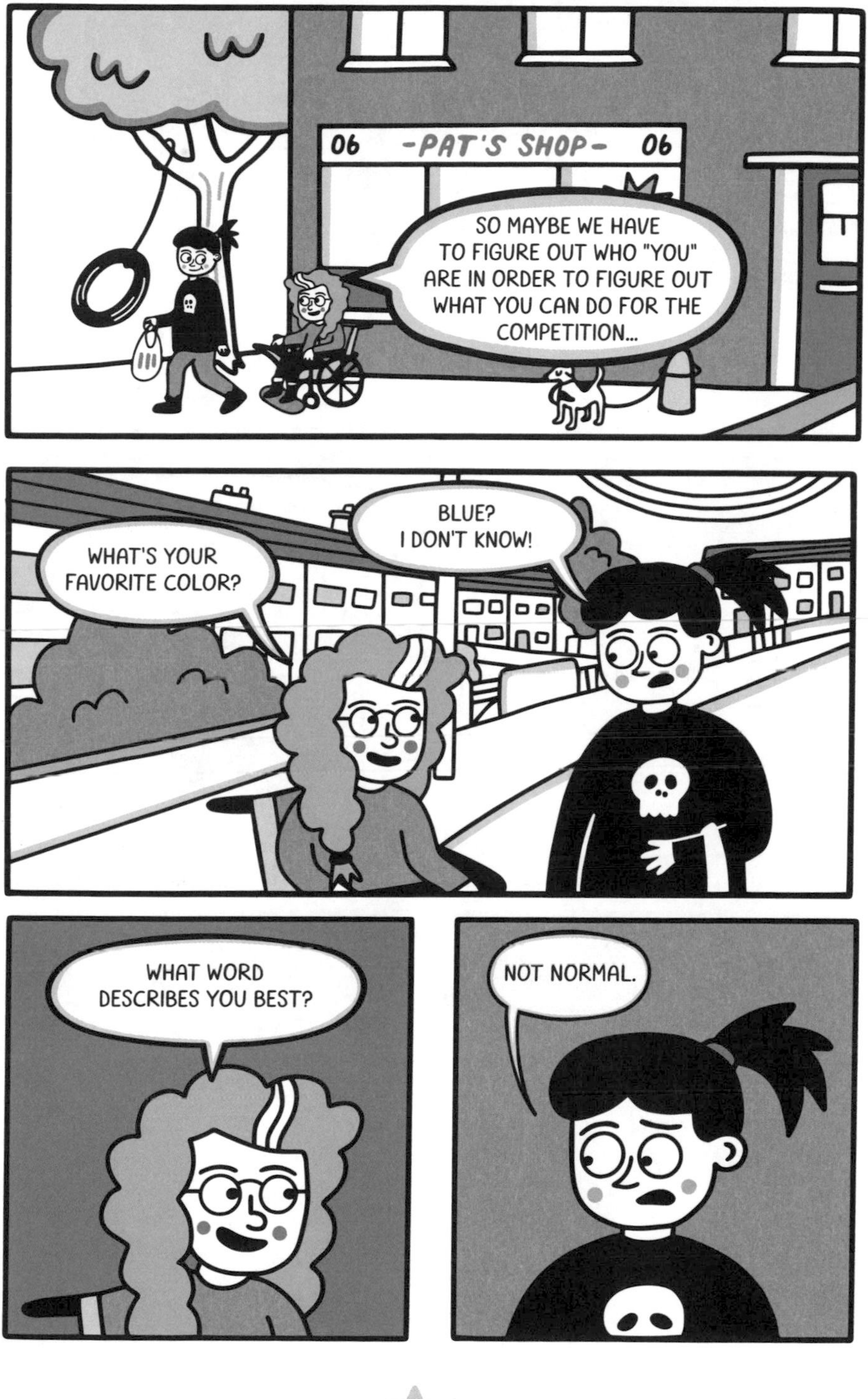
-PAT'S SHOP-
06
06
SO MAYBE WE HAVE TO FIGURE OUT WHO "YOU" ARE IN ORDER TO FIGURE OUT WHAT YOU CAN DO FOR THE COMPETITION...
WHAT'S YOUR FAVORITE COLOR?
BLUE? I DON'T KNOW!
WHAT WORD DESCRIBES YOU BEST?
NOT NORMAL.

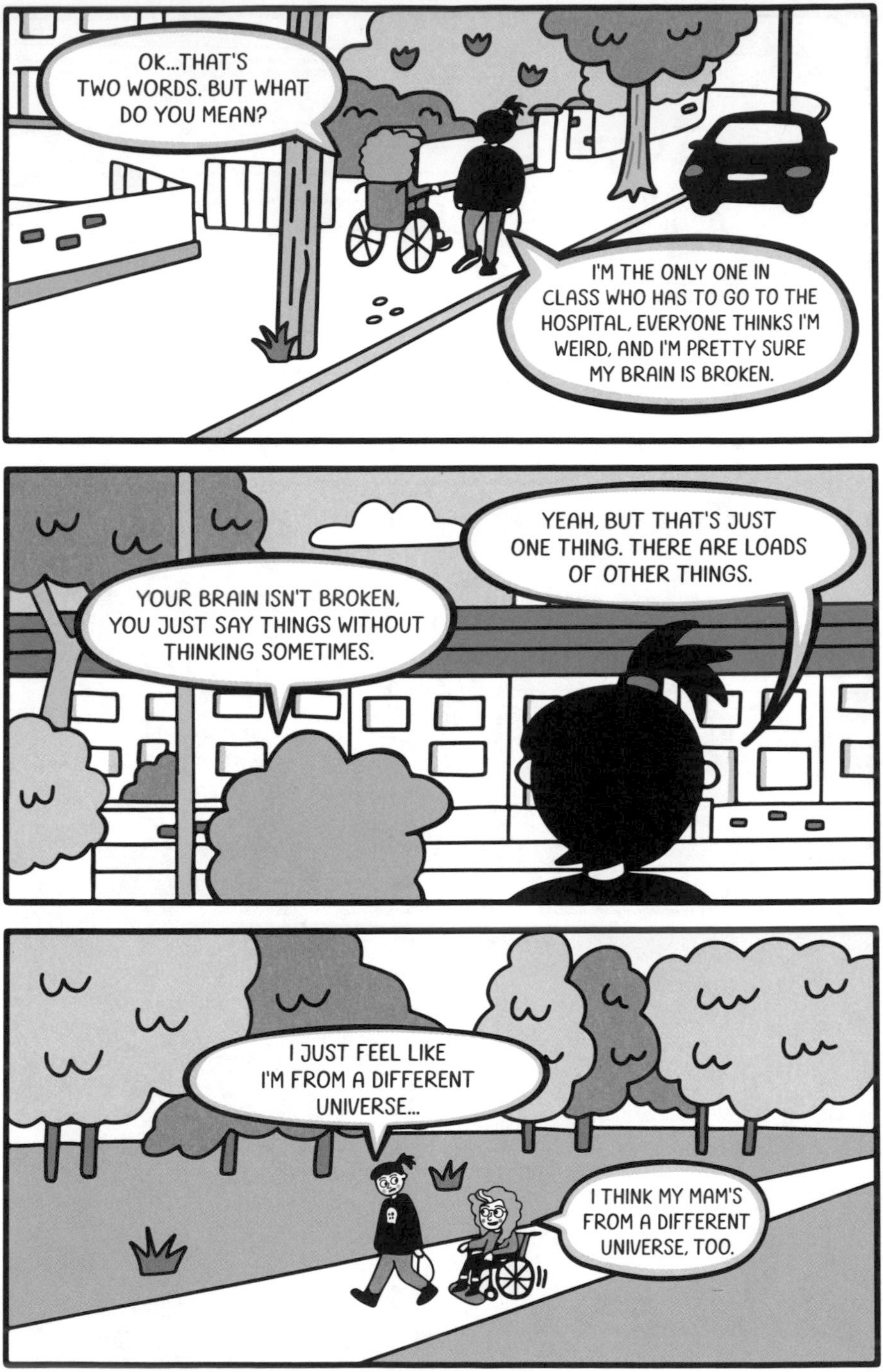
OK...THAT'S TWO WORDS. BUT WHAT DO YOU MEAN?
I'M THE ONLY ONE IN CLASS WHO HAS TO GO TO THE HOSPITAL, EVERYONE THINKS I'M WEIRD, AND I'M PRETTY SURE MY BRAIN IS BROKEN.
YOUR BRAIN ISN'T BROKEN, YOU JUST SAY THINGS WITHOUT THINKING SOMETIMES.
YEAH, BUT THAT'S JUST ONE THING. THERE ARE LOADS OF OTHER THINGS.
I JUST FEEL LIKE I'M FROM A DIFFERENT UNIVERSE...
I THINK MY MAM'S FROM A DIFFERENT UNIVERSE, TOO.

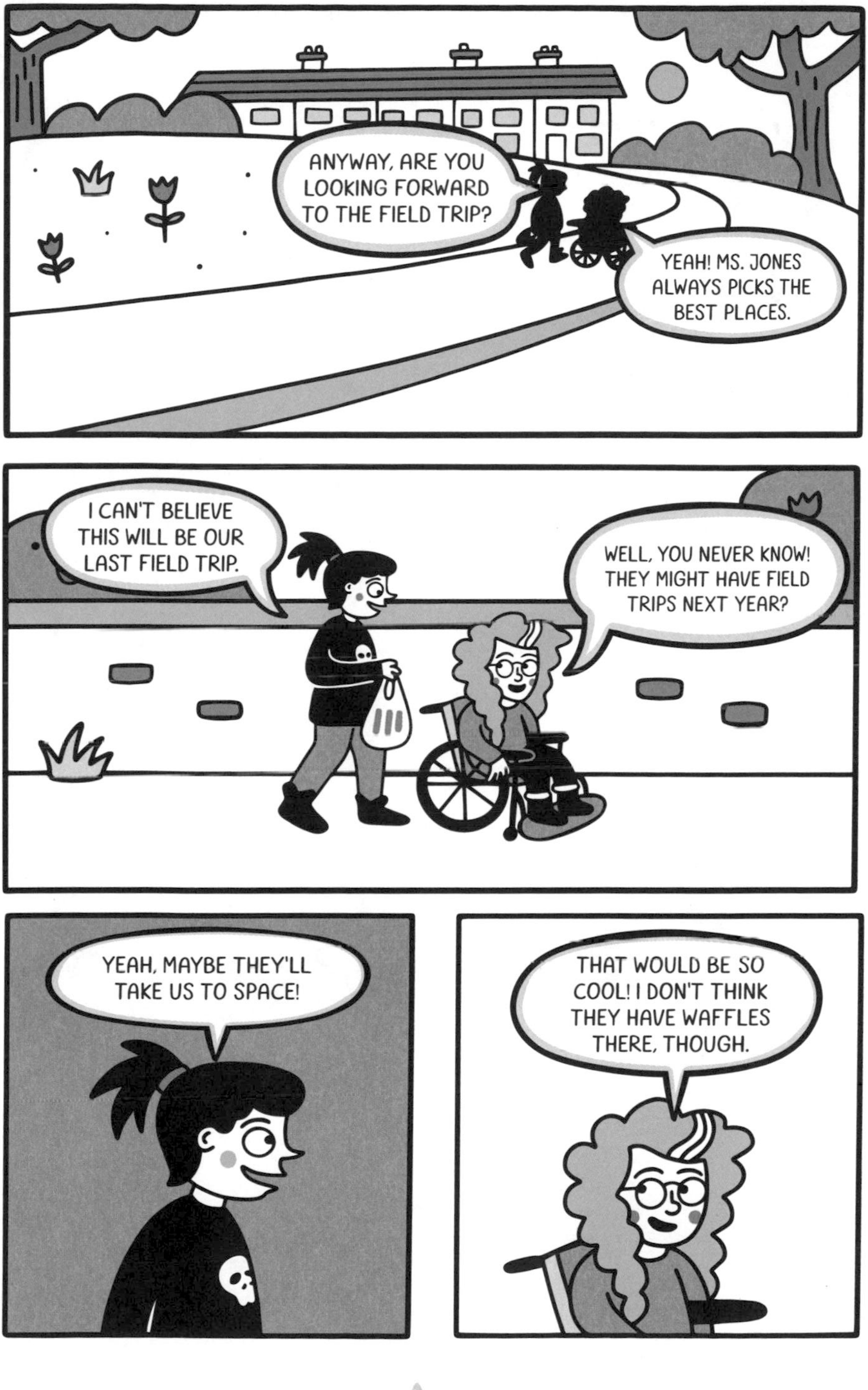
ANYWAY, ARE YOU LOOKING FORWARD TO THE FIELD TRIP?
YEAH! MS. JONES ALWAYS PICKS THE BEST PLACES.
I CAN'T BELIEVE THIS WILL BE OUR LAST FIELD TRIP.
WELL, YOU NEVER KNOW! THEY MIGHT HAVE FIELD TRIPS NEXT YEAR?
YEAH, MAYBE THEY'LL TAKE US TO SPACE!
THAT WOULD BE SO COOL! I DON'T THINK THEY HAVE WAFFLES THERE, THOUGH.

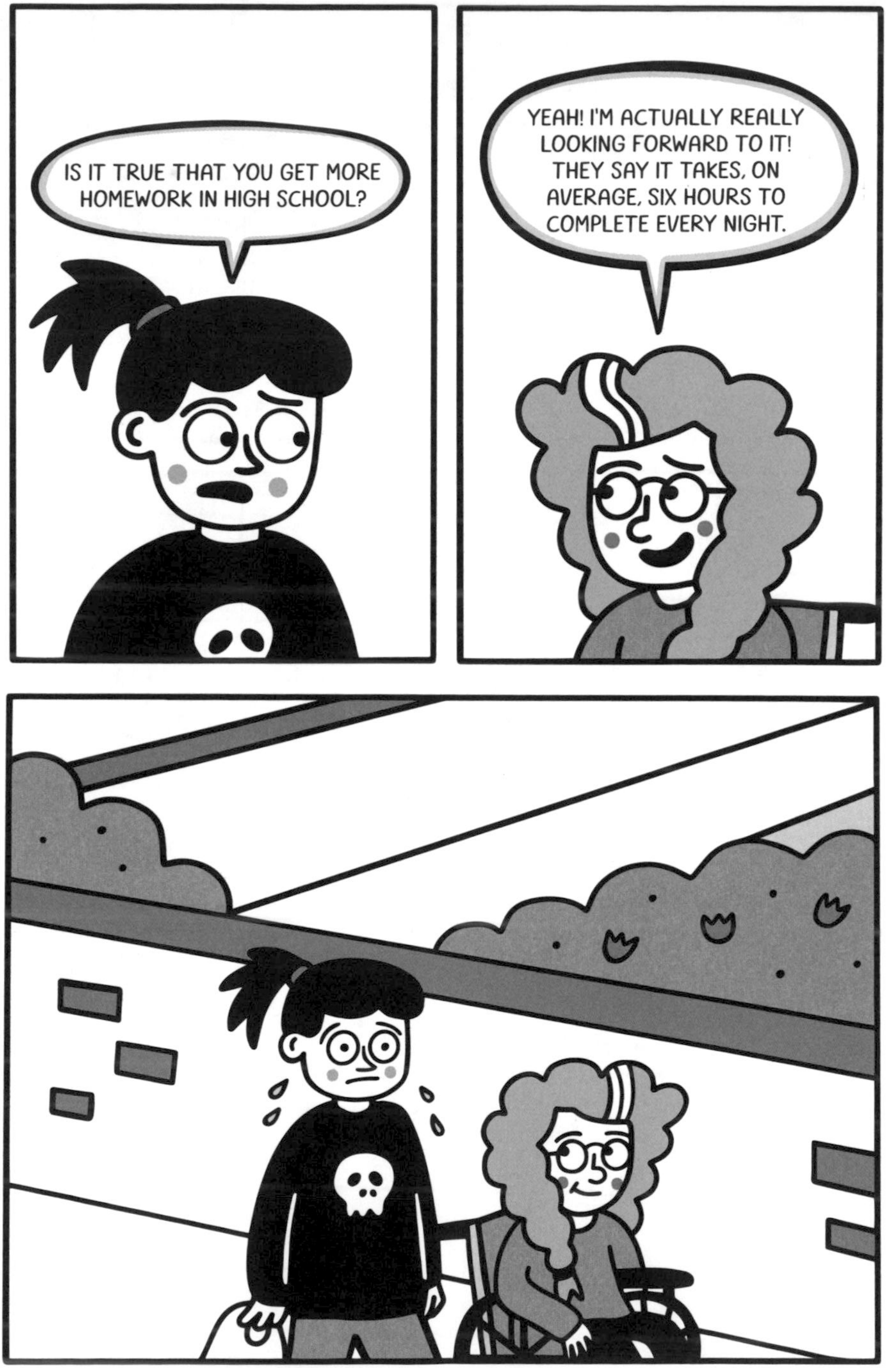
IS IT TRUE THAT YOU GET MORE HOMEWORK IN HIGH SCHOOL?
YEAH! I'M ACTUALLY REALLY LOOKING FORWARD TO IT! THEY SAY IT TAKES, ON AVERAGE, SIX HOURS TO COMPLETE EVERY NIGHT.

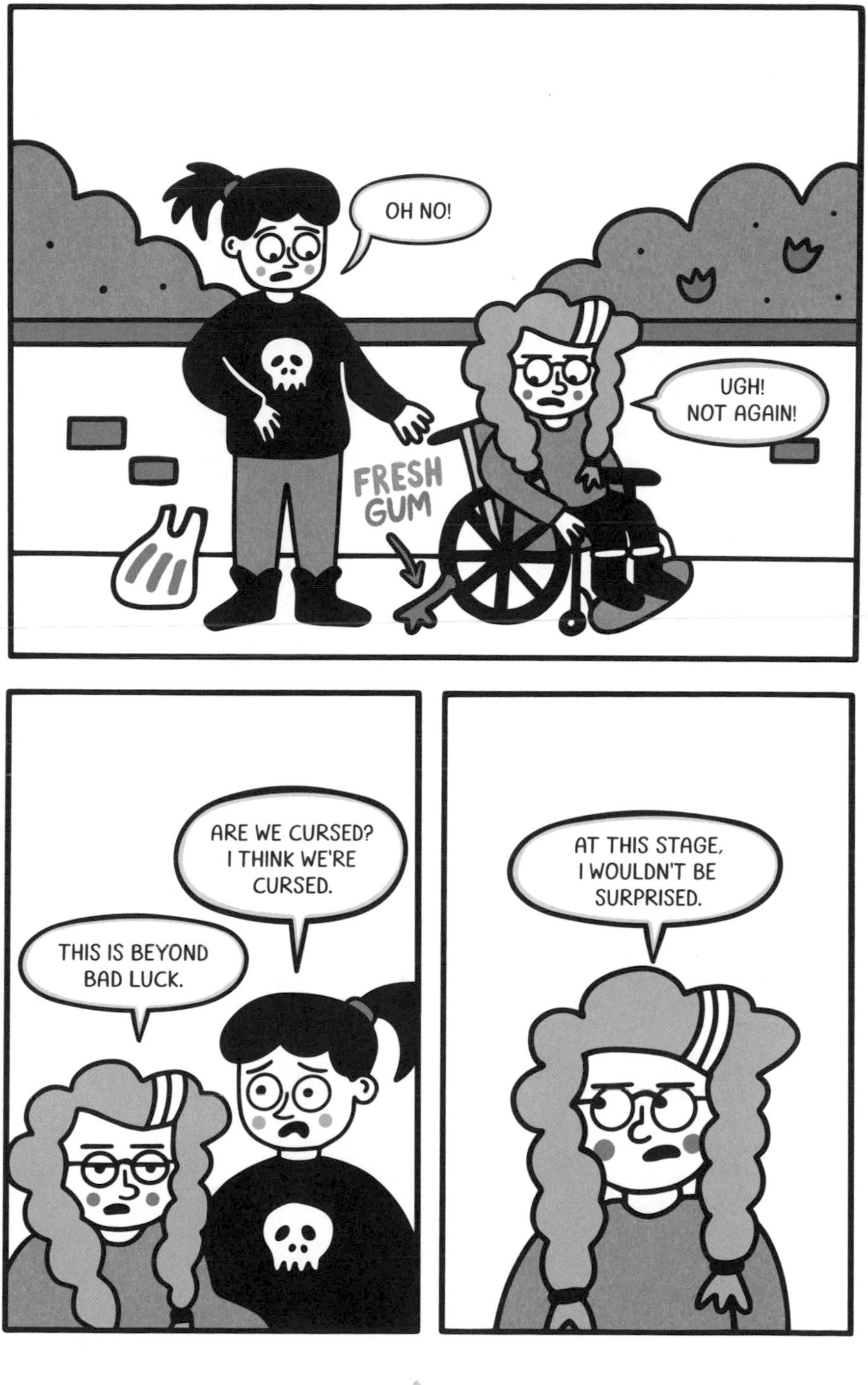
OH NO!
UGH! NOT AGAIN!
FRESH GUM
ARE WE CURSED? I THINK WE'RE CURSED.
THIS IS BEYOND BAD LUCK.
AT THIS STAGE, I WOULDN'T BE SURPRISED.

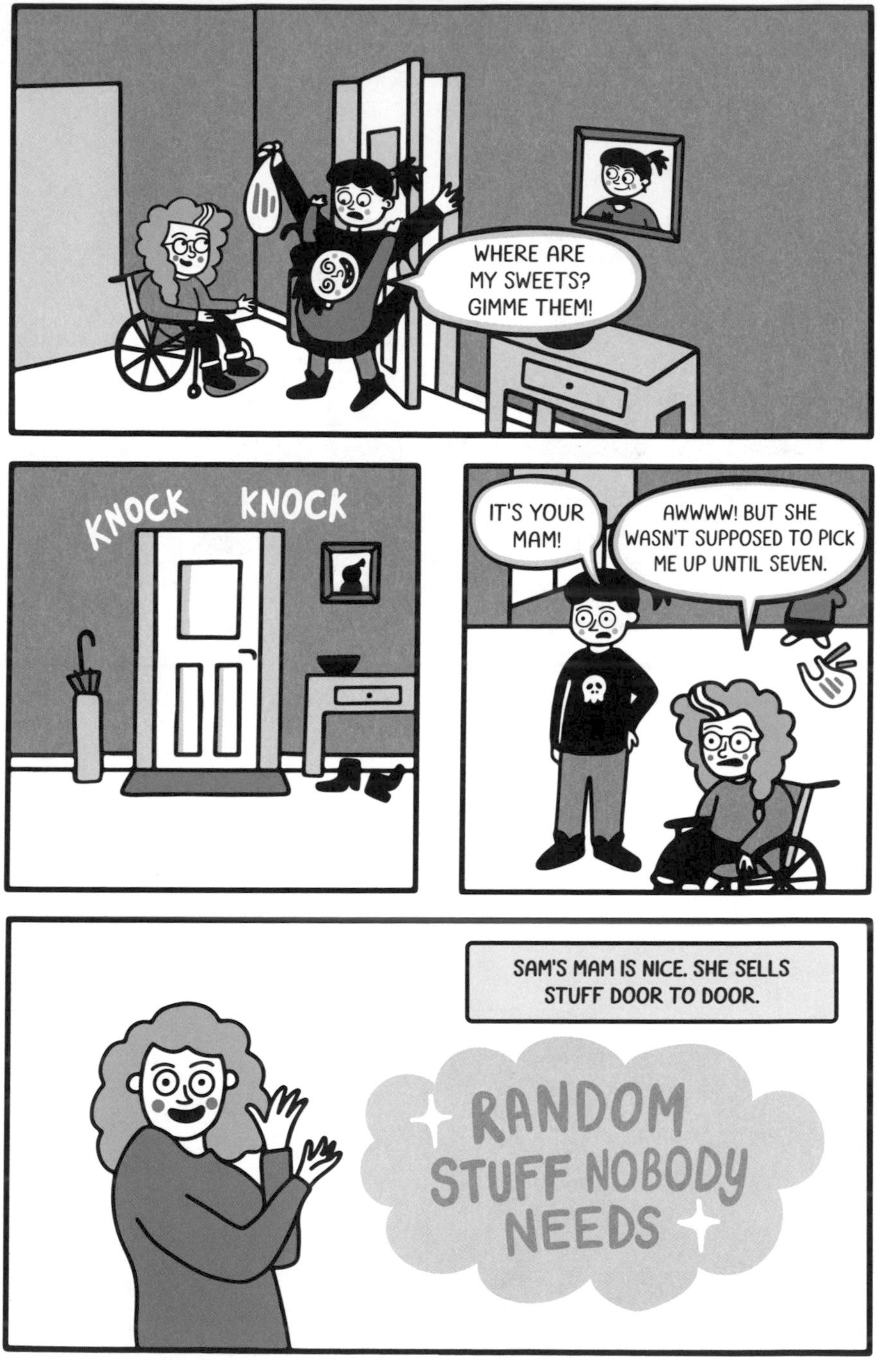
WHERE ARE MY SWEETS? GIMME THEM!
KNOCK KNOCK
IT'S YOUR MAM!
AWWWW! BUT SHE WASN'T SUPPOSED TO PICK ME UP UNTIL SEVEN.
SAM'S MAM IS NICE. SHE SELLS STUFF DOOR TO DOOR.
RANDOM STUFF NOBODY NEEDS

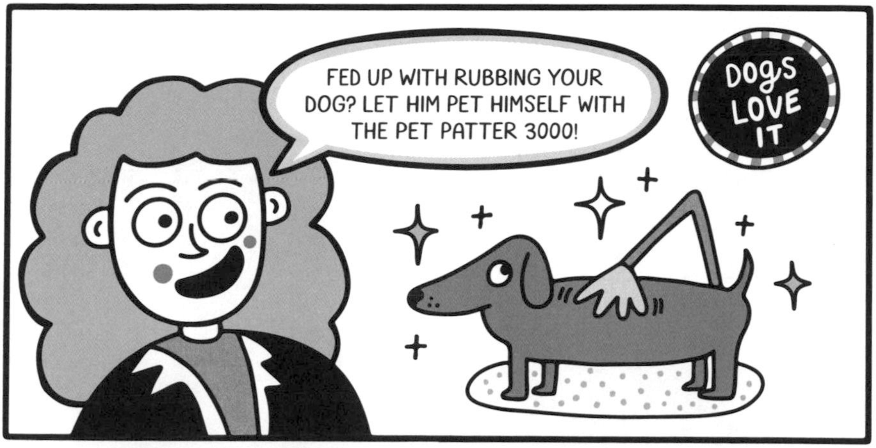
FED UP WITH RUBBING YOUR DOG? LET HIM PET HIMSELF WITH THE PET PATTER 3000!
DOGS LOVE IT

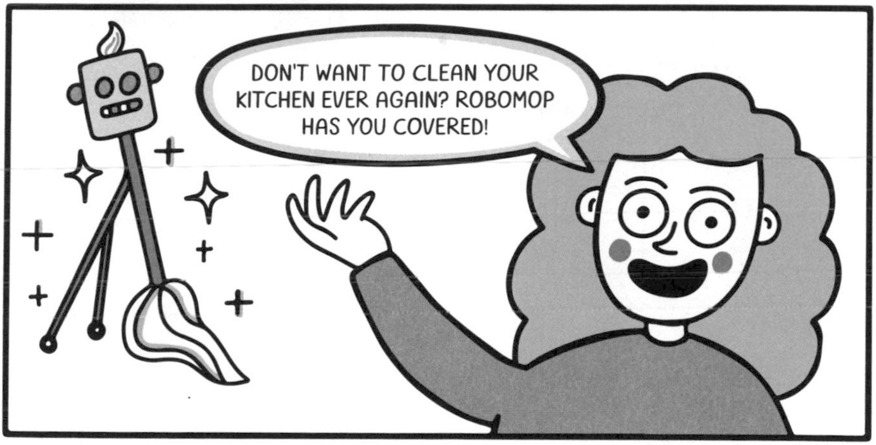
DON'T WANT TO CLEAN YOUR KITCHEN EVER AGAIN? ROBOMOP HAS YOU COVERED!

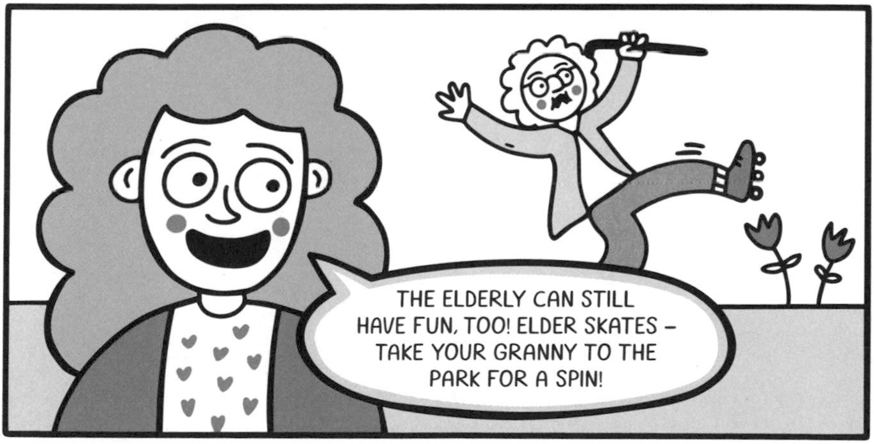
THE ELDERLY CAN STILL HAVE FUN, TOO! ELDER SKATES – TAKE YOUR GRANNY TO THE PARK FOR A SPIN!

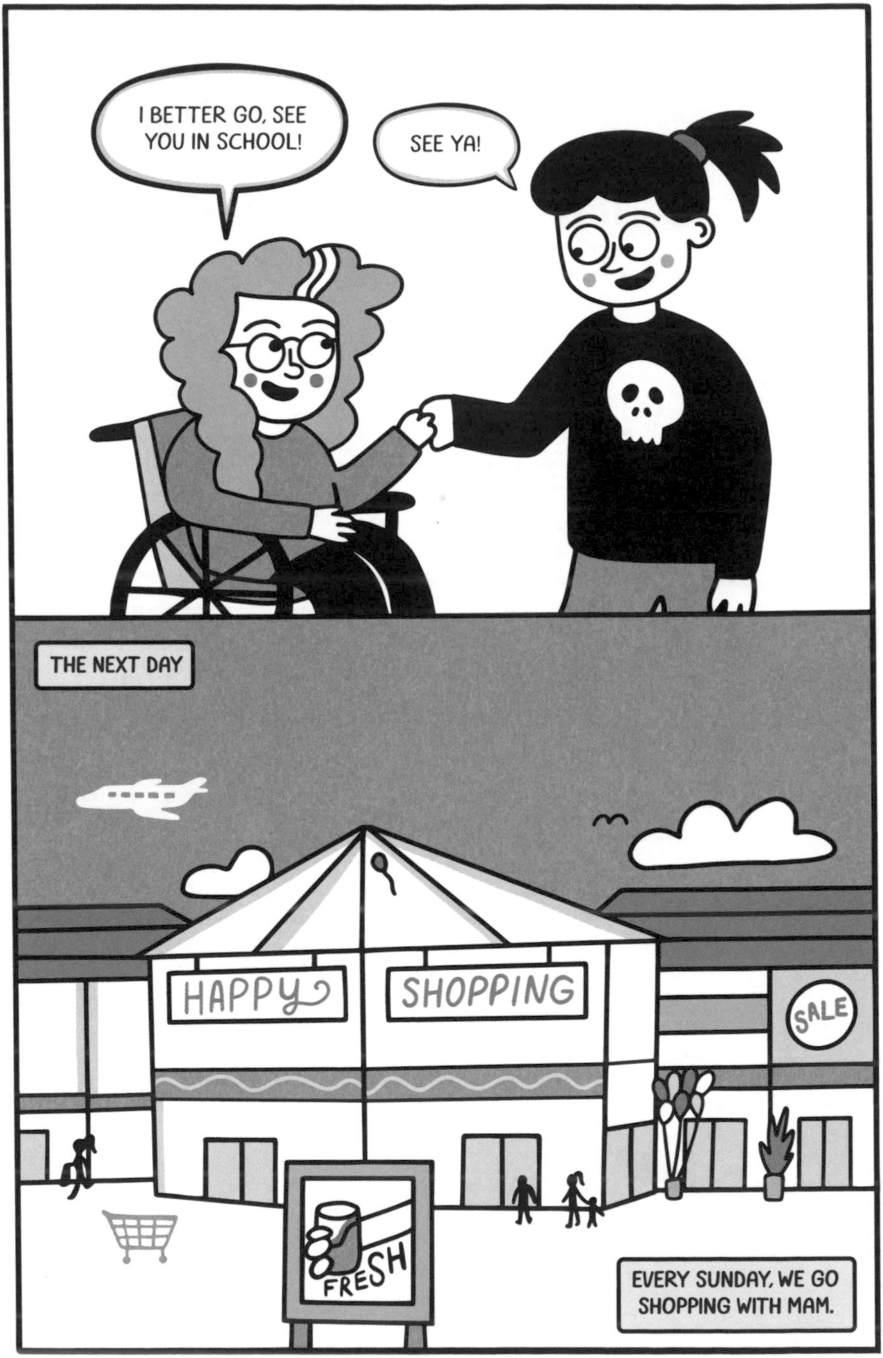
I BETTER GO, SEE YOU IN SCHOOL!
SEE YA!
THE NEXT DAY
HAPPY
SHOPPING
SALE
FRESH
EVERY SUNDAY, WE GO SHOPPING WITH MAM.

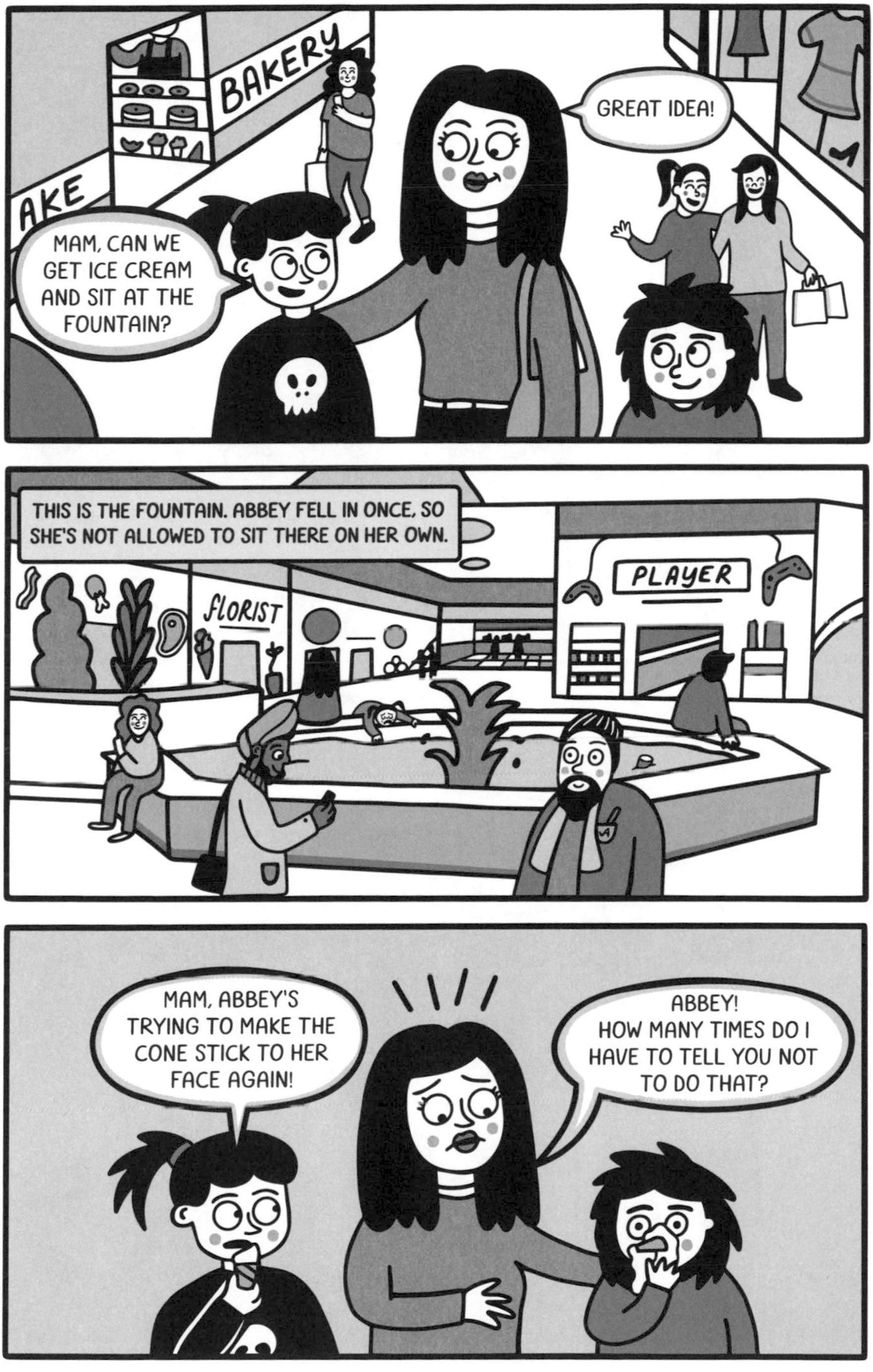
BAKERY
AKE
MAM, CAN WE GET ICE CREAM AND SIT AT THE FOUNTAIN?
GREAT IDEA!
THIS IS THE FOUNTAIN. ABBEY FELL IN ONCE, SO SHE'S NOT ALLOWED TO SIT THERE ON HER OWN.
FLORIST
PLAYER
MAM, ABBEY'S TRYING TO MAKE THE CONE STICK TO HER FACE AGAIN!
ABBEY! HOW MANY TIMES DO I HAVE TO TELL YOU NOT TO DO THAT?

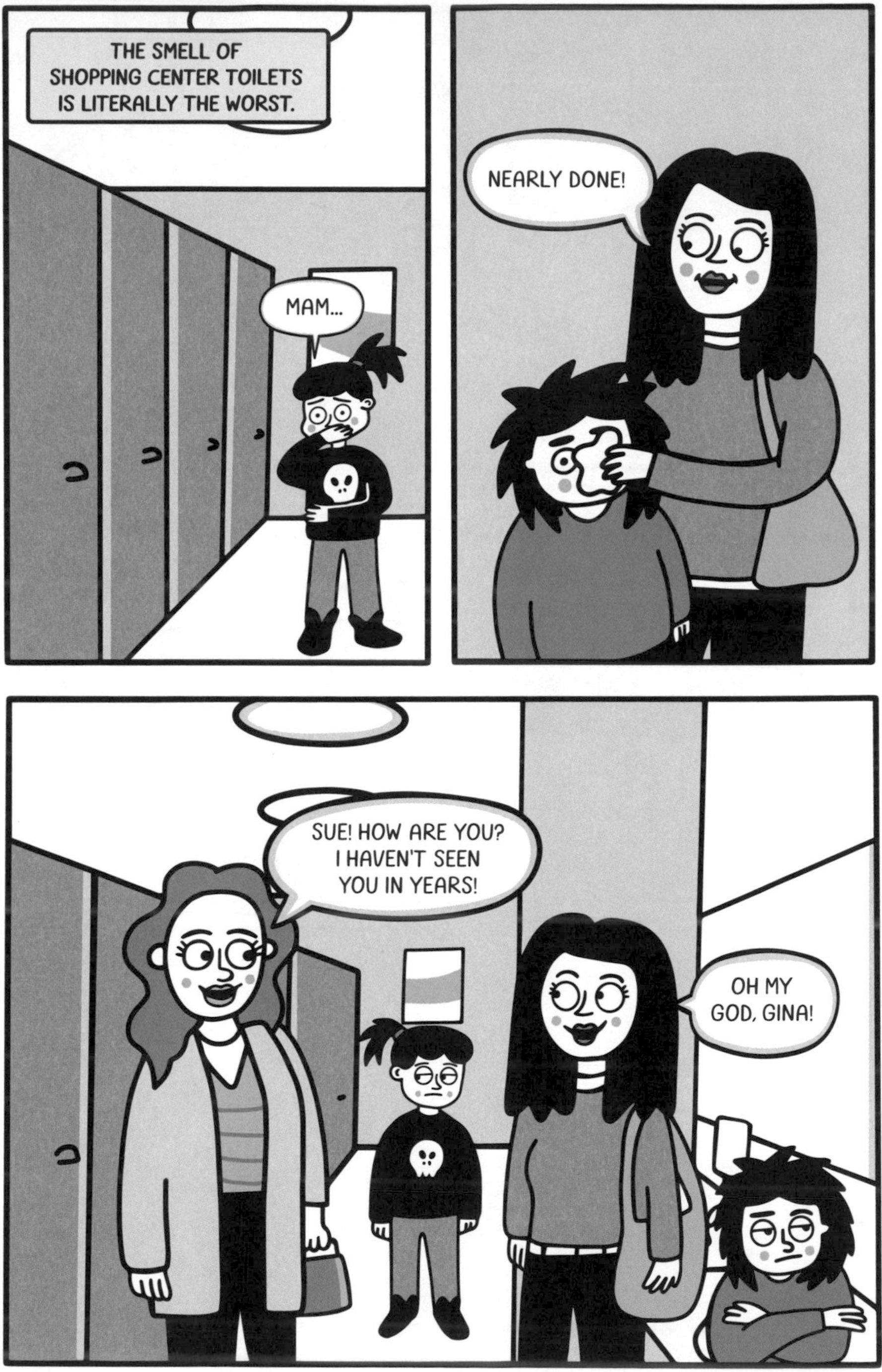
THE SMELL OF SHOPPING CENTER TOILETS IS LITERALLY THE WORST.
MAM...
NEARLY DONE!
SUE! HOW ARE YOU? I HAVEN'T SEEN YOU IN YEARS!
OH MY GOD, GINA!

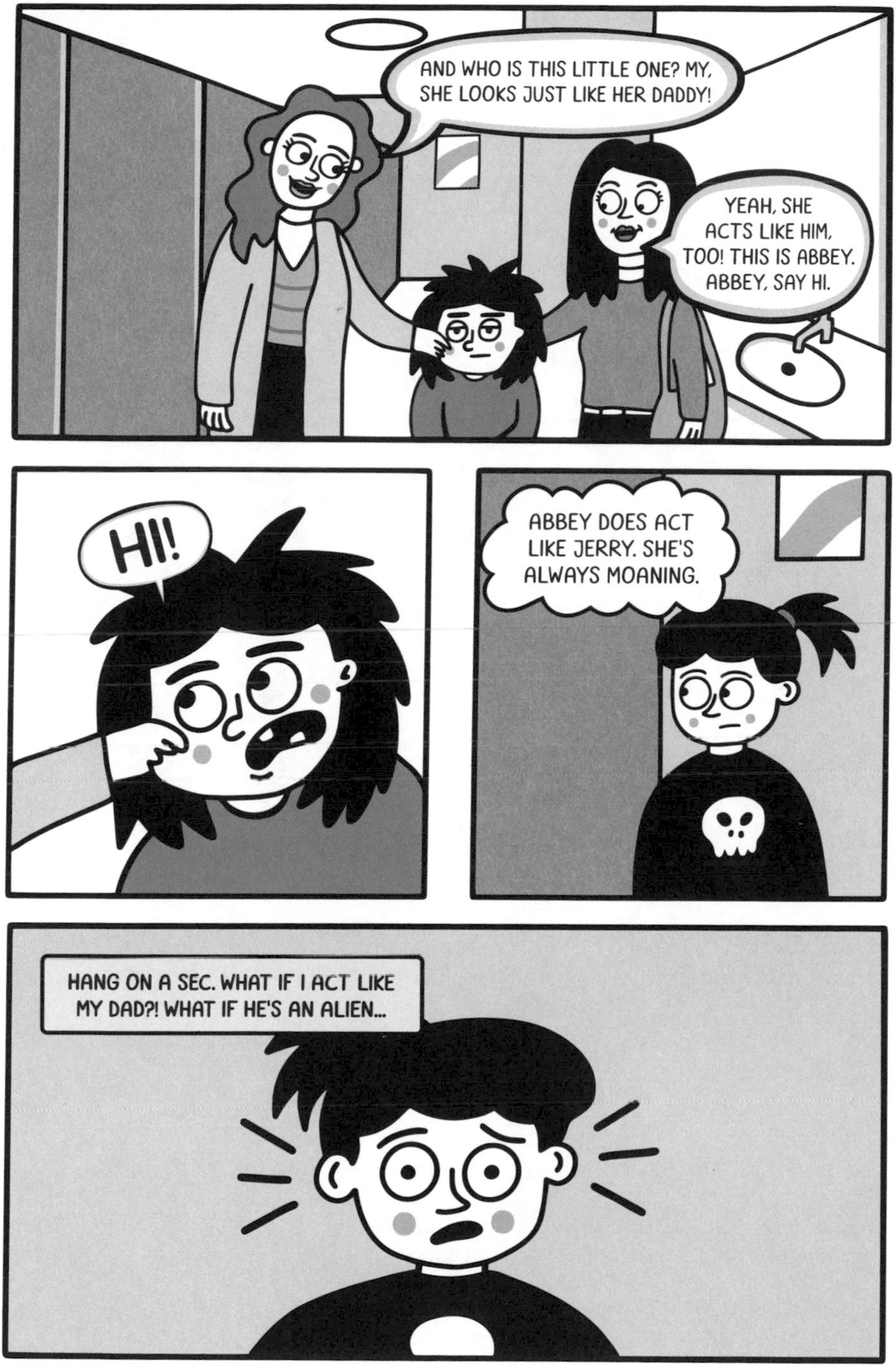
AND WHO IS THIS LITTLE ONE? MY, SHE LOOKS JUST LIKE HER DADDY!
YEAH, SHE ACTS LIKE HIM, TOO! THIS IS ABBEY. ABBEY, SAY HI.
HI!
ABBEY DOES ACT LIKE JERRY. SHE'S ALWAYS MOANING.
HANG ON A SEC. WHAT IF I ACT LIKE MY DAD?! WHAT IF HE'S AN ALIEN...

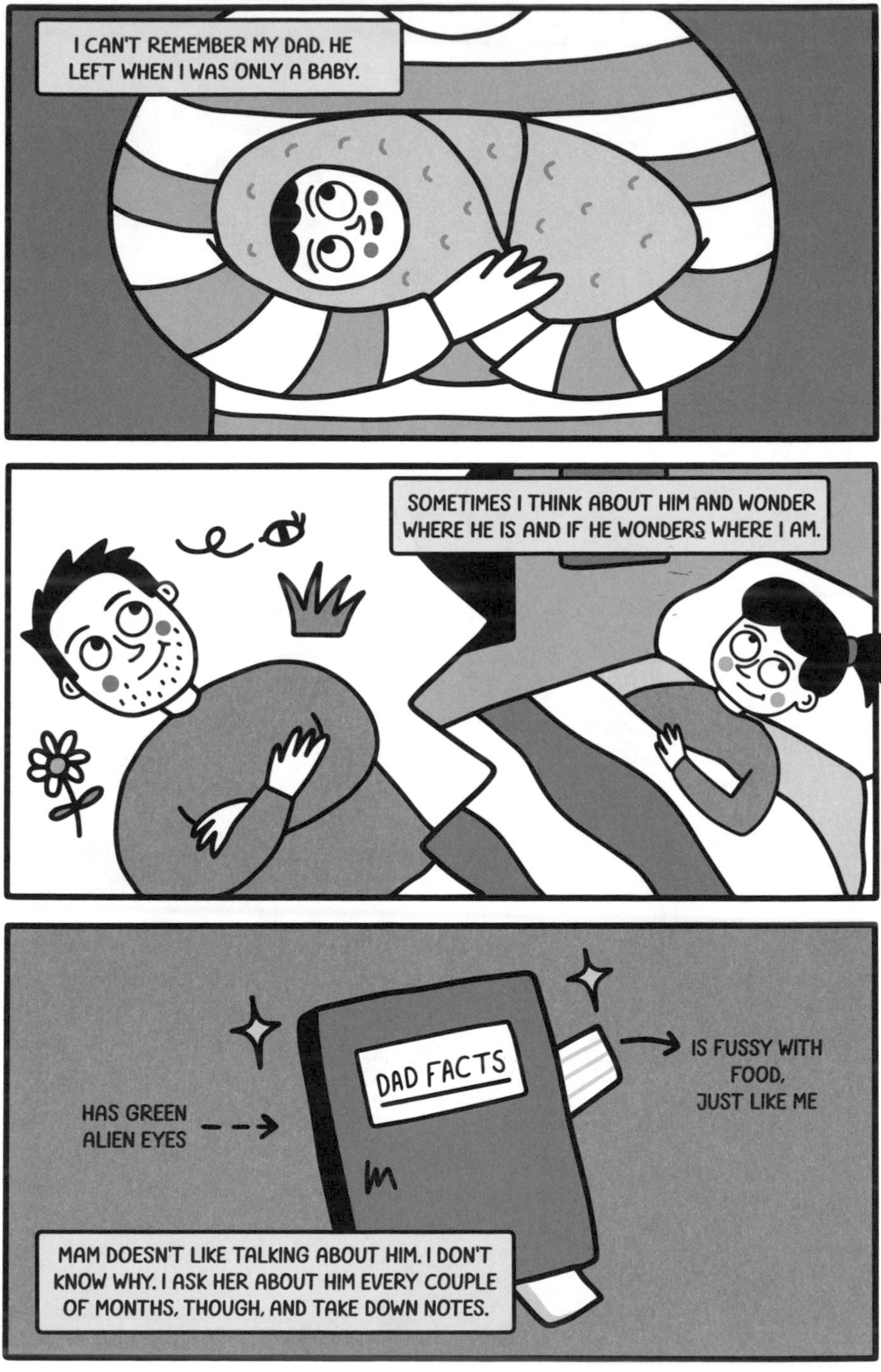
I CAN'T REMEMBER MY DAD. HE LEFT WHEN I WAS ONLY A BABY.
SOMETIMES I THINK ABOUT HIM AND WONDER WHERE HE IS AND IF HE WONDERS WHERE I AM.
DAD FACTS
HAS GREEN ALIEN EYES
IS FUSSY WITH FOOD, JUST LIKE ME
MAM DOESN'T LIKE TALKING ABOUT HIM. I DON'T KNOW WHY. I ASK HER ABOUT HIM EVERY COUPLE OF MONTHS, THOUGH, AND TAKE DOWN NOTES.

WHAT I THINK MY DAD IS LIKE

FUNKY HAIR
COOL LEATHER JACKET
ROCK 'N' ROLL
LISTENS TO ROCK MUSIC
NOT AFRAID OF ANYTHING
AMAZING GUY

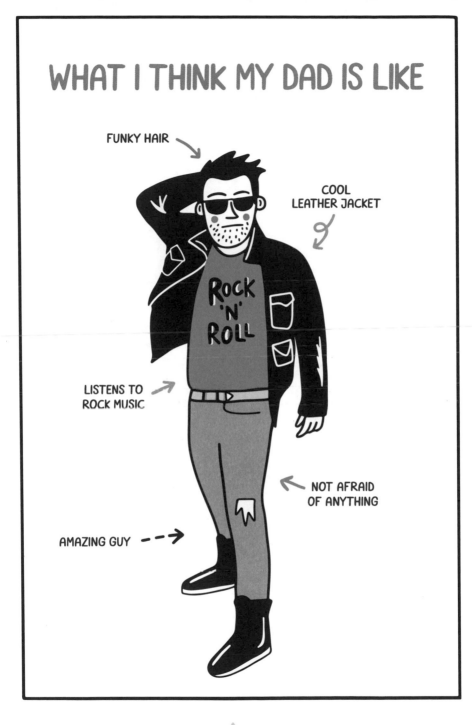

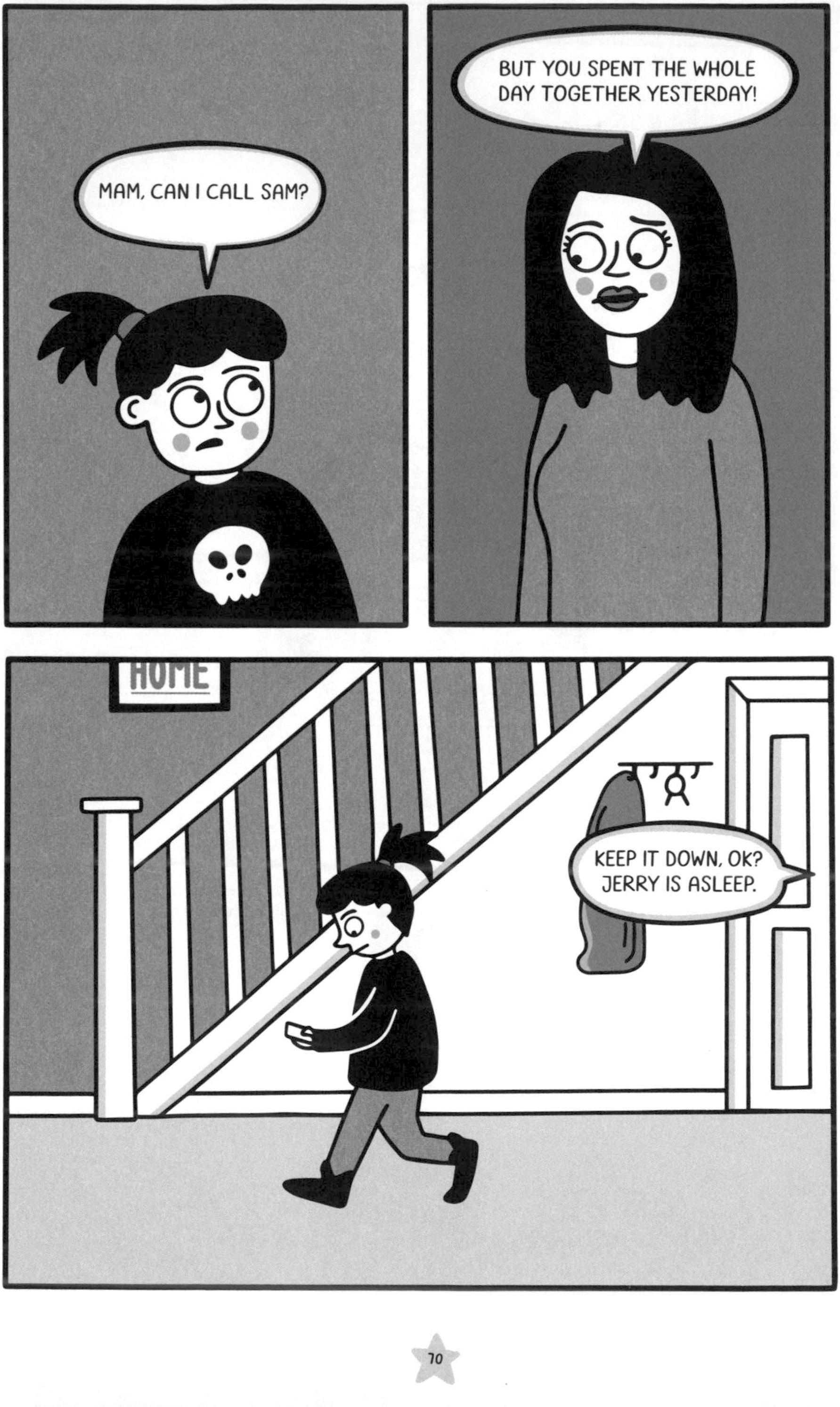
MAM, CAN I CALL SAM?
BUT YOU SPENT THE WHOLE DAY TOGETHER YESTERDAY!
HOME
KEEP IT DOWN, OK? JERRY IS ASLEEP.

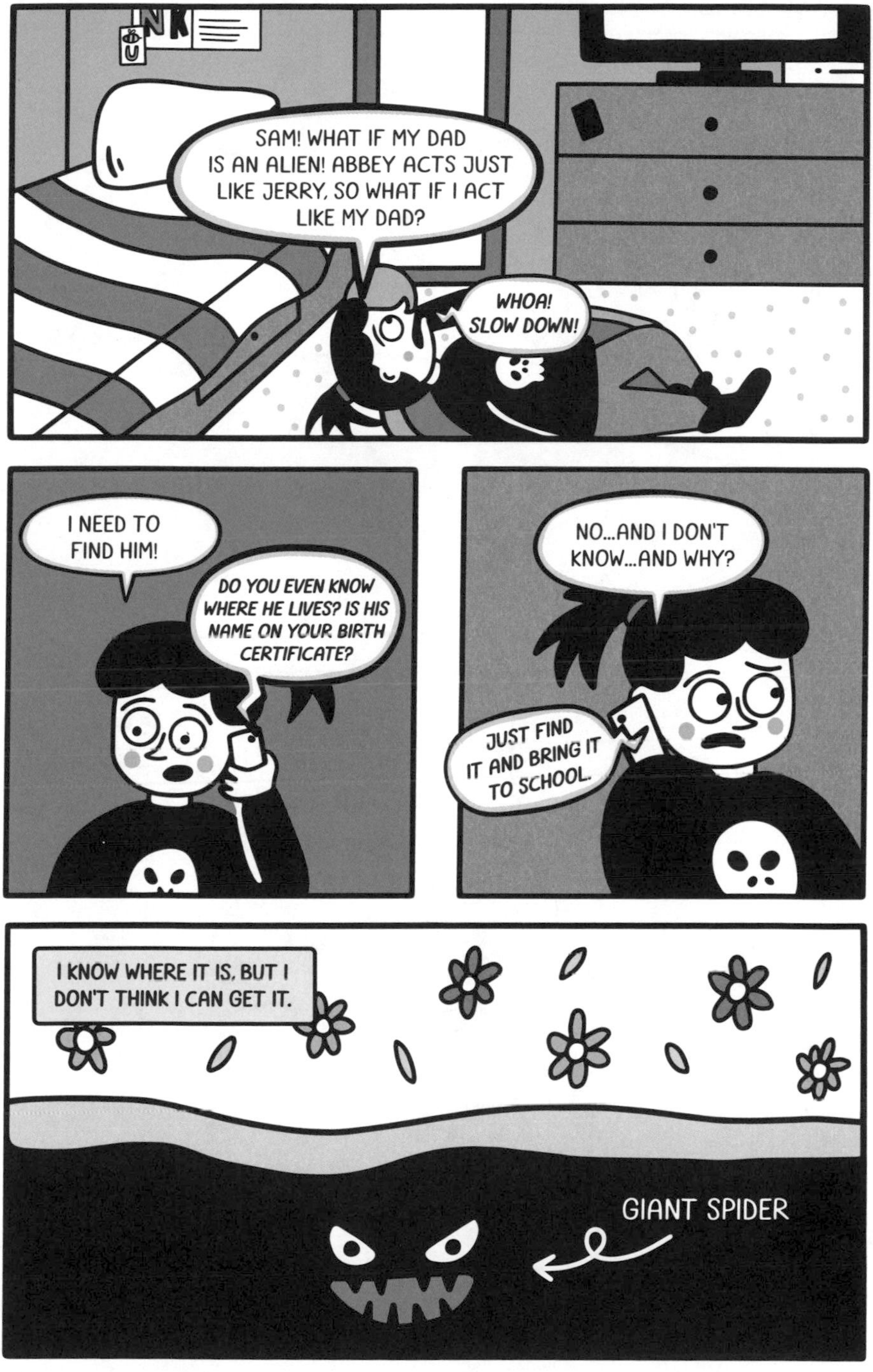
SAM! WHAT IF MY DAD IS AN ALIEN! ABBEY ACTS JUST LIKE JERRY, SO WHAT IF I ACT LIKE MY DAD?
WHOA! SLOW DOWN!
I NEED TO FIND HIM!
DO YOU EVEN KNOW WHERE HE LIVES? IS HIS NAME ON YOUR BIRTH CERTIFICATE?
NO...AND I DON'T KNOW...AND WHY?
JUST FIND IT AND BRING IT TO SCHOOL.
I KNOW WHERE IT IS, BUT I DON'T THINK I CAN GET IT.
GIANT SPIDER

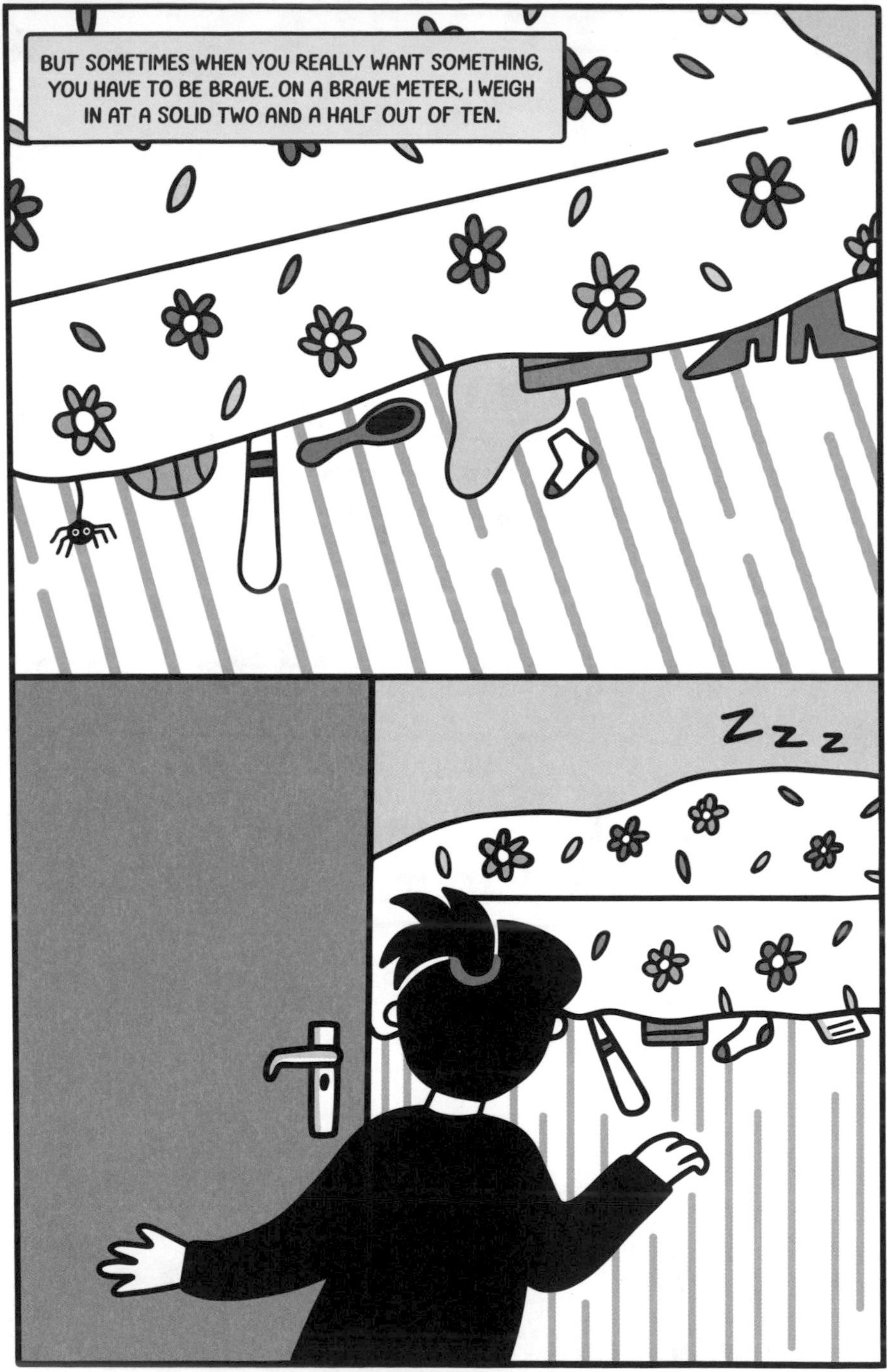
BUT SOMETIMES WHEN YOU REALLY WANT SOMETHING, YOU HAVE TO BE BRAVE. ON A BRAVE METER, I WEIGH IN AT A SOLID TWO AND A HALF OUT OF TEN.
ZZZ

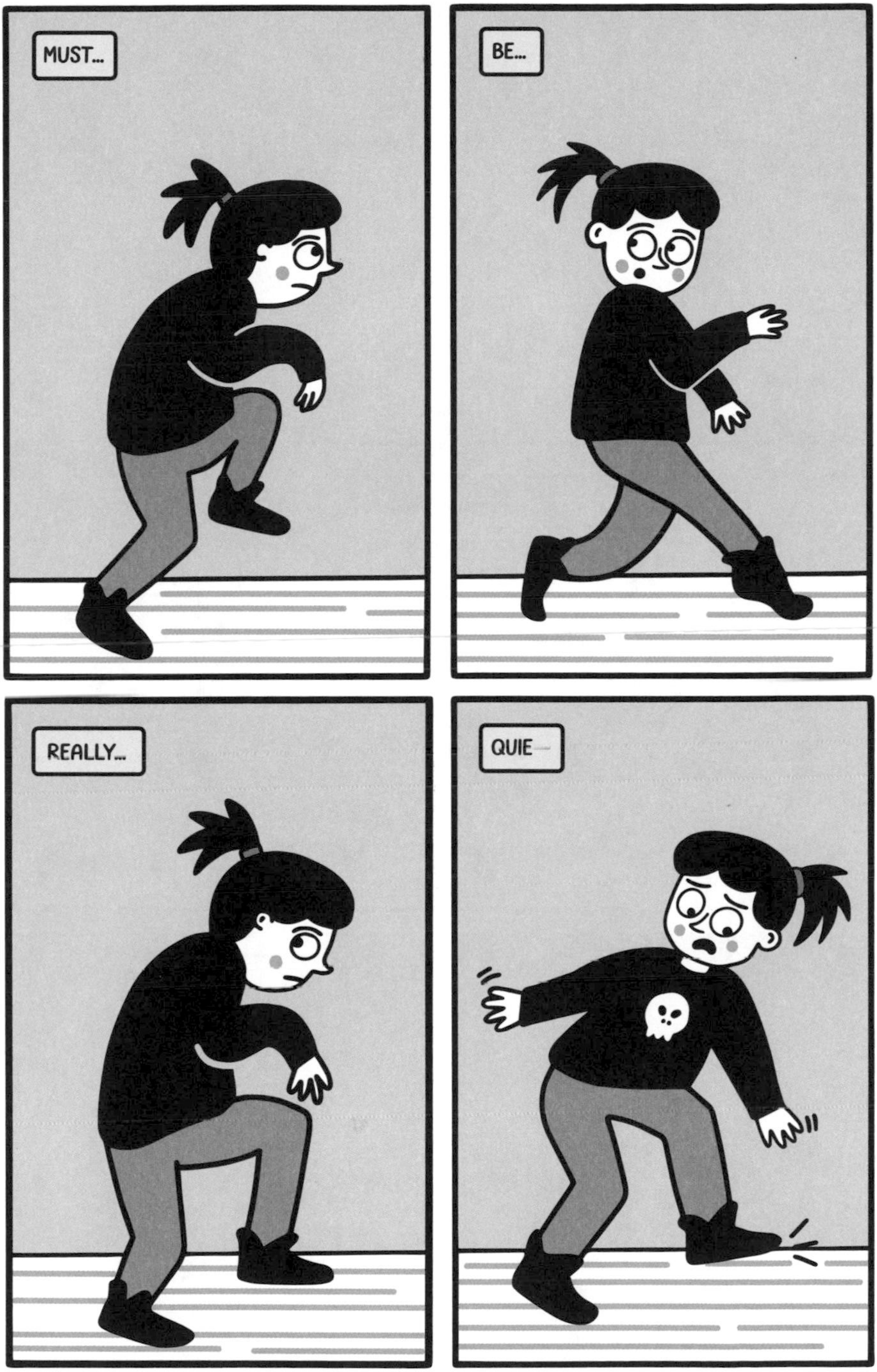
MUST...
BE...
REALLY...
QUIE—

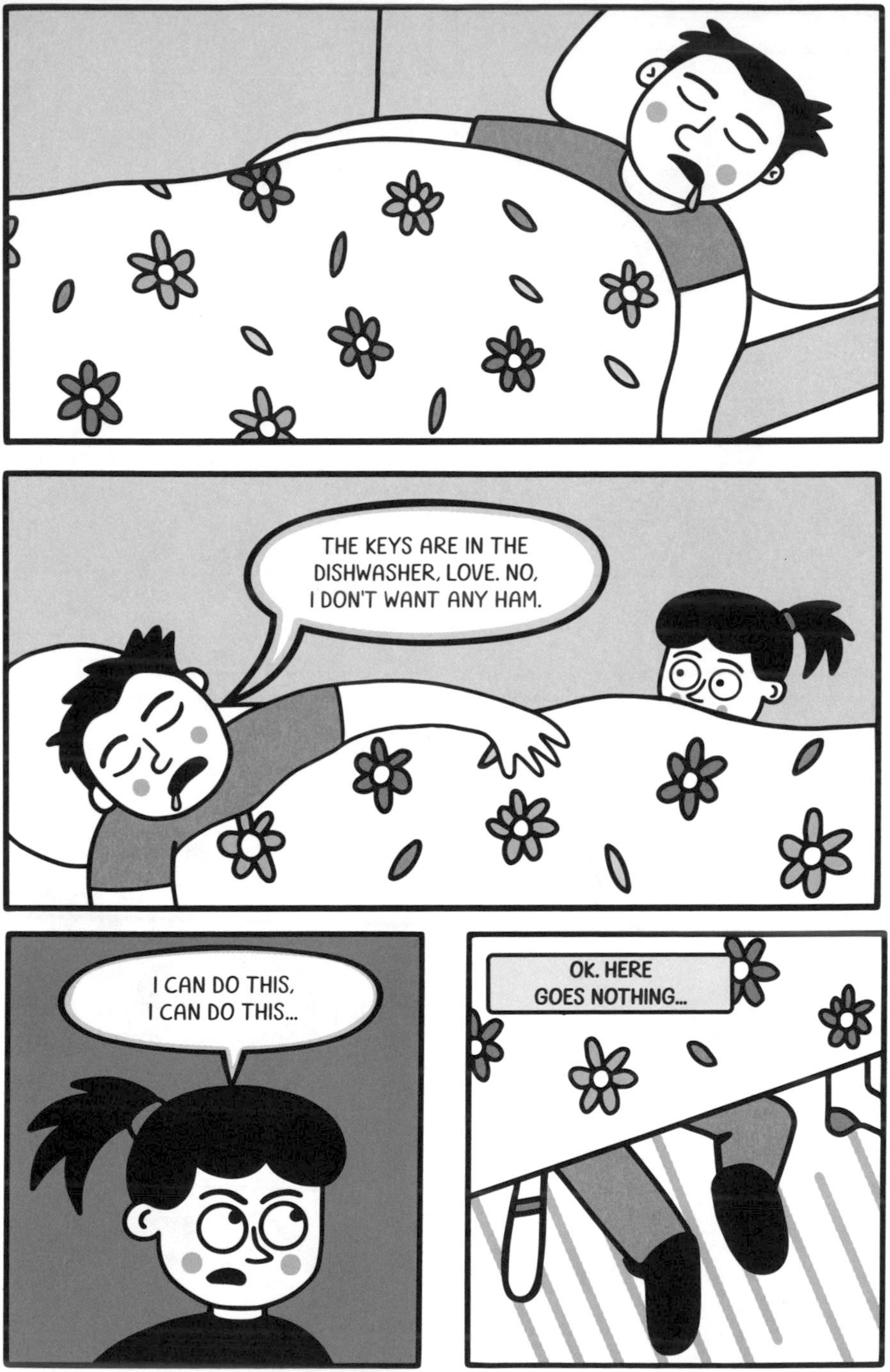
THE KEYS ARE IN THE DISHWASHER, LOVE. NO, I DON'T WANT ANY HAM.
I CAN DO THIS, I CAN DO THIS...
OK. HERE GOES NOTHING...

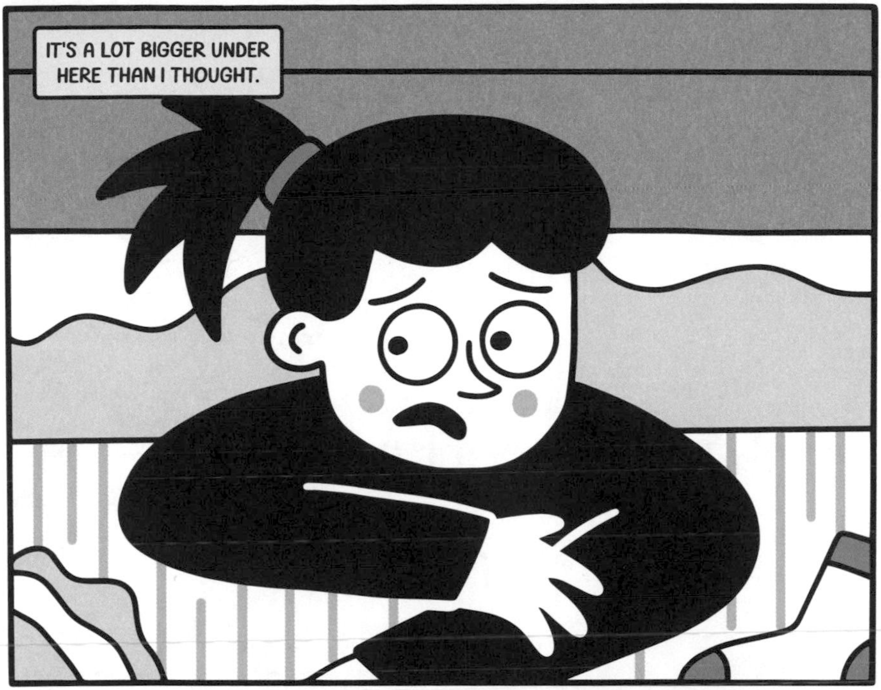
IT'S A LOT BIGGER UNDER HERE THAN I THOUGHT.

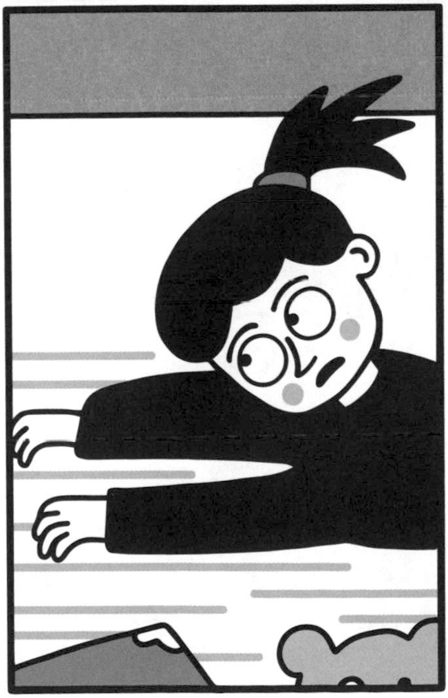

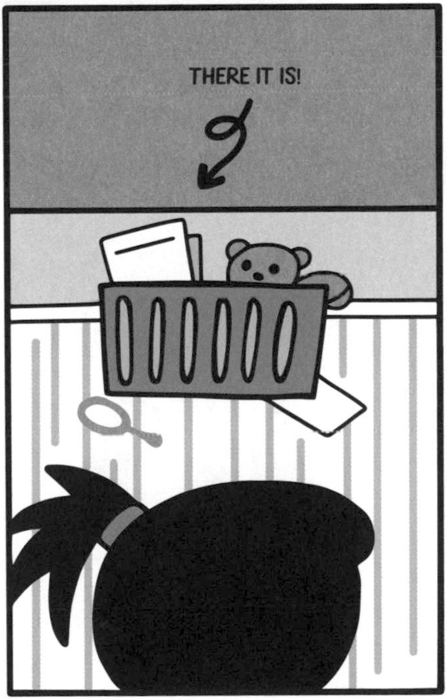
THERE IT IS!

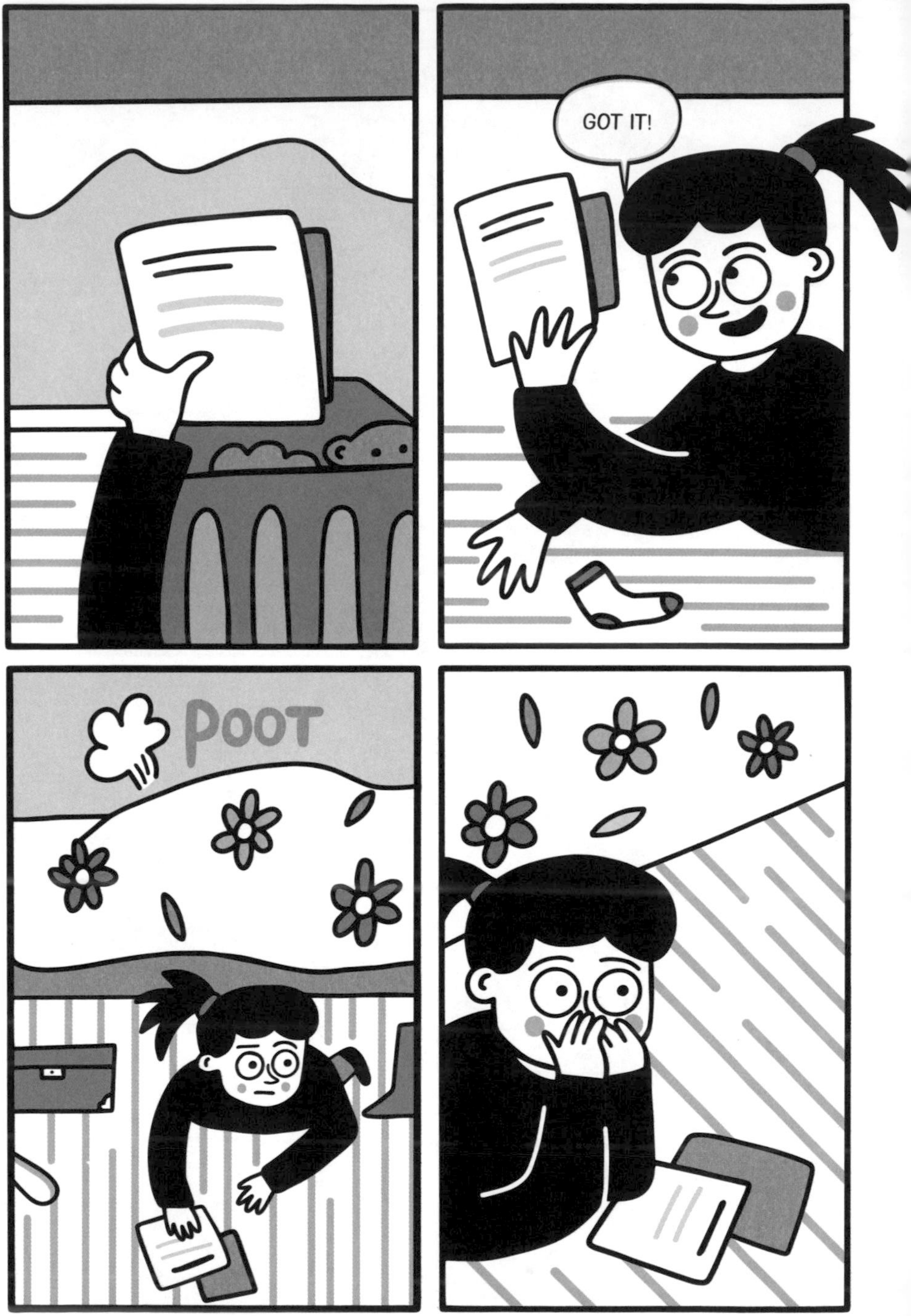
GOT IT!
POOT

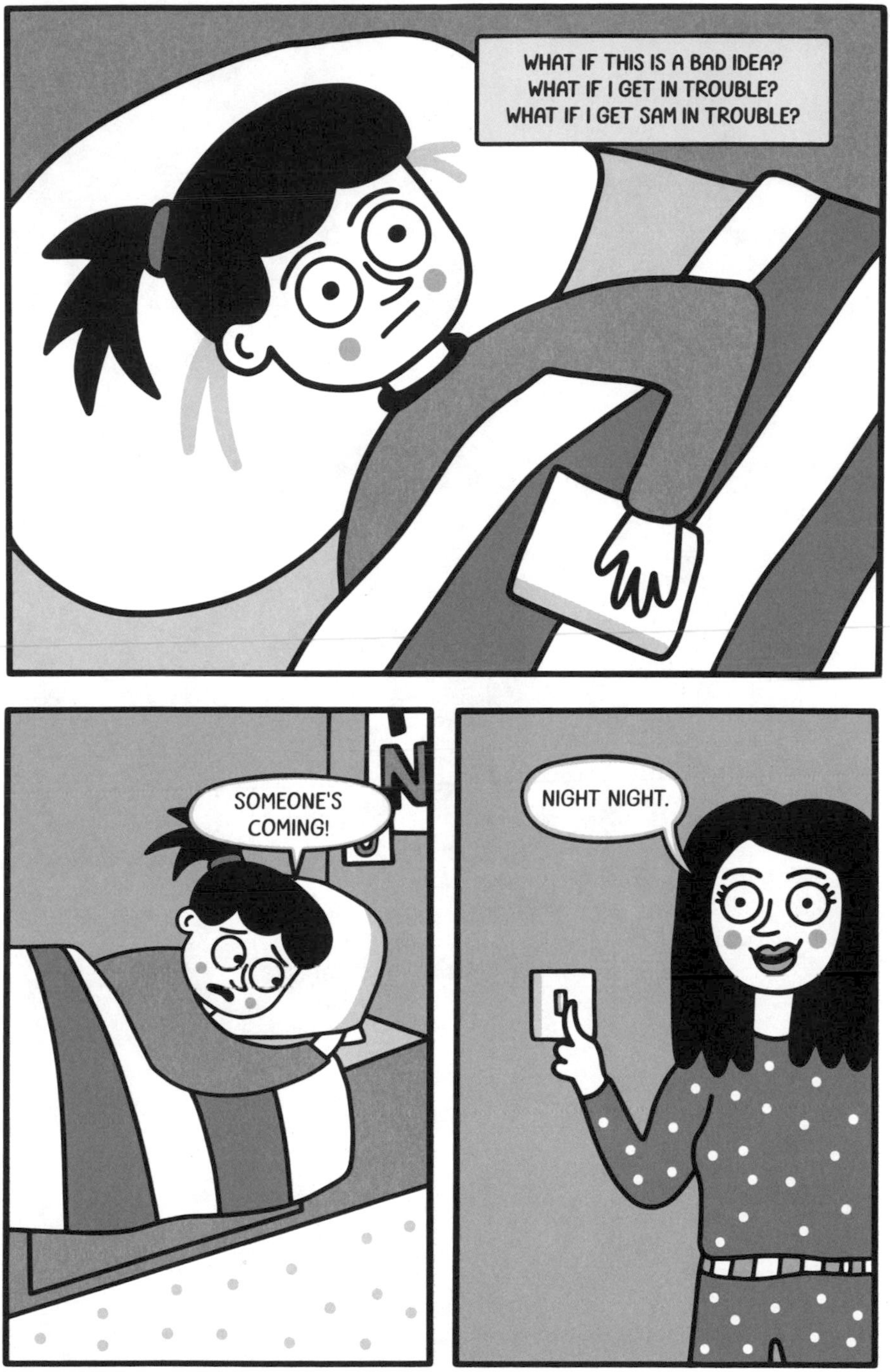
WHAT IF THIS IS A BAD IDEA?
WHAT IF I GET IN TROUBLE?
WHAT IF I GET SAM IN TROUBLE?
SOMEONE'S COMING!
NIGHT NIGHT.

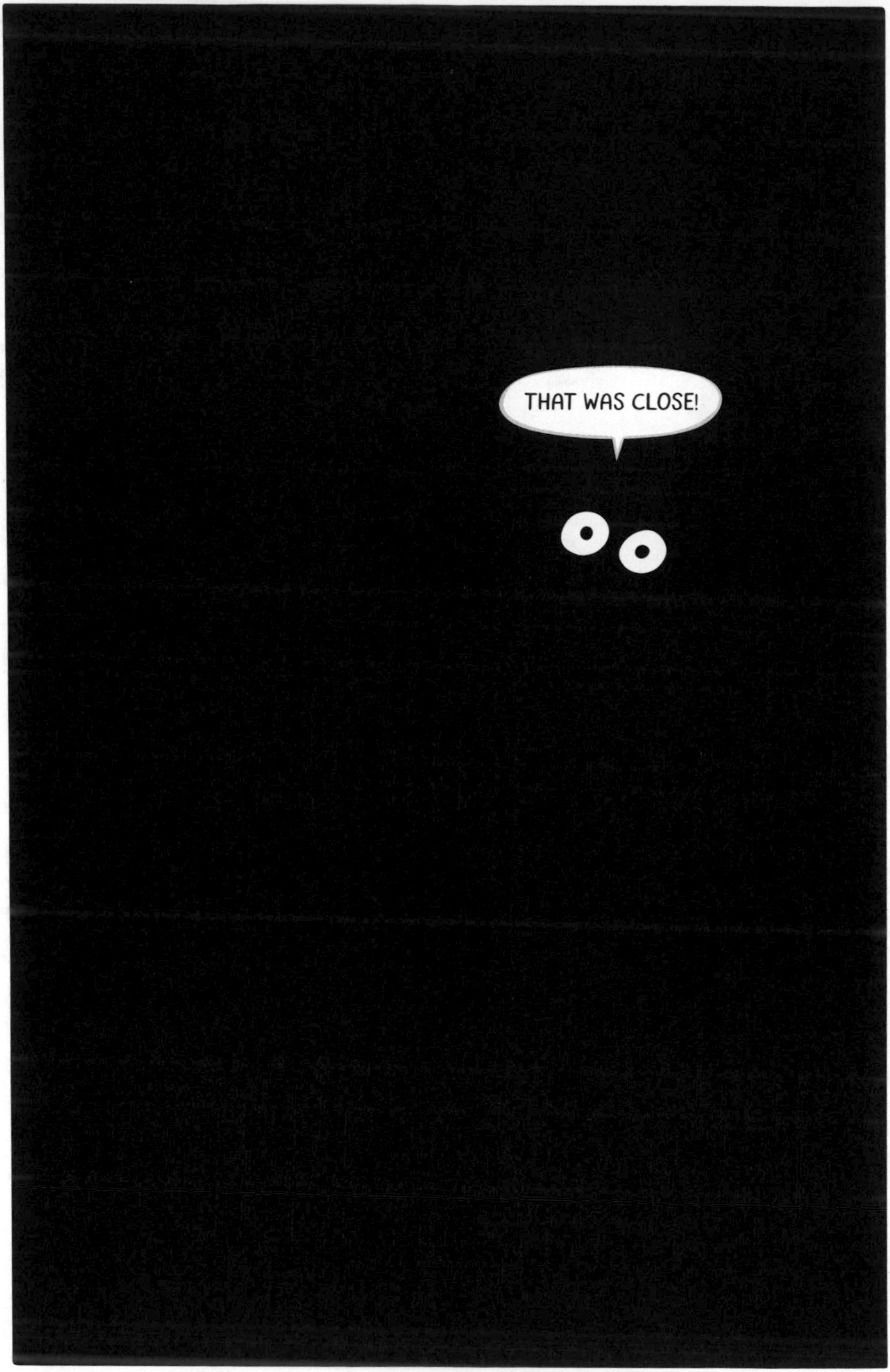
THAT WAS CLOSE!

CHAPTER 4

SUPER WEIRDOS UNITE!

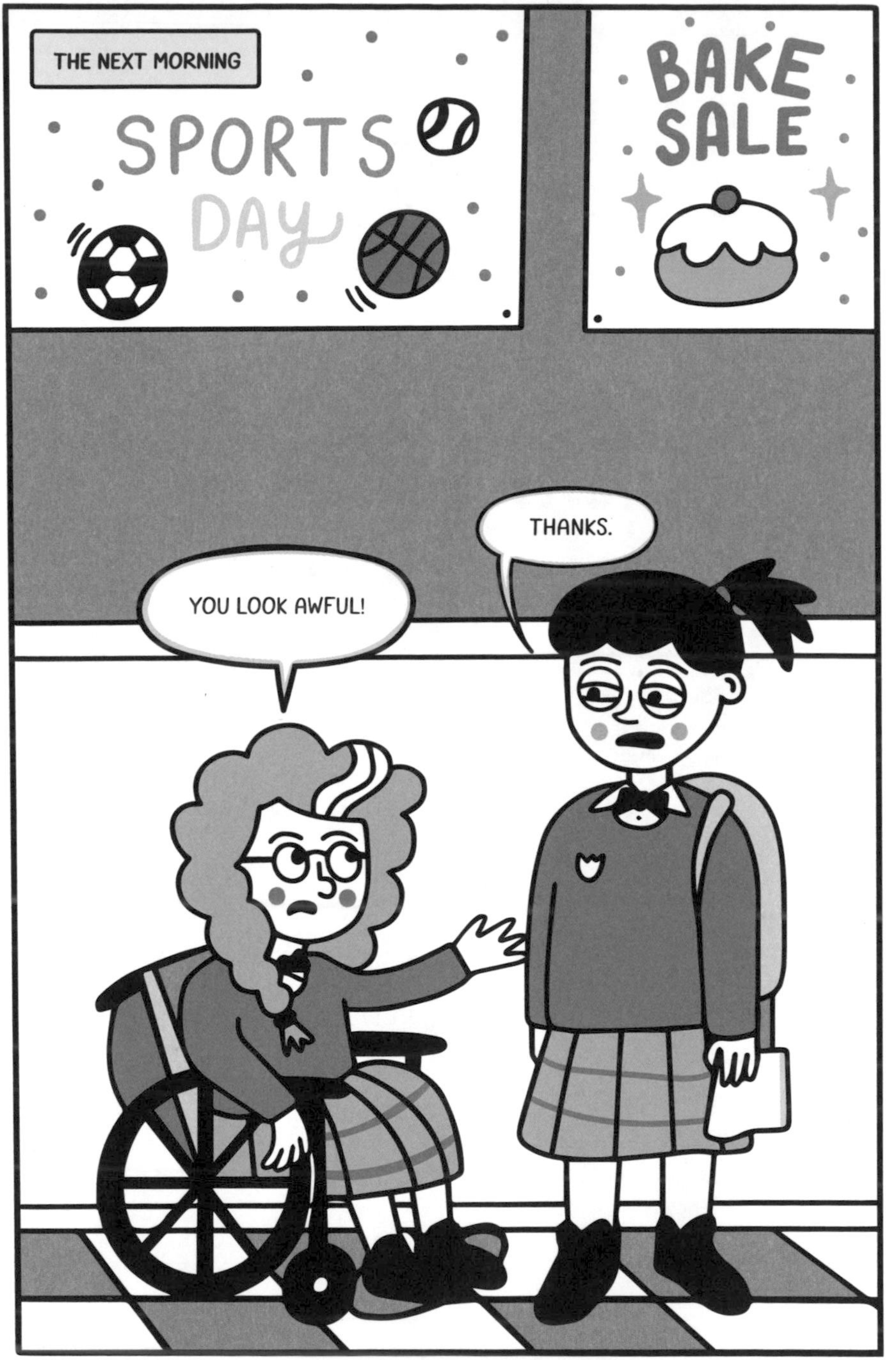
THE NEXT MORNING
SPORTS DAY
BAKE SALE
YOU LOOK AWFUL!
THANKS.

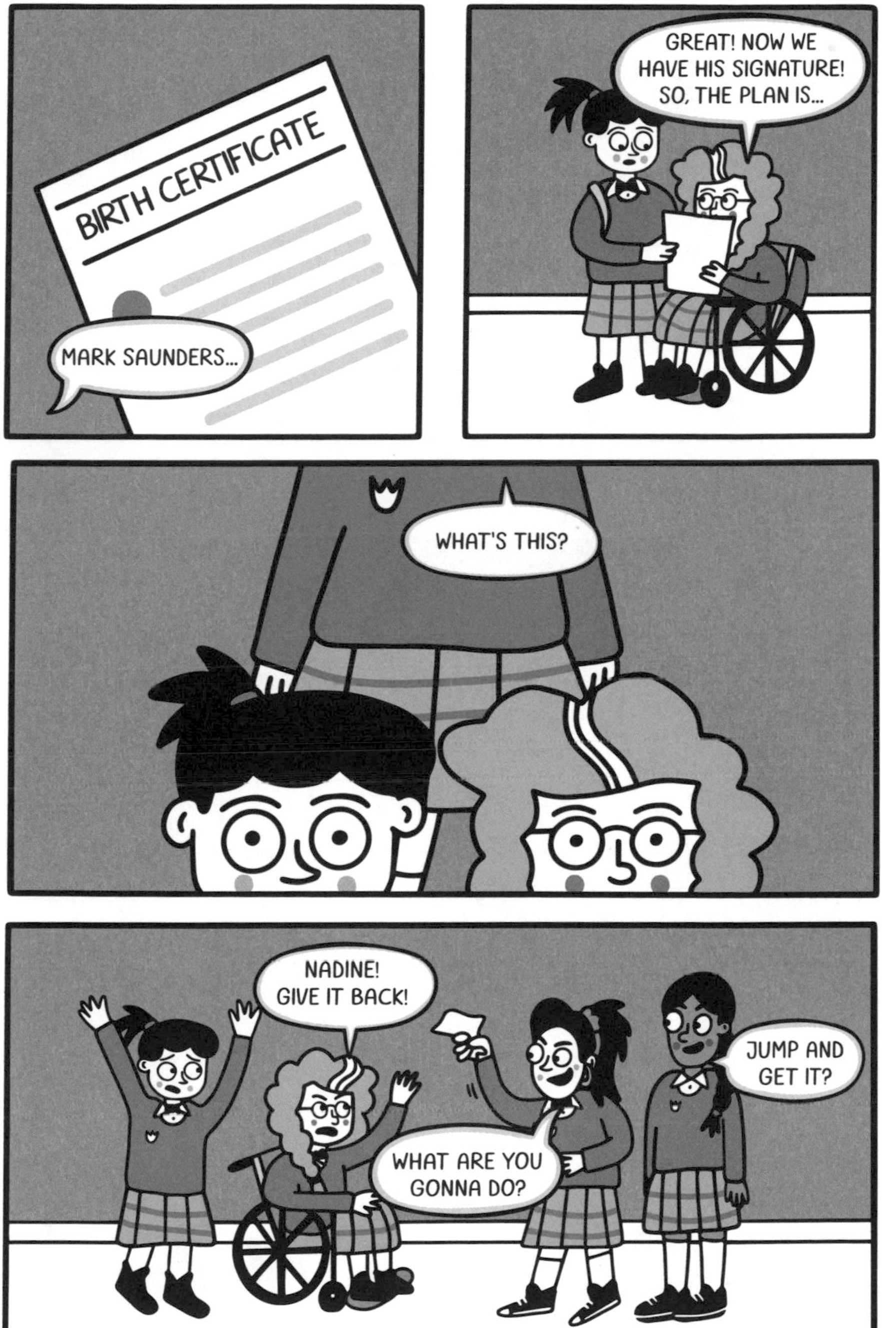
BIRTH CERTIFICATE
MARK SAUNDERS...
GREAT! NOW WE HAVE HIS SIGNATURE! SO, THE PLAN IS...
WHAT'S THIS?
NADINE! GIVE IT BACK!
WHAT ARE YOU GONNA DO?
JUMP AND GET IT?

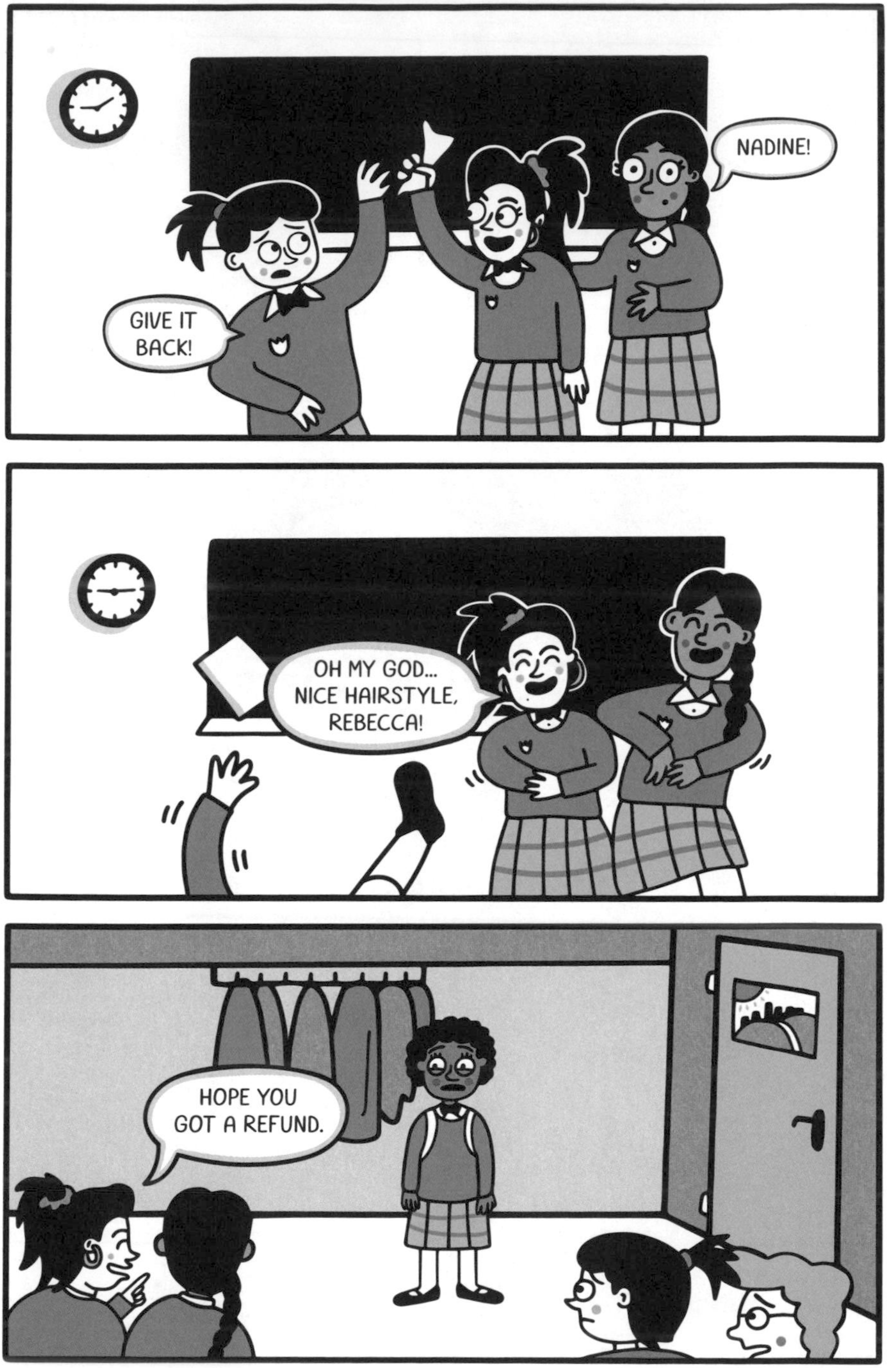
NADINE!
GIVE IT BACK!
OH MY GOD... NICE HAIRSTYLE, REBECCA!
HOPE YOU GOT A REFUND.

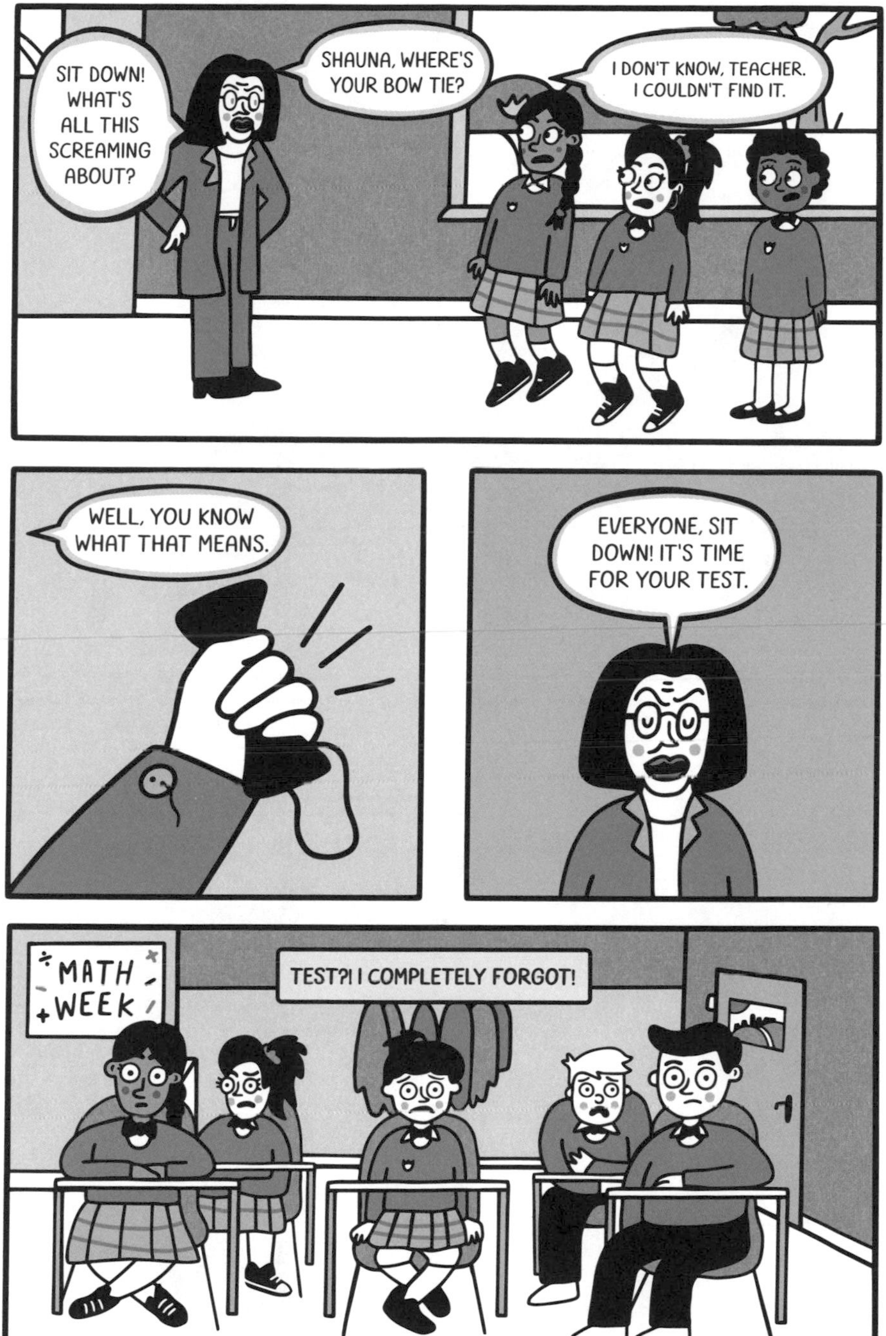
SIT DOWN! WHAT'S ALL THIS SCREAMING ABOUT?
SHAUNA, WHERE'S YOUR BOW TIE?
I DON'T KNOW, TEACHER. I COULDN'T FIND IT.
WELL, YOU KNOW WHAT THAT MEANS.
EVERYONE, SIT DOWN! IT'S TIME FOR YOUR TEST.
MATH WEEK
TEST?! I COMPLETELY FORGOT!

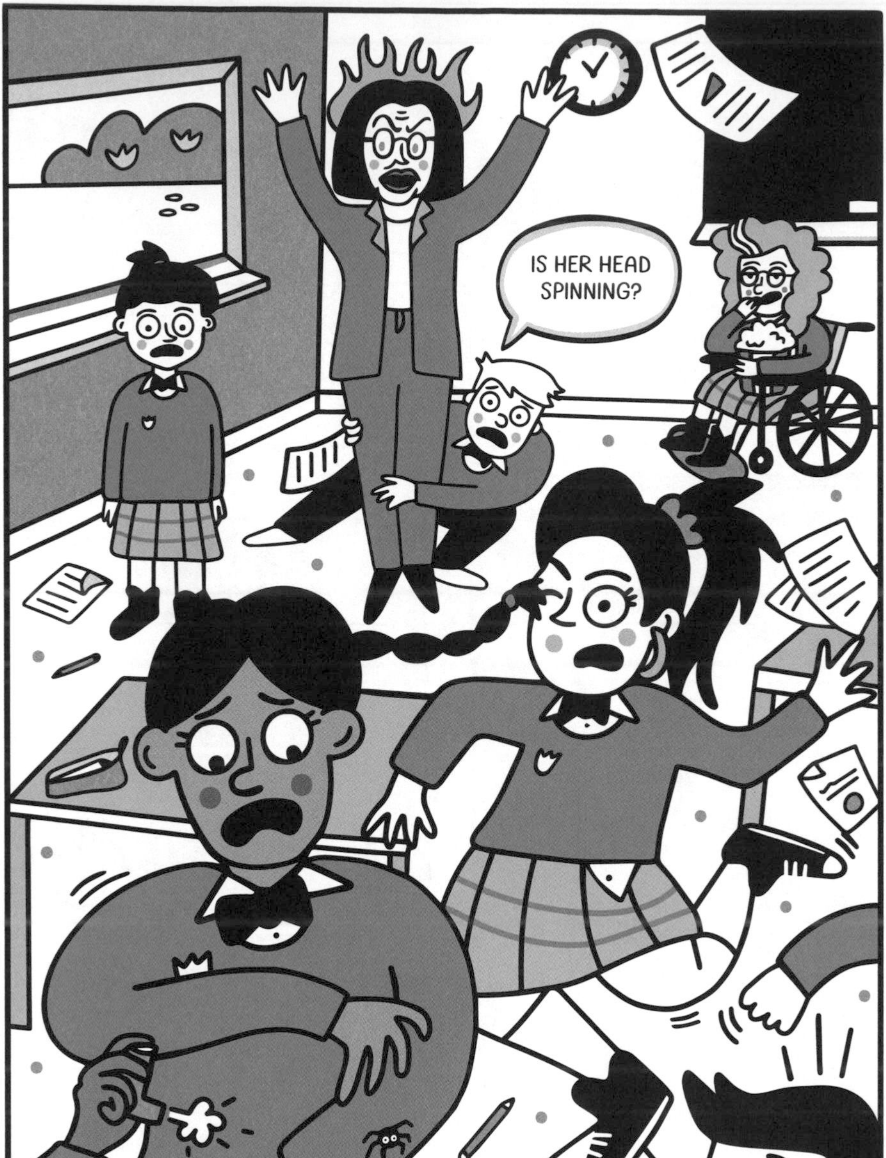
IS HER HEAD SPINNING?

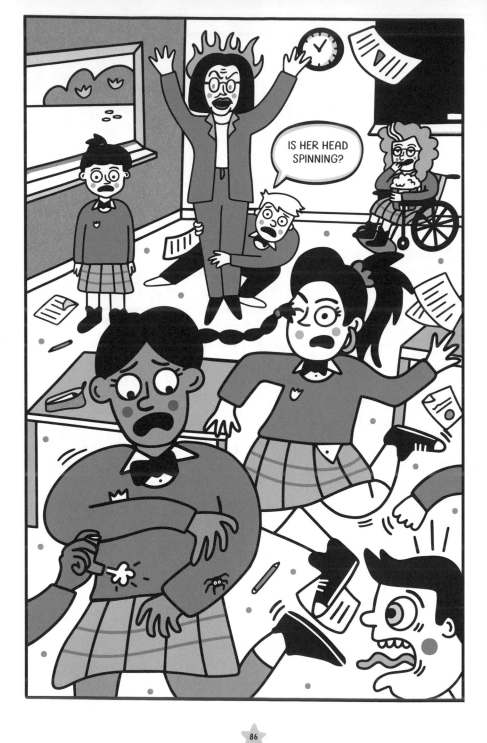

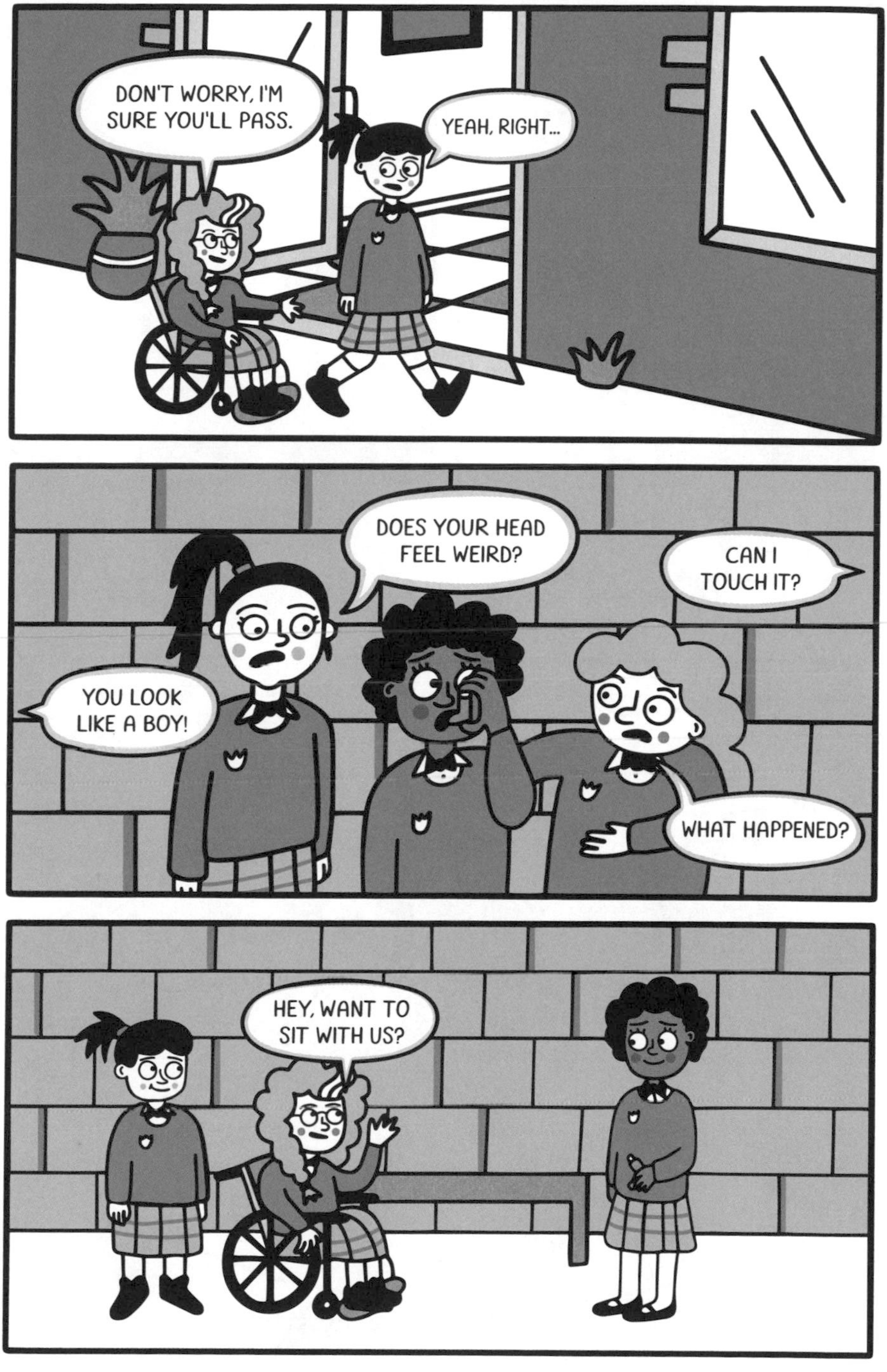

DON'T WORRY, I'M SURE YOU'LL PASS.
YEAH, RIGHT...
DOES YOUR HEAD FEEL WEIRD?
CAN I TOUCH IT?
YOU LOOK LIKE A BOY!
WHAT HAPPENED?
HEY, WANT TO SIT WITH US?

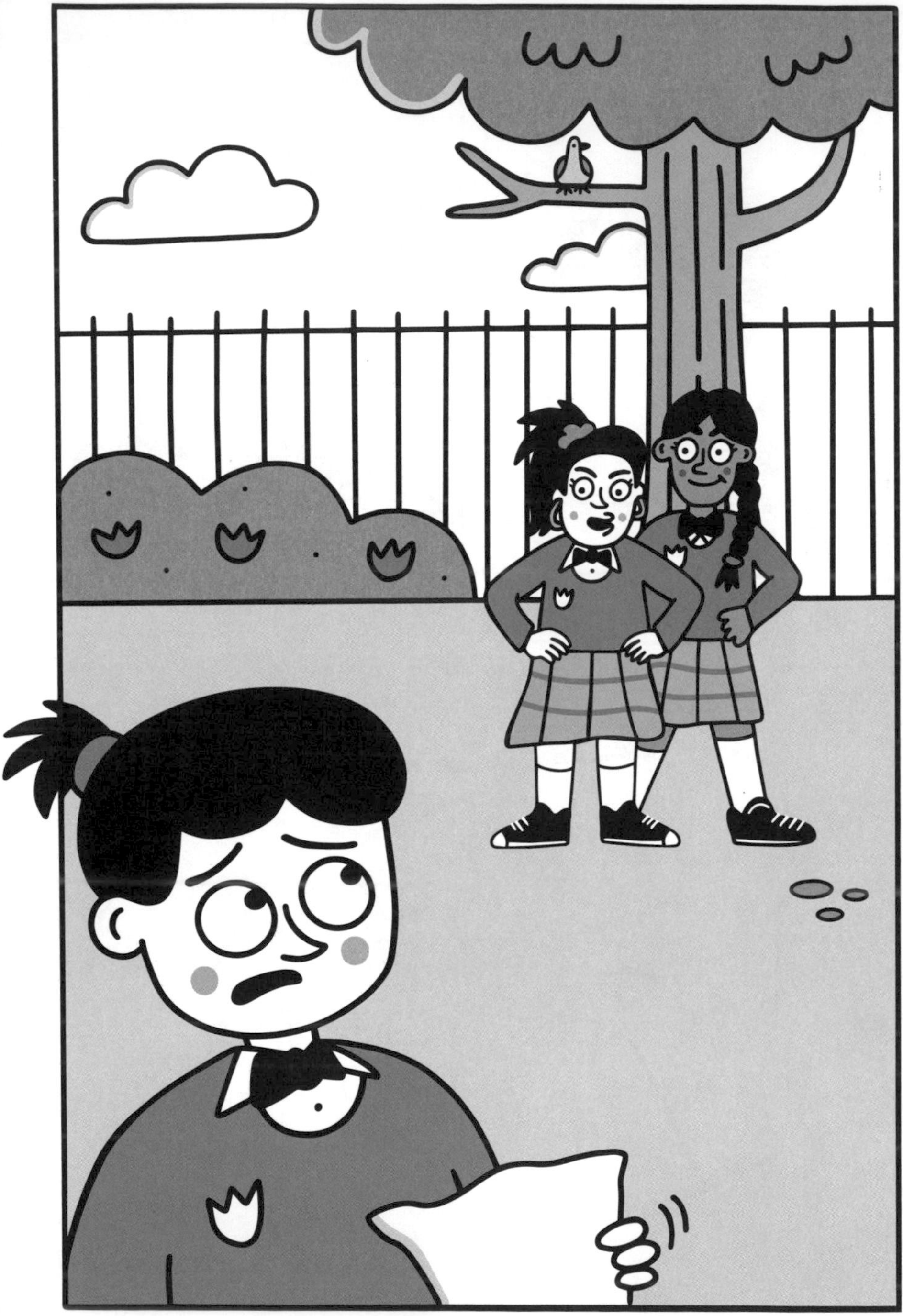

93

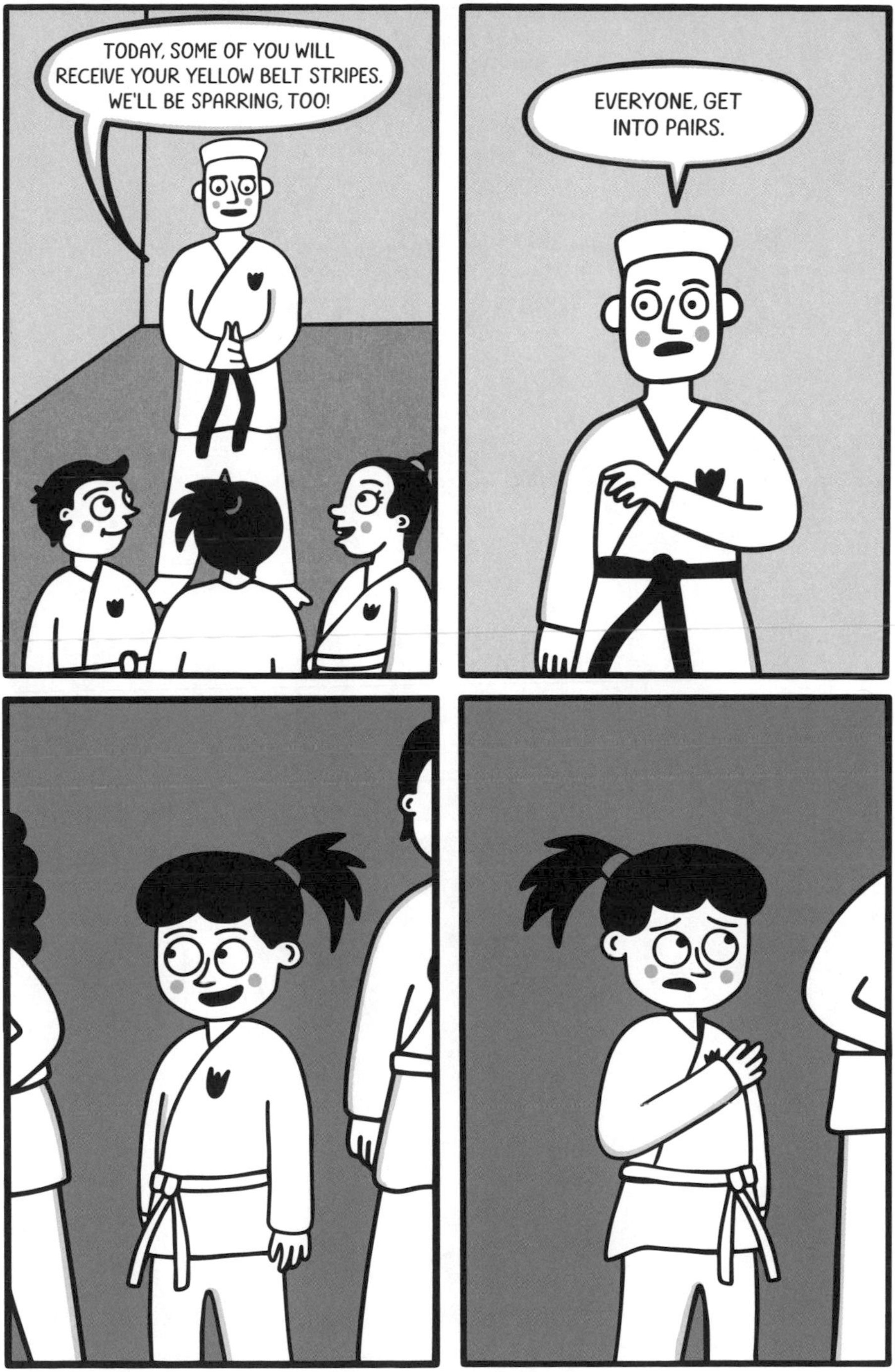
TODAY, SOME OF YOU WILL RECEIVE YOUR YELLOW BELT STRIPES. WE'LL BE SPARRING, TOO!
EVERYONE, GET INTO PAIRS.

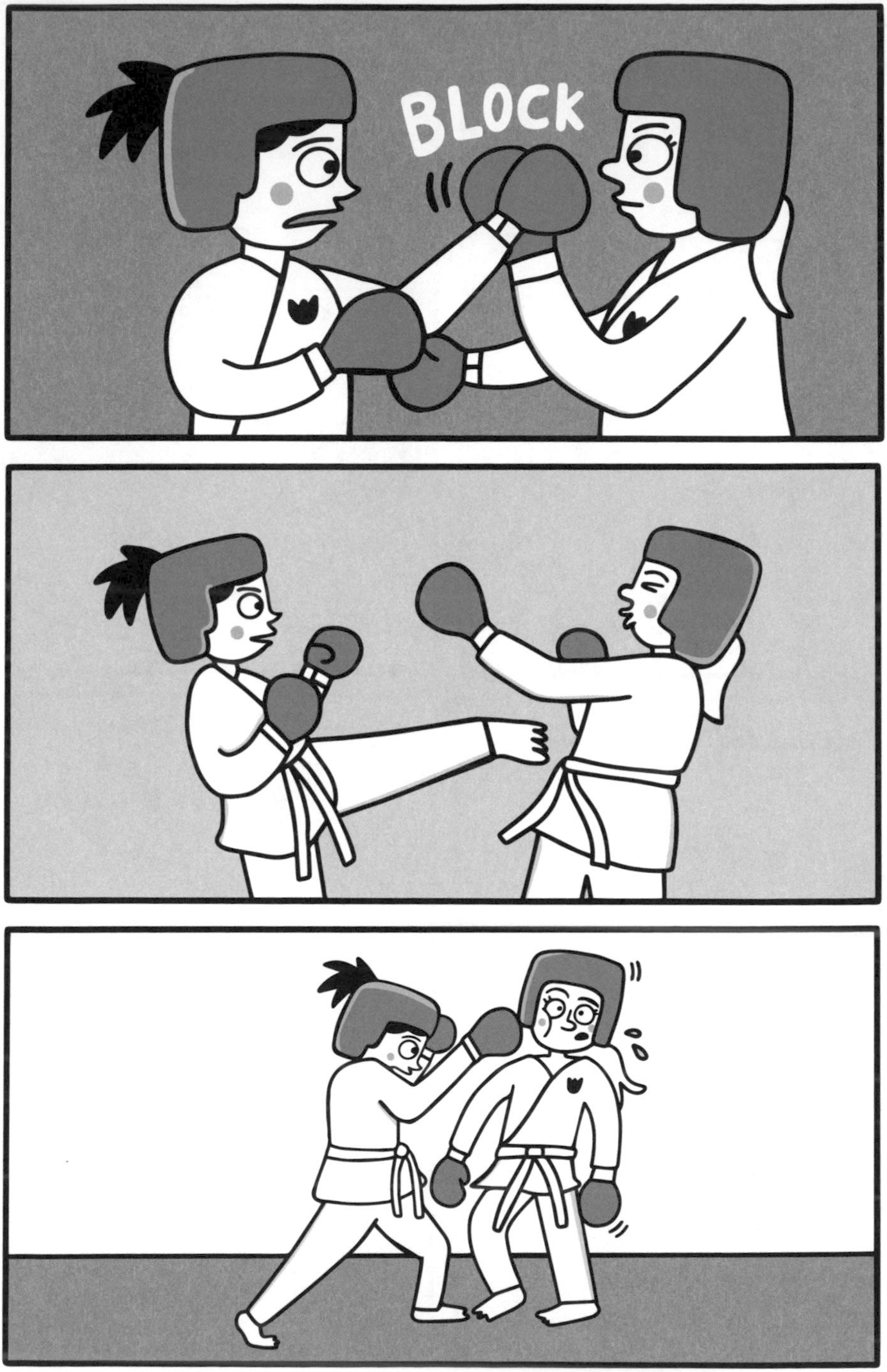
BLOCK

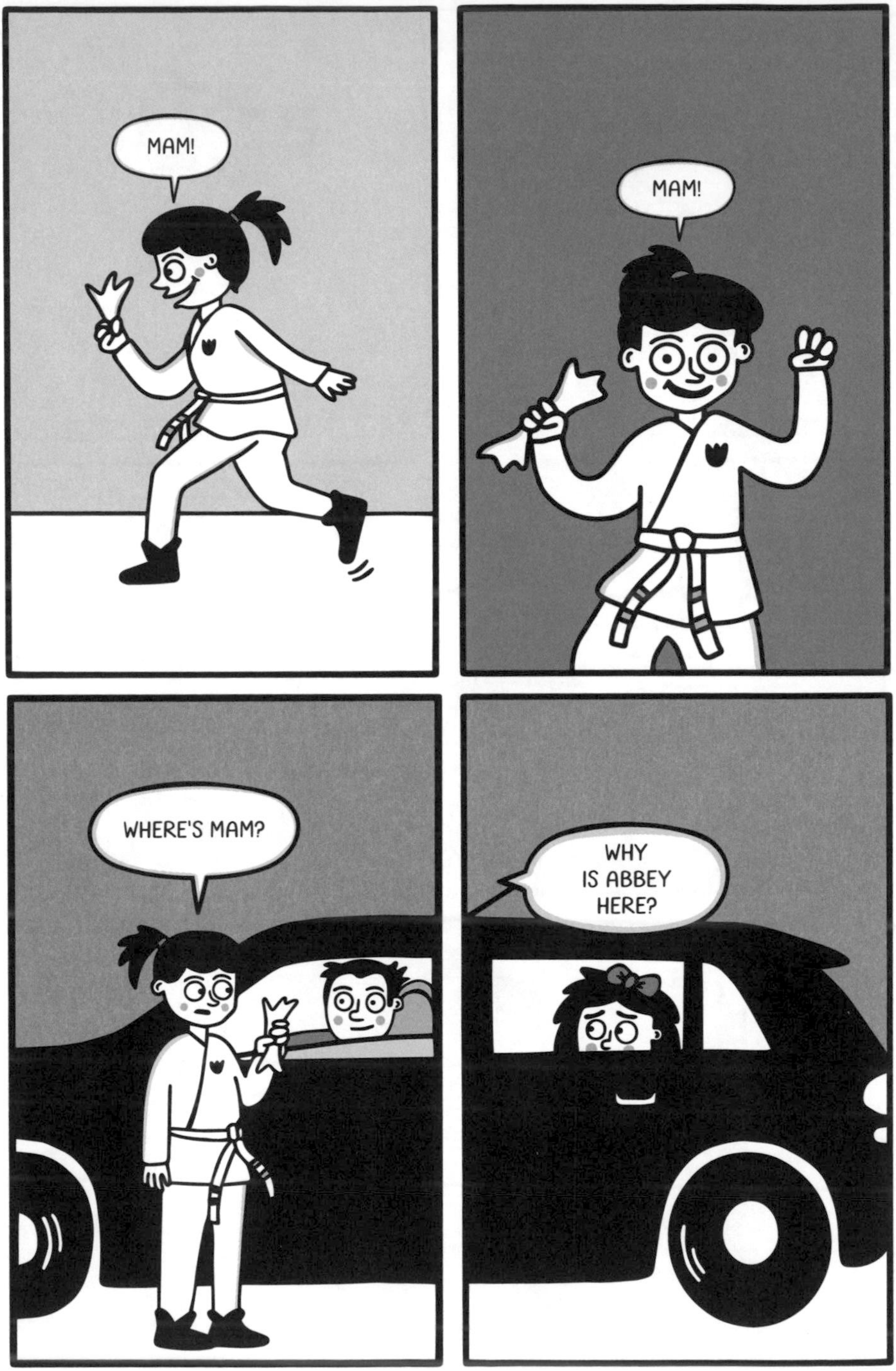

MAM!
MAM!
WHERE'S MAM?
WHY IS ABBEY HERE?

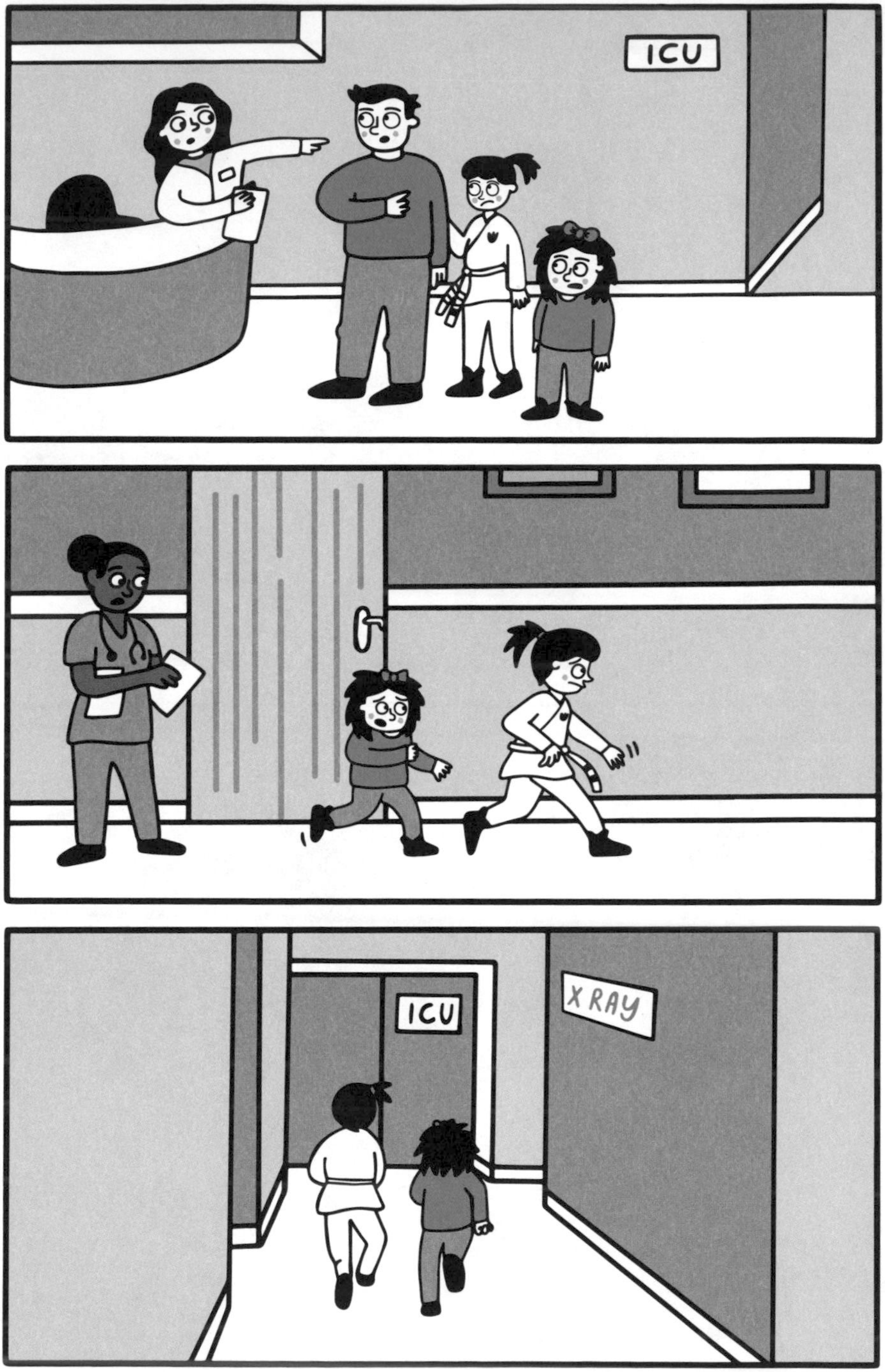
ICU
ICU
X RAY

CHAPTER 5

NANA AND GRANDAD'S HOUSE

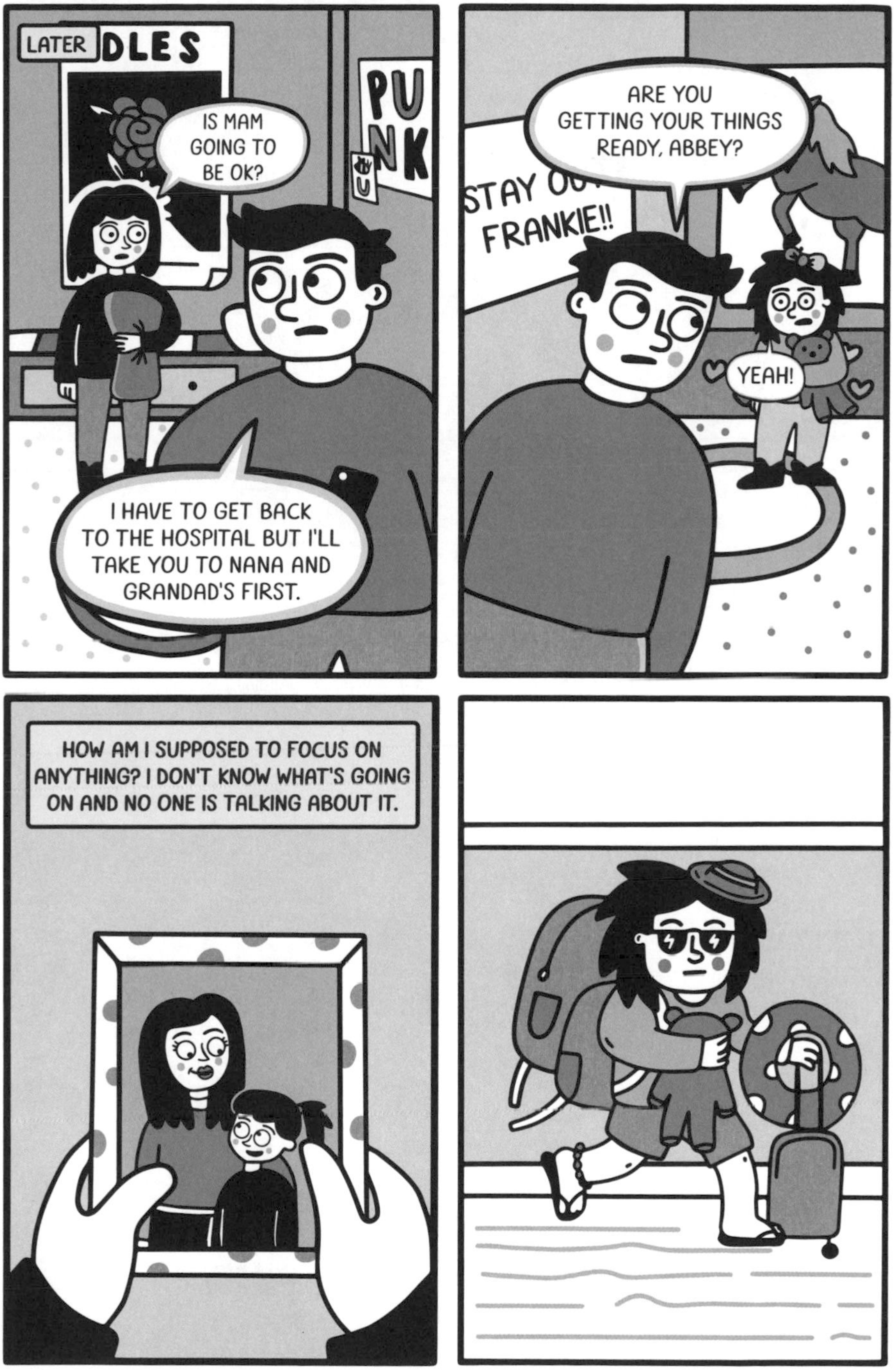
LATER
DLES
IS MAM GOING TO BE OK?
PUNK
I HAVE TO GET BACK TO THE HOSPITAL BUT I'LL TAKE YOU TO NANA AND GRANDAD'S FIRST.
ARE YOU GETTING YOUR THINGS READY, ABBEY?
STAY OU
FRANKIE!!
YEAH!
HOW AM I SUPPOSED TO FOCUS ON ANYTHING? I DON'T KNOW WHAT'S GOING ON AND NO ONE IS TALKING ABOUT IT.

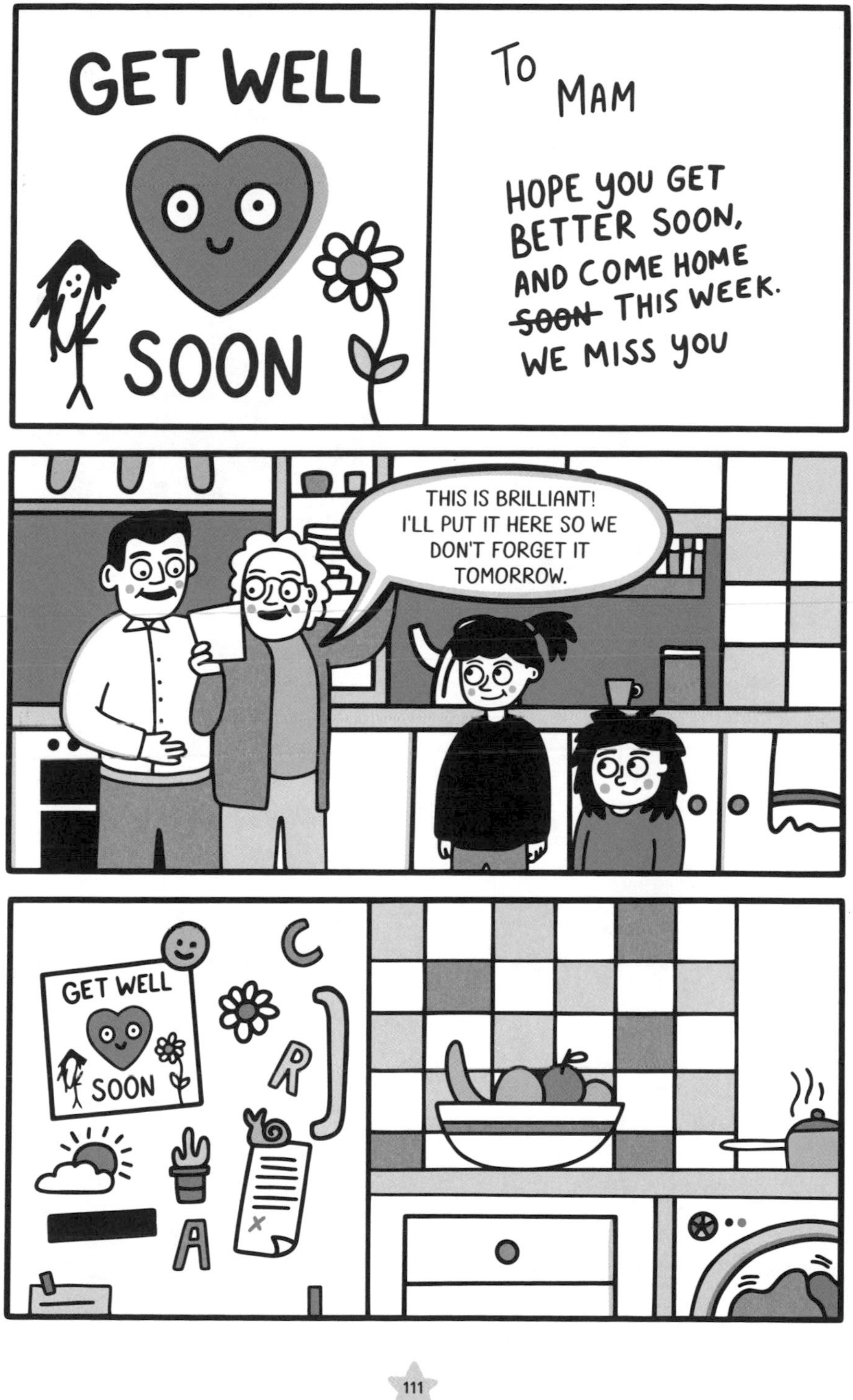
GET WELL
SOON
To
MAM
HOPE YOU GET BETTER SOON, AND COME HOME ~~SOON~~ THIS WEEK.
WE MISS YOU
THIS IS BRILLIANT! I'LL PUT IT HERE SO WE DON'T FORGET IT TOMORROW.
GET WELL
SOON
C
R
A

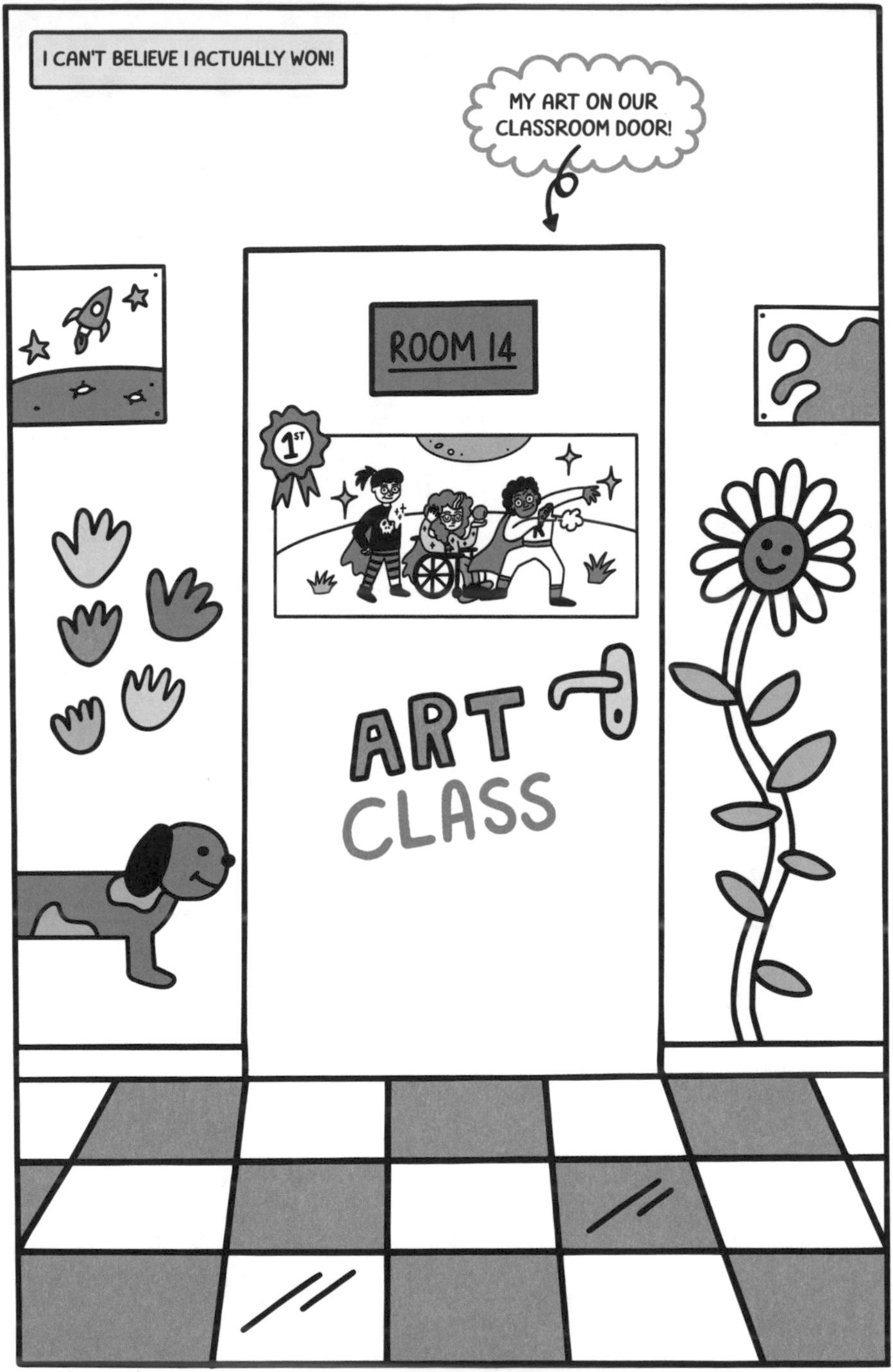
I CAN'T BELIEVE I ACTUALLY WON!
MY ART ON OUR CLASSROOM DOOR!
ROOM 14
1ST
ART CLASS

125

CHAPTER 6

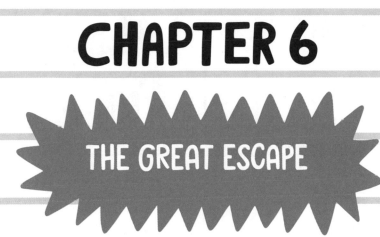

THE GREAT ESCAPE

135

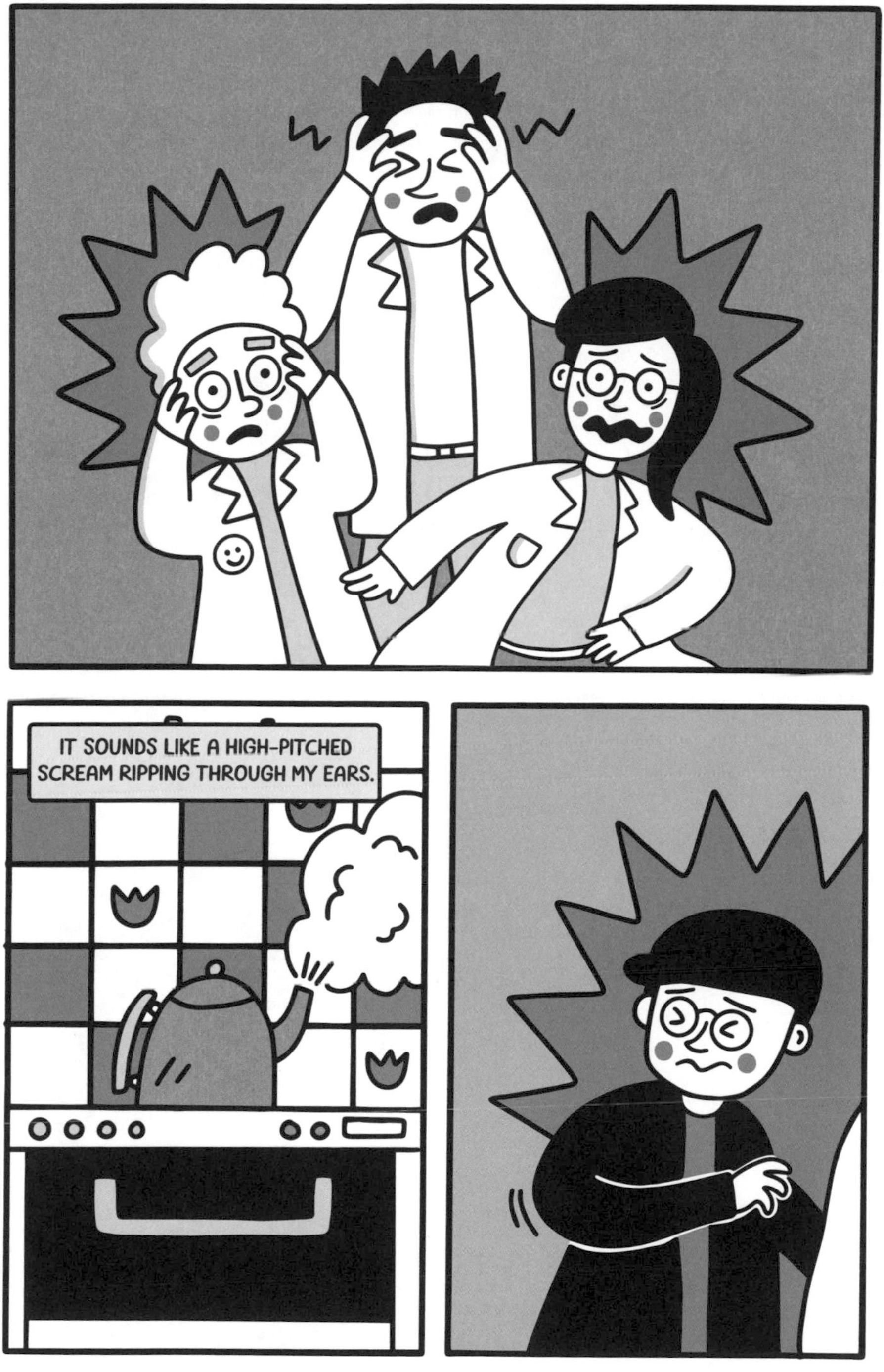
IT SOUNDS LIKE A HIGH-PITCHED SCREAM RIPPING THROUGH MY EARS.

138

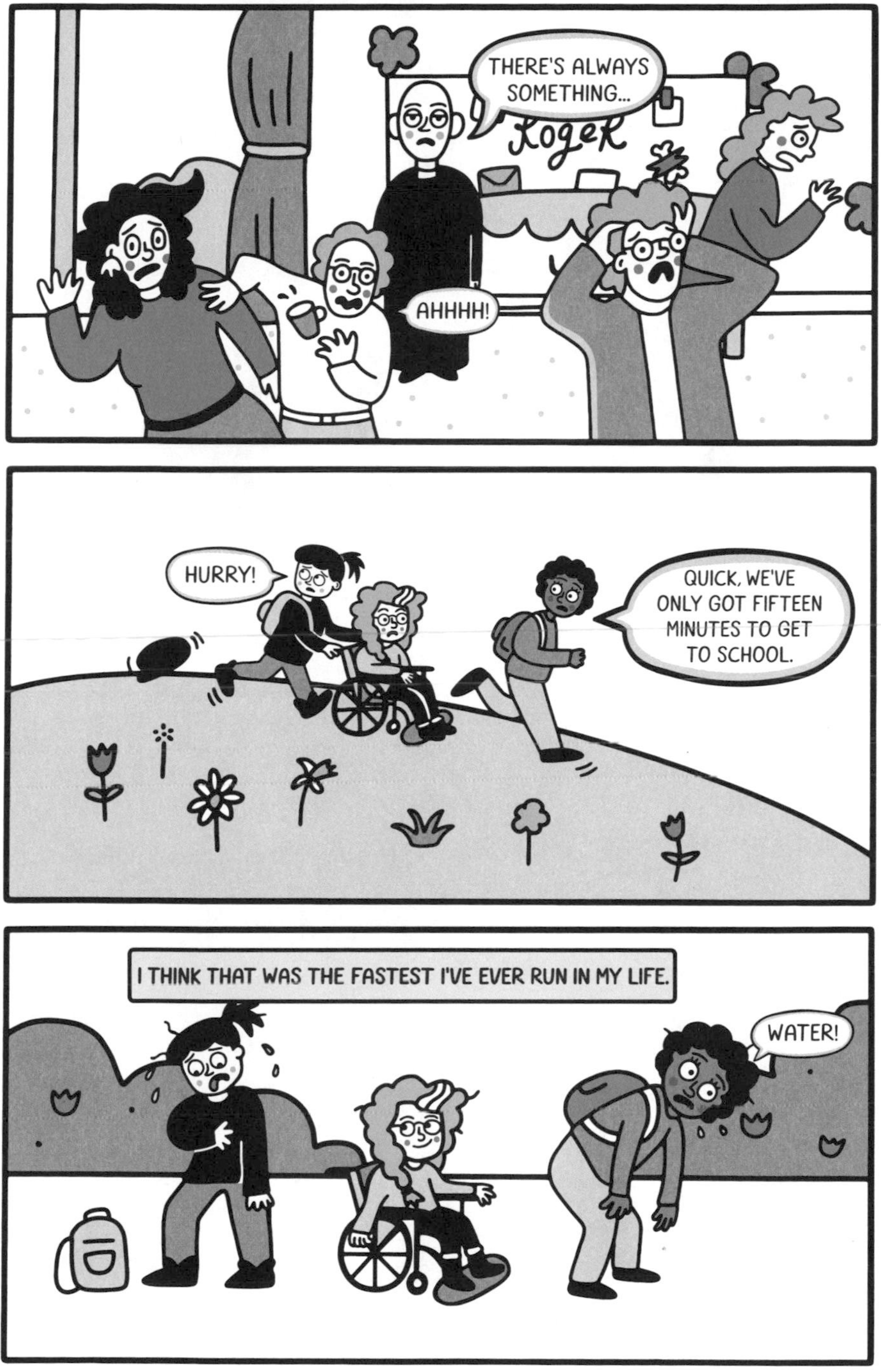

THERE'S ALWAYS SOMETHING...
Roger
AHHHH!
HURRY!
QUICK, WE'VE ONLY GOT FIFTEEN MINUTES TO GET TO SCHOOL.
I THINK THAT WAS THE FASTEST I'VE EVER RUN IN MY LIFE.
WATER!

149

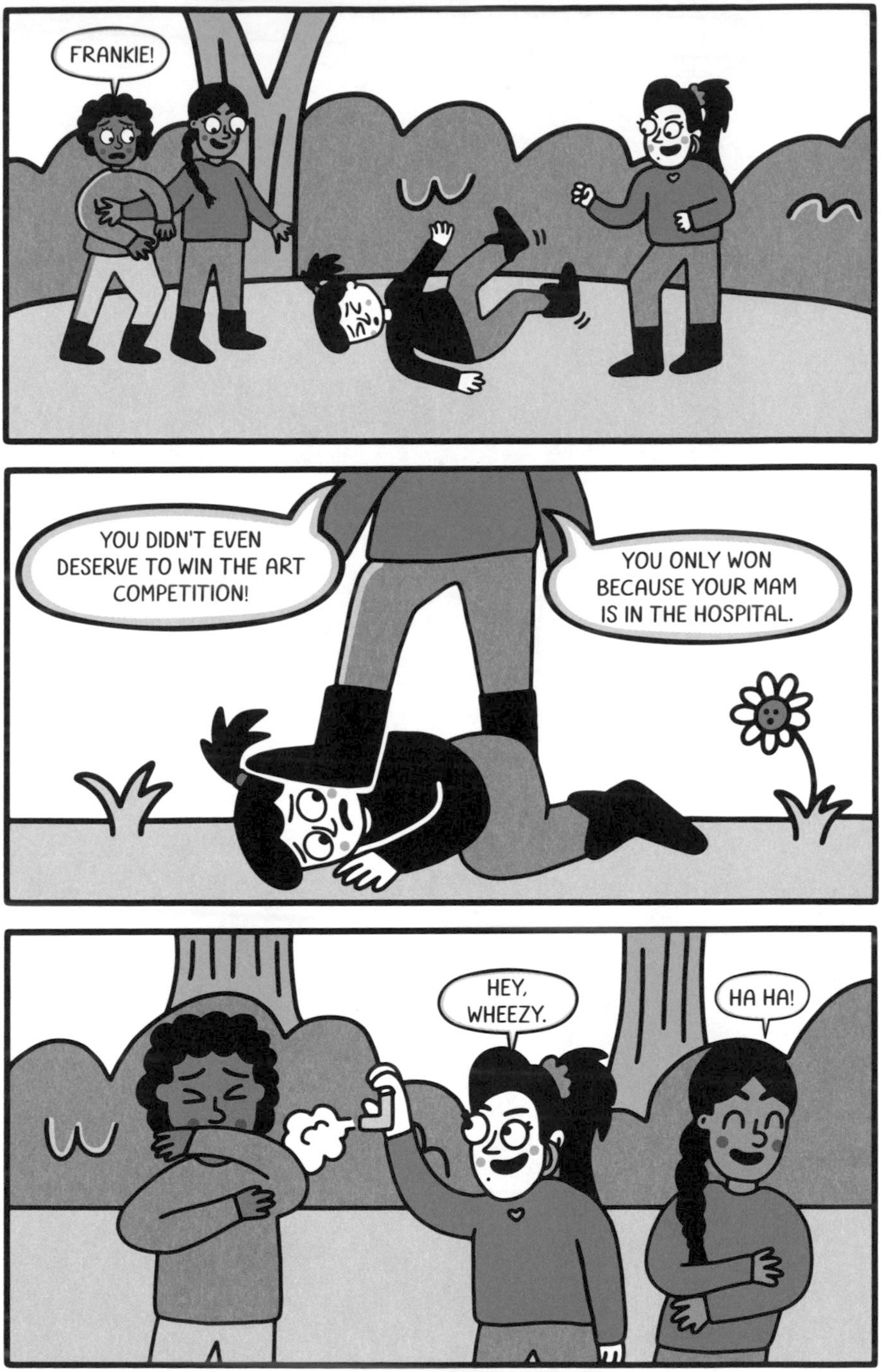
FRANKIE!
YOU DIDN'T EVEN DESERVE TO WIN THE ART COMPETITION!
YOU ONLY WON BECAUSE YOUR MAM IS IN THE HOSPITAL.
HEY, WHEEZY.
HA HA!

CHAPTER 7

BEING NORMAL IS BORING

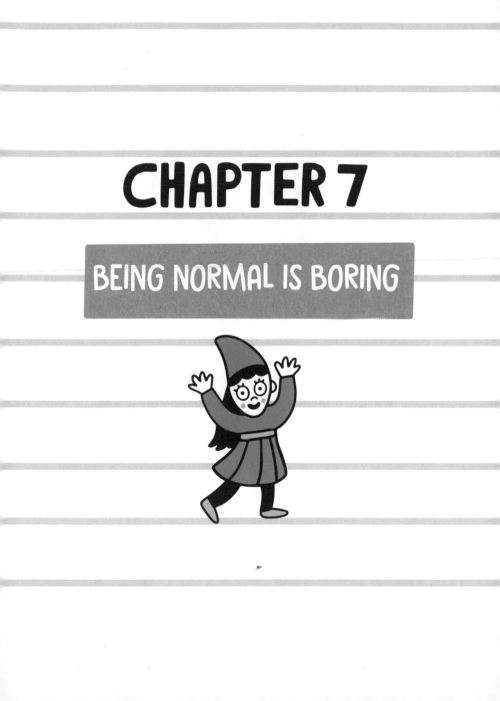

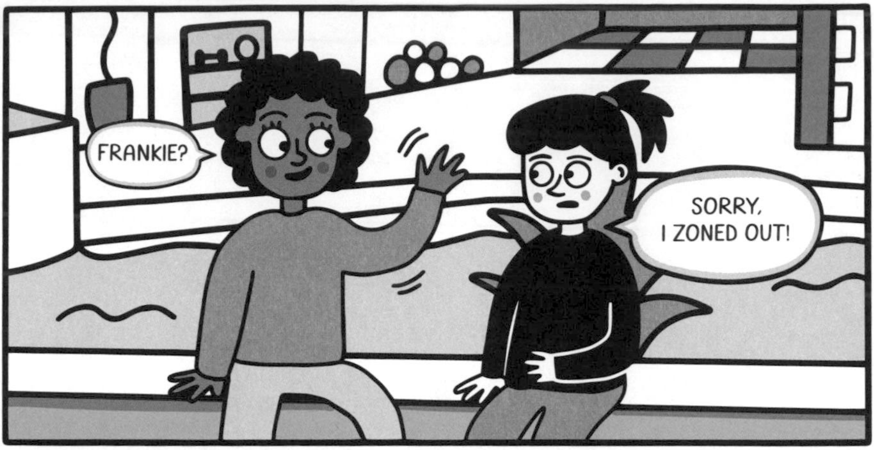
FRANKIE?
SORRY, I ZONED OUT!

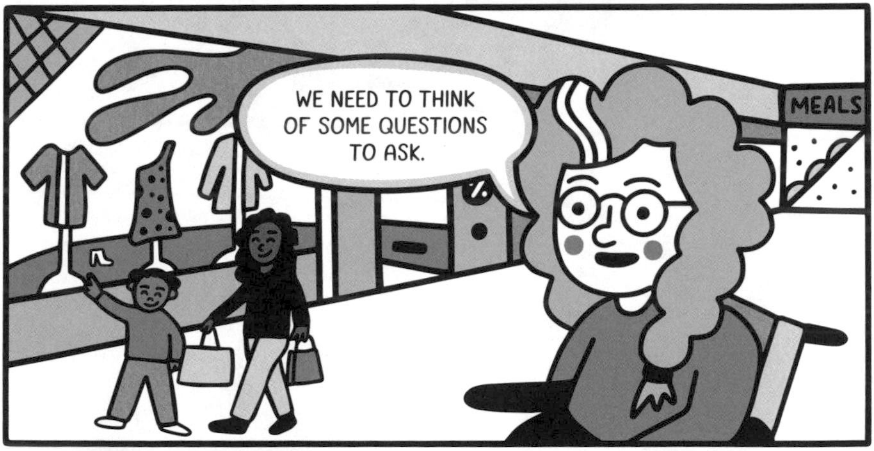
WE NEED TO THINK OF SOME QUESTIONS TO ASK.
MEALS

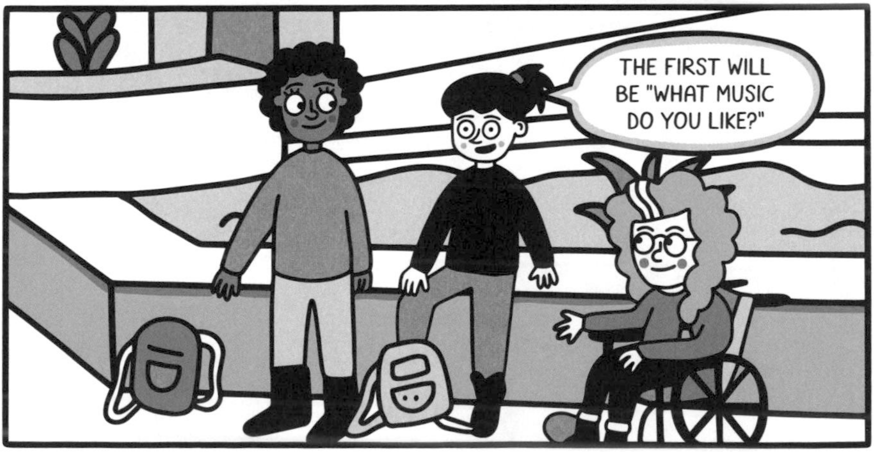
THE FIRST WILL BE "WHAT MUSIC DO YOU LIKE?"

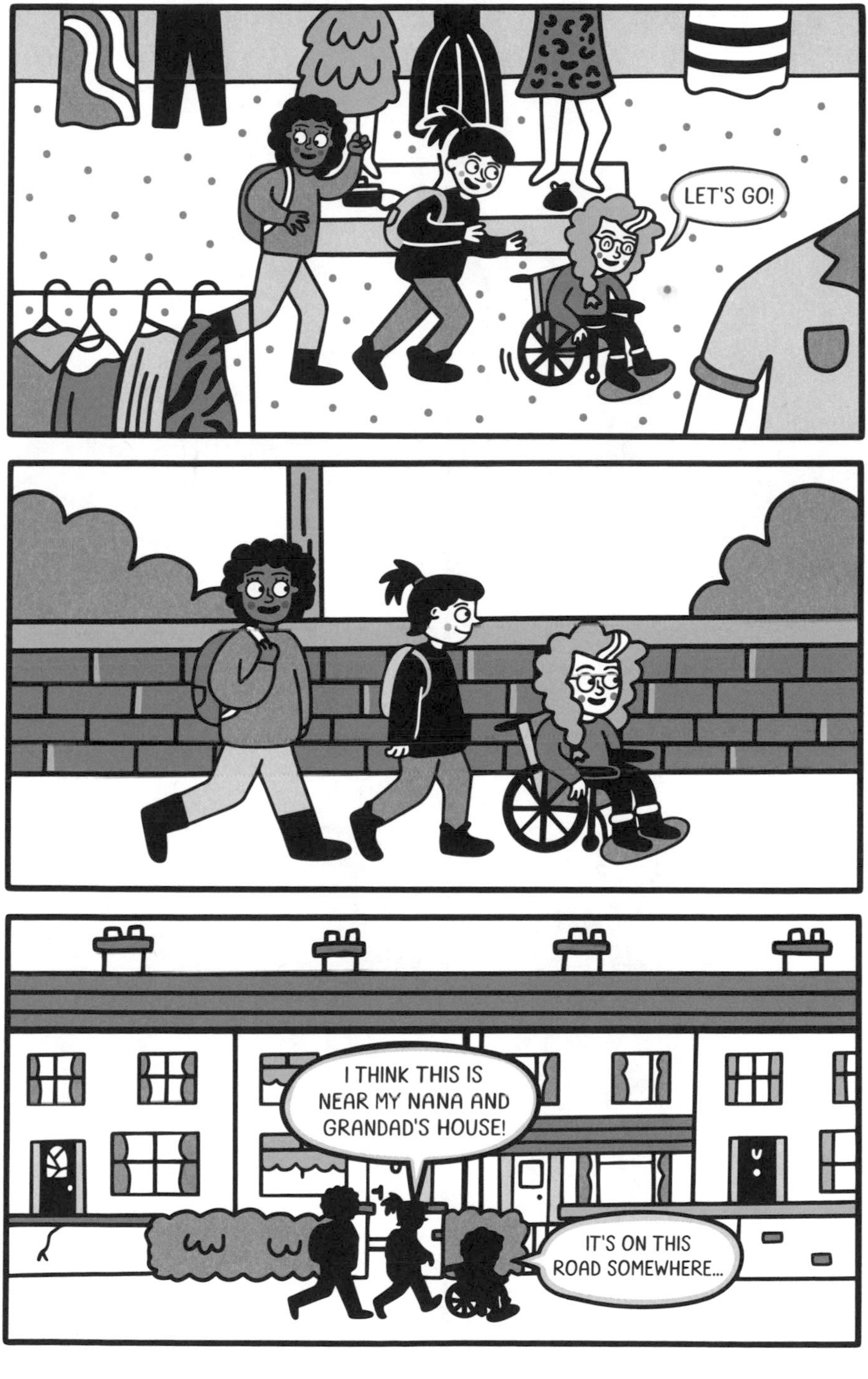
LET'S GO!
I THINK THIS IS NEAR MY NANA AND GRANDAD'S HOUSE!
IT'S ON THIS ROAD SOMEWHERE...

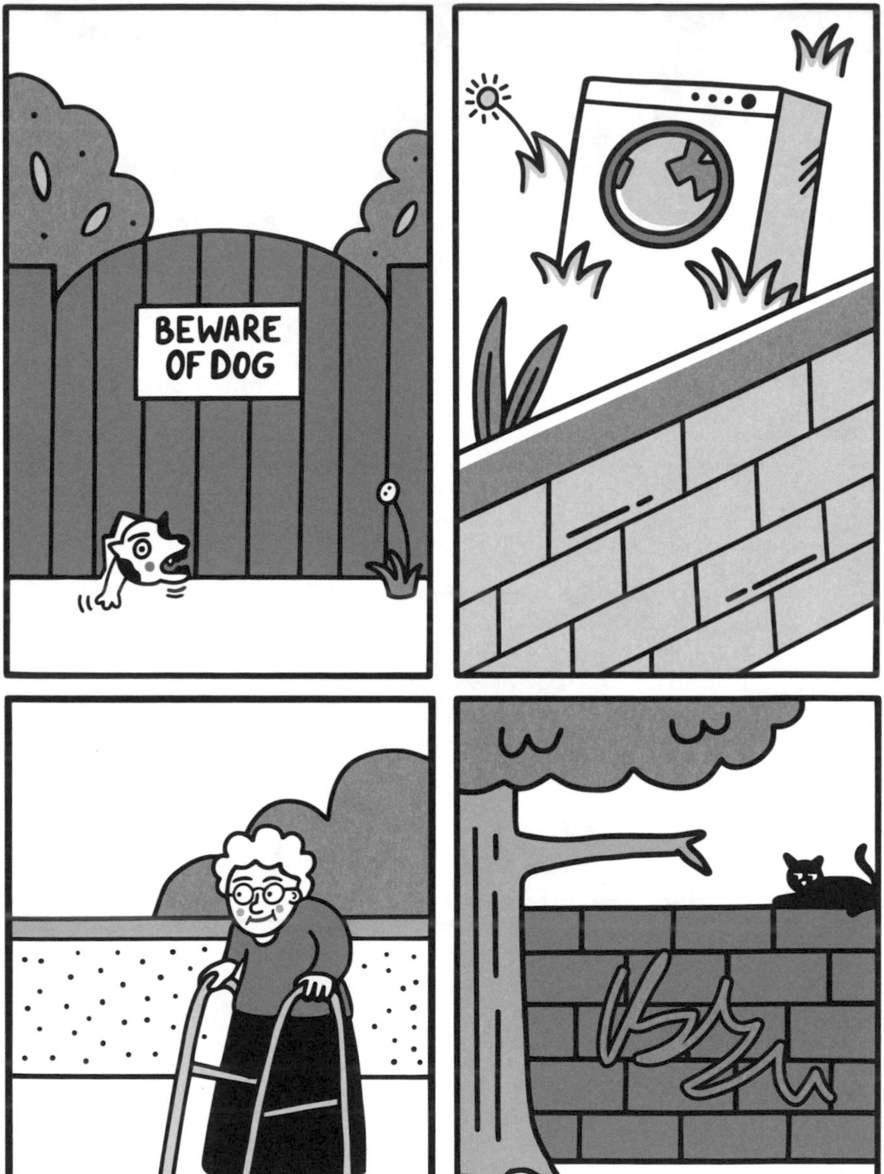
BEWARE OF DOG

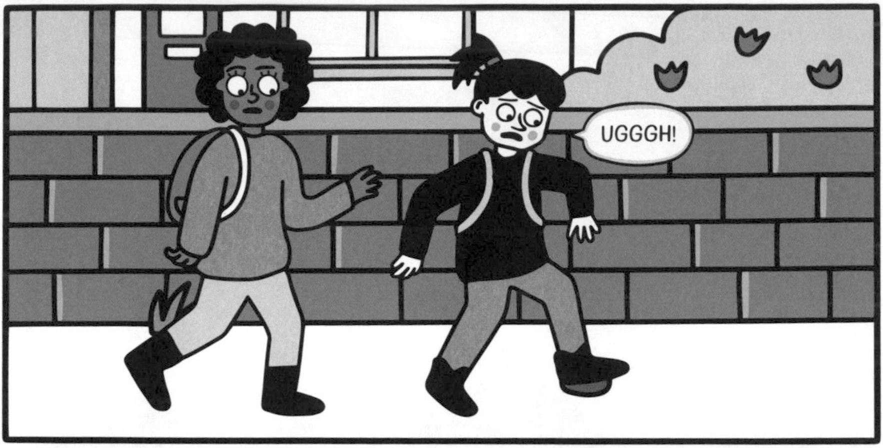
UGGGH!

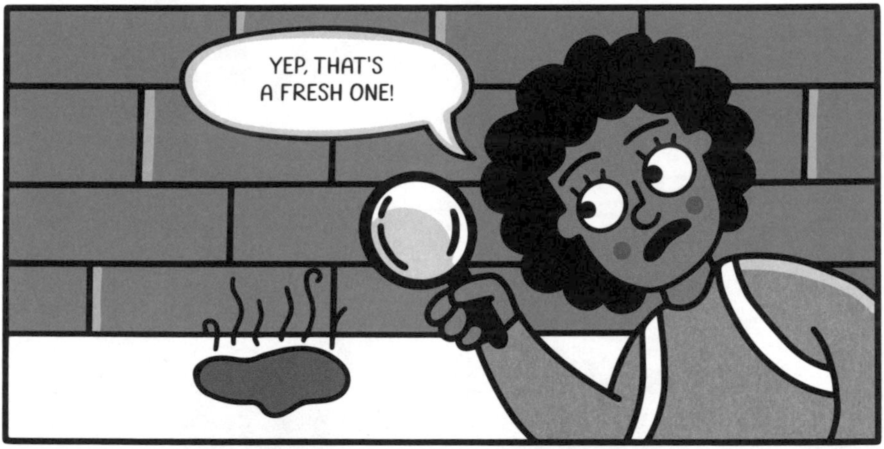
YEP, THAT'S
A FRESH ONE!

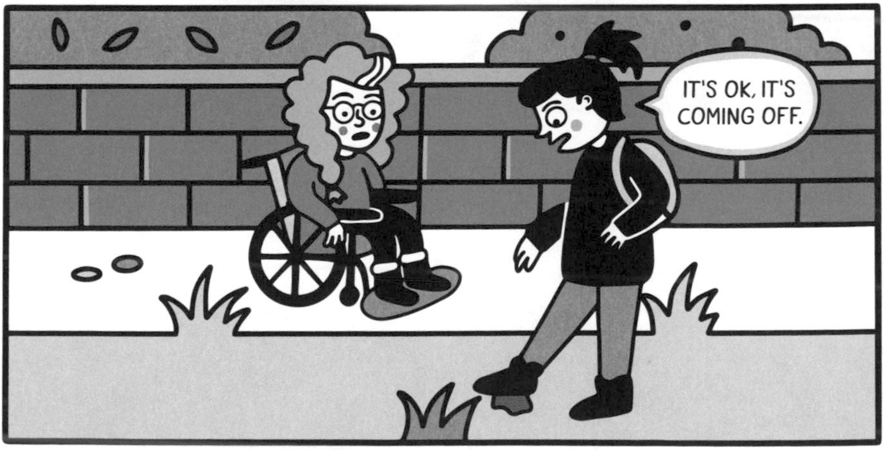
IT'S OK, IT'S
COMING OFF.

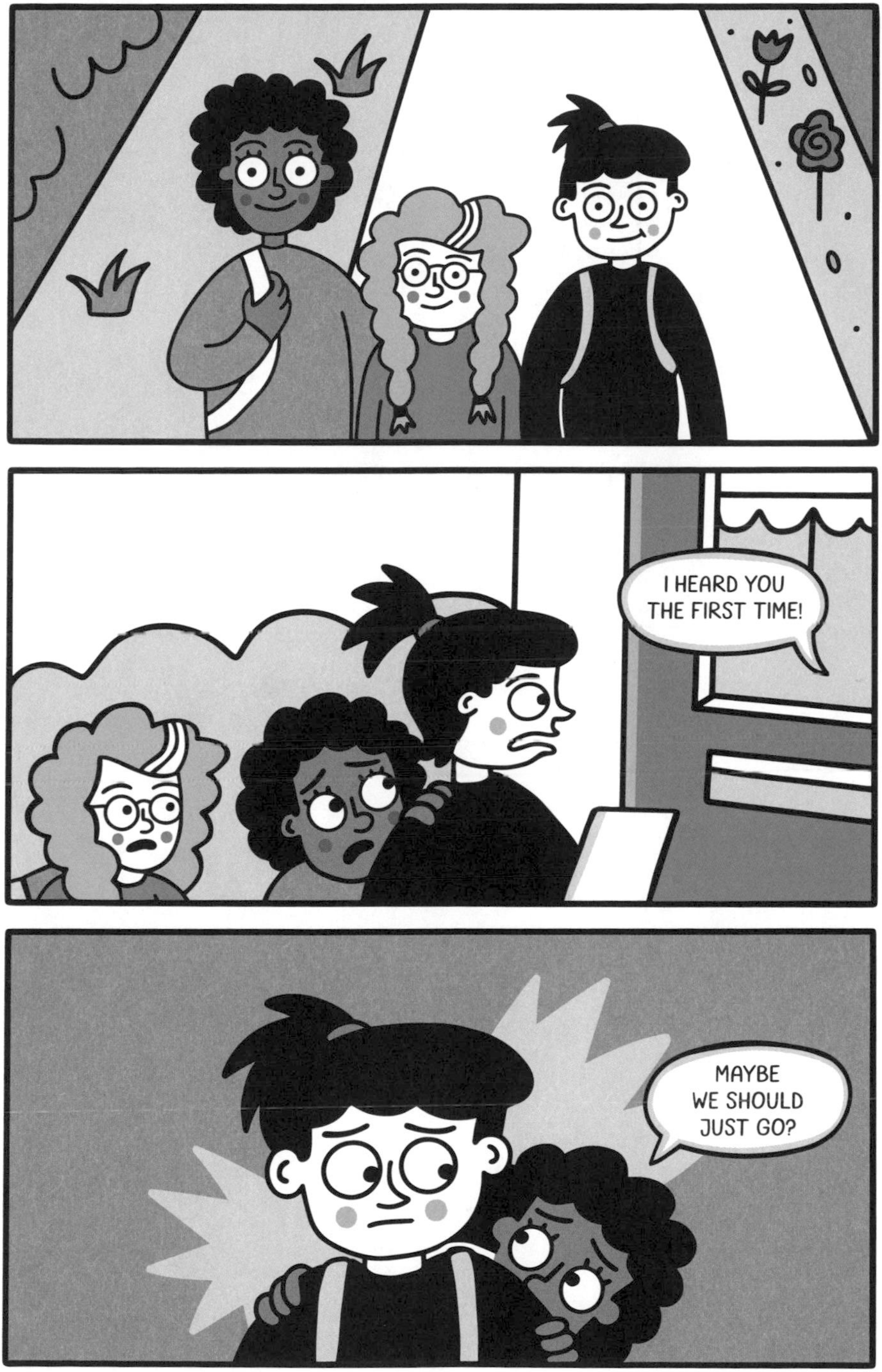
I HEARD YOU THE FIRST TIME!
MAYBE WE SHOULD JUST GO?

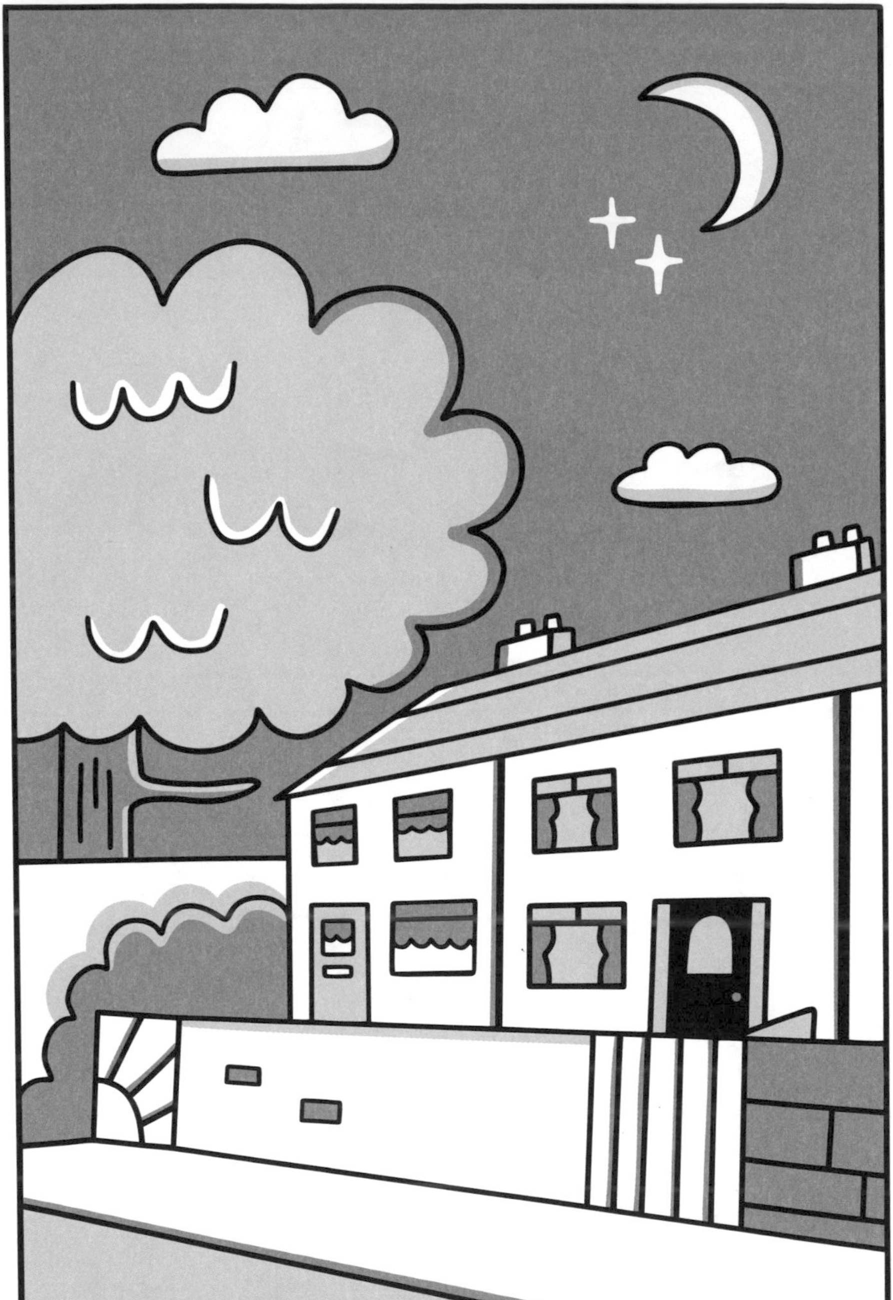

CHAPTER 8

GRADUATION

185

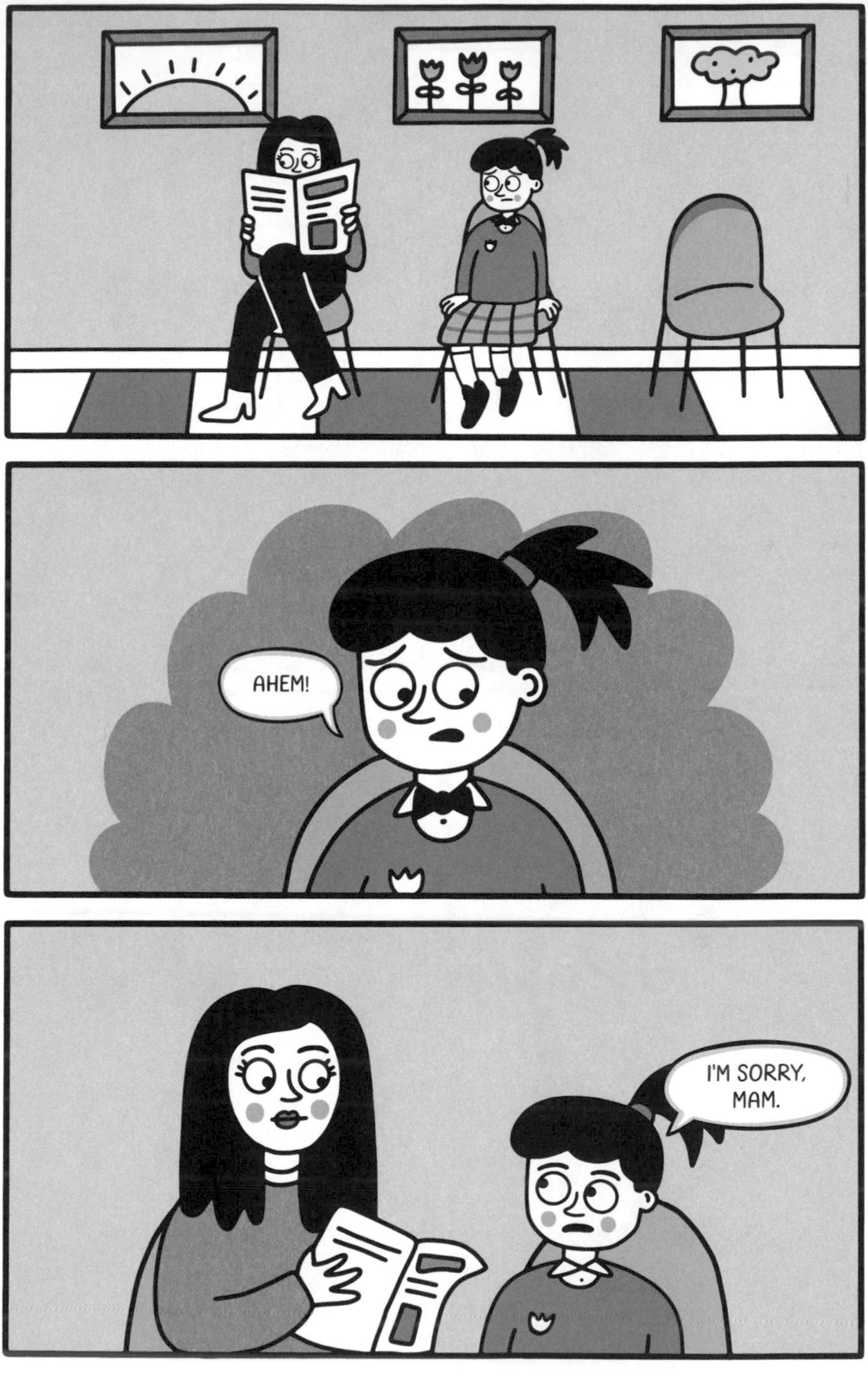
AHEM!
I'M SORRY, MAM.

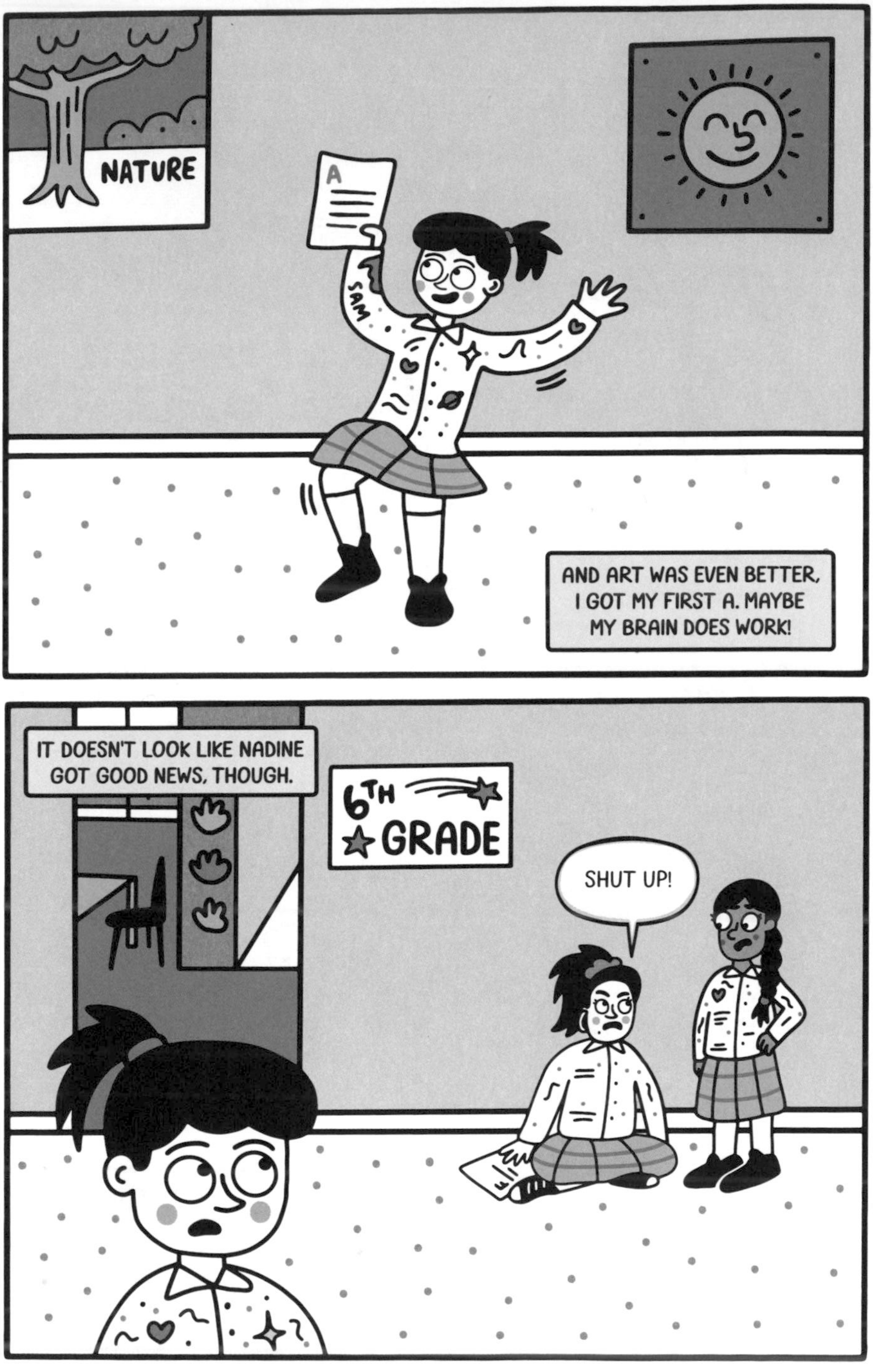
NATURE
A
SAM
AND ART WAS EVEN BETTER, I GOT MY FIRST A. MAYBE MY BRAIN DOES WORK!
IT DOESN'T LOOK LIKE NADINE GOT GOOD NEWS, THOUGH.
6TH GRADE
SHUT UP!

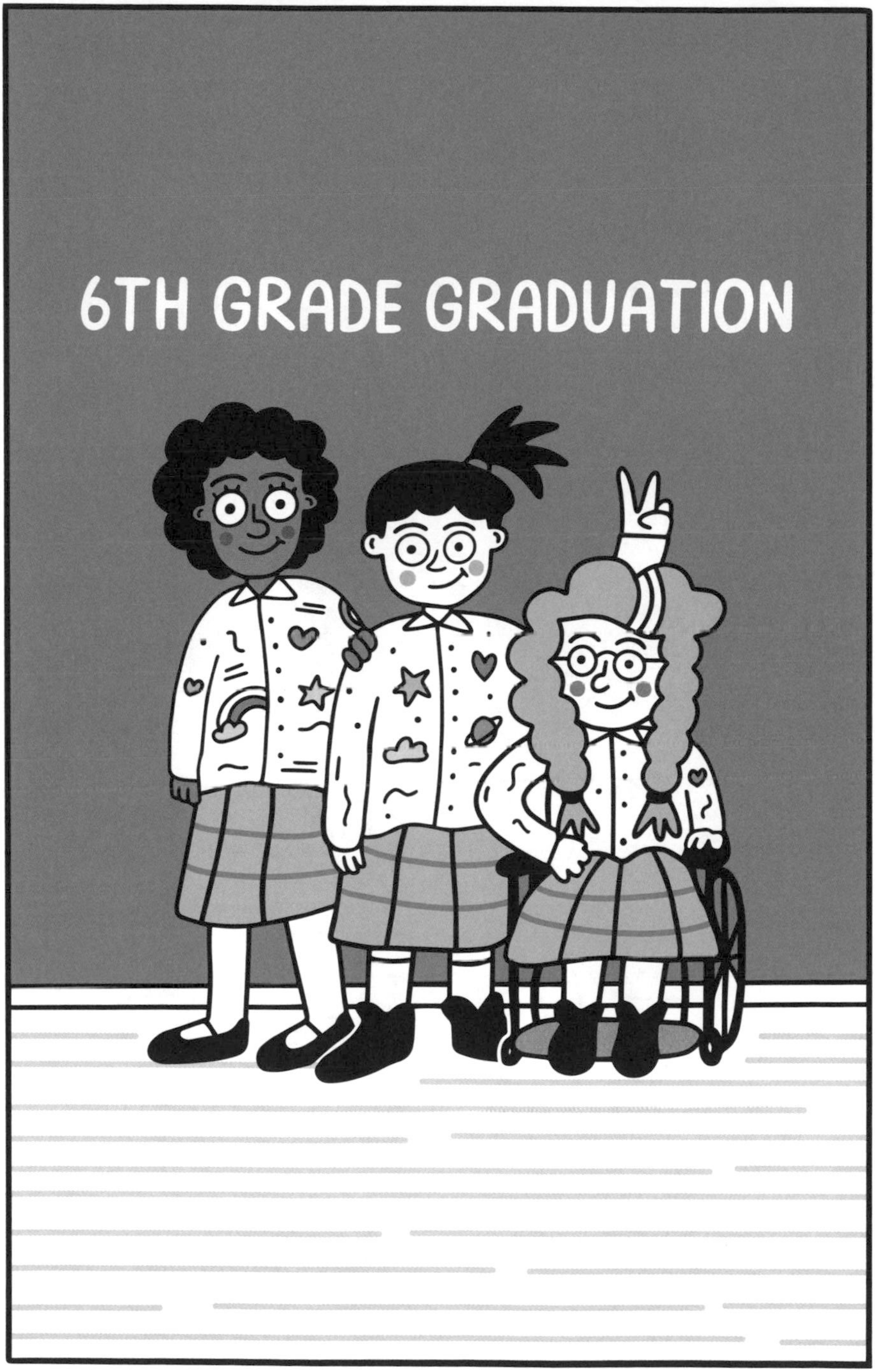
6TH GRADE GRADUATION

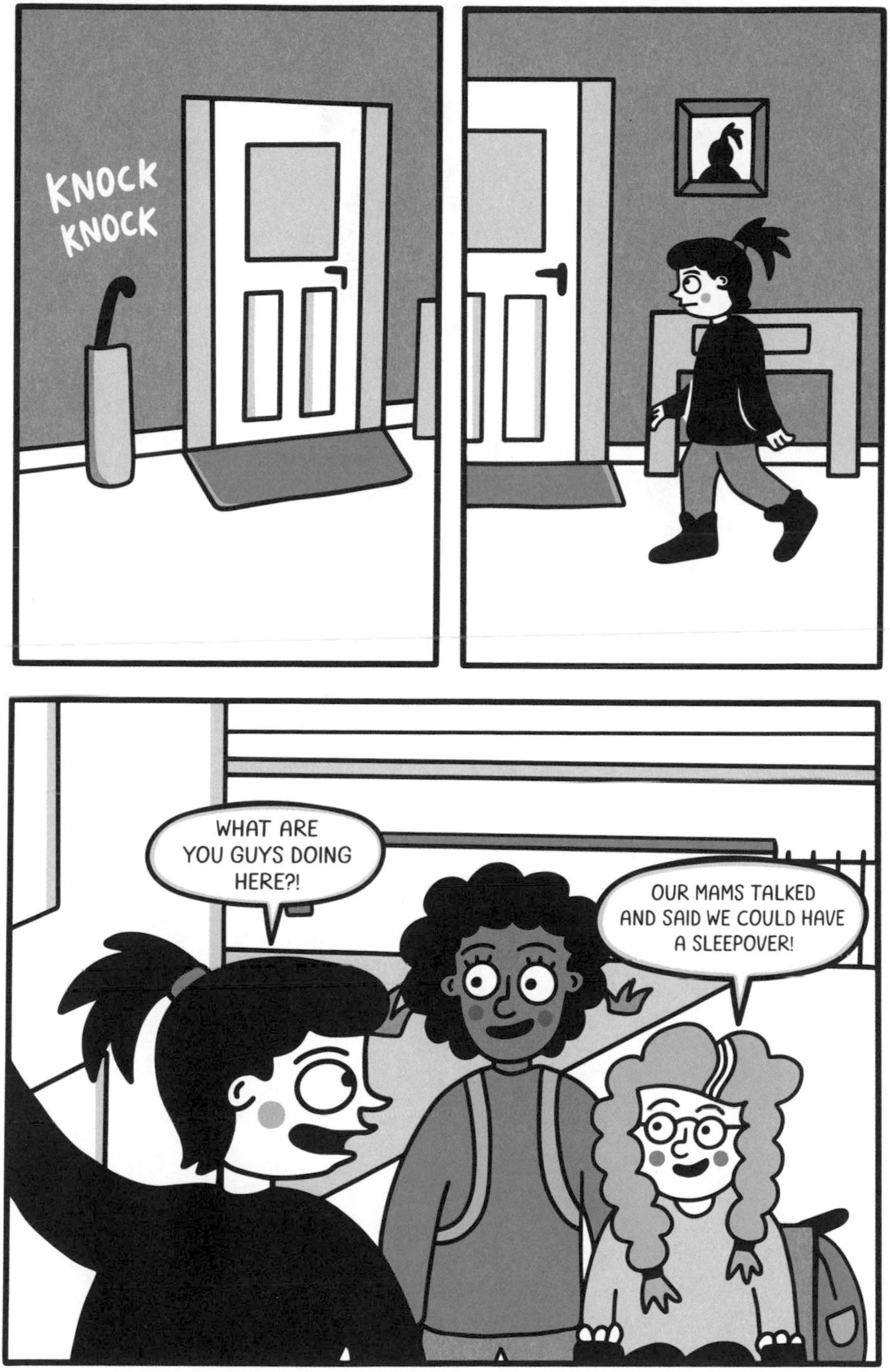
KNOCK KNOCK
WHAT ARE YOU GUYS DOING HERE?!
OUR MAMS TALKED AND SAID WE COULD HAVE A SLEEPOVER!

CHAPTER 9

DAD'S HOUSE

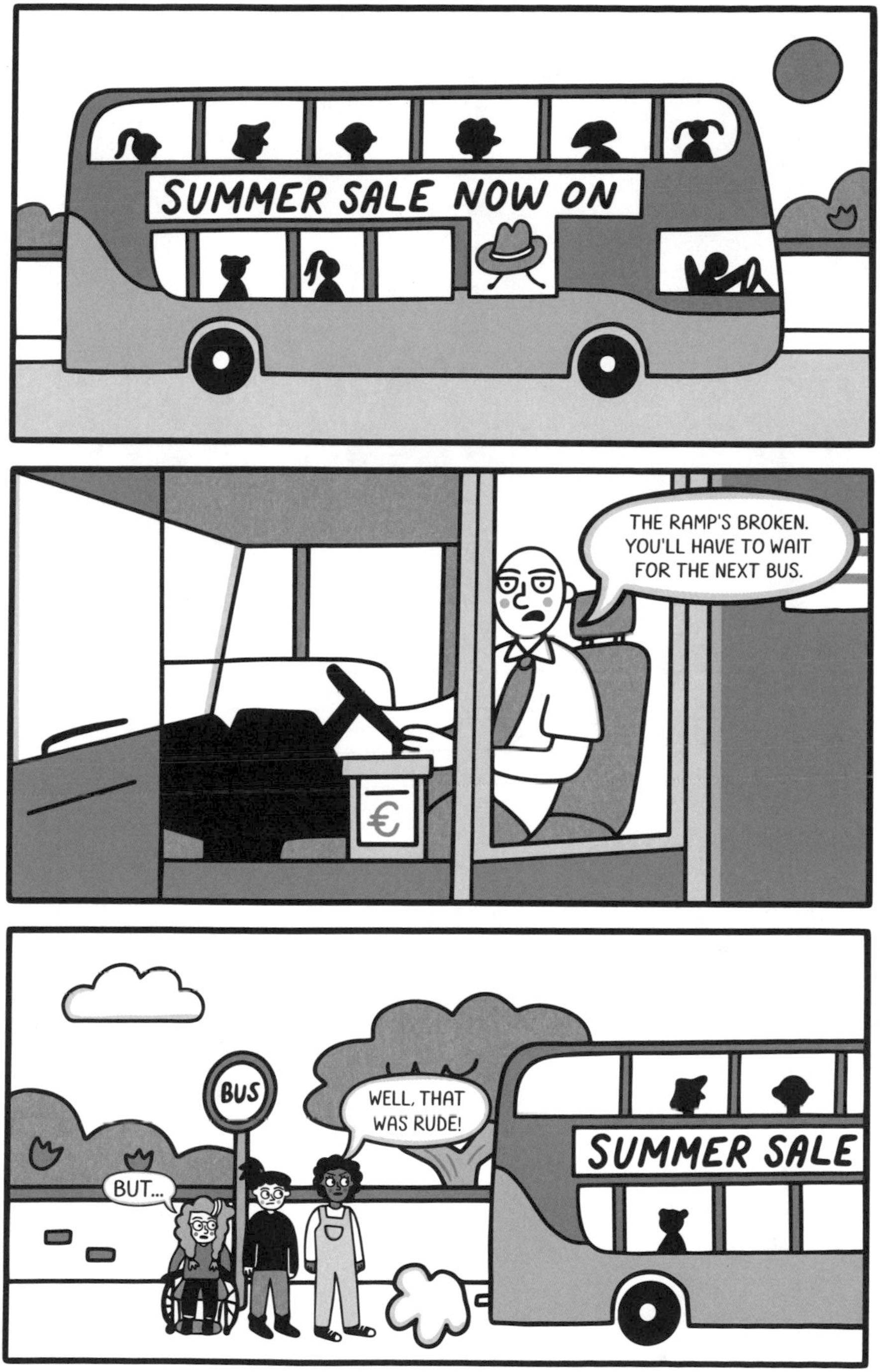
SUMMER SALE NOW ON
THE RAMP'S BROKEN. YOU'LL HAVE TO WAIT FOR THE NEXT BUS.
BUS
WELL, THAT WAS RUDE!
BUT...
SUMMER SALE

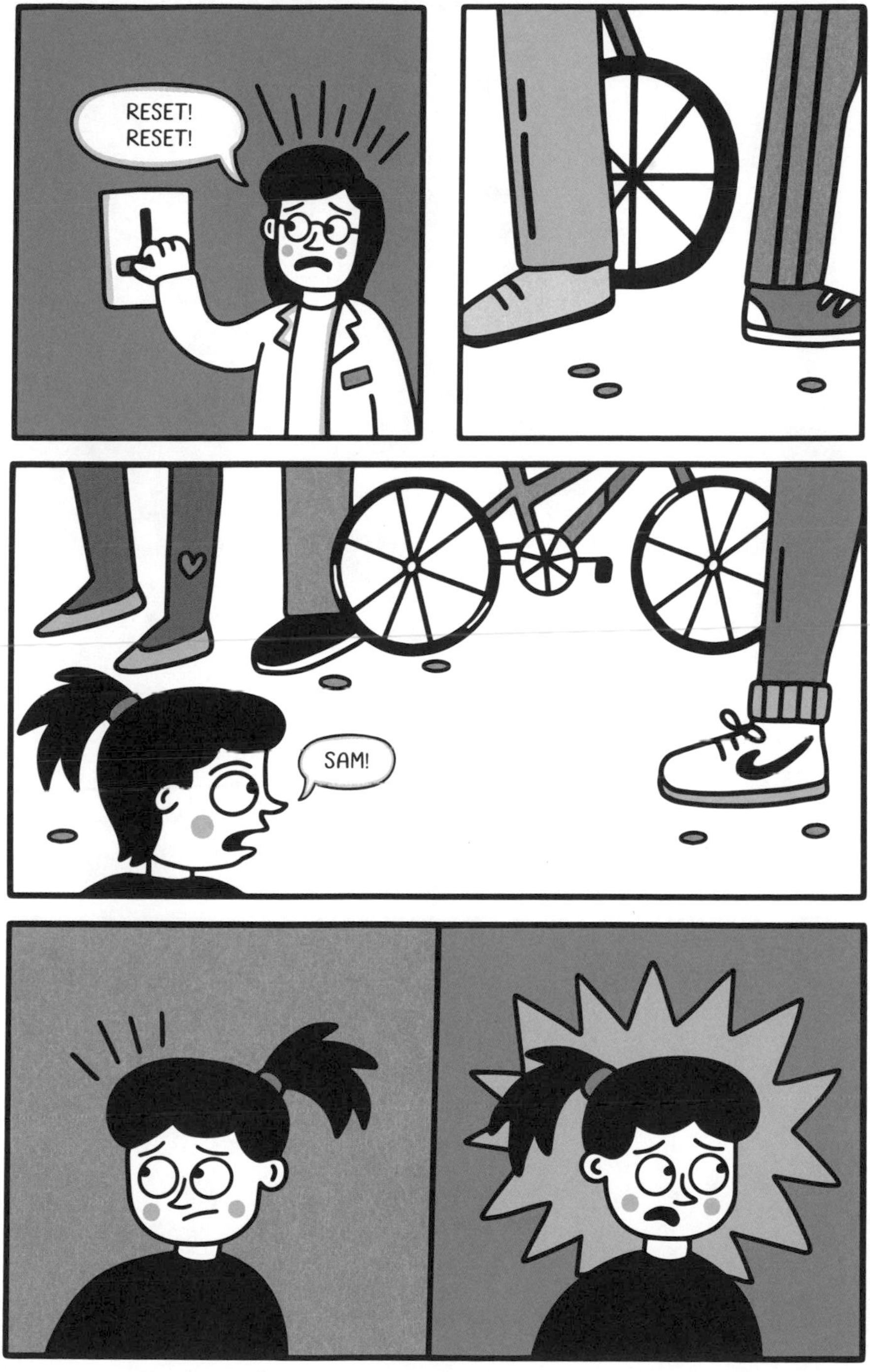
RESET!
RESET!
SAM!

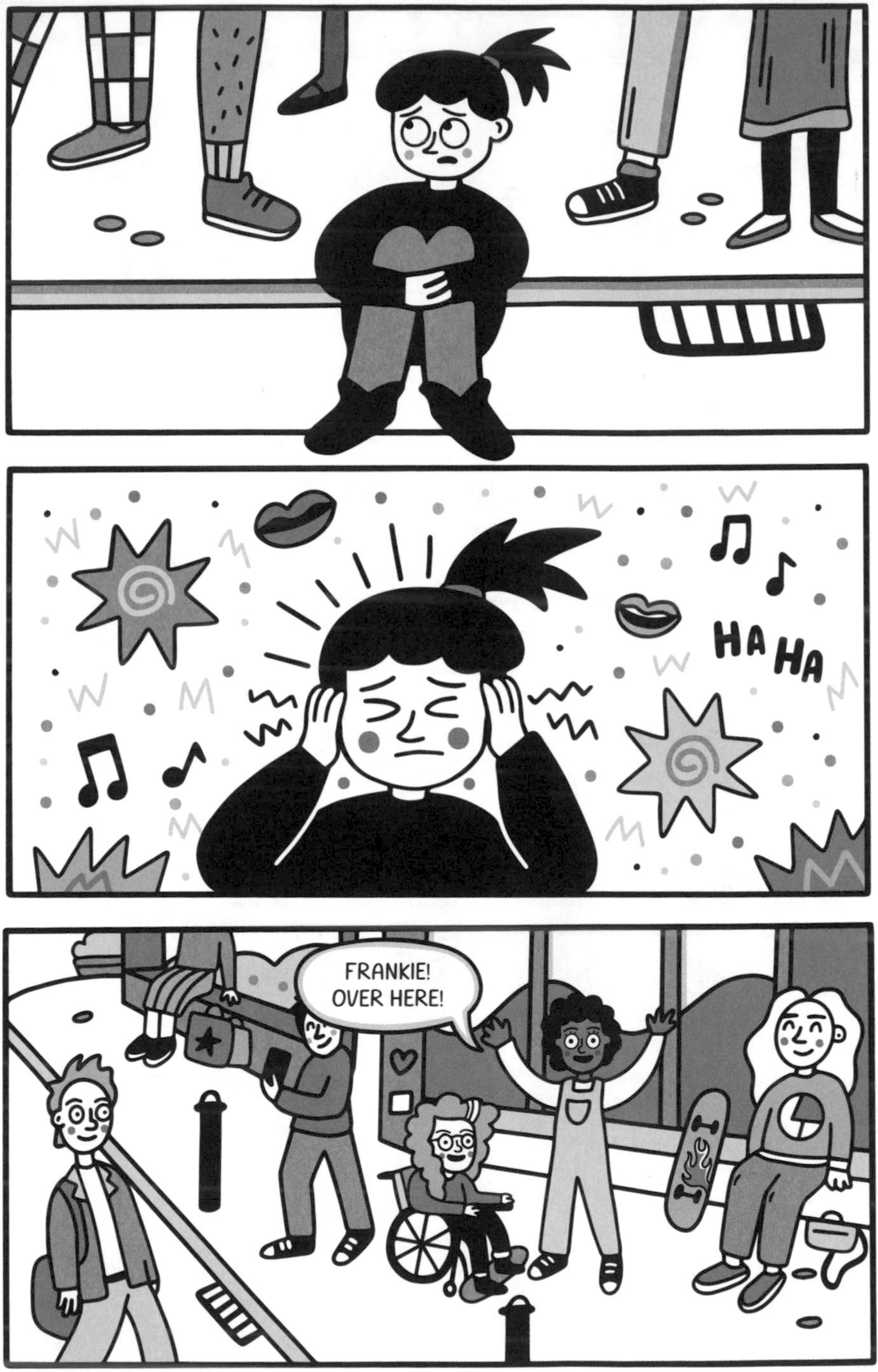
HA HA
FRANKIE! OVER HERE!

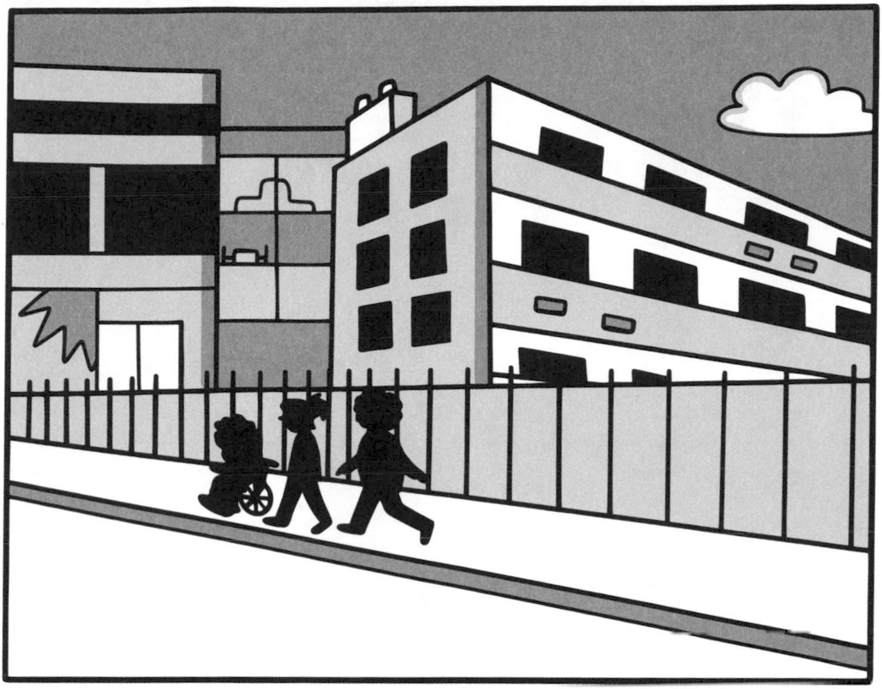

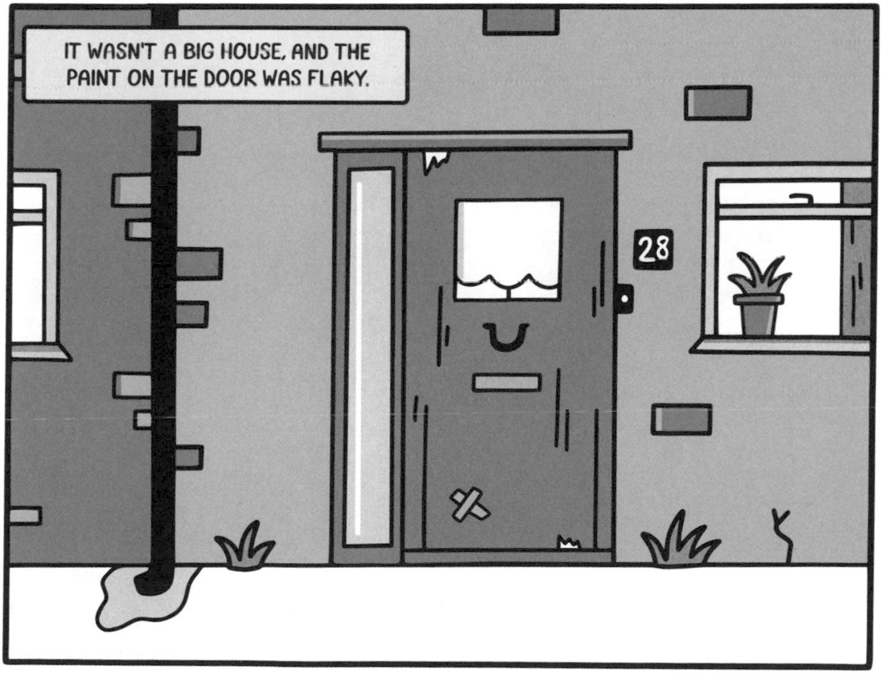
IT WASN'T A BIG HOUSE, AND THE PAINT ON THE DOOR WAS FLAKY.
28

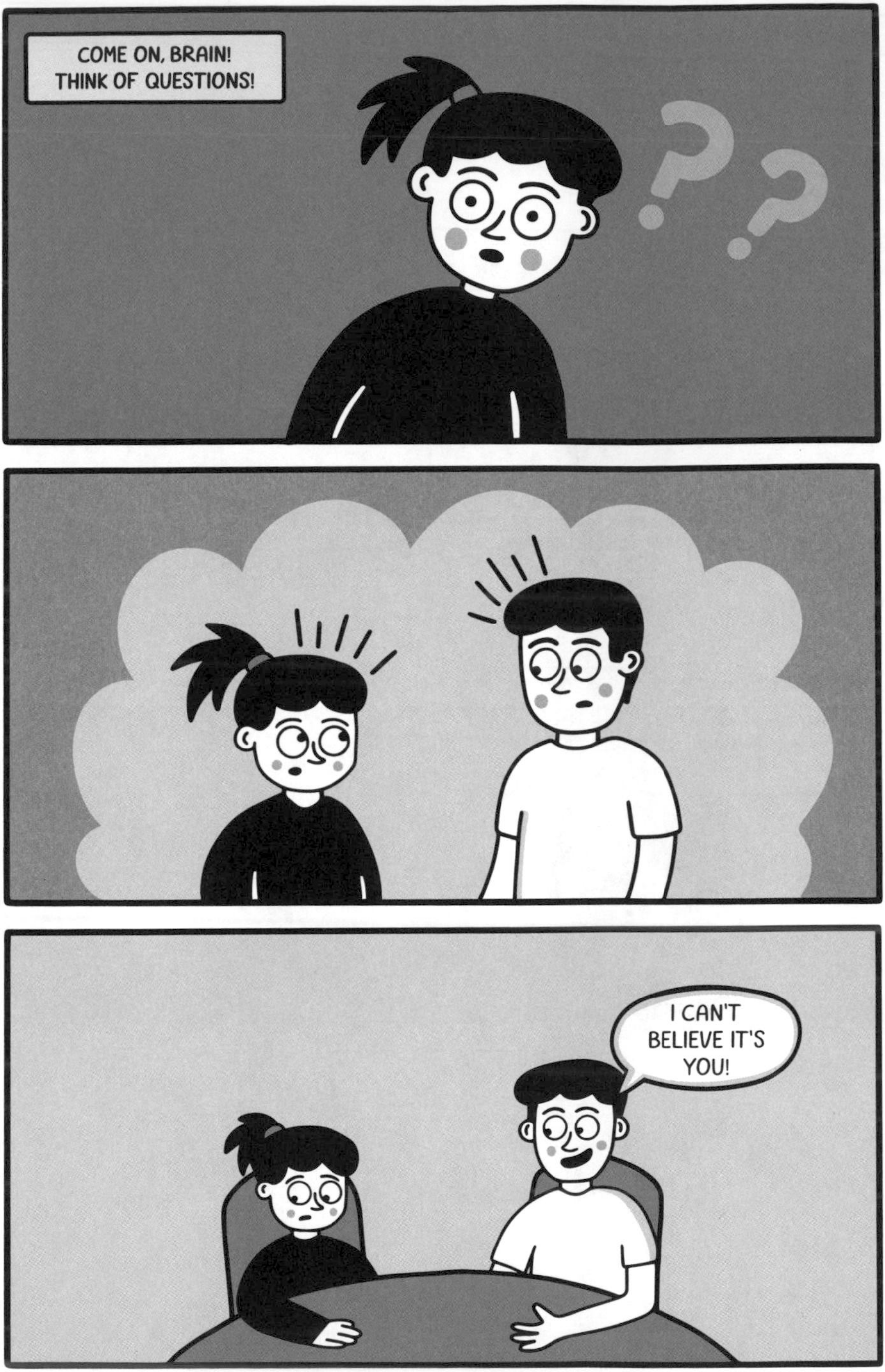
COME ON, BRAIN! THINK OF QUESTIONS!
I CAN'T BELIEVE IT'S YOU!

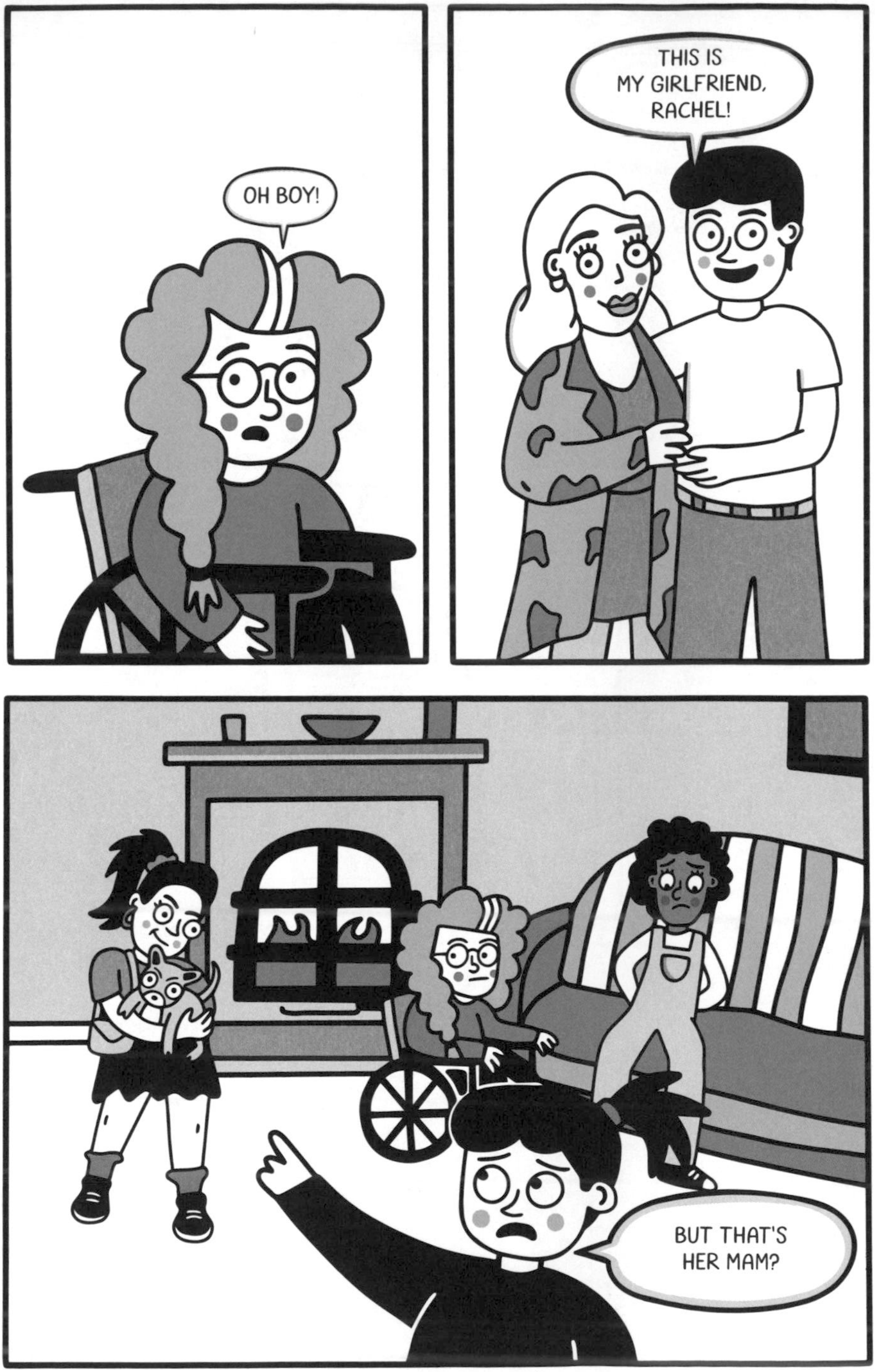
OH BOY!
THIS IS MY GIRLFRIEND, RACHEL!
BUT THAT'S HER MAM?

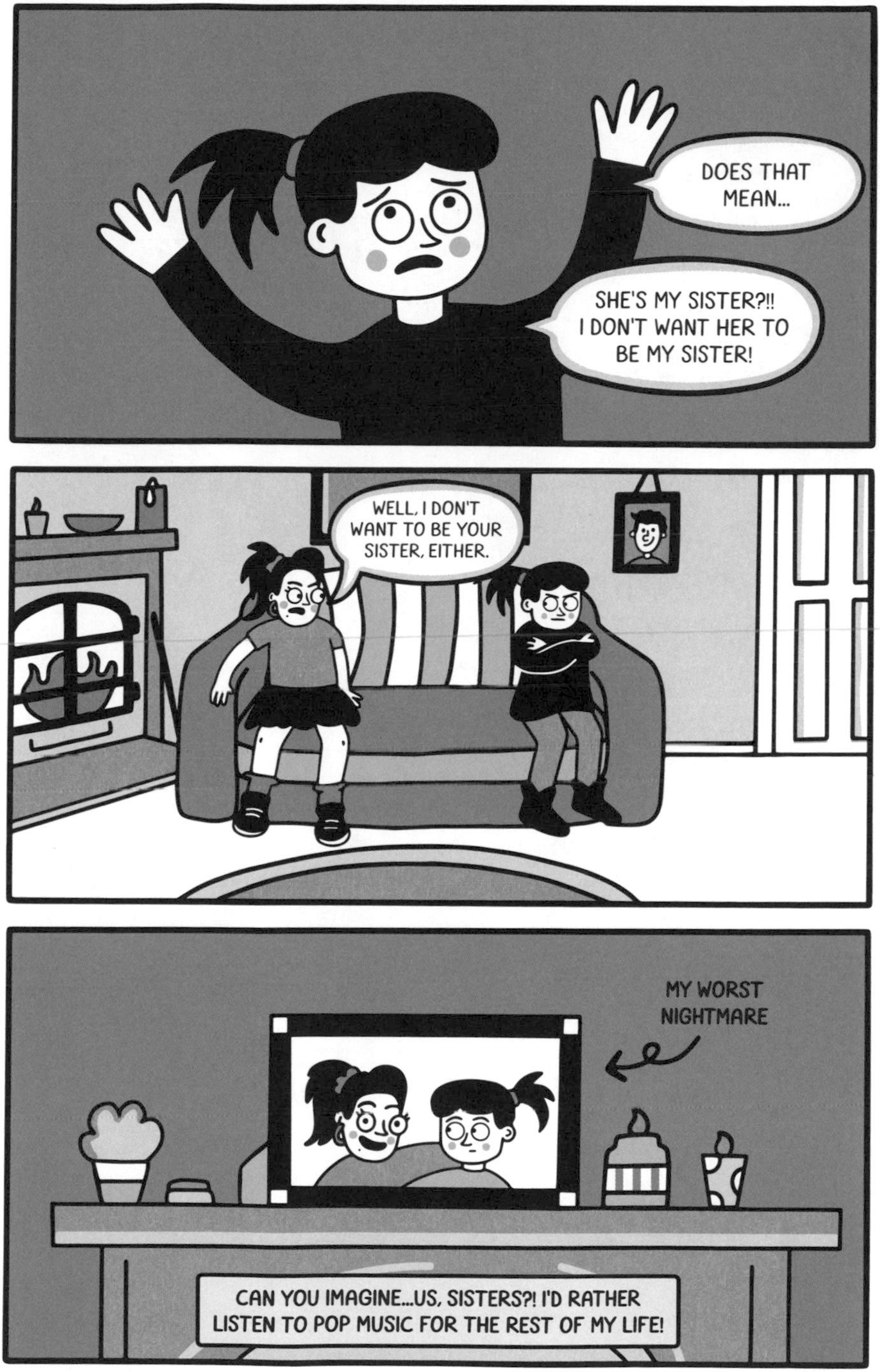
DOES THAT MEAN...
SHE'S MY SISTER?!! I DON'T WANT HER TO BE MY SISTER!
WELL, I DON'T WANT TO BE YOUR SISTER, EITHER.
MY WORST NIGHTMARE
CAN YOU IMAGINE...US, SISTERS?! I'D RATHER LISTEN TO POP MUSIC FOR THE REST OF MY LIFE!

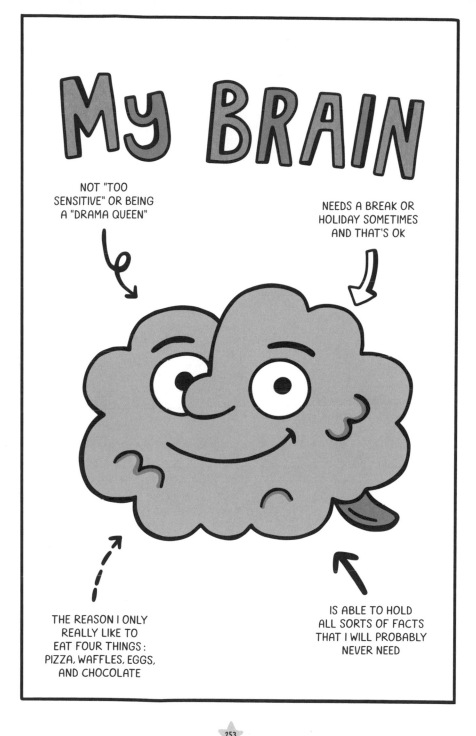

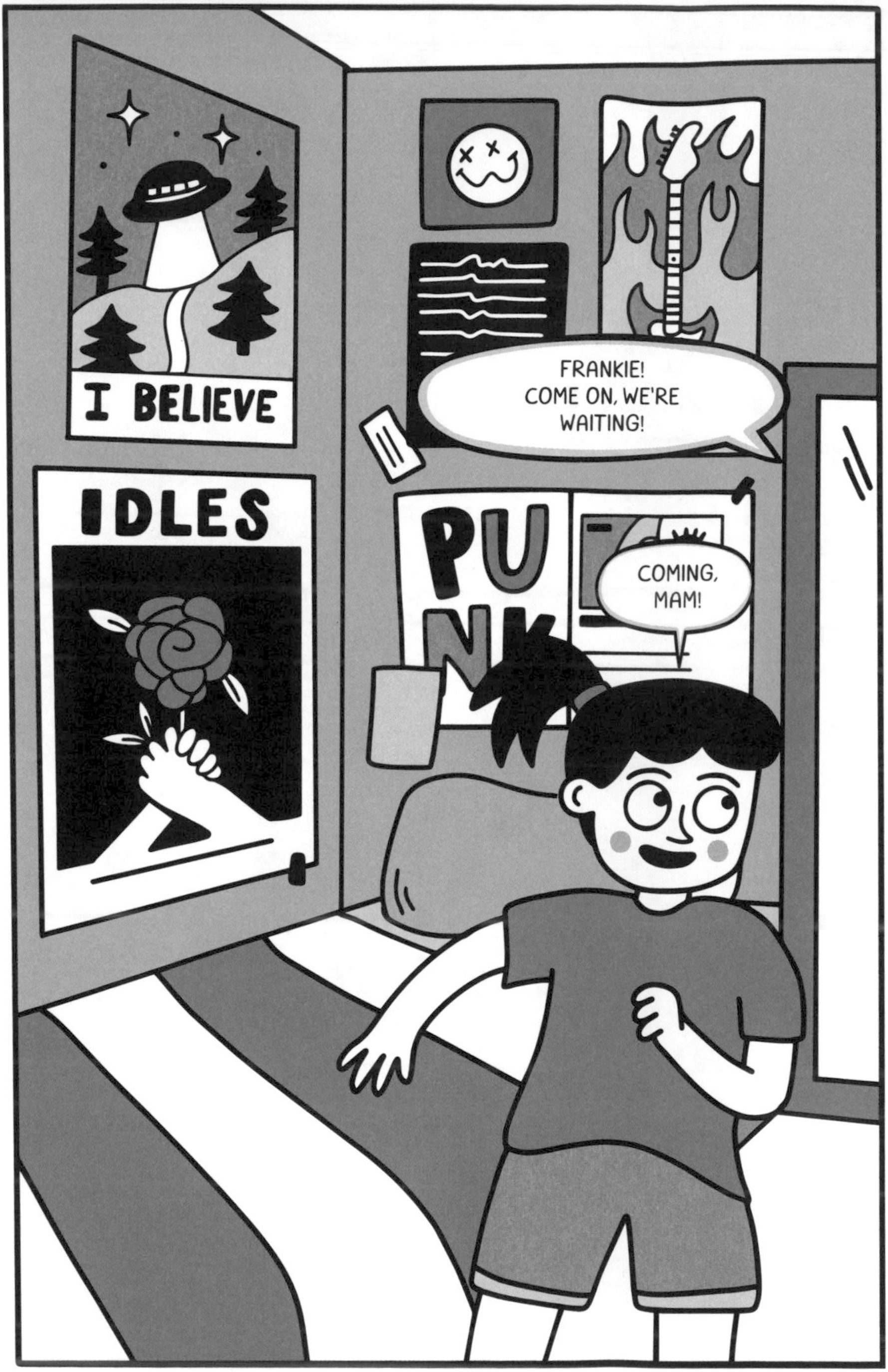
I BELIEVE
IDLES
PUNK
FRANKIE!
COME ON, WE'RE
WAITING!
COMING,
MAM!

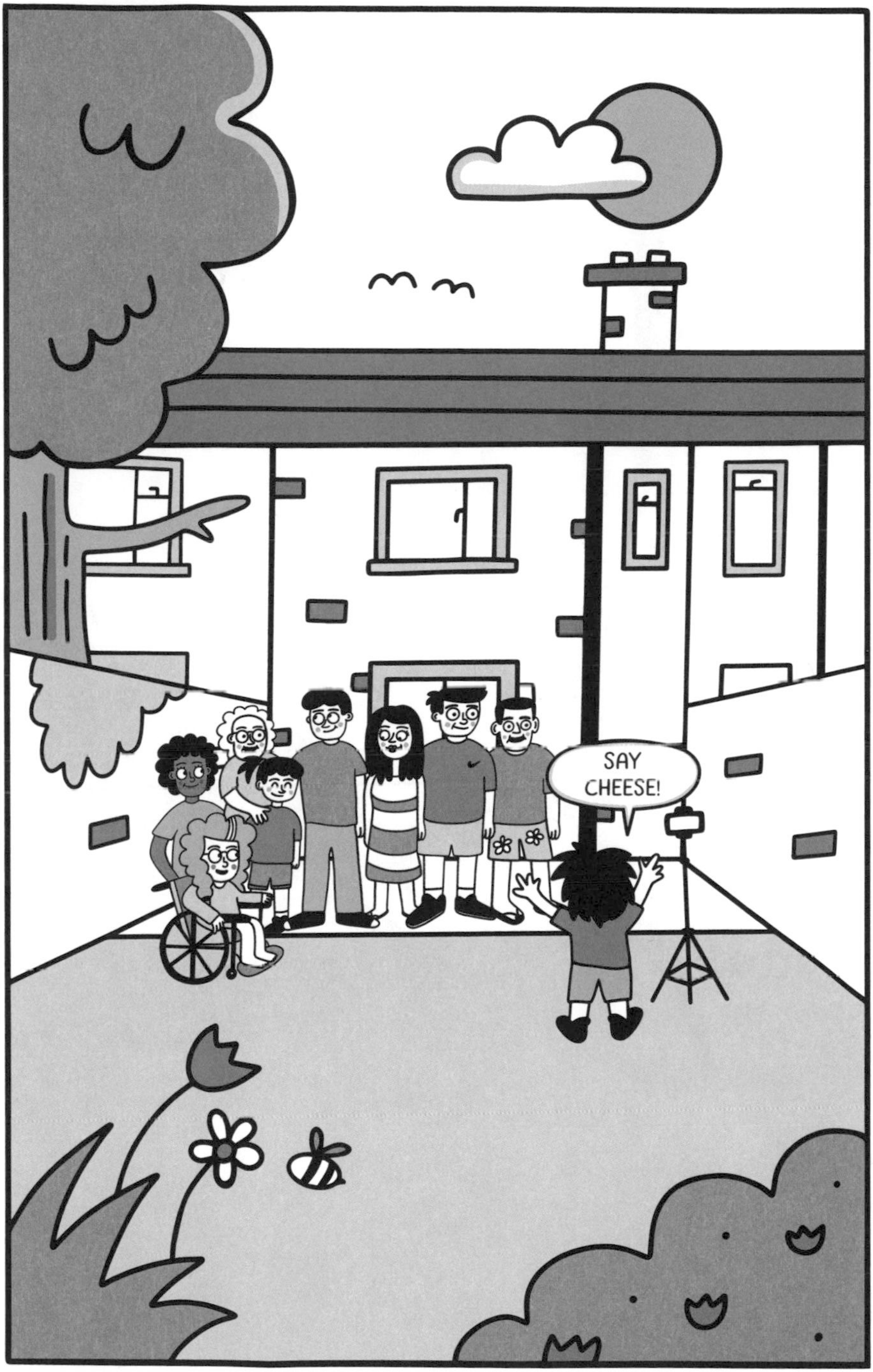
SAY CHEESE!

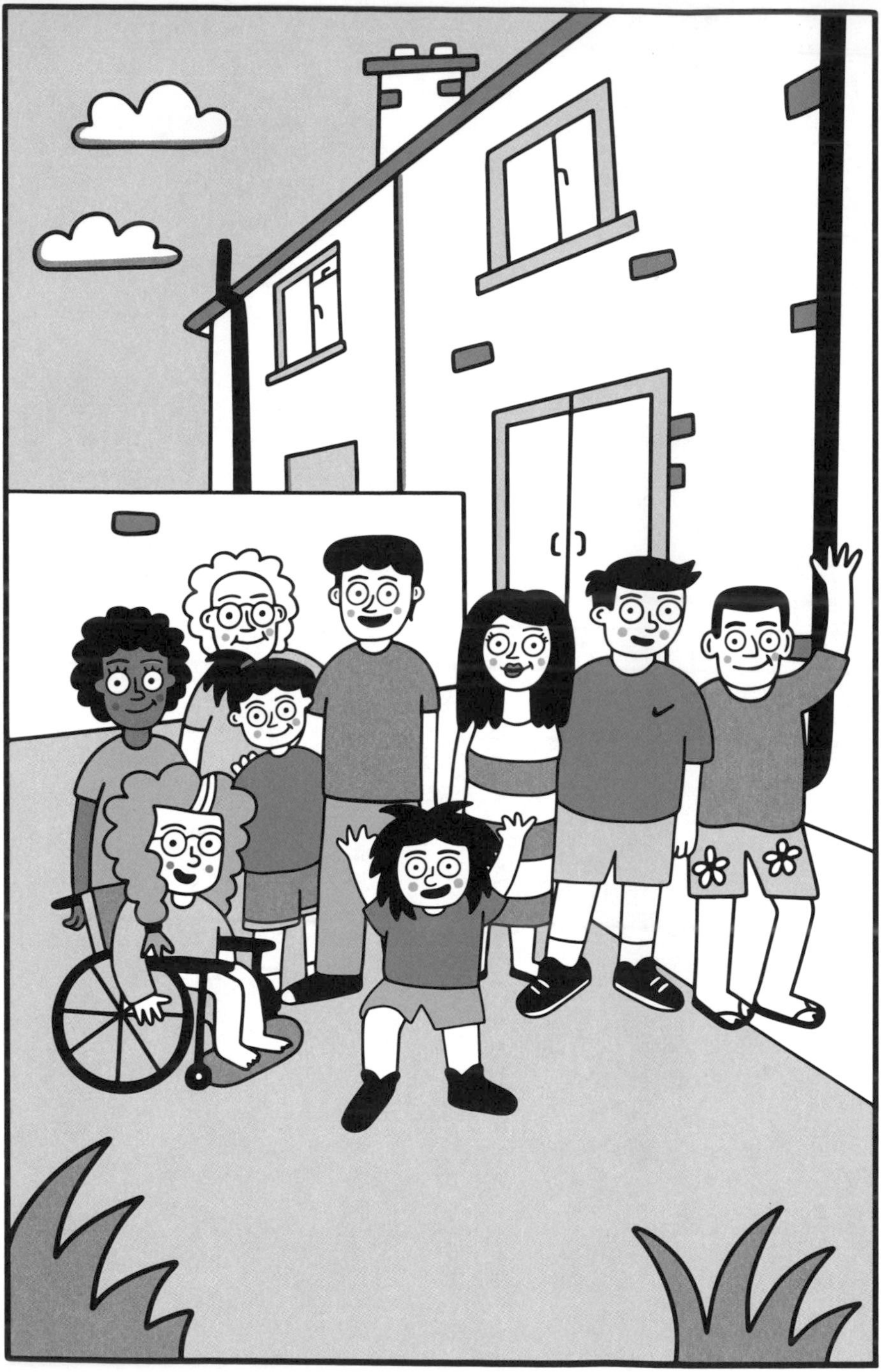

ACKNOWLEDGMENTS

I would like to start by thanking my amazing editors Yasmin Morrissey and Ruth Bennett along with Lauren Fortune for their continuous support throughout working on *Frankie's World*. Your energy, encouragement, and patience have been next to none. It has been one of the most uplifting experiences of my life to work with such an epic group of people who are just as excited about *Frankie's World* as I am. I have felt that energy with every interaction and it means everything to me, so thank you.

To all the team at Scholastic who I have met virtually and those I have yet to meet, thank you for all the time and energy you have put into *Frankie's World* and helping to bring this book to life.

To Andrew Biscomb, Tracey Cunnell, and Rachel Lawston, for giving *Frankie's World* a magic touch and who with their expertise have taken this book beyond what I ever dreamed.

To Alex Hynes, for helping make the typeface for my book possible and always supporting from afar.

To Faith, my agent. Thank you for believing in me and supporting me through all my endeavors. You have been a driving force in my life and took a chance on me when not many people did. I thank you for your patience, kindness, and everything you have done for me since the day we first met.

To my partner, Karl, thank you so much for all of your support. You have gone above and beyond over the years (and that's an understatement) and have been by my side through absolutely everything. You are truly the most amazing person I have ever met.

To my friends Bonnie, Marisa, and Chris, for showing me what true friends really are and for accepting me for who I am. You always show up. Even when I least expect it.

To my mam and dad, who are not with me anymore, but I know are shining down on me every day.

To my sister Orla, my niece Calla, and to all my family for everything.

To my nana, for supporting me and being by my side through college and always cheering me on from the sidelines.

To Uncle Dan, for always walking to the shop with me and introducing me to a world of imagination and fun.

And finally, a special thanks to: Will McDermott, who gave me a chance in my college interview and years later would give me an old drawing tablet. You made such an impact in my life and I will be forever grateful for your kindness.

Marc Doyle, who encouraged me to draw even more after looking at my notebooks. "Aoife, this is your niche!" is what you said. I have never forgotten that day in the National Art Gallery.

Tom, John, and Con, my lecturers from DIT, for always keeping it real. Thank you for your continued support (even after college) and for all the fun memories.

WHAT IS AUTISM?

Autism is a complex, invisible condition that a person is born with. Autism is a developmental condition, which means that the way a person communicates, interacts, and understands other people and the world is different from those who do not have the condition. It can be described as a "spectrum," which means it impacts different people in different ways, to differing degrees, at different times and in different situations.

Autism is not a linear scale or line with people at one end being "mildly autistic" and experiencing few challenges in any area and then people at the other end being "severely affected" and experiencing all the challenges all the time. This does not reflect how people experience autism.

Thinking of autism as being a spectrum is a much more helpful and accurate concept to understand the variation and individuality across autistic people.

Autism is said to be a spectrum because while autistic people can experience the world differently in specific areas, like sensory processing and communication, not all people will have the same profile of differences. So, you could have one autistic person who enjoys public speaking and has a very strong preference for routine. But another autistic person could find spoken communication very challenging but quite enjoy going to new places with little preparation. The autism spectrum is a very wide one, with people affected in a variety of ways, to a great number of varying degrees, and no two people on the spectrum are affected in entirely the same way.

Text from ASIAM with kind permission.
Please visit ASIAM.IE for more information.

FACTS & MYTHS

When talking about autism, it is as important to know what is not true as what is true about the condition. While autism awareness has greatly grown in recent years, we are still a long way from having a society that truly understands autism. Although many people have heard the word or even know someone with the condition, many people still cannot explain what autism is or understand the way autistic people think.

AUTISTIC PEOPLE LACK EMPATHY

This one always makes me giggle, and I know a lot of people on the spectrum can relate, but I think that we actually feel all the feels.

BUT YOU DON'T LOOK AUTISTIC?

"What does an autistic person look like?" is a question that doesn't acknowledge autism is invisible. It doesn't have a shape, size, or color.

AUTISTIC PEOPLE DON'T WANT FRIENDS

Most children want friends and to be included, and that is no different for autistic children.

AUTISTIC PEOPLE DON'T GET HUMOR

Sometimes a joke will go over my head, sure! But I love comedy and very much get most types of humor.

AUTISTIC PEOPLE ARE MATH GENIUSES

I'm sure there are many people in the world great at math, autistic or not. I, however, am not one of them.

AUTISTIC PEOPLE CAN'T...

Every person has abilities, including autistic people. We should never assume an autistic person can't do something, but rather talk about how we can empower autistic people to be able to participate.

HOW TO BE A GOOD FRIEND

There are many ways to be a good friend, like Sam and Rebecca are to Frankie. To me, a friend is someone who supports you, is there when times are tough, someone who listens, and most importantly, someone you can trust. I found it hard to make friends growing up, and sometimes it can be lonely when others don't really understand you. Below are some things I've learned along the way that have helped me to be a good friend, and to notice when someone is being a good friend to me. It costs nothing to be kind and you might just make someone else's day.

A REAL FRIEND SUPPORTS YOU AND CHEERS YOU ON.

I LIKE TO TREAT OTHERS THE WAY I LIKE TO BE TREATED.

DON'T STAND BY WHEN SOMEONE IS BEING BULLIED. STAND UP AND SPEAK OUT. YOU COULD REALLY HELP SOMEONE.

A REAL FRIEND IS SOMEONE WHO LISTENS AND WANTS TO HELP BECAUSE THEY CARE.

REAL FRIENDS ACCEPT YOU FOR WHO YOU ARE.

WHAT'S YOUR SUPERHERO NAME?

PICK THE MONTH YOU WERE BORN AND THE FIRST LETTER OF YOUR NAME TO FIND OUT YOUR FUNNY SUPERHERO NAME!

JAN	Captain	A	Barnacle	N	Brain Storm
FEB	Turbo	B	Storm Slayer	O	Space Doughnut
MAR	Magic	C	Lightning Strike	P	Justice Juice
APR	Danger	D	Broccoli Beam	Q	Iron Shadow
MAY	Galactic	E	Banana	R	Cookie Slayer
JUN	Doctor	F	Wonder Wizard	S	Rainbow Ray
JUL	Supersonic	G	Star Shooter	T	Illusion
AUG	Epic	H	Space Pizza	U	Sprinkles
SEP	Mystical	I	Thunder Beam	V	Steel Arm
OCT	Crystal	J	Waffles	W	Milk Menace
NOV	Cosmo	K	Thunder Fart	X	Space Slayer
DEC	Frightening	L	Hot Dog	Y	Waffle Warrior
		M	Nugget Ninja	Z	Ice Blaster

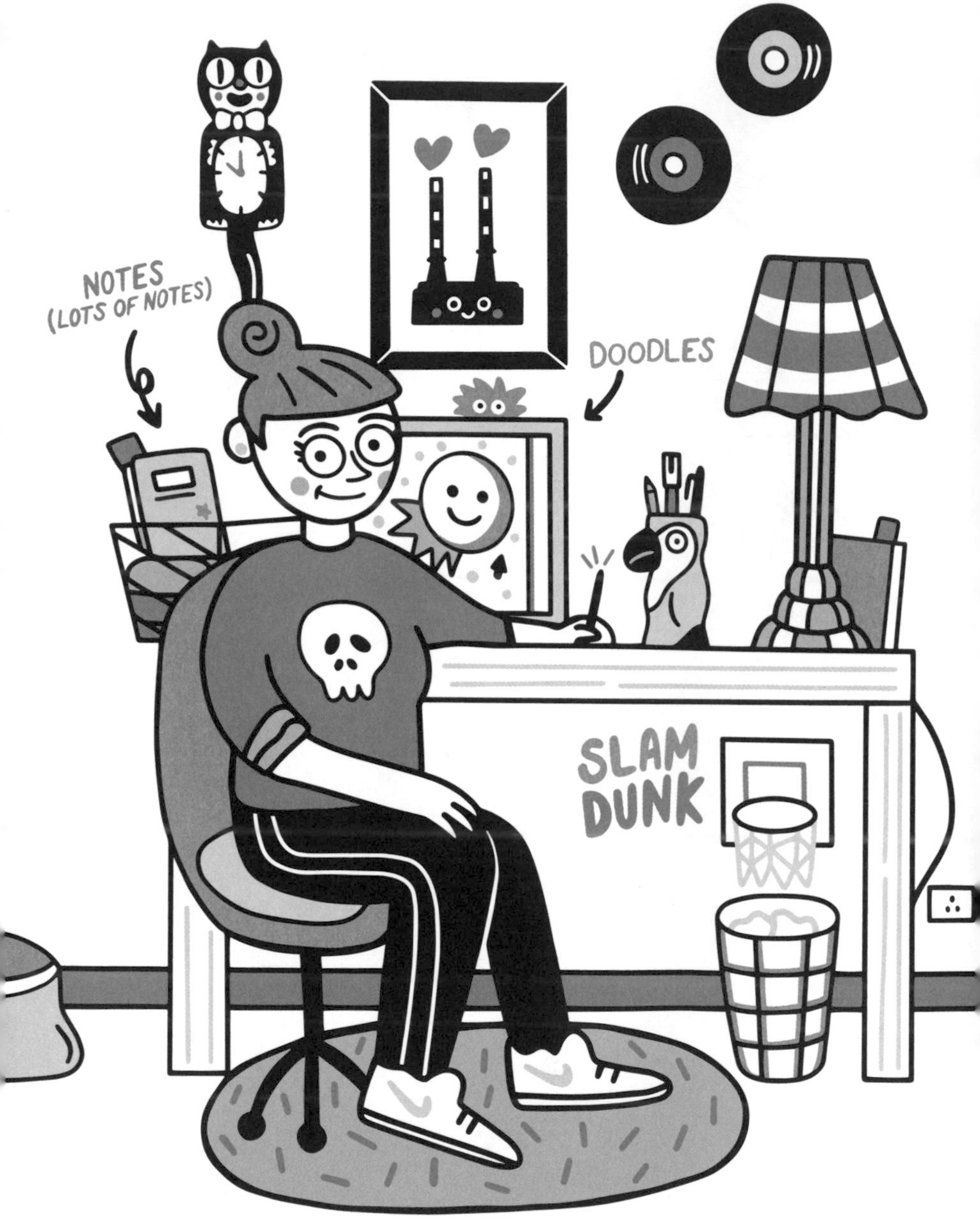
NOTES
(LOTS OF NOTES)
DOODLES
SLAM
DUNK

ABOUT THE AUTHOR

AOIFE DOOLEY is an award-winning comedian, writer, and illustrator from Dublin. She's the creator of a counting board book, *1 2 3 Ireland!*, which won an Irish Book Award. She is also the creator and animator of *Your One Nikita*, a web series of TV shorts that has a loyal online fan base. Aoife openly shares her experiences of being diagnosed with autism at the age of twenty-seven and how her diagnosis has helped her to truly understand herself. Visit Aoife online at aoifedooleydesign.com.

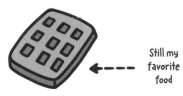

Still my
favorite
food

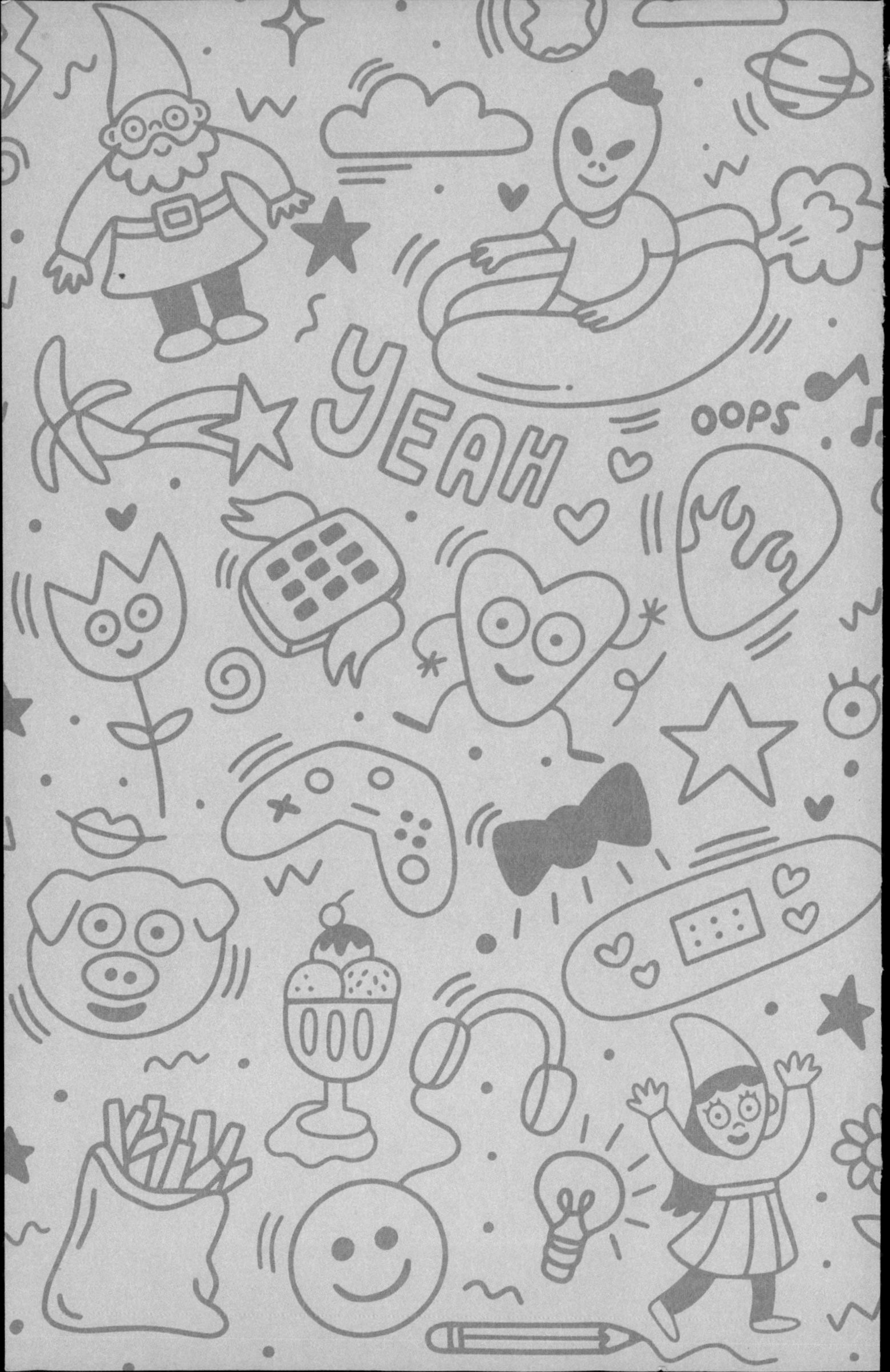
YEAH
OOPS